Wild Colonial Girl

p.d.r. lindsay

Copyright © 2021 p.d.r. lindsay

Published by Writer's Choice for p.d.r. lindsay

All rights reserved.

ISBN 978-0-473-56056-0

ISBN 978-0-473-56057-7

ISBN 978-0-473-56058-4

ISBN 978-0-473-56059-1

ISBN 978-0-473-56060-7

ISBN 978-0-473-56061-4

BLURB

What? Leave India? Move to the colonies and make a new life there? Melisande, appalled, gazed at her brother and fiancée. She loved her life in India. She'd been cossetted, loved and happy there. Of course the plague meant a radical change, but they could still live on the family's small estate couldn't they? But, no. Brother Jeri didn't want to live in India, neither did fiancée Richard. Both young men, filled with excitement at the thought of adventure in the colonies, were determined to go, and Melisande must go with them. Her life turned upside down, rushed into her wedding, onto a ship and off to Australia, and finally New Zealand, Melisande has to learn how to run a home and cope with colonial New Zealand, a life so different from her Indian one. Can she make a home and a life as happy as her Indian one?

REVIEWS

'p.d.r. lindsay succeeds in such a way that on finishing the book I was surprised to find that I was, in fact, still in the twenty-first century, and not back in the nineteenth century, so wrapped up was I in the story.' Beta reader review

'I finished your book about a week ago and I really enjoyed reading it! Sometimes I feel like Melisande – poor girl! – was talking to me and she did make me laugh.'   ARC Tina

Thank you again for your interest in our website. We read and reviewed your book and enjoyed it very much. Here is a copy of our review:
    Five Stars *****
The premise is delivered in a unique way that really makes the novel stand out from its counterparts, and I wholeheartedly recommend it to anyone looking for a top-notch historical drama seasoned with a touch of mystery and a good pinch of humour.

ACKNOWLEDGEMENTS

Grateful thanks to all the following for their invaluable assistance:

Cover Artist Peter Langdon: https://reedsy.com/peter-langdon
Editor: Fiona Brown: https://reedsy.com/#/freelancers/fiona-b

In New Zealand, the National Maritime Museum, The National Library, Waitaki Museum and Archive -Te Whare Taoka o Waitaki, and Port Chalmers library and museum.

DEDICATION

For Ailsa and Lorna who kept me sane

and

For all the brave women who followed their men to a colonial unknown.

and for my readers

FREE SHORT STORY for you. Details on the Resources page

CONTENTS

Blurb
Reviews
Acknowledgments
Dedication
Contents

Ch. 1 - What happened and where am I?
Ch. 2 - India, a beginning
Ch. 3 - Disaster strikes in India
Ch. 4 - The men take over as adventure beckons
Ch. 5 - Reasoning fails and tantrums never work
Ch. 6 - What? Go to the colonies? Where?
Ch. 7 - Married? Now? Not a perfect wedding
Ch. 8 - Australia's out, New Zealand's in
Ch. 9 - Port Chalmers and the first taste of colonial life
Ch. 10 - Learning the skills of a colonial wife
Ch. 11 - Learning how to get on with the locals
Ch. 12 - A farm is bought and a trip arranged
Ch. 13 - Exploring the Sounds and making friends
Ch. 14 - Secrets and plans
Ch. 15 - An engagement is arranged
Ch. 16 - Social disgrace
Ch. 17 - Great changes for all
Ch. 18 - Melisande's plans fall into place
Ch. 19 - Organising the move to the farm
Ch. 20 - The elopement
Ch. 21 - Settling in, finding new friends
Ch. 22 - Melisande remembers everything
Ch. 23 - Melisande rearranges memories
Ch. 24 - Melisande reveals all

Resources
About The Author
Writer's Choice Quality Fiction

Chapter One

In this end was my beginning

Why was it so dim? Where was the light and why was she lying down, down here on ... on the floor? She couldn't see properly, her eyes wouldn't open but she knew she'd been carrying a lamp. She remembered that ... so why was it dark? And ... oh dear Lord, please God, no. Her hand crept along the wooden floorboards, fingers pricking on fine splinters of glass and into a sticky pool of ... something moist. Fingers snatched back, an involuntary revolted reaction. She forced her hand to reach out again, an inch further. There. A clump of cloth. Her stomach lurched, heaved, and an acrid liquid soured her mouth. Something, someone else, lay on the floor beside her. She had seen ... it was ... men ... that man, the dreadful neighbour yelling but ... oh, her head ... something happened ... something ... happened. Tentatively she touched the back of her skull. Pain exploded, radiating through her head as her eyelids squeezed shut, she failed to ... she couldn't ... couldn't remember anything as she dipped and swooped in a terrifying descent into looming blackness.

"Melisande."

A voice ... she knew that voice.

"Melisande."

***

That's where it started. With a name. Melisande. Poor Melisande. How ridiculous a name for someone like her. She'd disliked it so much she begged for another, but her parents, who were, in all other things, an indulgent mama and a kindly papa, stood firm. They were romantics, loved to read the poetry of Keats and Shelley, adored the paintings of the Pre-Raphaelite Brotherhood, Holman Hunt and Burne-Jones being their favourites. They had a book of glossy reproductions of the group's paintings and sighed over what Melisande privately thought of as the faux mediaeval worlds those painters created. Faux mediaeval worlds with faux mediaeval names, hence the preposterous Melisande. Her poor brother, christened Jervais Shirley (he barely escaped Claudio Valentine), at school in England, managed to adopt the more acceptable Jeri, but what could she do with Melisande? She might have felt happier if she looked like a Melisande: tall, slender, fair of face, fair haired and willowy delicate, like the women in those paintings, but she was simply medium in everything – figure, height, hair, and eyes. A medium brown girl.

***

"Keep calling her, it's a head injury, she must stay awake." A man's voice, she knew that voice. She'd heard it before. But why was it so dark and difficult to see? And oh how she hurt, her back, her arm. What had she done?

"Melisande, Melisande."

***

How she hated that name.
"Stop complaining and call yourself something else," her brother told her on her fifteenth birthday.
"But I can't," Melisande protested. "You could make something useable from your names. What can I make from mine?"
Jeri gave her a brotherly grin. "Mel? Melli?"
She eyed him suspiciously, gave him her warning Look. He winked. "As in smelly Melli?" she asked sweetly.

Her brother backed away, putting the chaise longue between them.

"There's always Sand or Sandi."

"As in sand on a beach? I think not."

"Well …" Jeri paused and his grin expanded into a thoroughly wicked smile. "Now how about Jane, there's a nice *plain* name?"

Melisande grabbed a cushion and hurled it at him. "As in *plain* Jane, you rude, unkind …" She grabbed another cushion. Jeri fled, laughing.

***

"Keep calling. Keep her awake. Good Christ! It's a right mess."

"Melisande, Melisande."

Voices, kind voices, but she was still afraid. She knew that man's voice, but it was not her man's voice. Richard, he was her man … not Richard's voice. She knew … his voice, his face, Richard …

***

It was Mr Holyman, Richard, who solved the naming problem. He'd become one of the family ever since he'd arrived at their home delivering a collection of Arts and Crafts furniture and ornaments Papa had bought from Richard's senior supervisor, who was returning home to England. Papa could never have afforded to ship from home the William Morris or Charles Rennie Mackintosh pieces he and Mama so admired, but when the more affluent English families, their tour of duty done, left India to return home they would sell most of their goods and chattels rather than ship them back. Melisande felt sure every auctioneer in their part of India knew that Papa would buy the weird Arts and Crafts stuff and sent it to him. Certainly collections came downriver or upriver every time an auctioneer fancied he could sell something to Papa. She did like her William Morris chest, but this plain and angular furniture neither fitted in nor looked right in their house, which was so traditionally Indian in most ways. It gave her the artistic shudders.

It was Richard who brought her chest, and when introduced to her as "Miss Allmark, our daughter, Melisande," had not even raised an eyebrow. But he had smiled a most gentle and understanding smile at her rueful expression.

"Dreadful isn't it? Do I look like a Melisande? I'm trying to change it," she'd said.

"Melisande is a beautiful name," Richard had said, as Mama and Papa exchanged pleased smiles. "But I can understand why you aren't happy with it." His face had expressed such kindness and sympathy.

That fifteen-year-old Melisande sensed his empathy, his understanding, like an explosion of joy. Someone who understood without teasing or denials. "The problem is finding the right name, a simple one. My family refuse to call me Patience or Prudence, and they don't like Ruth."

"All too plain for our daughter, and too Puritan," Papa had said.

Mama had nodded. "Melisande is a lovely name, my dear."

Richard had inclined a gracious bow to Mama, and turned to Melisande, "With your permission, Miss Allmark," he'd said, with a little bow to her, "if you prefer it I shall call you Lisa."

And Lisa it was. Such a relief to an awkward, still growing girl.

***

That man's voice, agitated, distressed. "We've to move her out of this. We've got to move her and clean up."

"But should we lift her?"

That was a friend's voice, her name was ... was ... was ... but her head disintegrated into waves of pain beyond pain. Explosions of dark and light as someone moved her arm. She tried to protest, but her voice faltered in her throat which would not open, as a tight collar of agony enclosed it. She began to be afraid.

"We can't wait for the doctor. We've to make all right here before he arrives. He'll not get here for at least an hour."

"Oh, poor Lisa."

More voices, safe voices. Now why did she want safe voices? What was it she'd seen? Her eyelids remained glued together. She could not lift her head, moaned as someone touched her temple. Arms slid round her shoulders, her waist, grasped her tightly, raising her. She wanted to scream, "Leave me on the floor!" but her voice remained trapped inside her mouth, her throat sealed by that collar of pain.

"Oh her head, her poor head, look."

"Sweet Jesus, he smashed her skull. We need that doctor now. Let's carry her to her room. We've got to get this sorted."

Too much pain and a red roaring behind her eyes and in her ears. Then the pillowed, padded downiness of a bed ... it felt like her Indian bed .... Where was she? Scents she ought to know, soft little hands wiping her face and brow, the nostril-tickling odour of that herbal mixture ... her ayah .. she used that same silk cloth across her eyes. Usha, her ayah, India, she must be home in India.

***

India. Home. Mama and Papa. Afternoon tea on the verandah of that lovely large brick house beside the Ganges, surrounded by its formal Indian garden, walled off from their farmland as it rolled down towards the river. A perfect place to sit with invited visitors for their peaceful daily afternoon tea ceremony. "A way," Mama said, "to introduce you, my dear Melisande, into society in forgiving surroundings." And a way for Mama to remind her gently not to be so quick with retorts to her elders.

It rounded off each family member's day, set them up for dinner and the evening social activities, in a setting Melisande had so often tried and failed to paint. The brilliance of the light and the vivid depth of colours were not in her paint box and hard to mix. Only once did she succeed, in one tiny painting her mother had framed to treasure.

"We are the most fortunate of families," Mama would say, smiling at them all as she accepted her cup of tea from Advik, their sircar, a man who combined the role of butler and steward with much aplomb. He always supervised afternoon tea himself. With white gloves, red turban, and a brass-buttoned tunic smelling faintly of starch, he might have been a British Club steward. He certainly treated afternoon tea as a British custom even though some of the comestibles were their Indian favourites. He would make the main biwarchi, their senior cook, bake ginger biscuits and tiny sponge cakes for English visitors, and wondrous cakes for birthdays were an Advik speciality.

Melisande accepted her cup of tea in the delicate bone-china cup with a grateful smile. She was very fond of Advik, and she loved afternoon tea on the shaded verandah, with its spectacular view of the Ganges, the delicate scent from the honeysuckle climbing the nearest pillar, and today, a rare treat, no visitors, just the family, to enjoy the spring weather and a collection of savoury Indian snacks, and to talk. Melisande agreed with her mother, they were indeed a fortunate family and she the most fortunate of them.

Papa discreetly pulled a face as Mama extolled the joys of their simple Indian life, but Melisande spotted it, and so did Mama, although he had smoothed his expression into an agreeable one as she turned to face him fully.

"Money," Mama said, sweet in tone and honey of voice, "money does not bring happiness." She'd caught him out and would tease him for it.

Papa's eyes brightened. Now he had her. Melisande hid her smile, waiting for his reply. "Ah, but it does bring good fortune," he riposted, beaming. He'd tripped her and had managed to make a pun at the same time.

Melisande laughed. Jeri and Mr Holyman, Richard, tried not to. Papa didn't really mind being the younger son and having to earn his privileges, rather than inherit them; he liked India and his work here was of great use to scientists and doctors. He only wanted extra money for printing his books, for more botanising trips in the far north, and for paying more researchers to bring him more plants. She and Richard would do that for him when they married and could travel around India on Company duties, for Richard worked for the Calcutta Trading Company, and she would be a valued Company wife. A future she looked forward to.

Mama tried to frown Papa down, but her face was not made for frowns. Instead she waved a finger at him and then, in warning, at Melisande.

"Take care, Melisande, or your father will marry you off to one of the Maharajah's sons."

"In exchange for a casket of rubies and emeralds, Mama? For me?"

"Why not," came her fond Mama's reply.

Richard shook his head. "Not nearly enough for this jewel of a lady."

Melisande felt the blush steal up and pink her cheeks. Oh, it was not official, after all she was only eighteen and should see a little of the world, take the voyage home to England, tour Europe, before settling into married life, but Richard – slim, elegant Richard, with his hazel green eyes and wavy chestnut-brown hair – had been accepted by Papa and her family as her beloved, who would one day marry her.

"On her twenty-first birthday," her father promised them. "If Richard can support you in the style you deserve."

"That would prove impossible," Richard replied, "but I promise I will be able to support her like a princess."

Amidst affectionate laughter, and a hug from her brother, Melisande blessed the day her handsome Richard had arrived with the furniture. Secure, she thought, life in India, with a man she loved with every inch of her being. A man who respected and adored her, who didn't mind her being a plain Jane, who called her his 'Nut Brown Maid', who said she was better than pretty.

"You are striking, elegant, unusual, talented and intelligent. What's more," he went on, "you have ideas in your head, and can hold a conversation. Who wants pretty when you, my lovely Lisa, offer all that?"

She could live with that. They all could. If only it could be forever.

***

The appalling ache wouldn't cease. She couldn't rest her head in any way which would ease it. She wanted a trap door in her skull to open and release the pressure caused by the pain. Opening her eyes seemed impossible, something sealed the lids, or a weight closed them, and where was the light? She couldn't see, her throat and mouth, dry and parched, wouldn't open either. She felt the fear rising again, someone held a damp cloth to the back of her skull and she surged on a wave of agony almost into unconsciousness.

"Melisande, the doctor's here, Doctor Allinson from the hospital. Don't try to talk, just let him examine your head."

Hands, voices, then touching, poking, prodding, holding her skull, sliding over the bone. She tried to swallow and ah, thank God, someone dripped liquid into her mouth drop by drop. It had an oily bitter taste and numbed her tongue.

"Measure this amount of the medicine every seven hours. Drip it in slowly. Be careful, it's strong and addictive. She needs fluids, lemon and barley water, beef tea, even a little black tea, drip it in as often as you can." The voice took on a coaxing, persuasive tone. "Mrs Holyman, you must rest and sleep, do not try to move or sit up. Your head took a bad knock, it shook your brain, which is why you cannot see properly yet, or speak, but believe me, if you remain still, swallow the medicine, and sleep as much as you can the injury will heal. The medicine will put you to sleep, so please rest quietly."

Melisande heard other voices, angry, demanding to speak to her. The doctor, voice sharp and commanding, tried to silence them.

"She must tell us what she knows. She must have seen ..."

"Be silent. Do not disturb her. Questioning her now is not possible. Her head injury means quiet, rest and no anxiety."

We must know who to arrest ..." A scuffle? Loud men's feet tramped away, hustled out by someone else, not the doctor, for he took her wrist.

"Are her family available to visit? A mother's touch is often remembered and can soothe and help to restore the mind."

Those friends again, their voices. "Her parents are dead. We'll care for her. We'll keep her safe and quiet. Thank you, doctor."

"I will arrange with the police to have my father stay here. He specialised in brain and head injuries and can watch over her. Someone tried to throttle her and smashed her skull, but we must wait for her to tell us, and she may never remember."

Never remember? Surely she could. Mama, Papa, could she remember them? She still couldn't recall names for those voices she knew she ought to have names for, but the sleeping draught began to work, and even the pain faded under a smother of darkness. Could she remember her parents? Surely she might.

***

Melisande, carrying out Mama's daily duties at the riverside, collecting the mail and ordering fruit, vegetables and fish required by the household from the market, found herself one of a crowd watching the unexpected arrival of a ship. The rather imposing river boat created much noise and fuss as it shuffled and sidled its way into the Merchants' Wharf. She soon discovered that it had been hired for a tour along the Ganges by wealthy passengers, who had sailed into Calcutta from Asia on a much grander cruise ship, which waited for them at the port downriver.

She brought Papa and Mama, at a leisurely stroll, to their jetty beside the ghat, to watch respectfully as the river boat tooted and huffed its way into berth. Melisande admired its trim white and blue paint, the smart decking, rails and portholes, and the shining brass. It was a toy boat magnified to full size, amusing and harmless, a novel distraction. She would always remember how harmless it seemed.

There was to be a two-day stop for visits to a ruined temple, a shrine and the local markets, as well as the buying in of provisions for the boat from the local farmers. It only took half a day for the guests to learn of the British family nearby, and of her papa's books with her mama's illustrations. Cards and invitations were exchanged.

One elderly gentleman claimed acquaintance of distant kin and Melisande, collecting letters and parcels for Papa from the mail boat the following morning, also collected a message from the gentleman.

Melisande's ayah, Usha, and the syce, Vinay, their groom, tutted and frowned, indignation at a rude sailor's whistling and calling to Melisande and even crosser at her laughing at him. Such behaviour from their charge made them cease their usual bickering to unite in telling Melisande her demeanour was not fitting for a memsahib.

Vinay smacked the reins on the donkey's rump to set the cart moving away at a quick trot, much to the little jenny's surprise. She twitched both long ears and sneezed.

Melisande's ayah scolded all the way home. "What would Mr Holyman, the Richard-sahib think? Such shocking behaviour to encourage!"

Melisande closed her ears, smiled at Usha, and poked the parcels. Surely one held the silver wire she required? And did this one hold the gems, semi-precious beads she needed for the earrings she wanted to make? It rattled as she shook it. Thank goodness the driveway wasn't any longer or she might be cross with Usha. She wasn't a little girl any more, but Usha wouldn't see that.

She sprang from the cart in a flutter of petticoats. "There's a message from the ship, Papa," she called, running up the steps, across the verandah and into the hallway. She hovered as he checked and distributed letters and parcels to Advik. At last, he finished. He'd held back her parcels and now exchanged those packets for the sealed message.

"Come along, Melisande, I'll tell the tale just once. Your mama is in the library."

The library, on the cool side of the house, had latticework shutters which allowed good light to filter through, enough for Mama to work without too much sun and its heat. It was the least Indian of the rooms in their house, with its English library tables, glass-fronted bookcases, and her square piano, but it smelt Indian, of hot dry air, cooking spices, cedar, sandalwood, jasmine and marigolds.

Jeri stood beside Mama, discussing her latest illustration. He looked up and spoke before Papa could. "I've done the rounds, Papa." Oh, he knew how to avoid a fatherly scolding for not being out on the estate. "The storehouse roof is being rethatched even now, and I'm here to find out where that order of roof ties and wires is."

Melisande, clutching her parcels, tried to see Mama's new work. Papa and Jeri blocked her access to the library table. She wriggled and squeezed between them to see what Mama had done. She had been working at this page for some time and had been rather secretive about it. Usually Mama painted the flowers and plants Papa's books, but sometimes, when she could get it, she used fine rice paper which she coloured, cut into petals and leaves and then glued together on the page. It made for a textured and vividly lifelike appearance, but was difficult work. This time she had created two perfect camellia blossoms.

Melisande drew in a quick breath of pleasure. "That is exquisite, Mama." The message remained unread as Papa examined the work. In fact it would have been forgotten if she hadn't reminded him. "What is in the message, the note from the ship, Papa?"

It turned out to be a query about one of Papa's books and an invitation to dinner on the ship. Melisande watched her parents' faces, knowing that they were thinking about the inconvenience of wearing tight, hot, uncomfortable European evening dress, and eating European food, weighing it against the pleasures of possible book sales and news from home.

Her roly-poly parents wore comfortable clothes, European adaptations of Indian clothes for, as Mama said: "Only an Indian lady can wear a sari with the correct grace and elegance." But she and Mama could wear the soft kurtas, long-sleeved tunics, over loose skirts, so much cooler than the heavy materials of the stiff European styles.

Melisande knew what they would do. Jeri flicked her a quick glance, a smile lurking round his mouth. She smiled back.

"I think we should accept, Christabel, my dear. Sales of our books, you know, and we might hear more news about this African trouble and the government's decisions."

"Oh dear, yes, it will be a hot and uncomfortable evening, but you're quite correct, I agree and I too think we should go."

And they went.

Melisande waved them off in the dusk, watching the carriage lamps bob and sway as the two large jack donkeys picked their way round the lumps and bumps in the driveway. The evening air felt silky-soft and the birds had settled from piercing calls into silence. The river gave off its night scents, warmer and richer than the day's, and the night crickets creaked and chirred. She loved India most on soft-scented nights like this, and always would.

Chapter Two

"Can we ask her what happened? Does she know?"

That's an anxious male voice. She isn't certain if that's Papa. Something snags her thoughts ... it isn't Papa? If she could rid herself of the pain perhaps she could think, but it's growing again like zags and jags of lightning inside her skull. If only she could see. Her eyes will only half open and she can't lift her heavy hands to pry open the lids more than a crack. All she can see is a dim, dusky light in front of her, but she can smell people around her, lye soap and disinfectant, lavender water, a man's tweed jacket and pipe tobacco. She still only hears in waves of clear sound then shushing and crackles ring in her ears.

"No, she must remember for herself." That's a firm voice of ... of ... the older Doctor Allinson. He's been a constant presence, scratchy woollen suit, faint scent of pipe tobacco, and a steady breathing and heart beat at night when she ... but she can't think through the noises in her head.

"But we need to know what she saw." The male voice strained to whisper and keened with anxiety. "The police ..."

"Hush, don't. She thinks she's in India. We can't force her." That was another voice she might recognise. A friend ... it was ... She gave up, it was all too much.

"Mrs Holyman, Melisande, it's time for your medicine." The doctor again. "Let me drip it into your mouth. Remember to keep your head still now. And then you must sleep."

The oily taste didn't improve but it did take her away, drifting further from the pain and home to safety.

"Beef broth now, wash the taste away for you, Lisa." That's her friend, her friend ... from church?

Hurrying footsteps, a swish of skirt. "I've more news, worse news."

"Oh no, Ruth please not more bad news."

News? Who was this Ruth bringing news? A neighbour in India? Richard brought the news and newspapers. She remembered that and that was bad news too.

***

Richard ran, ran in the heat, from the Merchants' Wharf. He staggered inside, disturbing a quiet breakfast. 'It's your parents, they're to stay on the ship."

He collapsed on a chair and gulped the spiced, milky Marsala tea Melisande provided. Jeri sat, mouth open, stunned. Such humiliation, and dishonour for them both, Melisande thought, flushed with the disgrace of it. She'd not noticed her parents' absence. Shame curdled inside her, spoiled her breakfast.

"Did you notice, Jeri?" She clutched his arm and turned to Richard. "If they were very late, Richard, they wouldn't disturb us. I assumed they lingered in bed after a boring and tiresome evening."

Richard mopped his face with the towel Usha provided and looked ghastly. "They ... your parents ... can't leave the ship. The Company doctor and the captain forbid it." He drank more cooling tea and towel-dried his hair. "Your father shouted to me from the ship. He orders you not to leave the house, all servants are to be kept from crossing the river to the Merchant's Wharf, and any of the servants or field workers who have been near the ship must be isolated in the guest house at the bottom of the garden."

The sun might glow, the air beginning its dance, quivering with early heat, but Melisande shivered, something deep within froze, chilled her heart so that its beating faltered. "What is it? What do they fear?"

Jeri staggered to his feet. "Those travellers have been in China, it's not … they've not brought the plague with them? It's rife over …"

Melisande whirled round, skirts flying. Jeri grabbed her as she sprang past. "No, Lisa, no. Papa forbade it and you will only distress them."

She struggled, words beating in her throat, wanting to call out 'Mama', but only a whimpering sound emerged.

Richard hoisted himself up and flung his arms tightly around her, enclosing her against his chest. "Lisa, no. The doctor is in charge. Those who are ill are quarantined in the manager's office on the wharf. They will be cared for. Your parents have to stay on the ship."

She pushed away from him. "But it isn't right. They need me to look after them." She, who hated fussy weeping women, fought a bout of weeping. "Is it the plague?"

Richard pulled her close. "I don't know, Lisa. No one is sure, or they won't say. Your father said the elderly gentleman had been coughing all evening and then collapsed."

Melisande rested her head against his heated chest. His heart boomed in her ears and she could feel the blood thrumming through his veins. "Isolation means some dread illness surely. Some dangerous disease. Oh please God, not cholera."

"No, your father would recognise cholera. He would have told me and asked for you to gather some of his plant cures."

Jeri shook his head. "What then?"

Melisande raised her hands to her cheeks. They felt cold, they were wet. She mustn't weep, tears wouldn't help.

Richard brushed his cheek against hers, wiping off both his and her tears. "Don't fret, my love. We will go to your jetty and somehow shout, or float, or sail messages to your parents. Somehow we will send them things they might need."

Jeri patted her back and his voice wasn't steady either. "Let's find some of Papa's remedies which might be of use." He gently touched her shoulder. "What will we need?"

Melisande shook herself and thought. Illness, a serious illness meant fevers, so a remedy for fever, a lotion for parched skin, a liquid to ease a dry throat, and perhaps a palatable drink?

"Herbs, potions, what do we have? Richard, please ask the servants for containers, we might …"

Advik arrived in an undignified rush, a grey pallor over his skin making his face look sick. He laid his hands over his heart. "Sahibs, memsahib, I have heard. I am distressed. What can I do?"

Jeri issued Papa's orders and he almost ran to command the servants and set up the protective quarantine.

Richard followed the steward, seeking clean, safe containers. "Courage, Lisa. We can help them if we are careful," he called back.

Melisande tucked her hand into Jeri's, as she'd done when she was little. It comforted her. He squeezed back, and she knew he needed reassuring too. "You look up fever cures in Papa's notebook, I'll find the plants," she said, giving him something to do, something which might help. That thought consoled her too.

They carried two packets and a basket of remedies and delicacies down to their jetty, defying the servants, and making them obey the quarantine. Melisande gazed across the water to the Merchants' Wharf. The river boat appeared deserted, the deck empty, no sounds except the water lapping gently against its sides. The Ganges was not a vast and wide river but "It may as well be on the moon," she said. "Try a yell, Jeri. I think your voice is strong enough."

Richard joined in and 'Hello, the ship,' echoed across the water.

"I think we should try the bugle," he said when no one appeared on the ship's deck. Jeri groaned. In their family a blast on the bugle meant a warning of danger.

"I don't want to scare Mama," he said.

Melisande pulled the bugle out of the basket; Papa had made them both learn to blow it and she could manage to sound a couple of musical notes. Jeri only made a rude blarting, but loud enough to hurt the ears.

"Let me try," she said, and moistened her mouth, then pursed her lips against the mouthpiece. Two little squeaks and finally she hit the notes, repeating them until she ran out of breath and her cheeks ached.

"There's your Papa." Richard pointed to the stern of the boat. "Mr Allmark," he yelled.

"Hello, Papa," Jeri called. "And, thank God, that's Mama too," he added, his voice lowered to a more reasonable volume. "Just behind him. They're both well, Lisa."

Melisande squeezed her eyelids over threatening tears. Thank God indeed. She truly needed to stop being a milksop miss and see if her idea would work. She waved vigorously and mimed what she was to do. Papa waved back. Right, now could she do it?

"Arrow, thread, have we enough thread do you think? Will it be strong enough?" She looked at the suddenly vast expanse of river between herself and the boat.

Richard held up the spool of thread. "More than enough, Lisa, Now prove the old fairy tale is true."

Jeri wrapped the thread around the first arrow and handed it to her. He was holding a coil of thin rope, and a coil of thicker rope which he'd linked together. "Aim true little sister, and Papa will haul in the thread and then the rope and finally the thick rope with the packets and basket." He gave her a brotherly nudge with his elbow.

"Ow! Warn Papa, please, and mind that bony elbow, dear brother." Melisande returned the nudge then drew in a panting lungful of air and tried to breathe steadily and not shake. The bow was only a child's and the three arrows small and not well made; what if she missed with all three?

Richard watched her, his confident smile showing his steady belief in her. She angled her body away from the more agitated Jeri and set her gaze firmly on the top railing of the boat's deck, near her father. She straightened herself, fixed the arrow, and began a slow count in her head, timing her breathing. The arrow slipped. Her hands were damp. She slid them over her muslin stole, flexed her fingers, and tried again to place the arrow between her first and second fingers. She closed her ears and all her senses to everything except the boat railing. She deliberately imagined blinkers either side of her head, forcing her to see only the narrow path the arrow must take.

"Remember, elevation," Jeri said.

His advice came too late. Melisande had aimed true but low. The arrow skittered off the side of the boat. Mama raised her arms, waved them, reaching skywards, a hint to aim higher. Papa called something, but she failed to make out his words. Melisande covered her face with her hands, inhaled a scented breath of the warm Indian air, rubbed her hands together, and wiped them again on her stole. Richard handed her the next arrow, more thread attached, the excess loosely spooled beside her.

"It doesn't matter if the arrow flies over the ship," he told her, "they will be able to catch the thread."

Of course they could. Melisande gave him a grateful smile and her taut shoulders seemed to float in release as the load of worry lifted. She knew now she could ease the bow into full draw and discharge the arrow. Again she carefully blanked out all distractions, held the arrow, and grasped the bow. "Knock, draw, release," she muttered to herself. She aimed for the banyan tree on the far bank, pulling fiercely on the string. The bow snapped, and the string stung her fingers as it shredded and frayed into bits, but the arrow sped on its way with a furious wobble which nearly took it off course.

Melisande watched, hands to mouth, horror waltzing round her stomach. She willed the arrow to hit the boat. It soared over the boat, and Richard, clever Richard, had been correct. The fine thread trailed low in loops and coils behind the arrow and Mama caught at it, then she and Papa tangled their hands in it, pulling it towards them.

Jeri rushed to ease out the thin rope tied to the thread and all three of them watched as the rope dipped in the river, twisted and twirled, dragging its way across until Papa leant over the side and pulled it in. Now they only had to get enough of the thick strong rope safely over the river for Papa to safely haul in the parcels.

Melisande observed her mother wrapping the thread into a neat hank, and coiling the thin rope. That was mama, tidying up as was her wont. She squeezed away tears. How she needed Mama home and safe.

"Don't Lisa," Richard patted her arm. "We'll have them home soon. Attend please to our task and tie the bags and basket on to the rope."

Jeri and Papa meanwhile had been exchanging a conversation in sweeping arm waves, articulate gestures, and shouts. The message established, Papa and Mama took in the slack of the heaviest rope and attempted to make it taut as they fastened it onto the deck railings.

"Higher," Jeri kept muttering and raising his arms, pushing his hands into the air palms up and jumping to show height.

"They can't tie it anywhere else," Richard decided. "They can hardly reach up and tie it to the funnel."

Jeri snickered as he grasped the rope and passed it back to his sister. Melisande managed a smile as she measured out lengths of rope. She must fasten the parcels far enough apart along the length nearest the river so that the rope could be held up by both men and keep the parcels dry. She and Advik had wrapped each packet in several layers and then together in more paper and cloth before putting them in woven reed bags. The reeds were meant to be waterproof; Melisande eyed them hopefully. And the layers of dried banyan leaves covering the basket's contents of well-stoppered jars should protect them, surely.

She sighed and patted the leaves once more to be sure. "It's done. I think that's fixed each parcel so nothing will be damaged if we do plunge them in the river."

Jeri and Richard inspected her work, then Jeri tested the knots, and Richard grasped the rope.

"You'd better call again," Melisande said. "Tell Papa to haul in the rope when you raise your arms. Make sure he understands and mind your hands against rope burn."

"Sisters," Jeri growled. "Don't fuss. Come on Richard, we'll call for Papa's attention and raise the rope over our heads so he can see what we're doing."

Richard smiled at Melisande. "Then we'll bellow 'Pull'. Best cover your ears."

She smiled back and leaned against the low branch of a handy Arjuna tree, reaching up to gently pull the petals of its nearest yellow blossom to enjoy its scent.

The shouting began. After more arm waving, shouting and miming what they would do, Richard and Jeri raised the rope and began hand over handing it towards the boat.

Melisande looked across the river and held her breath. The rope dipped badly as the parcels moved out over the water. Another man – was it the doctor? – had appeared and joined in hauling the rope. Slowly and cautiously the rope bobbed, dipped and swayed. Time crept tortoise wise until the first parcel reached the boat railings and Mama had it safe in her hands.

Melisande felt too dizzy to cheer, realised she was holding her breath, panted a little, and then shuddered as the rope at the ship's end began to sag. The heavier basket dipped, slipped down, pulling the rope with it, and sat on the water with a splash. It wobbled and tipped to one side. Melisande squeaked in alarm, but a sharp yank and hauling in of the rope – Papa's work – and the basket fetched up against the ship as the second packet reached Mama's hands. She released the parcel, then went to help Papa. Melisande watched the basket. Surely it was lower in the water?

The doctor leaned over and lent a hand, two in fact as he pulled and tugged until Papa could grasp the handle and lift the basket, then pass it to Mama. "All safe," he bellowed, stentorian in his tone, so that Melisande could hear him quite clearly. "Nothing broken or soaked," he added.

Mama leaned over the railings and kissed both her hands towards them, an extravagant display for Mama. Melisande was kissing her hand in return when Papa copied Mama. Melisande had never seen him use such an emotional gesture before. She returned their kisses twice over and then waved vigorously. Jeri and Richard yelled farewells, she called as loudly as she could, and watched her parents wave a last time, framed in the doorway, as the doctor led them away into the main cabin. A picture to remember.

Chapter Three

Firm hands on her head again. Doctor, the voices calling him that. then damp cloths, lavender scented, on her forehead and another bandage wrapped around her skull, covering her eyes once more. And she still couldn't hear properly. Sounds, voices, came in rushes and spurts, fading then exploding. She felt something like a ball bouncing inside her head. It hurt as it struck the sides of her skull. At least the lightning bolts had faded, were less frequent.

"We must know what Mrs Holyman did. She surely saw …"

"No," more men's voices, loud, then thankfully fading, the doctor talking them down.

"She must not be forced to remember or speak." The doctor. Yes, that was his cross man's voice anyway. "Her memories might never return, although I am fairly certain that her voice and vision will increase. Leave her now."

Blessed peace. Just gentle hands making her comfortable.

She could drink for herself now, sip through a tube from a glass or cup, and yet she was lost somewhere inside her head, trying to find herself again. There was something she must remember.

"She keeps muttering about India." Voices again. Ruth and … and?

"Oh, Charlotte, if only we knew what she'd seen. Such a death."

Charlotte? But Charlotte wasn't at the funeral …

***

The huge funeral pyre burnt all day. Melisande stared at it from the house verandah. The manager's office, across the river, forming the pyre's wooden outer shell, burnt well. All the bodies tossed inside, not placed by loving hands, remained hidden. The perfumed funeral oils were overpowered by the stench of fuel oil with which the whole building had been drenched. But death had a distinct smell Melisande knew well. The crematorium downriver had made her familiar with the odour. The burning bodies stank, the heat currents swirled sparks and flakes upwards, snaking in a sooty smear across the lovely blue sky.

No more tea here, Melisande thought, no more evening concerts, singing new songs, playing new music, no more entertaining their friends from Calcutta, and no more family time on the verandah, with that spectacular view of the Ganges, the delicate scent from the honeysuckle climbing over the pillars perfuming the air. Her family no longer existed. Her sense of home and family collapsed into a void which she didn't know how to fill. How do you learn to live without the guidance of two people who have been your whole world? Jeri was no help, Richard devastated too.

Five days since the boat arrived, five days in which all those who sat with the old gentleman at his table, or served him, or tried to help him, all those who had contact with him, were gone, dead and gone. The captain had survived, the Company doctor had not. Nor had Mama and Papa.

Jeri and Richard, as stunned and leaden of life as she was, struggled to sort through Papa's orderly papers at his neat desk in the library, trying to find a will, addresses of people to inform, and some idea of what to do next. Jeri had been expecting to leave for England and Papa's family home at the end of the year. He was to learn estate management. Melisande had expected to travel with him, if a suitable companion could be found, or perhaps with Mama and Papa, who had talked of a six-month visit home and then a European tour. After which it should have been a return home to India and marriage.

Richard was as heart-struck as Melisande or Jeri. "They were like parents to me," he explained. "I'm desolate. My affection for them was as for my parents. I can't understand why this had to happen."

Melisande, weeping into his shoulder, felt his sobs and could not stop her own. Jeri joined them in a three-round hug which they held, physically supporting each other until they could control their emotions once more. Then it was back to simple tasks they could do without thinking, without feeling, which Melisande prayed for devoutly. She felt another brush with any emotion would shrivel her away. She was all raw skin and nerve endings. She could bear no more.

"Come, eat something, Little Missy, please, eat." Usha appeared at her side.

Downcast servants had been offering meals, but time staggered and faltered, Melisande had no notion of what meal was on offer. Weariness wrapped around her, encased her like stone, pulling her down, pinning her to the ground until night fell and she could collapse into bed. Time stopped altogether at night. Melisande never knew if she'd slept or not. She certainly felt tired, pounded, as if her bed had been made of tumbling rocks, jolting her bones, crushing and draining her of energy and life. Such weighty grief.

"Come Little Missy, come sahibs, eat a little of the nourishing dahl cooky has made." Usha and Advik coaxed and persuaded. They shepherded the three into the dining room where they had arranged food on the low table under the window.

Melisande sat on one of the square floor cushions, Jeri and Richard lumbered floorwards after her, rigid and uncoordinated, clumsy as camels. She found her throat stiff, reluctant to swallow. Some soft dahl and a carrot pottage slipped down, a sip, a pause, two sips, then tiny spoonful by spoonful, until she'd managed half a bowl. The meal, many little dishes, tempted them all to eat. The food did not vanish but they tasted most offerings and the scattered remnants only evoked a smile from Usha as she supervised the kitchen maids scurrying to clear the table.

"What are we going to do?" Melisande meant without Mama and Papa, but couldn't make herself say that. "Money, the printing, the books …" so much she'd never had to concern herself with. The thought of all she needed to learn overpowered her; she pulled herself up to her feet, wobbled two steps, then slumped in a large chair.

Jeri held his head as though he feared it might fall off. Richard massaged the back of his neck and groaned.

"You need to think of returning to your work, Richard." Melisande reached a hand out to him. "Not that I want you to leave but …"

He clasped her hand, massaging her palm with his fingers and smiling wearily at her. "I know, but there is our future to consider."

She opened her mouth to speak, to ask why there might be a problem, but Jeri shook his head at her.

"No one expected … Pa … our father …" he swore under his breath, got to his feet and paced round the table. "They didn't expect to die." He contrived to say the words, his mouth twisting them out as if they pained him physically. "He borrowed money for the new printing press and to build the printing shed."

Melisande gaped. "We are in debt? Can we not pay? Must we …"

"No, no." Jeri stopped pacing and grasped her other hand, giving it a reassuring squeeze. "But I am not yet twenty-one, not until November. I am under age, as you are too."

"And how does that affect this debt?"

"Come outside, let us take a turn round the garden and discuss the problems. Richard, being so much older and wiser …" Here Richard gave him a punch on the upper arm which he returned. "As I said, Richard will give us the wisdom and experience of his twenty- four years."

The evening offered a mild warmth and a superb view of the sun setting over the water. Melisande walked between her two young men and took comfort from the sounds of the river and the scents from the spring blossoms. She loved this place so, it was the best of India, and by the sacred Ganges. Their pace was slow, she found it hard to step out, but

Richard shortened his stride to match hers and Jeri copied his action. None of them moved in sprightly fashion anyway.

"Our official guardian would be our uncle, in England."

Melisande wished her head felt clearer, grief sneaked in like a river mist invading her head, wrapping her thoughts in fuzziness. Thinking became a struggle, like wading against a current in knee-deep water; it required concentrated effort. "I think I knew that."

"According to Mr Know-Everything," here Jeri indicated Richard, "we are not obliged to pay the debt because we are under age and therefore …"

"Not liable by law." Richard finished.

Melisande looked at them both. "You can't mean … you wouldn't dishonour Papa so. We must pay."

Her brother stood tall and looked down his nose. "Sisters!" He glared at her as Richard slipped an arm round her shoulders and turned her towards him. "Lisa, dear Lisa, would I let your brother behave in such a manner? Yes, the debt will be honoured, but things are difficult because Jeri is not twenty-one. We have to involve others."

Melisande managed a fraction of a smile into his face, and linking arms with them both, led them past the fountain into the flower garden. The garden was not truly Indian in the grand Mughal style with terraced lawns and large water features, but it did have a small rectangular waterway, with pretty scallop-shell fountains at either end, and a rose garden laid out in squares beyond it. The water gently splashing into the fountain bowl made a comforting background of sound to their talk.

"You said the debt was not large, Jeri? Can we pay it off with the jute crop after harvest?"

Her brother and Richard exchanged glances above her head. She mistrusted that look.

"Oh, yes, we could. Papa's …" Jeri still found it difficult to say Papa, "the will is simple and all is left to provide an income for Ma … our … mother." He could not bring himself to say Mama. "After which the property is mine and there is money for you. But it is all tied up legally until we come of age. We have to find a way to use what we have without waiting for our uncle's permission." He released her arm, turned away towards the fountain and sat on the lip of the bowl, with his back towards them both.

Melisande moved towards him, but Richard barred the way with his outstretched arm. There were tears in his eyes too. She found a handkerchief and used it, listening to a jackal yap across the river, leaning on Richard, and trying to find balance within herself.

The night crickets began their chirruping as she strung two thoughts together rather as she strung her beads to make a necklace, slowly and carefully, linking her way from the thought that September was five months away, to the thought that five months might be long enough to receive a letter of instructions from their uncle.

"I think, Jeri," she paused, waiting for him to turn and listen. "Jeri, we could surely stay here until we hear from our uncle. That should be by September. We would have paid off the debt by then and we can continue our lives. You have this estate to run, I will learn to use the printing press, and make the books."

"You forget, I am to leave for England in September. You cannot stay here alone."

"I can come with you."

"No."

"You could stay."

"No."

Melisande waited for an explanation, but nothing was said. "Jeri?" In the gathering darkness she could only see his profile outlined against the pale cream stone of the fountain. She looked up. "Richard?"

No reply. "What are you not telling me? And why?" Melisande addressed them both.

Jeri sighed, came over and tucked his hand under her elbow. Richard caught her other elbow. Between them they swung her round and walked past the roses, heading towards the house.

"Lisa, why am I going to England?"

"You're the spare," she managed to put a touch of humour into her voice, hoping to add a little cheer. "You are to learn to manage the estate in case the heir cannot. Aunt Lillian produced the heir but not a spare. Only our cousin George and our girl cousins have survived." She remembered her parents' comments about how fortunate they were never to have lost a child whilst poor Aunt Lillian had buried half her babies. She blinked back more tears. Another thought that hurt.

"The chances of my hearty cousin, George, failing to inherit are slim. I will spend ten months learning all I can in England, but then I want an estate of my own."

Melisande slowed from a stroll to a halt. "But you have this lovely place. Our home." She turned, made an embracing gesture which encompassed the fields, the orchards and the river, all wrapped in the velvety warm Indian darkness.

"Yes, well ... Come on in, Lisa, the mosquitoes have started buzzing round me." Jeri hurried her up the verandah steps. Richard followed slowly, as if waiting for Jeri to finish what he intended to say.

Melisande reached out to her brother. "I don't understand. This is our home."

"Lisa, I went to school in England, I spent my childhood years there ..."

"I know that."

"You didn't and you have spent most of your life here. You were only two when we came to live in India. You've had ayah Usha to care for you, syce Vinay to run after you, sircar Advik to guard you, servants for every task, and the best of tutors in our parents ... " he broke off, swallowed, flicked his head sideways as if he could toss away his grief, "I've spent more time in England. I prefer the green countryside. I hate the heat of Indian summers. I want my children to grow up in a decent Christian country with children like them for friends."

Melisande stared. She'd never worried about friends for she had been surrounded by her family, her parents, ayah and syce and the other servants who, with Mama, cosseted her with loving kindness. Then she had met Richard who filled in any gap with his companionship. Also she'd had tasks to do, her piano, embroidery, painting and jewellery making. She shook her head. "I don't understand."

Richard urged them inside but she stopped, let them pass her, and stood under the porch lantern watching the moths blundering against its sides to scorch their wings and fall. She knew how they felt.

"Lisa." Jeri pulled her inside. "Richard understands. He would not choose to stay in India forever."

Melisande stared at Richard. He gave her a rueful look. He knew what she felt about her home and India, but he nodded. This was betrayal. She turned and fled to her bedroom.

Chapter Four

"Melisande, Melisande, medicine time, just one little spoonful. Come, open your mouth for me. Then you can go back to dream time." That wasn't Doctor Allinson.

She had something to do, something hidden in those memories, but oh her head still ached and rang, her ears still buzzed and crackled, and all her eyes saw were little flashes of light.

"Will she dream her way back to us, do you think, Ruth?"

"She'd better. Only she knows who killed ..."

"Hush, don't say it. She mustn't be upset and I can't bear to think of it. You'll make us both fretful."

"But we must know, all of us are under suspicion, all of us watched by this Doctor Allinson for the police ..."

"We have told the police all we know, we simply have to be patient. You and I are considered 'safe' to be near Lisa, we have to nurse her back to health and hope her memories ..."

"Oh, Charlotte, now you're making me fretful."

***

Fretting was what she was doing now. After a fitful, restless night, Melisande finally gave up trying to find peaceful rest and rose as the sun made its appearance. She determined to read Papa's will and see what she could make of it, then she could make her own plans. This was her home, all she asked for was this fine secure place for the rest of her life. Usha, sleeping on a pallet on the floor, insisted on rising and clothing Melisande and then dressing her hair. It was as well she did for Richard and Jeri, who looked as though they had not slept, sat round her mother's work table in the study with papers scattered between them and maps open across the whole surface. No chance of finding Papa's will and reading it privately now.

Melisande walked up to the table, stood beside her brother's chair and frowned at him. He raised his eyebrows. Richard avoided her glance.

"Can you please explain how you are going to leave India with the debts paid. I don't understand. Please tell me what all this," she waved her arm over the contents of the table, "is about." She didn't add her last thought out loud, but clamped her teeth on her tongue and held back the words "There is no possibility of me leaving home." She did, however, feel like indulging in a three year old's screech of 'You can't make me leave.'

Richard finally met her gaze and the look he gave her was full of sorrow. "Lisa, my Nut Brown Maid," he held out his hand to her. "We are trying to arrange something good for us all out of this disaster."

"Looking at all our problems I don't consider leaving India is a good conclusion." she replied. "Mama and Papa gone, we are under age, our guardian is in England, and we must wait for his instructions which will surely reach us before September. There, I've reckoned four reasons why we have to wait here."

Advik padded quietly into the room, and bowed his small half bow. "Sahib Jeri, memsahib, it is more than a week. Do I follow my instructions for those in quarantine?"

Melisande remembered first. "Are the servants well, Advik? We should have asked sooner. I am sorry."

"No, Little Missy, you have your sorrows. They are well. They had not been on the boat, only across the river nearby."

"Then we are pleased to see them released to their old positions, are we not, Jeri?"

"It may not ..." Jeri began, but broke off when Richard touched his arm and gave a slight shake of his head. "Indeed, see to it, please," he finished.

Advik regarded Jeri, a long thoughtful look, bowed again and departed.

Melisande sighed, watched Advik depart and then glared at her brother. "What is happening? What are you planning?"

Richard answered. "Lisa, you must be brave. What has happened has radically altered all our lives. But with courage we can go forward into a different future, a good future, although I understand how difficult it is to see that today. In a year's time we might even be able to say that we triumphed over tragedy, made something good out of our despair. We can make decisions now which will give opportunities for Jeri and myself, ultimately for us all."

"The death of our parents a great opportunity?" Her voice rose to a shriek. She clapped a hand to her mouth to hold in the noise and her head shook with the effort. When she had control she spoke again. "I can't believe this. Had you planned this for when you went to England, Jeri? Did Papa know this?"

"What 'this'?" he demanded.

"That you would not return."

"No."

Melisande sank onto the nearest chair. "I am bewildered." She knew she was complaining and her voice had risen shrilly ending in something like a cricket's squeak. She waited for an answer.

"Listen, sister mine, I did not know. Once in England, when I felt I'd learnt enough to manage a small estate, I was going to look for a position managing someone else's. That was all I could hope for. But now ..." His voice died away as he leaned across to pat her hand. "Now I can own my own estate."

Melisande pressed her fingers to her temples, fearing her head might explode. "But you have this estate here in India and ..." She lifted her head, felt her jaw drop again. She forced her mouth to form the words. "No, you can't mean … it is not possible. You wouldn't sell … you can't sell. This is my home."

"But I can. The Calcutta Trading Company have already made an offer. Business is expanding and they can use the house for their manager here and the land for growing opium poppies."

Melisande shook her head slowly in denial. This was her home, her only home, her safe place, full of memories of her beloved parents, that Jeri talked of selling, as easily as if it were a set of Papa's books.

"It's a good offer, Lisa," Richard said, "generous even, for I think the management feel guilty about your parents, because of allowing that ship to use their wharf. And your father's loan came from the Company bank, thus they are pleased to make the offer and settle the debt at the same time. It avoids the under-age problem as your uncle's cable gave permission for the sale."

"You've already been in touch with my uncle?"

"Of course, listen Lisa, we must set things straight now, and then …"

"No!" She didn't see how, and gripped the chair seat to prevent herself sliding to the floor. She closed her eyes against the flashes of light as the walls spun around her, and the floor seemed to heave and dip under her. She opened her mouth and heard her breath pump in and out in a rapid pant. She couldn't believe this. Losing Mama and Papa had been a devastation, to lose her home in India hit her with such a shock she thought her heart had stopped.

"I am determined, Lisa. As my sister you are my responsibility. You will come with me. We leave at the end of May, we have six weeks to pack and depart."

Six weeks? Impossible. How could she leave? Her home, the servants, Mama's paintings, the press, all the books. In those short weeks? Underneath the pain, anger flickered.

Richard left Jeri at the table, and knelt in front of her. "We've arranged a scheme for you, Lisa, don't be afraid, don't be upset. We're here to take care of you." He lifted both her hands and slid them between his own. "I know we were to wait until you were a little older and had seen something of the world, but how would you like to see the world on your honeymoon?" He pressed her hands together gently. "We can marry now, there will be no problem about your age. I am of age, it is well known that your parents had given their consent, your brother does. You see, this means you are safe and looked after."

That flicker of anger grew until she found herself bent over, gripping Richard's hands so tightly she hurt him as well as herself. "I'm safe here, in my home."

"Don't you wish to marry me, Lisa, my love?" Richard eased her grip on his hands, and clasped hers.

"Married, when? Now, next week? Leave India so soon? And what about our uncle and what he might say?"

"Lisa, Lisa my love. Don't be afraid, I will take care of you."

Melisande lifted her face and inspected Richard's, noting the anxiety in his eyes, and his expression of genuine loving concern. He did care. She held back the anger, tried to be calm, but couldn't stop clenching her hands inside his.

If only her tongue didn't feel weighted down, heavy, immobile, too solid to lift and shape words. She tried to explain. "I haven't even got decent mourning to wear and you talk of a wedding. Papa can't give me away nor Mama give me my marriage morning talk. Our family and acquaintances won't be able to attend a ceremony. What sort of wedding is that? And you want me to abandon my life here and go … go where?"

Jeri slapped his open hand on the table top. "That's your duty as a wife, that's what you must do, follow your husband. Don't be missish." He dropped his hectoring tone and turned from bully to her dear elder brother, coaxing her.

"Melisande, my little sister, Lisa. Where is your sense of adventure? Our life here is finished. Could you really continue in this house without Mama and Papa?" He paused as his voice wobbled, he inhaled and began again. "I can't. We would look for them, hear them, forever bumping into their ghosts because of our memories. We can make a new life for ourselves. Yes, I must learn how to manage livestock and farm in a different climate from India, but then I want position and an estate of my own."

She had to make him understand. He wasn't thinking sensibly. "Jeri, you must have heard Papa talking about this, even I know selling our Indian estate will not give you enough money to buy anything other than a small farm, a yeoman's family affair, in England."

"I know that. So does Richard, but together we could break in land and create an estate in the colonies."

The colonies? What colonies? Melisande simply gawked, she knew she did, unable to find a word to say or the breath with which to say it.

Jeri eyed her. "If we leave quickly we'll have time to travel, take a ship to Australia and even on to New Zealand if we can't find what we want in Australia. We can seek land, something suitable, before I travel home to England."

Australia? New Zealand? Melisande could only flap her hands as though wafting away the idea, gasping in a struggle to breathe.

Jeri sought Richard's attention with a meaningful look. Richard continued. "If we find good land," he told Melisande, "you and I will begin to make the estate, have a house built, farm livestock whilst Jeri continues to England, and he'll join us after a year, full of knowledge, new ideas and anything useful he might transport on the ship. He can bring plants, seeds, even trees, you know. Anything we write to ask him to find. " He smiled and caught her hands again, pressing them gently. "Be brave, my love, be adventurous."

"No, no, no."

"Don't you wish to marry me?"

"Richard! You know I do."

"Well then, my little love, a quiet wedding, because we are in mourning, a comfortable voyage, enlarging your experiences of the world as your parents wished, and then we'll build our new home together."

Melisande looked at her two men. Her brother, almost quivering with excitement and hopeful for his promising future, the way he desired it, and Richard, the green flecks in his hazel eyes glinting as they did when he anticipated something pleasurable, giving her his most loving look.

She tried to think. How could she delay them, stop this rush from everything she loved into a sure disaster. She knew she had none of the skills an adventurous colonial woman needed and what did her men know about farming without servants. Were there servants in the colonies? How could they plough, plant or sow, grow any corn crops? Her eye fell on *The Lady* magazine tucked down a chair cushion where Mama had left it. Clothes – she didn't have proper mourning dress nor did she have winter clothes for colder countries. What Mama had stored away would not fit her, though perhaps a cape or mantel might be made over. And then there had to be gloves and hats, stockings and undergarments. She daren't wear her lovely Indian clothes in countries as cold as Australia and even more so, New Zealand.

"Clothes, I don't have proper clothes." Another thought surfaced in her fuzzy mind. "And you are surely not considering leaving from Calcutta, where the plague is still dangerous?"

"Oh, my practical and prosaic sister. We shall leave in a month's time from the port and you can order all you need now and it will be on the ship ready for you."

"Money ... how do we ...?"

Both Jeri and Richard interrupted. "Banker's draft for travelling," Richard said.

"Papa has cash in his safe, we are secure until the sale is finalised."

How could she make them understand? "But how can we sell when you're underage? I don't wish to leave, I don't have the slightest inclination to leave, nor do I want to. This is my home. I want and need a home."

Jeri combed his hair with his hands, grasping chunks of it to twist and tug. "For goodness sake, Lisa. You cannot remain in this house when it has been sold. You cannot live in India on your own, it is not conceivable. Who will protect you, escort you to social occasions? What sort of life would it be? Our uncle would never permit it and nor do I."

She could manage this house with Advik and Usha, surely that would be permitted? All she needed was ... ah, but she did. "I have money, you said I had money."

"And our uncle and I control that money and will not allow you one penny until you are married and installed on our land, wherever that might be."

How could he, her brother, do this to her? She sobbed in furious anger. "Jeri, you can't force me."

"I can and will." He turned to Richard, frustration and exasperation colouring his face with a patchy red flush, putting a snap into his voice. "For God's sake talk some sense into her." He slammed out of the room, bellowing for Advik.

Talk sense? How dare he! He needed the sense, not she. Melisande had no tears left, but her eyes tried, her throat convulsed with dry sobs and her cheeks burned with resentment. Richard, who had always been a true gentleman, and never tried to do more than put an arm round her waist or kiss her cheek, surprised her by scooping her up, swinging her round and sitting both of them down, with Melisande firmly on his knee. What did he think he was doing? She tried to wriggle free but his arms hugged her in a close embrace and he kissed her, little kisses running from her temple to her throat, along her jawline to her lips and back again.

That was a distraction, should she let him do this? Melisande's dry sobbing stopped. She tried to break free, to stand, but Richard's arms clamped her tightly to him.

"You must listen, my love." He now began nibbling kisses to her ear and the nape of her neck, then back to the hollow of her throat and finished with one long fierce kiss to her lips. Melisande found herself breathless. Richard's arms relaxed, his grip eased and he kissed her again, long and demanding. She found herself responding. She wasn't experienced at this kissing business, but Richard seemed pleased, for he kissed her a third time.

"There now, my love." He resumed his little kisses and his hands moved, one to cradle her head, fingers woven through her hair, thumb stroking her cheek, the other round her waist to pull her as close to him as possible in a more comfortable embrace. It felt lovely.

In between the kisses he spoke softly, gentle murmurs showing his good sense and his understanding of her feelings. "This is Jeri's future, you wouldn't deny him the opportunity to make more of himself now he has this chance?"

But what about my future, she thought but found herself feeling shaky, trembling rather. All the kissing and touching stirred sensations she didn't know or understand.

"It's not only Jeri's opportunity, Lisa, my Nut Brown Maid." Richard stopped the kisses, and spoke earnestly. "You have scope now to do so much more in your life. You are very young and know so little of the world beyond this sheltered paradise." He put his hands either side of her head and turned her face so that she had to look into his eyes. "Lisa, I would like to travel, see new places, and if we can make a better life for ourselves and our children in Australia or New Zealand then shouldn't we?"

Melisande watched his hopeful expression and thought about the changes. It was all too much, she didn't know what to do. "If things become difficult then we can return to India?"

"Only if we need to make our fortunes again."

"Richard, I can't. I can't go."

He rocked her in his arms as though she were a little girl again. "Lisa we've tried to give you a choice, tried to let you understand and agree. But you have to accompany your brother. Your uncle might well demand you return to England. Do you want that? To be in a strange place with people you don't know. That is not family. We are your family, Jeri and I. If you are safely married you will have Jeri, the last of your family, and," he smiled and kissed her again full on the lips, "me."

She rested her forehead against his, thinking.

"Your only other choice, my Nut Brown Maid, if you cannot bear to marry me and go to Australia, will be to return to England and your uncle. The magistrate's wife is sailing soon, taking her children to school and chaperoning her daughter for the London season and a debutante's coming out. She will chaperone you on the crossing. That's the best we can do for you." He sounded so disappointed, his eyes darkened, his mouth downturned. "Think about it well, my love. Consider what I've said. You do have a choice. Choose well."

It was not an easy choice All she wanted was a home, a safe place to be, a home like this one, with servants, a garden and what was left of her family.

Chapter Five

Dull aches and ringing ears annoyed her now, but that was far better than the dreadful pressure both inside and outside her skull with that crushing, squeezing sensation on the top of her head. And her eyes leaked tears again. They'd been dry and sore, full of woody sawdust like grit, but now she could blink comfortably against the bandage the doctor insisted she cover them with. She felt perhaps her head was improving. The doctor made approving murmurs as he rebandaged it and moistened the pads covering her eyes.

"The bandages must remain, Mrs Holyman. They support your skull. You must keep quiet and still, and I am sorry, but your eyes need to rest in darkness. I am sure you will see again once your head has recovered from the concussion. It was a severe blow but your skull is healing well, and sleep is the best thing for you. When the pain ceases and when you are able to tell me where you are and what happened, only then will I allow you to move around."

Someone offered her another teaspoon of the medicine. It made her sleep and truly she was grateful to rest in a deep blackness out of the pain, but that linctus still tasted vile.

She knew something had happened, but what did the man, that doctor, mean by asking her to tell him where she was. She was home wasn't she? India of course ... but no ... home was ... home was ... She gave up and sobbed, actually cried. She never cried. "I can't remember."

A chorus of voices, dominated by the doctor's, spoke the same theme. "You will remember. When your head heals."

Hands patted her hands. Her friends, kind women's voices, Ruth and ... and ... Charlotte. "Rest, dream and you will remember."

But who was the male whose voice muttered "She'd better or we're all in trouble."

She drifted away into a drug-induced sleep remembering, remembering her parents had died.

***

Usha put her to bed that evening, and she let her prattle in gentle and sorrowful tones as she massaged Melisande's scalp, brushed and lightly oiled her hair, then applied the scented cream of Papa's making to her face and neck. She heard nothing, but her body responded to the musical murmurs. Her strained neck and aching shoulders eased, her scalp ceased its tight crawl. Hoping to make sense of her brother's attitude and Richard's reasoning, she struggled to work through the things Richard had said.

She had never wanted more of life than she now had. India, loving parents, a home here by the Ganges, her beloved Richard, and her friends among the servants who would have gone with her to her married home. She could have continued her sketching with Mama, her jewellery making, and helping Papa with the printing press and his books. She'd assumed marriage to Richard would be like the marriage her parents shared, and it had been a sharing partnership and a loving one. Wasn't that what Richard intended their marriage to be? Yet he had given her a choice, marriage with him or return to her father's family, sent to England, accompanying the local magistrate's wife. She must not be alone and unprotected. Proper, socially correct young ladies from 'good families' must be under their father's or a senior relative's protection until they married, and then they would be 'protected' by their husband. She knew this even if she had not seen its consequences in a less than ideal life. Now she wondered.

She heard his voice again. "Do you wish to be with me loving you like this, or this or this?" Her skin tingled at the memory of the sensations, she'd not realised that touch could make her feel so ... so ... she didn't quite know what it was she felt. Her mother told her that she would explain about married life and having babies on her wedding morning. Mama's plump cheeks had pinked up with a rosy glow as she spoke. "It will sound peculiar but it isn't." This time her face flushed with pleasure not embarrassment. "The physical side of marriage is something you and dear Richard will learn together."

Usha had folded her clothes, cleared her dressing table and now sat back on her heels, beside the bed, the mosquito net draped round her like a veil. She looked up at Melisande, patiently waiting.

"What do I decide, Usha? What should I do? I don't want to leave India, it's my home."

Usha's large, dark eyes were liquid bright, but she shed no tears. "I know. You must go with your men. Plan, you need money. Money makes freedom. Have you money, Little Missy?"

Melisande wrinkled her nose, puzzled, but did some reckoning in her head. "I have some."

"And jewellery? Valuable enough to sell?"

"I think so. Why, Usha?"

"My first family here, the memsahib was later wife. She had her babies and his two big daughters. Sahib's grown daughters but not hers."

"Oh, I think I ..."

"Hush, Little Missy, you listen. They wanted to be home, never wanted to come to India. Their mama's family, in Ireland, was home. Sahib Papa said 'No'."

Usha rubbed the soles of Melisande's feet, such a soothing feeling. "I hear about the young man Papa did not approve, and young man's welcoming family in Ireland. The daughters took jewellery, sold it, used allowance money, ran off to ship and Ireland."

Melisande blinked, watched her ayah's smile hidden in her eyes. "Did you help, Usha?"

Usha lowered her head, wouldn't answer, but she patted Melisande's feet again. "You make a secret place for your money. Keep some good jewels. Then you have ship ticket home." She smiled, gave a swift glance at Melisande. "We Indian wives do that, guard our family's money, wear our savings." She jangled her gold bracelets and anklets, touched her earrings and nose stud.

"Sahib Richard, good kind man. But he wants exciting life, with your brother, seeks adventure, find fortune."

"But what about me?" Melisande tried not to wail. She was not a child but the descriptions of Australia and New Zealand had little to recommend them compared to India. One was mainly hot dry desert with weird animals, the other cold and wet with sheep. Talk of gold and farming land did not impress her, although the new idea of supplying chilled meat to Europe sounded fascinating. The government men from New Zealand, who came to India encouraging half pay officers to take up land grants in New Zealand, were full of the chiller technology and the farming opportunities, gold even, available to find in streams.

"You marry good man, Richard sahib, he generous, gentle, he's good to you. My Little Missy will be safe, will be in good place."

"I do care for him, Usha, but …"

"And he for you Missy. You go with him and live good life with him."

But Melisande didn't dare admit that she had no courage, felt afraid, was a coward, not to her ayah who told her she was so brave. Leave everything she knew and loved … for what? What she wanted in her life was a lovely home like this, a home full of love and kindness. Her men talked of adventure, a little prospecting for gold, 'seeing the world'. She'd much rather see India. And what did they expect her to do if they rode off chasing gold or adventures? Was she supposed to keep camp for them in some wilderness, waving off ferocious beasts with her bow and arrows? That made her smile and Usha clapped her hands softly, making chirrups of encouragement. "I go chase that lazy derzi, that tailor man," she said. "We make you ready as for England. Memsahib Mama had cloth for cold clothes, for you both." She paused. "And maybe you use some of Memsahib's pretty things?"

A reminder, a tangible reminder, of the dearest Mama a young woman could have. Shawls, wraps, scarves, fans, so much to choose from.

"And Usha, my best of ayahs, after I have decided which things to keep, would you organise all the women servants so they can pick something too. After they have chosen what is left is yours."

Usha ducked her head to wipe away a few tears.

"It would be best if I saw to Papa's things as well. Should I ask Advik to help? He and Papa respected each other. Perhaps he'd like Papa's chess set too if Richard does not. And the menservants might like a memento."

"There now, Little Missy, don't you worry, you sleep, sleep 'til morning. Tomorrow we'll do all things, tomorrow comes a better day for you."

She forgot to add that tomorrow never comes.

***

So where was her home? And where was Richard? What had they done? She was Mrs Holyman. The doctor called her that. When did she marry? And where? They removed, yes, they removed in a great ... in a great fuss. Jeri made a fuss, but Richard was kind. Where was he? Jeri had had to go ...? Oh, the utter frustration of not remembering properly but in fits and starts, scraps and oddments floating through her brain.

Chapter Six

Jeri wanted to go across the river to ask about booking their berths on a ship. He intended to leave after breakfast, but Melisande prevented him, standing in the doorway, arms spread out.

"You and Richard have matters to discuss," he said, trying to walk round her.

"No, brother mine, you and I have matters to discuss."

Jeri raised his eyebrows. "Oh yes?"

"Yes, Papa's things."

"Leave that to Advik."

How like Jeri to dodge the difficulties. "I mean clothes and personal things. The servants would surely cherish a memento and wouldn't you wish to keep some things?"

Jeri shrugged. "The servants can pack everything in a couple of trunks and we will ship it …"

"A couple of trunks? Jeri, there is an entire house full of furniture, a huge library of books. Then there's the herbal collection, the printing press and books, the artist's studio. Where will you find the money to pay for shipping all that and where is it to be shipped?

Jeri's mouth gaped open. "But …" he stuttered, and fell silent.

Hah! And he wants us to leave in four weeks? Melisande glowered at her brother. He had grown to rely too much on the efficiency of Advik and the other servants.

Richard regarded her with a distinct twinkle. "That's my Nut Brown Maid. What do you suggest, Lisa, my practical commonsensical one?"

"Serious thinking," Melisande said. "How civilised are these colonies? How easy is it to buy good furniture and silverware and …"

"Enough," Jeri begged. "We don't need much. I planned to sell the printing press and books. What else do we need?"

If only screaming and a fit of hysterics would make Jeri think of the simple practicalities of life. And under no circumstances was he selling the books and press. "You are not selling all the books. I wish to keep some and there will be universities, even the Royal Society librarian, who would be eager to have them. The medical department of the university here might welcome the herbs and notes."

Richard managed a laugh. "Jeri, you and I must consult the experts, and organise that. Lisa has the right of it. We must consider and not be in haste."

Jeri opened his mouth.

"There's money to be made from all this," Richard gestured round the room, "for our estate." He gave Jeri a friendly shake of the shoulder. "And you know, if we think about it carefully, it makes sense to arrive with the basic equipment for our new home. There's a good book in my office about what a gentleman needs to take to the colonies. It actually applies to India, but some of it will be useful. We must take our time and become organised." He linked arms with Jeri and they turned to leave.

All they could think of was their adventure! She nearly seized the brass incense bowl from the side table to hurl at them and knock sense into their silly heads. "Wait, there is so much we need to do to honour Papa and Mama." Melisande forced her throat to open, swallowing the lump which threatened tears. "We have to see the servants have work, either here in the house, or somewhere in the village. We must give them all a gift in farewell. What about the animals? We can't just leave them. The donkeys will need a caring home."

Jeri scowled, then glanced at Richard. Richard raised his eyebrows and sighed.

"Don't try to leave, there's more." Melisande hurried around Richard and Jeri, blocking their exit again. "What do we need for a wedding?" She felt warmth blush into her cheeks as Richard smiled his special smile for her. "What documents do we need to travel? How do we move our things?"

Jeri shrugged. "We leave the house clearance to Advik, of course, what is a steward for?"

How can he be so unfeeling? Melisande regarded her brother, puzzled by his indifference. "You are asking me to leave my home, my whole life, all the familiar furniture and everything which has made this home for me. There are things I cherish and would like to have with me. I'm not leaving my piano or Mama's art equipment." She reached out to shake his arm. "Surely you have favourite items you would want in your new home?"

"I don't wish to waste money for my estate shipping goods we can probably buy in the colonies."

"How do you know?" Melisande's voice rose; she strove to control the irritation she felt like venting with a good sharp smack on her brother's arm.

Richard stepped in, catching Melisande by the elbow before she could explode into unwise speech. "I have an idea. We can have a sale, raise money to ship your things, Lisa. Advik can organise the other servants to help with that."

Jeri nodded. "Excellent, Richard. We'll take the launch upriver to town and organise an auctioneer for the sale, even find answers for Lisa's questions." He grinned, ducked around his sister and left the room calling back over his shoulder to Richard, "Come on."

Richard squeezed both Melisande's hands, gave her a loving look, and followed Jeri.

"Men!" she exclaimed. "Do they never grow up?" She flung her hands up, clutching the air to make fists, wishing it was their necks she was squeezing. She tried not to wail. How she needed her mother's advice and help. She had never had to manage a house or servants. What should she do? What could she manage in this time? Perhaps distributing Mama's things if Usha and the other women servants came to help? She went to find them herself, hoping a personal approach rather than orders through the steward would succeed.

She discovered the women in their waiting place at the back of the house, near the rear doors. Talikha, Madhuja, Padma, Kala, Prema and Ramita clustered together as a group. Sitting on their heels, their heads covered by their stoles, hands busy, they murmured together. The lowliest woman servant, Basanti, the gardener, handed round baskets of marigold flowers and tulsi leaves – that scented herb called Holy Basil they always used for religious ceremonies – and nimble fingers deftly threaded them together.

They were making flower wreaths, garlands of bright yellow and orange marigolds, signifying trust in the divine, and a symbol of surrender, surrender of the soul, and tulsi leaves for Vishnu. Usha had taught her that. These were for her parents, she knew. Touched, Melisande blinked away tears and cleared her throat.

The women all bobbed their heads and rose with a graceful swaying motion in a rustle of saris and a jingle of anklets. Usha greeted Melisande, gesturing to the strings of strongly scented flowers and leaves. "Come, to the ghat. We go to the Ganges, a final farewell to sahib and memsahib."

"Oh, Usha, for Mama and Papa?" Tears did leak slowly onto her cheeks. It was part of their Indian tradition, not hers, but it touched her that they cared enough to do this. She turned quickly, hands over her mouth to hold in the sobs. Ganga and Vishnu, and the rest of the Indian pantheon, were not her family's gods, but she didn't believe that prayers lovingly given would offend her Christian God.

The women surrounded her and she became the centre of a group of mourning women, wailing according to custom. She wrapped her stole over her head and walked with them. Usha gave her a garland and they processed down the main garden path to the ghat on the river bank. Villagers washing, bathing or gossiping bowed respectfully, moved aside, and allowed the group the full width of the steps and access to the river.

Melisande watched and listened, as the women swirled, swayed and bent at the water's edge in a pattern of movement and sound. She closed her eyes and said her own prayers as the women sang-said theirs in that special drone. The scent of the garlands, the smell and sound of the river, the rustle of fabric and the tinkle-clink of bracelets and anklets, made a musical, scented picture she would always remember.

Ankle deep in the river the women released their garlands, floating them away. Melisande bent and set hers free and watched the raft of orange and yellow brighten the grey-green waters. The ceremony alleviated some of the guilt and hurt coiled tightly inside. She thanked all the women as they returned to the house, a silent group who perhaps wondered about their future. Time to reassure them.

She addressed them all. "I came to ask, firstly you, Usha, to help me select and choose those of Mama's things I might need. Then I would like each of you to choose something to keep or sell as a present from her."

Pleased whispers reached her ears. "I also want you to know that if the new sahib does not wish to employ you then we will find you a place in the village, or help you start some small, money-earning business."

Dark eyes brightened and faces smiled at her. There were little bows, hands pressed in the namaste mudra, thanks from the heart. She could almost hear her parents say her idea was well done.

"Yes, they are only servants, not our equals in the world's view," her papa would say, "but they are God's people too."

"And besides," Mama would add, "treat servants with kindness, never allow them an opportunity to be tempted to steal or do wrong, and you have a happy household."

Melisande blinked away the too ready tears and led the way to her parents' bedrooms. A happy home was all she asked for. A safe and stable place to be. Was that too much to want for her life? One thing she began to understand, her men were not going to supply it.

***

They were quite correct, that doctor and her friends. Flashes of memory, pictures in her head, tumbled about. She had to slow down the jumble, un-muddle them into some form of order. The feelings came first, the emotions, and she had to connect them, glue them to the correct pictures. And that was the trick, matching the right emotions to the pictures from the memories.

Only there was something, something she didn't want to remember and when she thought of that, terror grabbed her, choking her. Best go back to her wedding. And she had remembered now where Richard was, the traitor!

***

The derzi had employed two tailor's boys, who wouldn't have a moment to themselves for weeks. Usha and Melisande required their skills first, for they had gathered a collection of what Mama had called her England wardrobe: woollen capes, jackets, coats, cloaks, skirts and dresses to be made over into current styles or used as fabric for what Melisande thought of as her colonial clothes.

The dye vats were in steady use, turning as much as possible into the black she needed for her mourning clothes. She sighed, a whole year of black, not her favourite colour nor becoming to her olive skin and dark brown hair, but for Mama and Papa she'd wear it. Her men could get away with black formal wear and then black armbands for their daily business, but perhaps she could have dark grey dye on the silk for the European-styled evening dresses she had to have.

The servants were contented though. It had taken the rest of the day, but every servant now had cloth, clothing, stoles, scarves, some one thing or more of Mama's to turn into a new garment. Usha took the remaining clothing, her perk, which she had well earned. She would probably sell it and invest the money in another gold bangle or anklet, perhaps even gold drop earrings. That reminded Melisande that Mama's jewellery was safely locked away and she must find a way to pack it securely. Jeri promised he would not sell any part of it.

"Honestly, Lisa, sister mine. How dare you think I would sell the family jewellery or those pieces our parents bought? I know Mama promised them to you." He glared, nostrils flaring in disdain, and then he continued eating his lunch.

Richard kept his smile to a mere upward twitch of the corners of his mouth, but he raised his glass to Melisande. When Jeri frowned at him he raised both eyebrows and tipped his head at Melisande. "You and I must arrange our wedding, my dear Lisa. Your brother and I have spoken to the Company manager. Apparently, as the new bishop is in town, we can present ourselves to him with our documents, and he will let us have a special licence. Otherwise it's the usual three weeks of the bans read in the nearest church if we cannot obtain a special licence."

Ah. That was why Jeri was frowning and looking gloomy. "Three weeks?"

"The problem is that you are both not of legal age." Richard sounded smug. At twenty-four he had no such problems and ragged Jeri about it. Melisande noted his teasing sideways glance and her brother's facial twitch. My superiors at the Company will provide testimonials, to explain the situation, but you, Lisa, will have to charm the bishop into believing that this is what you want."

Jeri pulled a face, and wagged his finger at her. "No unwilling brides allowed. You must convince him. No wailing about leaving India."

If only she dared to do so. Melisande surveyed both her men. She contemplated screaming, throwing the dinner plates at them, or trying to stage a convincing fit of hysterics. But that was not her way, she was the sensible, practical one of the family, full of common sense. Instead of screaming she attempted to speak in reasonable, pleasant tones.

"But I don't want to be married now." Tears threatened. I am not going to cry, she told herself as she willed them away. She despised herself for being so weak. "Am I not allowed my dreams too? I don't want to leave India forever. It's my home. But I've always dreamed of going to England with you, Jeri. I want to see England, the Lakes, the Welsh mountains, and Scotland, then tour the Continent, and have a wonderful year. After that I would like to return to our uncle's home and have a socially proper engagement announcement in The Times newspaper and an engagement ball, then a proper society wedding with all our relatives and Richard's present, and finally a honeymoon in Venice before coming home, home to India."

Jeri groaned, banged his fists on the table, and roared, "Well, you can't."

No use asking why not, still she had to try. "But you are trying to make your dream become reality. Why is mine not to be?"

Richard, a troubled expression on his face, glanced at Jeri, then swung round to face Melisande, who could no longer hold back her tears.

Had she hurt him? Did she see wounded feelings clouding his eyes?

He regarded her steadily before resting his head on his hand. "Lisa," his voice, though muffled, carried tones of long-suffering patience. "Lisa, the magistrate's wife is an option for you, she will escort you so that you may go to your uncle."

Oh Richard, my love, she wanted to say, it's not that. How to make him understand? She mopped her tears with her muslin stole, brushed her wet cheeks and tried to speak reasonably.

"No, no, you see, you are both so full of plans for your own dreams …"

Jeri, cheeks mottled red and white, threw up his hands with an exasperated shout. "Your dreams are about a comfortable life and marriage. Female stuff. That's what we're trying to give you. We men have to be able to support ourselves, our wives and families forever. Can't you comprehend that we must do something different now our parents are dead?" His voice hit a top note sharp enough to crack a looking glass.

Melisande rubbed her temples. "Please don't shout at me. I understand that if you were content to stay in India we would have our future organised here for us. You are talking of travelling and adventure and becoming colonial landed gentry, and I am being carried along by you as if I were a parcel and have no rights in the matter."

Jeri thumped the table again. "Lisa, you have been little sister and favoured baby in our family. But our family is no more. Be sensible. I know what Papa said, I remember his words …" his voice thickened, he swallowed several times. "You were to marry when you were twenty-one, when you were of age. It's all changed, we have to manage our own lives now. We have no choice. This way we care for you, make things safe for you."

No, they couldn't see what she meant. "But you are making the choices. I have no choice."

Jeri spluttered, opened his mouth to roar, but Richard reached out a hand and clamped his mouth tight shut. "Hush Jeri, let Lisa speak." He released Jeri's jaw and observed her.

"What do you truly wish for, Lisa, my love?" He held out his hands. "I would give you your wishes if I could, but, if we are to make anything good grow from your parents' death, we have to be brave and step out into a different, difficult future."

Melisande sighed. It was all so uncertain. She was sinking under a flood of sorrow, fear and a desperate feeling that leaving India was wrong. But what could she do? Jeri was all the family left to her and Richard she loved. She sighed, knew she must capitulate, although that idea of Usha's was worth reserving for her own future. Money of her own, she needed that. She managed a smile. "I don't feel brave."

Richard reached over and patted her hand.

She looked up into his face. "Very well. Do we visit the bishop tomorrow then?"

He exhaled noisily, relief like a cloud streaming round his head. He picked up his knife and fork and began to eat again. "That's my Nut Brown Maid," he declared. "I will take care of you, I promised your parents. You know I did."

"It's not quite how I imagined it though. And after luncheon," Melisande reminded them, "you are both to help with Papa's things and the sorting of the furniture. We all must decide on the things to take."

"Bishop first. We can take the steam launch downriver to town, as he's dining with the board members at Company House and will be free to speak to us this afternoon. The manager told us."

Melisande nodded and looked at herself. Wrong clothes for the bishop. "We had all better wear something suitable. Visitor Sunday best." She pulled a face – that meant English-style clothes and a rigid English corset. And it made her remember that night and Mama and Papa, and their fuss over clothing before setting out to dinner on the boat. Would she never be able to think of anything without a painful pang of grief?

Jeri cast his eyes over her and nodded at Richard. "She'd better start wearing proper memsahib's clothing all the time."

Well really. How rude of Jeri, she always wore proper clothes. Melisande opened her mouth to protest.

"Married ladies do not wear Indian garb except at fancy dress balls," he added. "Melisande, you must realise how other English ladies dress."

Of course she did, that's why she and Mama had worn adapted Indian dress, much cooler and more comfortable. "Richard," she turned to him, "Am I improperly dressed?"

He gave up attempting to finish his meal. "Jeri, you sound like a pompous colonel in Poona. You aren't Squire Allmark yet."

Dear Richard, she did love him. "Thank you, Richard."

Jeri scowled. "I'm her brother I'm the one ..."

Richard cut him off. "No, Lisa has to realise what changes are ahead for us all." He stretched out a hand to her, almost a beseeching gesture. "Lisa, your mama and papa created a special place here. You lived in a style that was comfortable for India's climate and your health. This allowed you to become part of the community and beloved by the natives. Your parents did not maintain a strictly British household or keep to a typical British way of life. That is what I have found so distinctive, extraordinary, and in fact superior to what the government people or the Company people do. You have lived here adapting to the Indian way of life, and I found a haven here, and I am sure the reason I have survived my time in India is because of your parents showing how it was possible to live well in this difficult climate."

It's his tone that gives him away, Melisande thought. She cocked her head, and gave him the Look. "But," she said, "there is a but, an objection, coming, is there not?"

"Oh, Lisa, all our lives must change. You are going to be my wife, a proper English lady with a home to manage and children to rear in a British colony. You must look and act as that lady should or you will not be accepted by society as you should." He smiled at her, his special smile. "You can't dine at the captain's table in that fetching outfit, but dinner gowns you shall have to dazzle the ship's company. Please go now and find something sober for the bishop."

Corsets, thought Melisande, gloomily, and all that heavy black fabric, so stupid in India. Full of doubts, she departed to find a suitable costume for the bishop. It was easier for men, they had uniforms or suits. She needed a proper English lady's black hat, not her Indian style veil. She began to see that there would be a chasm between her new life and her old, and began to wonder about servants. How did one manage without Usha and Advik, and perhaps Vinay?

Melisande must learn. She had to.

***

She had learnt, hadn't she? How? Who had taught her? But she must have because she'd been going to ... to set a sponge for bread and ... and ... something happened. Voices nagged her to tell them, but she couldn't remember.

What could she remember? The doctor, Mr Allinson senior, stayed with her overnight. He had a fatherly manner and soothed her panics and nightmares with gentle words, often reading aloud the day's Bible passage as her father once used to do. Her friends came in each morning to tell her what day it was, and what the weather was like as they helped her, tended to her needs as a nurse would. This day Ruth had brought flowers for her to smell. Charlotte had placed material, silk, in her hands. The silk slid through her fingers in a soft slither and she caught a scent of India again. Her wedding. There'd been something odd about her wedding, a bishop was it? And Jeri in a rush.

***

The river trip, speedy in the steam launch, put Melisande in a reflective mood. Would this be the last time she travelled in the family's river boat? Had it been included in the sale Jeri and Richard talked about? What about the boatman, her syce, Vinay, who dealt as well with the donkeys as he did with its temperamental engine? Vinay could never afford to buy the launch. She must make her brother take more care and thought for the servants.

Two river dolphins rolled through the water, shying away from the launch as it chugged out to midstream. Would she never see them again? She mustn't cry, surely she'd cried enough. She surreptitiously dabbed her eyes and watched her beloved Ganges, her river.

Vinay steered cautiously, dodging the smaller boats which ferried people from one bank to the other or downstream to town. There were enough of them to make the launch's course more zigzag than straight. She commanded her nervous tummy to settle and resolutely looked downstream.

The Company House was a Victorian red brick crenelated edifice so out of tune with Indian architecture that it seemed as if it had been flown in on a magic carpet from London and dropped down, plonk, beside the river, dwarfing the other buildings with its fiercely red top storey. Melisande thought of her mother's disparaging comments and wished she was making polite jokes with her as they approached. The rear of the building faced the road and the façade overlooked the river. Its well-painted wharf supplied berths for private launches or smaller supply boats. The space between building and river had been turned into a British lawn where the Company held its private garden parties for the sahibs and memsahibs.

Vinay nosed the launch into place alongside the dock. Melisande shivered. Her family had attended one or two, but never enjoyed the trivial fuss and constant harping about 'natives' and 'home.' Another dart of grief pricked as she remembered her family no longer existed.

Richard put his arm round her shoulders. "Are you cold, or …" he gave her that smile, "apprehensive, even nervous?"

Jeri sprang out of the launch, impatient as ever. "Come along you two. We won't be above half an hour, Vinay. Wait here for us."

How like Jeri, so insensitive. Melisande ignored him and smiled at Richard. "Apprehensive. I have not met the new bishop, Bishop Edward. Papa told me he is the Reverend James Edward Cowell Welldon and quite a scholar. Papa was pleased." She sighed.

Richard offered his arm and stroked her hand as she rested it on his forearm. "He'll approve of that bonnet. Most respectable. Up you come."

She dimpled up, wanting to laugh. "Mama's boating bonnet designed to protect the face and hair, flossied up with black crêpe and a veil? Respectable? Battered old bonnet is more likely. It's years out of style." She allowed her men to swing her up onto the wharf and walked between them, her hands cold in her gloves, her heart jumping.

The room in which they met the bishop was someone's office, but a grand one with a massive desk in one corner near the large windows and plenty of leather armchairs circling a small table set for tea. Melisande wondered if the bishop enjoyed Marsala tea, the spicy milky Indian tea, but never found out. They were obviously squeezed in between more important visitors and no tea was offered. She expected it would have been different with her papa present, and sighed.

The bishop entered at a brisk walk, followed by his deacons, the Company manager and a secretary. Melisande found herself lowering her head to hide her amusement, for the bishop was bewhiskered, chubby faced, quite young for a bishop, but rather pompous. He greeted her in an avuncular manner as though she were a panicky schoolgirl, not eighteen, and 'out' in the social sense as an acknowledged young lady.

"Please accept my sincere condolences for your recent loss," he intoned, not in the plummy tones she had expected, but in a nice light tenor's voice. He took her hand.

Melisande found herself giving a little bow rather than speak through the constriction in her throat.

The bishop had recently come to India and had yet to adapt. He seemed a little uncomfortable in the warmer climate for his nose and brow were sun-touched red, and he still wore traditional British-weight clothing, unlike the men with him. All the men, a band of clerical black, grey hair and beards, shook hands and murmured the usual greetings and correct comments. Melisande found herself ignored.

"Now, I understand you wish to see your sister safely married before you leave for England, Mr Allmark?"

Jeri inclined his head in a bow. "That is correct, my lord bishop."

"And I understand you young people wish for a special licence in order to marry." The bishop beamed at Jeri and Richard, then turned slightly to include Melisande in the smile.

They'd planned what to say and Jeri inclined his head again. "I am required to be in England in September. My uncle, Sir Aubrey Allmark, wishes me to study the management of his estate. This was planned by my father and uncle last year. I cannot leave my sister alone in India, and now we are orphaned she wishes to marry her fiancée and travel with him. My parents had given permission for the wedding, and, my lord, we all wish it."

There was a thoughtful pause as the bishop contemplated the three of them. Pompous he might appear, but a prosy fool he was not.

"It is a somewhat hasty action, you know." He surveyed the three of them. "Would not your uncle wish Miss Allmark to make her home with him?" He frowned and turned to Melisande. "Would you not prefer to go to your uncle, my dear, and be married from his home after your period of mourning?"

Now this was going to be tricky. Melisande knew she must speak well. "I am sure my uncle would offer me a home, my lord bishop, but I was an infant the last time I saw him, and do not know him. I have spent all my life in India and think I would prefer a home of my own with my husband, one where my brother will come and join us when he has finished his study. We will be a family again. Papa did give us consent to marry and he and Mama treated Mr Holyman as a son. We would be so much happier together especially now Mama and Papa …" She allowed her voice to fade without a sob, lowering her head to hide threatening tears.

"But you will not be in India will you?" This the bishop addressed to Richard. "I understand you intend to sail for the Australian colonies, Mr Holyman? Hence the speed and need for a special licence."

"Indeed my lord, and when Mr Allmark has learnt his business he will be joining us." Here Richard turned and took Melisande's hand, smiling at her. "Then we will be a family again on our own estate." He gave the bishop an earnest and sincere look. "We do have the means to be comfortable for two years. My own father supports my travelling to the colonies, and Mr Allmark and I will be partners growing wheat, sheep and cattle for the home market."

The bishop mulled over their comments. The silence grew. He coughed and frowned. "You are both under age." He looked at Jeri, than Melisande.

The Company manager cleared his throat. "Mr and Mrs Allmark thought highly of Mr Holyman. The engagement was known though not formally announced. Mr Allmark did indeed count Mr Holyman as a second son, I believe I am correct in saying that he welcomed the thought of Mr Holyman as his son-in-law."

More silence.

"You are very young, Miss Allmark. Are you sure you are ready for such a challenge as marriage and life in the colonies. Life in India is comfortable and easy. You have never been without servants have you?"

Melisande shook her head, and lifted her face up to look into the bishop's eyes. She read genuine concern. He did care. She managed a small smile. "I don't know what I can do until I try, my lord bishop. With Mr Holyman, Richard, to encourage me I hope I will learn to manage."

The bishop nodded his head, looking thoughtful. "Do not attempt to take your Indian servants with you, my dear. I saw several unhappy Indian servants in London. It never works, the weather is too cold, even in Australia, and they will face considerable prejudice in the colonies."

Melisande bit her tongue on arguments and inclined her head in a polite bow.

He turned to his associates and gestured to the door. "Write out the licence for Mr Holyman and Miss Allmark." One man, the secretary, Melisande thought, departed. "And I give my blessings to your union." Indeed, the bishop signed the cross over them and offered a short prayer for a joyful and faithful union.

Jeri and Richard joined Melisande in thanking the bishop.

He looked at them. "You know it is not socially proper or correct, with you in mourning, to marry so soon after your parents' death, but as your circumstances are so unusual … so difficult … and you are underage and need witnesses of good character, like myself," here he beamed at Melisande, " an idea has occurred to me. Your marriage should be a quiet private affair, and I suggest that Deacon Boyd conduct the ceremony now."

Melisande kept her head bent, face lowered, as she struggled not to cry out. Married now, in an old bonnet and tailored jacket and skirt, a walking costume of severe cut, newly made over from Mama's plain black twill costume. The only rings they had were of her making, on her fingers, twisted silver wire she had plaited and decorated with hearts and flowers.

And not even in church. Don't make me, she wanted to beg Richard and Jeri. Useless. They were already shaking hands with the bishop and deacon as they bustled her out of the door.

The actual ceremony was a dull, hurried affair in the Company hall. The bishop and Company manager delayed attending their meeting to act as witnesses, and Jeri stood up as the best man at the ceremony, if such you could call it. The deacon, an elderly and very proper gentleman, performed a shortened form of the service, frowned over the rings, but blessed them all the same, and wished the happy couple joy.

"Phew," said Jeri as they headed back to the boat, Melisande tucked in between them, her arms linked firmly to each man. "That's all done. Well, little sister, aren't you glad that's over?"

Melisande said nothing, but thought of plenty of rude things to say to him.

"Hush, Jeri," Richard said. He peered round the bonnet brim to look into her face. What he read there disturbed him enough to halt and make Jeri stop too.

"Lisa, Lisa, my little one, don't be distressed. I am sorry we couldn't arrange a better ceremony. I will make it up to you. We will have an anniversary every year more splendid than you can imagine."

Jeri sighed. "Be practical, Lisa. Having the wedding now, like this, is the best possible thing for us."

For you, you mean, thought Melisande, but "If you say so," was her reply. She swallowed down her misery, tried to accept the practicality of the situation, and make the best of what had just happened. She accepted Vinay's assistance and stepped into the launch. "Let's go home."

That was what she'd wanted: a home, and a proper wedding. And she wasn't going to have either.

***

"Is Mrs Holyman still sleeping most of the day?"

That was young Doctor Allinson. Of course she slept, that disgusting medicine forced her to sleep.

"Good. I want to decrease the dose again as I don't want her to rely on taking this as a regular sleeping draught, but I am worried about her skull fracture. You must see she remains quiet. I shall allow the eye bandage to be removed tomorrow but you must keep the room darkened for another week."

She wished she could speak and make them hear. She didn't know why her voice had disappeared, it must be her head. She framed words to say, to ask questions but they wouldn't issue from her mouth. The link between her brain and her mouth didn't work. The old harmony of thoughts to words was disrupted like the harmony — she was sure — the harmony of her life.

All she had to do was put the pieces back together and she'd be well again. That was what the doctor told her, but was it true? She hated the enforced dark, the noises she heard and could not understand. When Ruth or Charlotte left her alone she startled at every sound, and she missed Usha and Advik.

***

Usha and Advik had not always been in harmony, for Advik was sensitive in his position and place in the household, and Usha was pushy, but they united in horror when Melisande and her men returned from seeing the bishop. Advik met them in the hallway. Jeri demanded champagne to toast the newly-weds.

Advik's spine lengthened, his head rose on a stiffened neck. "The memsahib is wed?" He observed her hand, and saw only the silver rings Melisande had made. He regarded Jeri, with such a look, surveyed Richard in a down-the-nose glance.

"This cannot be correct. This is not how the memsahib should be married." Then, casting off his dignity he actually raised his voice. "How could you treat our Little Missy with such lack of respect, such unkindness? Where is her wedding party and where is …?" His words vanished under a torrent of shrieks and cries as Usha hurtled across the hall, wailing. Vinay had told the staff.

"No, no, this is not right …" more wails and shrieks and muffled words. Melisande found herself grasped and clutched to Usha's skinny bosom as Usha let rip in lightning flashes of abusive Bengali.

Advik continued looking down his nose at Jeri and Richard as Usha scolded both of them.

"Where is her wedding jewellery? Her silk choli, dupatta … gown?" Usha muddled Indian wedding customs with British ones. "Why no feast? Where her gold rings?"

Melisande, despising herself, her tongue turned to wood, her face flushing and her wretched eyes burning with unshed tears, disengaged from Usha's embrace. She knew she should tell her faithful supporters it didn't matter, that Richard and Jeri and the bishop had been practical and sensible, but Usha gave voice to all the lost dreams snatched away, all those things she felt.

Advik refused to bring champagne. "I will organise a wedding feast for tomorrow night, after proper ceremonies for our little memsahib. There is nothing to celebrate today." He bowed to Melisande, glared at Jeri, and actually turned on his heel and stalked away.

Usha promptly embraced Melisande again, then pushed her towards her bedroom. "You go, I come, we'll make your wedding feast." She gave her another gentle push then hurried over to Jeri and Richard, who stood stunned. Indian servants did not behave like this.

Exhausted, Melisande leaned on the door frame and listened to one of Usha's vicious scolds in English. At least she wasn't receiving it.

"What would Memsahib Allmark say? What would Sahib Allmark say?" Usha was short and had to look up, but her fixed gaze and waving hands made Richard and Jeri retreat a faltering step backwards. "Little Missy is still a child, needs care, loving. Her wedding must make her happy, then marriage will be happy. You sahibs, you don't think." She jangled her bracelets, flicked her earrings. "And where is her jewellery, her ring?" She turned on Richard. "You go now, down to the village goldsmith." She flapped her hands at him, shooing him away, before spinning round to attack Jeri.

Jeri flung up both hands. "That's enough, Usha, you forget yourself!"

"No, Master Jeri," Melisande noted the nursery title, understood. Usha reminded her brother that he had behaved like a schoolboy. "You forget. Your mama and papa never forget. They treat all fairly. You don't treat your sister fairly. All you see is big adventure. Little Missy doesn't see it. You forget to give her a reason to go with you."

Jeri spluttered. Richard had dodged Usha and reached Melisande. He took her left hand and touched the ring the Deacon had blessed. "Give me your ring, Lisa, my dear one, I need to know what size to have made."

Usha wheeled round, let him receive the ring, then chased him out of the main door. "You buy the best," she yelled after him.

Jeri sidled round the edge of the hall, aiming for the bedroom corridor. Usha scuttled after him. "You and I talk, Master Jeri. We arrange things. We plan for tomorrow's wedding feast." She steered him forcibly, step by step, into the library.

Melisande shook her head, even laughed a little as she went to her room. What would she do without Usha? Sudden realisation came with that thought. She sat with a thump on her bed. But would Usha come with her? How would she manage without her ayah who had been her nurse and now her maid and even more than that? She remembered the bishop's words. She knew here in India how Indian servants were treated by the British, by anyone who considered a white skin made them superior. How could she ask Usha to suffer that kind of treatment in a place as strange to them both as Australia or New Zealand? And Usha had family here. She'd never leave them.

Oh, why couldn't her men think of all these things instead of galloping her off in a hurry. She would need a lady's maid. How did one … oh, Advik, he who knew everything, he would know. Perhaps he'd help? What would she do without them?

She untied her bonnet strings, dragged the bonnet over her bun, tossed it on the bed and struggled out of her walking suit. Time to chase Advik, ask him, show him her lists, hope he could supervise packing, as well as badger her two impractical men, and oversee the sale of the family goods and chattels. Advik's bargaining skills were legendary, even better than his organisational skills, and they were superb. She slipped on her comfortable kurta and a soft silk skirt and went to find him.

She was still talking to him when Usha came seeking her. Usha waited until Advik had organised the male servants and then seized Melisande. "Come, we make your wedding bed."

Melisande blinked, felt her cheeks glow as she blushed and stuttered. "Marriage bed?"

"Guest house," Usha explained, tugging at Melisande. "Private place for wedding night. I sent everyone to help."

Melisande stopped holding back and followed. She hadn't thought about being with Richard. Her own bedroom, with its narrow childhood bed, certainly wasn't suitable. She couldn't bear to use Mama's bedroom – too many loving memories – nor Papa's rather spartan bedroom – too many scoldings. The guest house was charming, with a large bedroom and a big Indian bed, its own bathroom and sitting-cum-dining space leading out to its private garden-facing verandah.

By the time they reached the end of the garden Melisande had rethought the idea of the guest house, wondering if Richard had his own ideas about their wedding night. Then she saw the women servants, all smiles and happy faces, carrying flowers, bundles of material and baskets which clinked, or rattled, and smelled of oils and spices.

"But Usha," she tugged against the ayah's clutching hand. "Usha, what about Richard, what might he want?"

Usha gave her a dark look. "He wait until tomorrow night, after our festival feast."

"But …"

"Tonight we sleep in Little Missy's room, tomorrow the guest house is for you and Richard sahib." She pulled her up the steps to the guest house door.

Melisande sighed and followed. She'd never had that 'What to expect on your wedding night' talk with her mama. She really had no idea, she wasn't even sure of the anatomy involved and although she had secretly pried into many books of her papa's there had never been a medical one that she could find. None of the books had drawings of the human body. All she knew from glimpses of the villagers was that men's organs were external and women's were not, and that didn't help her much. Then she focussed on the room, looked at the preparations.

"Oh," she cried, finally seeing what had been done. "Oh, it's lovely."

There were marigold garlands, jasmine, honeysuckle and rose garlands, garlands of herbs and plaited rushes and grasses. The garlands made swags and wreaths twining up each bedpost, but outside the mosquito net. They also decorated the net sides. The net was held back by ties of red silk, and swathes of rainbow silk made a tent enclosure in the corner of the room to the left of the bed. Small dishes of spices and finger-length glass bottles of fragrant floral oils waited on the dressing table top.

"Tomorrow we paint hands and feet."

Melisande blinked, opened her mouth, rethought her words and then spoke carefully. "Usha, are you planning a Hindu wedding? Henna painting is traditional for one isn't?"

"No, no Little Missy, we plan a festival, special for you." She reached up, placed a hand on each side of Melisande's face, and gently eased her head down until their foreheads touched. "Not Hindu wedding. You are Christian, like your mama and papa," she said in an undertone, almost a whisper. "You have loving heart. We will have heart ache when you go."

"And I will miss you so, Usha. I wish you could come with me."

"Ah, Little Missy. My home is here."

And so is mine thought Melisande, hugging her. She straightened and found all the women servants in a circle round them. They pressed their palms together, gave the little bow and the namaste valediction. Only Usha spoke English well enough to communicate easily, but those seven faces, all with teary smiles, murmuring thanks, made Melisande sit down on the bed, press her hands over her heart and try not to cry.

"My heart is full," she managed to say. She had made Jeri insist that they were all employed by the new owners or given a little money. This celebration was their thanks.

Basanti, who was tending the flowers, clapped her palms together gently, slid her stole back to reveal her ears and touched the silver earrings she wore. The others, Padma, Kala, Talikha, Madhuja, Prema and Ramita did the same. They all wore them, Melisande's gift to each of them. She had made them as a farewell present for each woman servant, as she had made a twisted-knot silver button as a gift for each manservant. She felt honoured by their acceptance because gold was the preferred metal but she didn't have gold wire to work with. She'd made ornate peacock tail designs with different semi-precious stones for each woman and she felt proud of them.

"No tears," Usha said, waving a finger at them all. "We make all beautiful. Big surprise tomorrow. Little Missy, if you like what we do we will finish and you go help Advik organise packing your special things."

Chapter Seven

Little Missy, that's who she had been. She'd been cosseted and protected by Usha and Advik and her mama and papa, and then torn away from that safety by her husband and brother after that wonderful wedding feast. She'd always remember the bridal bower decorations, their heavy rich scents, and those servants who lovingly prepared it for her. That Little Missy had long gone, but who was she now? And what was it she must not remember because...because it would hurt, hurt...who? No, safer to think about bridal bower, a wonderful Indian memory.

***

Jeri and Richard were still in disgrace at breakfast time. Advik remained aloof, Usha scolded and breakfast consisted of all Melisande's favourite dishes, some of which Jeri did not like.

Richard had to go into town again. Fetching the rings, Melisande supposed. "Wedding gift for your bride," Usha ordered. Richard saluted, grinned ruefully at Melisande, and went.

Jeri, occupied with settling estate matters with the Company people, departed for their offices, bustled out by Advik with a warning to return to dress for his sister's wedding feast which would begin in the early afternoon. Jeri growled his assent. He did not like the servants behaving in this way, nor the fact that he could do nothing about it now as the sale had been completed and they were his servants no longer.

Advik bowed. "The men are packing your goods now, sahib, you have nothing to think about but your sister's wedding festival."

Jeri scowled, grunted something, and stalked off.

Usha seized Melisande. "We go prepare you." Her smile was full of mischief and delight. "Scented bath, henna, face, hair and clothes. All prepared in the guest house."

Melisande gave in and followed her through the front door and along the garden path. She'd been a spectator or visitor at Hindu festivals and wedding feasts before, but had never been involved at the centre of one. She'd enjoyed gift giving and the first feast, but had never taken part in the actual ceremony, which was always a more private family affair. "What have you prepared, Usha? What have you done?"

Usha waited for Melisande to catch up. "We prepare you as a bride for husband." She giggled. "We talk and paint and decorate you. We tell bedtime tales," she added with a cheeky smile.

Melisande didn't think she meant story-book tales – perhaps women talk? As they entered the guest house she hoped she'd find the courage and the words to ask Usha the questions she would have asked her mother.

Inside all the women servants waited, full of giggles and chatter. Only Usha helped her bathe and anointed her body with the scented oils, then it was henna painting time. Mama and Papa had been insistent that she learn both Hindi and Bengali so she had a reasonable knowledge of Bengali, but she wasn't fluent. Still, she caught parts of most comments as they painted her hands and each other's with the henna. It was fun, but tickled when the bridal patterns were painted on her feet.

Even the lowliest, caste wise, Basanti, was present, making flower wreaths for everyone to wear in their hair. After her hands were painted Basanti left to raid the gardens again for flowers to decorate the dining room for the feast.

"Hair, Missy's hair." The chatter broke up into giggles, and some comment about men's hands? Hands in hair? Melisande's hair, drying loose after her bath, hung well below her shoulder blades. She thought of her hair as her only claim to beauty, for it hung straight and richly brown in a thick, shining cascade.

"Pretty," crooned the chorus, who began a discussion on whether to braid and plait or twist and tuck. Usha, jealous of her position, allowed no other hand to touch Melisande's hair, but the other servants were allowed to offer wreaths and suggestions. Her hair went up and down in several different ways until all were satisfied when it was high off her face, piled in soft swathes, with wreaths and sprays holding it in place.

"Easy for husband to let down," they told her.

Surrounded by Usha and Padma, Kala, Talikha, Madhuja, Prema and Ramita, who were laying out various combinations of her clothes and arguing over them, Melisande struggled to find words, wishing they spoke more English or that she knew the Bengali words for 'What happens on my wedding night?'

Then she saw what they were now agreeing upon. "Oh," she said looking at the Indian clothes, a cream orna, the wide and long, all-enveloping stole of exquisite silk, heavily embroidered, reflecting the light with a rainbow sheen like peacock's feathers. The choli, the traditional blouse top, was scarlet silk, red for luck, and spangled with gold thread and tiny gold discs round the neck and hem. It appeared to be the short, midriff level style. Melisande had never worn one of that length. The long skirt, a pavada, made of heavy raw silk striped in dull yellow and dusky red, was beautiful and full enough for her to sit crossed legged.

Melisande eyed the choli, and held it against herself. "Oh, Usha, I can't …"

Big brown eyes widened and stared at her. All seven faces showed amazement then flashed into giggling mischief. "Yes, yes," they all cried.

"For husband," shy Padma explained.

Madhuja who, after Usha, knew the most English, ran her hands over her stomach and thighs in a lingering gesture and wriggled her body suggestively.

Everyone laughed.

"Husband like this." She danced around Melisande wriggling, undulating and peeping sideways at her through her eyelashes in a most forward manner. She stroked herself again and there were peals of laughter.

"Then husband do this." She waved a hand at Talikha, who jumped up and, with her bold bright eyes flashing, moved her hands round her buttocks and in an upward gesture along her back and over her breasts. "And like this." Again much laughter as Talikha and Madhuja undulated towards each other. "Husband like this, you like this."

Melisande flopped down on the bed amongst the clothes. Modesty, taking care not to show a naked body, had been ingrained. Girls mustn't be forward, they wore clothes to conceal but enhance. "Choose the right colours and shapes for your face and figure, my dear," her mama had said, "but don't flaunt or reveal. A modest décolleté on an evening gown is permitted and suitable for you, but be careful who you dance with. And a good corset is necessary if you wear a low-cut gown." How she wished her mother stood before her, helping her into a wedding dress. Now, how to explain. She'd never worn clothes which showed her midriff.

Even Usha entered into the romp and the women swayed and undulated around the bed, laughing. "We give Richard sahib a present," she said, "his bride to unwrap."

Melisande shook her head. "I don't understand."

Kala, so graceful and lithe, began a dance. The others patted their hands together in a soft clapping. "Wedding night dance for husband," Usha explained. "She dance, he touch, she touch, he take clothes away, he love her."

At last. "How?" Melisande cried. "What does he do?" There, she'd said it.

Silence, a long moment of no movement. Eyes down, heads bent, sideways glances. Usha sighed. All sank down to sit on the carpet. "Little Missy needs a mother," Usha said.

"And aunties, lots of aunties and married sisters," Madhuja said. "We help."

The women muttered and argued. Madhuja spoke again. "Don't you see carvings on temple walls?"

Melisande nodded. "I always look, which ones?"

With much shoving and pushing, a lot of laughter and helpless falling about, the women demonstrated the poses using their hands and fingers. Melisande watched the actions and puzzled over them. It couldn't be – surely not?

Ramita and Talikha jumped to their feet and chattered excitedly. Something about the street theatre, a play? Madhuja explained they would show her part of a street play performed during one of the religious festivals. Hands flew to mouths and the giggles verged on hysteria. Ramita's sari skirt was bundled around her hips so she looked like a man wearing a loin cloth. She waddled like an old man. Talikha became a sensuous woman draped in a rather revealing bedsheet. They revolved around each other pretending to touch and stroke in a languorous, lingering way. Ramita's floppy hand held in front of her 'loin cloth' suddenly jerked upright and Talikha arched her back and pressed forward against it.

Melisande let out a peal of laughter, clapped her hand to her mouth and gasped, "Not like the donkeys? Surely not." She didn't know whether to be shocked or amused.

Usha translated. Everyone laughed until they cried. Melisande felt pity in their mirth and knew a touch of shame for her ignorance. But the memory of strolling back from the stables with her brother last year, and seeing the jack donkey chase down the jenny, had remained. The jack lurching up upon the jenny to poke his member in her had puzzled her and then shocked her when Jeri, seeing what she was staring at, hurried her away.

"What's he doing?" she'd asked.

Jeri had spluttered, "Mating. Just don't tell Mama, and don't ask Papa."

"Why on earth not?"

Jeri had grinned. "It's not a sight for young ladies, nor for polite conversation."

But she'd never applied that sight to human mating. It had been so rough and clumsy for the jack had been fierce and bullied the poor little jenny.

Perhaps the women realised that Melisande feared this invasion of her body for they made soothing murmurs. She wrinkled her nose. Such loutish treatment for humans. The women darted quick glances at her, stopped laughing and in a babble of words told of touch and kisses, of feelings and, wonder of wonders, enjoyment.

Usha picked up a bottle of scented oil, the jasmine one. "Use oil, touching him, rub him with this. Ask him to rub you."

Melisande, thoroughly confused, inclined her head, waved her hands at the clothes and let them dress her. Modestly draped, wrapped and completely covered by the sari-length orna she found herself escorted by the women, singing and dancing, back to the house where the feast was prepared.

***

Melisande thought her head had improved. Her mind seemed clearer, only in patches, but she felt it. She smiled to herself, pleased she could remember a little of her Indian wedding and all that Usha and women servants had done for her. She needed cheerful memories to fend off the fear from the dark ones lurking. Best to keep to warm and positive thoughts for she was afraid of....No...remember the riot of noise and colours, remember all she could of India.

***

The villagers came to celebrate and say goodbye. All her people brought simple gifts, fruit, flowers, local cloth. They were her people and she was leaving them, and they regretted it too.

The local musicians played as she sat cross-legged beside Richard on their huge silk cushions. Before Advik bound their hands together with the traditional red ribbons Richard redeemed himself in Usha's eyes by producing the wedding ring. He slipped onto Melisande's finger a heavy gold band, a plain circle, over which another ring, a delicate filigree of gold with emerald chips caught among the fine tracery, fitted like a glove. Advik approved. Melisande was speechless. It was perfect.

The feast, enough wonderful food for all to enjoy, the music and the dancing, lasted until darkness fell in that swift Indian way. Advik made a speech, a formal farewell, a blessing of their marriage, and a prayer for a healthy and fortunate future. Led by the musicians, accompanied by a great snake of clapping, singing and cheering people, and guided by Usha, Melisande and Richard arrived at the guest house. At the doorway they turned and thanked everyone then entered, accompanied by raucous cries, whistling and applause. Usha breathed a few words into Richard's ear and left, closing the door firmly behind her. The crowd outside sang and clapped, full of noisy merriment, for several moments before Usha could be heard shooing them back to the house. They went, still singing and cheering, to finish the food.

"Well …" Melisande wriggled her hand free from Richard's, and stepped back, head down, struck dumb by a weird bout of shyness. This was Richard, her understanding friend. She thought she knew him, and now he stood, handsome in his Indian garb, and she really didn't know him at all. And they were alone and she didn't know what to say. She tugged the all-enveloping stole firmly round herself. "I …" she began, chin tucked on to her chest, then faltered. He was her friend, but he was making her leave home. He appeared to sympathise with her wishes to be and do something with her life but he insisted they sought another life in another country. But this was her wedding night, she should not think such bitter thoughts, yet what a miserable wedding ceremony it had been. If it hadn't been for her servant friends she'd have had nothing special to remember or tell her children. Resentment filtered into her voice. "And you, you know all about … this?" she waved her arms in a sweeping gesture which encompassed the room in all its festive glory and the wedding bed.

Richard sighed, removed his bridegroom's turban, and rubbed his forehead as if it ached, but spoke gently and calmly. "Ah, Lisa, my little love, I have upset you." He walked over to the bed, moved the mosquito net aside gently, avoiding the garlands and swags of flowers, sat down and patted the space beside him. "Come and sit beside me, my Nut Brown Maid."

She came, hesitantly, for he still seemed a stranger. She sat, leaving a small space between them, but Richard didn't try to touch her. He folded his hands one over the other and stared at them, then at her. "I never wanted to leave England," he told her, "never wanted to leave the Dales."

She sneaked a quick glance. He gave her the fleeting ghost of a smile. "We don't have proper English seasons in India but every April and May I remember an English spring, the primroses and cowslips along the lanes, and the air full of moist, growing scents and greenness. I remember the bluebells spread like a sea in our woods – they're so beautiful under the trees, Lisa, I would love to show you. I remember snow outlining the dark skeletons of trees on a winter's morning." He gazed into the distance as though he could still see them. "And summer, with blood-red poppies and blue cornflowers at the edges of the fields where the heads of the wheat whispered and rustled as they dried."

Melisande eased an inch closer. "Then why …" she began.

"Why did I leave?" Richard finished for her, and turned his face to hers. "Mainly for the reasons we must leave India." She sighed, looked down again. He carefully slid his arm around her waist and leaned towards her so that her head could rest on his shoulder if she chose to do so. She didn't. He inhaled deeply, began to speak.

"My family are like yours, comfortable, no great estate, nor really wealthy. My father offered me a commission in the army or navy, or, as I did not care for the idea of killing people, the church. None of them were to my liking. But then we heard about opportunities in the Indian Trading companies, and I applied to several. The Calcutta Company offered the best prospects and both my father and I agreed that I might do well in India, that this was the opportunity to make a profitable future for myself and be able to support a wife and family. I had to leave, which was painful, yet, for all the longing for my green and pleasant Yorkshire, if I had not come to India I would not have met you, and you, my love, make up for everything." He briefly rested his cheek on the top of her head. "My precious love," he murmured before straightening up, allowing her to choose how close to come.

Melisande let the tightness round her heart ease. She knew again the man beside her. This was her Richard, who showed consideration and let her decide. "It's hard, hurts the head and heart doesn't it, leaving what you love?" She slid across the final inches to lean her head on his shoulder. His arm eased her closer and she slipped her hand into his.

He remained silent and that was good. Melisande needed to think and the silence was easy, a gentle kind of waiting. A jackal yapped, one of the donkeys brayed. Oh, that reminded her. What could she say? How could she ask?

Richard squeezed her hand and exhaled a great gusty breath, spoke as if to himself, "And here you are facing your wedding night without your mother's advice."

She felt the blush right down to her toes. "I saw the donkeys … Jeri said they were …" Finally she managed to bend a stiff tongue round the words. "I can't believe humans behave like donkeys. It's … it's not decent." She looked up at Richard. "Are you going to do that to me?"

She saw Richard's lips twitch, the laugh lines crinkle beside each eye. He prevented the smile, but she'd seen the suggestion of it. He caught her hands in his, kissed them, then contracted his brow to look serious again. "Have you never seen pictures, medical ones, of the human body?"

"I've tried to find out." Her voice, tinged with indignation, made Richard press his lips together. He wanted to laugh at her, she knew it. She pulled a face at him.

"Don't laugh at me. I've hunted in all Papa's books and there's not one about human anatomy. Many about plant anatomy but no pictures of human bodies."

"Oh Lisa, my little love, you are an ignoranty aren't you?"

She pulled her hands away, shifted sideways from him, gave him a disdainful look and sniffed. "Do boys have such lessons at school? Is that how you know?"

"Ah, no. The lucky ones, their fathers take them to Paris." He reached for her hand, began to massage the palm with his thumb. It felt good. She relaxed a fraction then nipped his thumb hard between her fingers.

"Paris? I know about Paris. When Jeri's school friends visited I heard them talking. You mean a brothel don't you? Is that where you learned?" Melisande found her curiosity was stronger than her indignation; she leaned in against his shoulder again.

"Lisa! Do you think that of me?" Richard clasped her hands, pulled her closer, dropped a kiss on the top of her head. "Not me. I'm clean. But in Paris, more so than in Yorkshire, you can buy books which teach you about sexuality, about human bodies and how to enjoy them."

"Oh, can I look?" The words popped out before she could consider. Her cheeks warmed as she flushed. "Well, I am a married lady now," she added hastily as Richard's eyebrows rose and his mouth opened. She pressed her hands to her scorched cheeks, felt a bubble of – was it laughter or tears? More like something in between. Her lips quivered.

Richard's mouth twitched, his face relaxed into a grin. He gathered her into his embrace in a gentle hug. "We'd better study it together, I'm new to all this too."

Melisande spluttered, managing to turn it into a laugh and not tears.

"Here, I can't see you properly with all that, admittedly beautiful, orna, wrapped round you." Richard pushed the stole off the back of her head, so that it fell in folds around her shoulders. He touched the flowers in her hair. "They're pretty. I like your hair like that. Can I kiss you?"

Melisande pressed her lips together to hide a smile. This was her Richard, polite, kind and loving, well, she hoped he would be loving. "Do you want to?"

"What I want to do," he said, lightly touching the flowers tucked over her ear, "is ravish you from head to toe, but I'll start with a kiss."

Melisande pulled gently at the spray of flowers, allowing her hair to curtain the side of her face nearest Richard.

Richard laughed. "You tease." He tucked his hand beneath the hair, lifted it away, smoothed his hand round her cheek and gently tipped her face to his. His hand felt warm, the skin dry, slightly corrugated. He kissed the tip of her nose, ran a trail of kisses round her cheek, and Melisande found herself dodging his nose to kiss his lips. His lips tasted of the sugary preserved litchi the cook was so proud of.

"Sweet," she said touching a finger to his lips.

"So are your lips. Want some more sweetness?"

She obliged until they had to breathe again.

Richard gave her his loving look and began to run a line of kisses down her neck to her shoulders.

Goodness, she thought, it feels so strange, like goosebumps.

He began to ease the stole right off.

'I … oh … I'm …" She pulled away. She had bare feet and legs, a bare midriff and she felt undressed, and afraid, not ready for – for whatever. And she was undressed. Ladies wore stockings and corsets and petticoats. She wore a skirt, a brief, barely-bosom-covering blouse and that was all. Her whole body grew heated as if she had blushed all over. "I'm not decently covered. I don't …"

Richard kissed her firmly, stroked her hair, running his fingers through it until it fell down over her shoulder. He kissed her cheek and caressed her head. "Show me."

Well, he was her husband, and he was gentle … her thoughts trailed away as she slipped the orna to her waist, stood up and shed it in a cloud of silk. She blushed and twirled round the bed in her short choli and the graceful skirt. She felt wonderfully free without extra petticoats, stays and stockings, and, judging by his face, Richard approved.

"Tut," he said, gazing as though he could never see enough of her, as if he were hungry and might eat her. More goosebumps and shivers tickled her spine and slid across her skin.

"Shocking, Lisa, you should feel undressed, you're not a proper memsahib. How disgraceful." But he was laughing and he jumped up, grabbed her round the waist and swung her off the floor and round and around until they collapsed on the bed, giddy with something more than just laughter, with a physical sensation Melisande had never felt before.

"You are all mine, my beloved. Come here and be ravished." He reached towards her, but didn't grab at her.

Now if she was all his, surely he must be all hers. She hesitated then spoke. "And are you all mine?"

"Utterly, completely and devotedly. Come here and let me show you."

Smiling, she slid over to sit on his knee and discovered that the sensations of being slowly unbuttoned, eased out of her clothing and touched, of unbuttoning him and sliding her hands over his body were fierce, overwhelming and quite marvellous, and in the end, not a bit like the donkeys.

***

"Melisande, do drink this please. And stop muttering Indian words. Come back to us please."

That was Ruth, she'd recognised the tone. "I'm trying," she wanted to say, "trying to remember where I am." All that came out of her mouth were squeaks and huffy squawks.

"Don't nag her, Ruth." That was Charlotte's softer, kinder tone. "She must heal her head to regain those memories by herself." Her hand gently brushed Melisande's bandage. "You're safe on the farm, and your eye bandage will be removed shortly."

"But we need to know what she saw."

"Hush, Ruth. Be cautious. The doctor warned of brain fever. Then we'd never know. Think of what she said to us on the ship, how she's helped us. It's our turn to help her. Please do be patient."

A ship? Leaving India perhaps, but more than that she had fond memories of a ship, something to do with Richard and ... ah! That French book and stormy weather. When was that?

Chapter Eight

She was trapped in her bunk during much of the voyage to Sydney, with distressingly few happy memories to recall about those last days in India. Only misery and loss. But Richard never grew tired of ravishing her, and she loved being loved, which meant that the voyage to Australia, although a rough and stormy one, was a honeymoon to cherish. She felt it made their relationship all the more special and for her, and hopefully for Richard, it helped to obliterate some of the grief they shared.

Melisande treasured the many days when the captain asked the passengers to stay in their cabins. She studied Richard's Parisian book with him, and made him laugh as they learned to love each other, not always successfully but with care for each other's pleasure. The book, a translation from Arabic, with detailed drawings, Melisande determined to save for her daughters. They would not be as ignorant as she had been.

***

How much could she remember of Australia? It had been important, something she'd done meant they climbed aboard that ship again and bounced around on a buckish sea to come here. Wherever here was. If only she could see. She felt certain she would remember so much more if she could see where she was. The scents around her, green growing things, moist soil, fresh-cut grass, didn't really help but ... oh yes ... she could remember the scents of Australia.

***

The *Matiana* sailed into Sydney harbour in the early hours of the morning. Melisande and Richard woke fully, disturbed in their waking-up love-making, by Jeri banging on their cabin door, and announcing their arrival. "We're passing the heads, forty-seven days it's taken," he added through the door. "Hurry up and come and see the harbour."

"We've lost the passengers' guess-the-day- of-arrival competition," Richard muttered, kissing Melisande. "I guessed fifty days and you guessed forty-four days." He then proceeded to run a slow caressing hand down her back and kiss her breasts. Melisande lost interest in Sydney.

Over breakfast, with Jeri eager to land, and even Richard showing signs of interest, all Melisande could think about was the long trip, forty-seven days aboard the *Matiana*. She'd counted them carefully, enjoying the moon-dappled sea, the occasional magical phosphorescence glowing, lighting up the deeps on moonless nights, and the flying fish, sea-skimming birds and leaping dolphins, but always heart sick at going farther and farther from her home. Still, they had arrived. Perhaps this was where she'd make a home. She needed a safe place to be herself, to raise a family, to replicate what she'd had in India. Perhaps Australia would surprise her.

It did. The air tickled her nostrils with drier scents, the eucalyptus trees made her sneeze, the dust had a bitter tang. The light, its quality of brightness sharper than India, seemed harsher, clearer, outlining the distant buildings with a cruel clarity. The harbour was busy, a forest of masts, naval ships, warships anchored mid-harbour, small boats scudding over the waves and trading vessels, both sail and steam, putting in to the jetties. Melisande hadn't imagined the port would be as busy as Calcutta's but it had far more shipping and bustle than she'd thought. And Sydney had buildings a plenty, perhaps not as many as Calcutta, but it was a city with three- and four-storied buildings, broad and busy roads and houses spread along the wide harbour inlet.

Half a million people lived in Sydney, so a proud returning resident told them at the final dinner.

"You should see our St Andrew's cathedral," he boasted, "and the town hall."

"Well, Sydney looks almost civilised." Jeri propped his elbows on the rail and watched the city approaching. "This is much less colonial than I expected, Richard." Jeri sounded impressed.

The three of them leant against the ship's railing on the first class deck and watched the commotion of the docking, Melisande musing on what life might have in store for her next. She'd miss the fuss and service on the ship, especially the electric lights which did not require all the care oil lamps and candles needed, and the reliable steam heating. Altogether strange after India, but she felt chilly for much of the time, always needing a shawl when other ladies were warm. The heat in the cabin had been welcomed. Soon she'd have to manage on her own, and that worried her. How she longed for Usha and Advik. How did one find a cook and a lady's maid?

She watched the sailors fussing over the sails, which had been used to save coal when the winds had been favourable – not too often on their journey. Passengers stood by the holds, fussing over access to luggage.

"At least we don't have to rush to unload and unpack." Richard sounded relieved. They had all the household goods and chattels she'd insisted on bringing and Jeri had tried to abandon, until Richard weighed in on her side. They would be travelling on to New Zealand on the *Matiana*. Jeri believed that Australia would offer them the best opportunities, but wanted them to investigate New Zealand first. "As we're travelling we may as well go as far as we can," he had said. He would leave them there and take a ship to London. Melisande and Richard would have to organise the removal and repacking of their belongings if they did return to Australia, and she sighed at the idea. Oh, for Advik to weave his magic.

"It is knowledge, Little Missy," he'd told her. "You must find out who the useful people are, who can do things the best, and then you are polite and listen to them and pay them well." She remembered that advice always, for, like her mother's comment on servants and how to treat them, the advice had value and she understood it.

The *Matiana* carried, so the chief petty officer told them, thirty-four first class passengers, and twenty-four second class passengers. The ship had certainly carried a full complement of first class passengers; she didn't know about the second class. But most passengers were disembarking in Sydney, and only two other passengers, apart from themselves, had booked to voyage on to New Zealand. They had five days in Sydney before the *Matiana* sailed for Dunedin with a new load of passengers and refilled cargo holds.

Richard had cabled to reserve rooms in a city central hotel. Now they simply had to get there. It was not going to be a quick journey but plenty of transport was available. If only their legs would behave. Sea legs, the captain warned her, but they would soon wear off. However, she wobbled down the gangplank, thankful for its strong sides and rails. The boys looked little better. One of the stewards called a porter for them and he trundled off the ship with a handcart of trunks and boxes for them. Melisande nearly asked for a ride, anything would be better than her staggering footsteps.

Jeri whistled up a cab and they loaded the luggage on top and themselves inside, and were off. A bubble of something –... excitement she hoped – popped into her throat. Jeri and Richard hogged the windows, staring and exclaiming. She slid to the edge of the well-worn leather seat and wormed her head under Richard's arm. He stroked her cheek and moved his elbow to avoid knocking her hat.

"We'll explore the town tomorrow. Today we have to see land agents. Jeri's organised some introductions and meetings and I thought you might prefer to rest in the hotel and perhaps take a cab to the shops. We might go to the theatre in the evening. Would you enjoy that, Lisa?"

"Thank you, It would suit me perfectly. I'd love tea in a cup which didn't slide about." She tapped Jeri's arm. "Remember Papa's maxim about making decisions?"

Jeri wrinkled his nose at her. "Sleep on the idea and decide the next day?"

"Precisely. You haven't had Uncle Aubrey's lessons yet. We need expert advice."

Jeri laughed and promised to be careful. Richard gave her a quick sideways glance which reassured her that he would control any impulsive actions. "We won't sign your money away," he promised.

The hotel, tucked away in a quiet street, did not stand out as an imposing edifice, but rather appeared as a solid, four-square town house. The lack of bowing servants and a doorman, the absence of brown faces, seemed strange. There was a porter who hefted their bags, and a receptionist, but no one else. At least the rooms smelt of polish and not dust. The beds, made up with starched linen, had mattresses like boards and no mosquito nets. A chambermaid finally brought hot water, after three requests, and lit the fire. Jeri and Richard departed, washed and shined up, off to visit a bank before the land agents.

"I'll order tea for you, Lisa," Richard promised as he closed the door.

Melisande removed her hat, rearranged her flattened hair, changed her blouse, sighed over the unflattering black, and sallied forth to find her tea. Down the stairs she tripped, holding the banister with a firm grip as her feet still needed reminding that the earth stayed still. She found the ladies' lounge, guided by the receptionist, a smart young man with a celluloid collar of dazzling white and a flashing smile.

Melisande blinked as she registered the lounge décor: plum-flowered wallpaper, dark paint and shiny wood, a huge, carved wooden mantelpiece and floor-to-ceiling windows, which lightened the room considerably, despite their framing of bobble-edged, green plush curtains. The armchairs appeared well-padded, covered with flowered cretonne. All very English, Melisande thought as she headed for a comfortably plump one by the fire. She imagined her uncle had rooms like this.

A waitress entered through a side door carrying a tray. Advik would not have approved, the china rattled and the tray lacked a decent starched cloth, only a gingham napkin to cover the bare wood. Still, there was a fat brown teapot, a milk jug slopping over and sugar lumps in a bowl. The young woman plonked the tray down with a flourish.

"Here you are, Missus. Cook's got a nice batch of drop scones just off the stove. Would you like some with your cake?"

Advik would certainly have reproved her for her manner and her words. But this was Australia, not India; with an inward sigh at her pang of longing for the familiar, Melisande made herself smile. "Thank you, that sounds delicious."

"Did you say drop scones, Millie?" The speaker was the youngest of a group of three women – mother and daughters perhaps? – who entered the lounge, shedding coats, removing hats and peeling off gloves as they headed for the fire.

"A large plate of 'em for us, dripping in butter, Millie, and two pots of tea," the other daughter said.

"Don't forget cake," the first speaker again. "Any fruit loaf, Millie, for Ma?"

"Can you manage all that, Millie?" the mother asked. "Bring it all to the table here by the fire. I'm sure this lady won't mind sharing. Save you a bit of work if you bring us the one tray."

Ah well, Melisande sighed inwardly, I needn't stay long if they are overly talkative or inquisitive.

The daughters plumped their mother down in the armchair opposite Melisande and drew up two armless chairs for themselves.

"You don't mind, do you? I'm Betty."

"Now then girls. Be proper." Please excuse them, Miss …?" she sneaked a quick glance at Melisande's left hand, saw the elaborate wedding ring.

"Mrs Holyman," Melisande told her, her lips quirking round the words, still enjoying the sound and feeling of her married name.

"I'm Mrs Symond and these are my daughters, Betty and Nell."

"How do you do." Melisande offered her hand across the table. Mrs Symond hesitated then shook it. The girls jumped up to pump her hand and tangled with Millie and her loaded tray. The cake stand tipped, nearly tumbling off, but fortunately Nell caught it just in time and straightened it.

"Now girls!" But Millie, deft, dodged the worst of the collision. The girls helped unload the tray with pleased cries and Millie promised to bring the extra tea pot and a jug of hot water when she'd had a breather.

Hiding her laughter inside, because Melisande felt their innate good nature if not good breeding, she let Mrs Symond pour her a cup of tea – at least the cups were fine china and the plates matched – and listened to the girls. Betty, she guessed as sixteen or seventeen years, Nell a couple of years younger. Both had their mother's grey eyes, but Betty was shorter and plumper, Nell lean and spare. This was the girls' first visit to Sydney and they were full of the city, shops, theatre and churches.

Mrs Symond explained that they lived on a farm up near the Blue Mountains, about fifty miles away. "It's a bit of a day's journey, even by train, so we don't often get into town but Mr Symond had promised Betty the trip for her seventeenth birthday. We're buying …"

Betty interrupted. "A ball gown for me."

Nell cut across her sister. "It's her first grown-up ball gown, there's a dance we're invited to …" Her voice faded away as her mother coughed and her sister glared and nodded towards Melisande's black garb.

"I'm sure you understand the girls' excitement, this is their first dance. They're young," Mrs Symond said, "and so are you, you'll remember your first dance."

Melisande sensed a trap, a social one, of which she wasn't fully aware yet. How had Richard explained on the ship to those nosy women in the first class dining saloon, the women who were trying to ascertain their standing on the social ladder? Ah yes, she remembered, and it wasn't truly lying. "Shading the edge of truth," Jeri had remarked afterwards. "You need to learn how to do this, Lisa, to be on the upside of such social quizzing. It's what Mama and our aunt would have taught you in England."

Melisande raised her chin slightly, adopted a calm face. "My parents died unexpectedly, shortly before my engagement party." No need to explain more.

Nell gasped, glancing in distress at her mother.

Mrs Symond tutted at her daughter. "Please excuse Nell. I am sorry for your loss, we wouldn't have mentioned the ball had we known it would bring back such sad memories."

"No engagement ball and your wedding wouldn't have been …" Betty tailed off under her mother's censorious glare.

"You're correct. Both events had to be private and quiet. It would not have been proper to make those special occasions a large family and public affair." Melisande smiled to show she could speak of such a personal thing without overmuch sorrow. "And they would have meant nothing to me without my parents." That thought popped out, surprising her, but it was true, she'd never really thought of the situation in quite that way. Seeing the girls' faces touched by doubt and pity she began to tell them of the ship's amusements, starting with dressing for the formal church service taken by the Captain every Sunday.

""When we were not confined to our cabins by bad weather we could enjoy dancing, balls on Saturday evenings, many sporting activities, even a sweepstake on the daily log," she paused, remembering. "Fancy dress balls were a favourite, and no voyage was complete without the grand dinner and ball held during the last week."

"Oh," breathed the girls.

"The dining saloon each evening was a splendid sight. We all dressed for dinner as if we were at home, but I suspect many of the beautiful dresses, those low necks, and vivid colours, were created for the voyage. Ladies like to show off in such a charming situation. An officer sat in splendid full uniform at the head of each table, electric light made the jewels brilliant, shooting sparkles of light, and the dining saloon was always beautifully decorated.

"Ah, I would love to travel on a ship. What did you wear for fancy dress?" Betty leaned forward, lips parted, eyes bright with curiosity.

"I have lived in India for most of my life so I had some beautiful silk costumes, but it was not correct to wear them when my bereavement was so recent."

That brought further exclamations and questions about Indian silk and Kashmiri shawls.

Millie returned with another tray of tea, more buttered drop scones and little cakes. Melisande contrived to load her plate and even enjoy a drop scone, which was indeed dripping with butter.

Millie, quick and agile, flapped another napkin onto her knee which caught the drips, and did the same for Betty and Nell. "Don't let these chitter-chattering girls scoff all them scones," she said to Melisande, then turned to Mrs Symond. She gave her a saucy smile. "They need their pa to keep them in order, their ma's too kind."

The Symonds laughed. Melisande found their behaviour odd. Servants didn't or perhaps shouldn't be like this? But no offence had been taken. Perhaps this was the Australian way?

Two cups of tea and all the little cakes later Mrs Symonds turned chatty herself, and motherly when she heard about their hopes and what Richard and Jeri were doing. "Oh I wish Mr Symond was here. He'd put you right. There are land agents and … well … land agents. You have to ask about water and stock numbers per acre and …" she sighed. "A good farm like ours, we have water, fertile soil and can grow what we need. But it's hard to buy a good farm like ours, for they're not easy to find these days."

Betty had been listening as she ate heartily, enjoying a large slice of fruit loaf. "Pa would say tell them about the drought."

Mrs Symond hesitated.

Nell poured her mother and herself a cup of tea and peered over its rim at Melisande. "It's bad, the drought, over two years Pa says, and inland they're always too dry any year. Without water, Pa says, you'd have to keep putting down wells and even then they go dry. Eats up all the money for nothing."

Mrs Symond fussed and wrinkled her brow, concerned. "It's not a good time for buying an inland station. Did the land agent come with a government recommendation?"

"The land agent came with good recommendations from people on the ship. He's a Mr Geoffrey Scrimgeour, in partnership with a Mr John Fitzgerald."

Silence. An exchange of looks and pressed lips.

"I'll bet it's the Langley estate Mr Scrimgeour's trying to sell," Nell burst into speech, then pressed her hands over her mouth, holding back the rest of her words as her mother tutted.

"Yes, that or the Wallace one. He and Mr Fitzgerald are tricky, they'd love to catch a 'new chum'," Betty shook her head at her mother. "Mrs Holyman should be told, it's not right sitting quiet because it isn't polite to say bad things about local people. Mr Scrimgeour and Mr Fitzgerald give all of us a bad name. They behave shamefully, Pa says so."

Mrs Symond gave in with a gusty exhalation which scattered crumbs. "The Langley station, and the Wallace one, are always being sold to new chums. The poor fools put down another well, struggle to get cattle and sheep up to market weight and give up for it's hopeless. Neither station has ever been well managed and each new owner pours good money into a dust bowl, then has to sell."

"It's the water," Nell said, "there isn't any."

Melisande listened, and felt grateful for such advice. She hoped Jeri would be when she told him what they needed to know.

"Is there a government-registered land agent we should try?"

"Blaine's," the girls chorused.

"In Pitt Street, near the Post and Telegraph Department," their mother finished for them.

"Thank you. It's our whole future you have helped preserve. To set us on the correct path is such a kindness. We won't forget."

Mrs Symond blushed bright red. The girls chuckled and leaned across the table to pat their mother's hands.

"There, you see, we did right to say."

"Indeed you did," Melisande smiled at them. "Now tell me about your dress. What colour have you settled upon?"

They were still arguing styles and trimmings when Richard came to claim her.

***

And now she remembered, she hoped Betty had found the dress she'd dreamed of and enjoyed her first ball. A blessing on that family who saved them from a life-destroying error. They'd told her so much simply by talking about their daily lives. She was pleased to recall that she'd paid them back with a gift of Indian silk shawls for the girls. But how had Jeri reacted when he learned that he'd been taken in by a cozening rogue? In a fuss, she'd guess. She'd try to remember that next.

***

It was in an expensive restaurant that evening where Melisande listened to an enthused brother talking about the stations Messrs Scrimgeour and Fitzgerald had on their sales book. Knowing Jeri, Melisande let him wax lyrical, exchanging a swift smile with Richard. He knew, from her refusal to answer his early questions, that she had something to say.

"And what is your opinion, Richard?" she asked, when Jeri paused to eat a mouthful of steak.

"I'd want to see these places first."

"And of course Messrs Fitzgerald and Scrimgeour have many reasons why you must not do this?"

Jeri paused, mouth half open, knife and fork raised. "How did you know?"

"We are what the Australians call 'new chums' and Messrs Fitzgerald and Scrimgeour wait for new chums. They are not registered agents with the government but are rogues and cheats."

Jeri clattered his implements onto the plate, swallowed hastily, inhaled, swelling visibly, as he glared at his sister. "What would you know about them, and about buying land or these stations?"

Melisande let laughter lighten her face, brightened with mischief, and smiled sweetly at him. "The Langley and Wallace stations Messrs Fitzgerald and Scrimgeour want to sell you are without water. Did they tell you that you can drill, make a bore and find water?"

"Yes …" He eyed her suspiciously, then scowled at Richard, who was laughing.

Melisande managed to look apologetic. "There is no water, there never was much apparently."

"I did wonder. Messrs Fitzgerald and Scrimgeour seemed, shall we say, over keen, even pushy? We've been rooked, or nearly. Thank you, my good and clever wife. Do you have any more advice for us?"

Melisande longed to kiss him. His words gave her such a warm feeling of loving appreciation. "Yes, go and speak to a good government-approved agent, a Mr Blaine, in Pitt Street, near the Post and Telegraph Department."

"And here we thought you were indulging in feminine chitter-chatter about ball gowns."

She laughed. "The Symonds are a good farming family and know Messrs Fitzgerald and Scrimgeour and their reputation." She reached out to pat Jeri's arm. "I'm sorry Jeri. They tell me the drought has made many farms unprofitable and that a station is always risky because of the water problem. Mrs Symond said that Blue Mountain land is the best but hard to buy. She also said there was nothing for sale. Going inland for a sheep station with this drought lasting so long is foolish. A waste of our money."

Richard nodded. "I think we'd better see this Mr Blaine tomorrow and ask his advice."

"Well, according to the Symonds, we need coastal or Blue Mountain land because you want to grow crops as well as keep beef."

"We'll ask tomorrow." Jeri sounded grumpy. "How do we know this woman …"

"Jeri, please, her name is Mrs Symond, and she gave me real and honest advice. In fact if her daughters had not been there I doubt she would have said anything, because it's up to new chums to look out for themselves." Melisande dimpled up a small smile for her cross brother. "Australians seem to believe if one is stupid enough to be gulled by crooks like Messrs Fitzgerald and Scrimgeour then one should not be in Australia. At least that's what I understood."

Richard played peacemaker. "I think we'd do well to make a lot more enquiries, of anyone who should know. There are government offices in this city. We can start there. Would you like to come and visit this Mr Blaine, Lisa, since you found him out for us?"

How like Richard to actually include her in their business affairs. She gave him her loving look. "Yes, I would like that, for they are my affairs too."

Jeri humphed, but said no more. Richard gently nudged her foot under the table, but Melisande knew not to do more than smile kindly and struggle to eat even half of this huge Australian meal, which differed so from those lighter spicy Indian dinners she'd enjoyed.

***

The doctor had promised bandages off tomorrow, Melisande was sure she'd remember more when she could see. She still wasn't allowed to move around or sit up by herself, but her head only pulsed occasionally and the lightning flashes faded to nothing most of the time. The ringing, buzzing and clanging in her ears had diminished but not vanished. She knew not to force her memories, because it hurt, and something lurked and threatened in the blackness of her mind. She was afraid to seek for it, yet she knew the others wanted her to remember. She tried. Australia, that's where ... where what?

***

The wind nipped and the pavement was not always as smooth or clean as Melisande preferred. She was glad she had Richard's elbow to tuck her hand under as they walked to the Blaine office. He sheltered his hat with one hand and her with the other and she felt his warmth close to her side. His warmth she needed. Mr Blaine did not approve of women in his office or taking part in business discussions, although he tempered his disapproval in deference to their mourning state. Melisande longed for India with a pang sharp enough to make her wince.

After the to-do of handshakes, cards and introductions, Mr Blaine dusted off his chair for her, back rigid, head high. He didn't need to say a word, Melisande saw his disapproval.

"Thank you," she said, settling herself, and smiled politely.

"Aye, well I didna expect to be seating the ladies," he responded, his Scottish ancestry clear in his voice, "not in my office."

The office, slightly dusty round the edges, had clean window panes, plants on the windowsills and a loaded desk. Decorated with wooden panelling, practical brown paintwork and a cream ceiling, Melisande understood it was a working man's office, a busy working man and hopefully an honest man.

He was. He pushed his spectacles down from his forehead onto his generous nose, listening intently to Jeri's enthusiastic explanation. His first questions showed his quality in sorting out financial and legal matters, and he even took account of their hopes and wishes. It was his final questions which floored Jeri and Richard.

"How do you expect to farm? How much work are you willing to do? How much work can you do?" His face expressed mild interest; he didn't look her men up and down to make a point about their well-cut mourning wear, city suits, double breasted overcoats, suede gloves and matching trilbies, a contrast to his easy-fitting suit and low-collared shirt. He did nothing to point out that Jeri and Richard looked what they were, well-to-do young men, not manual workers, but his questions brought the contrast to mind.

Jeri lifted his head. Melisande hoped he wasn't going to lose his temper. He did develop a touch of red over his cheekbones and his mouth muscles tightened but he controlled himself. "I'm sailing on to England to learn estate management. In India I managed our small estate of fruit, vegetable and hemp crops," he replied.

Mr Blaine turned to Richard. Richard nodded, "I have dealt with livestock as a boy," he said, "and we'll need livestock to provide our own meat and milk, but I am no farmer, neither of us are, but we are learning."

"Managing an estate, Mr Allmark, will provide some useful skills, but can you milk? Can you clip a sheep? Can you plough and reap? Can your wife manage the poultry and nurse lambs, Mr Holyman?"

That was it. Melisande didn't speak, but wanted to exclaim with satisfaction. Mr Blaine had touched on what made her uneasy. She couldn't milk or manage poultry. She could barely cook, or carry out household duties, though she could manage servants to do those tasks. Richard had little or no farming experience, Jeri was only experienced as a manager of workers, people who did the hard work.

"We can learn," Jeri said, "but we will need help first, and can pay workers."

Mr Blaine pushed his spectacles up and down the bridge of his nose, enlarging the red mark already there.

Melisande tried not to, but a little puff of air escaped her lips as she sighed internally.

He heard her. "Mrs Holyman? Regretting India? It must have been an easy place to live with so many servants."

"Mr Blaine, I believe you are about to tell us that finding good farm workers is not easy in Australia. And yes, I miss my home in India but my husband and brother are my family and their wishes become my own." Loyalty made her say it and she knew their wishes ought to be her own, but she intended to see some of her wishes included in their future, chiefly a welcoming home like she'd had in India. She intended to work hard to achieve it despite her men.

"Your good lady wife has been chatting to the locals, I see." Mr Blaine fixed his spectacles firmly in place and looked at Jeri and Richard. "She's right. To find a good man to teach you or manage for you will be costly. Nor are there many such around. In Australia you'd have to settle for an inland station and I'll not sell you any without you and me both seeing the place and me being sure of water. Australia is a harsh country at times and I have a reputation to keep or I will lose my licence. Now have you thought about New Zealand?"

Richard nodded, Jeri spoke. "We have considered New Zealand."

"Frankly," Mr Blaine went on, "for what you want to farm I'm saying it's more than likely you'll find good land there, aye, and the climate's better for what you wish to do as well."

Melisande suppressed a shiver and Mr Blaine laughed at her, but spoke kindly. "It's easier to warm a home, Mrs Holyman, than it is to cool one. New Zealand has much to offer and the land is good. My son's farming sheep and cattle on New Zealand's North Island. It's a good living an' I'll be joining him when I retire."

"Then," said Richard, "you recommend New Zealand as a better place for us to find a good farm and men to work it?"

"My son tells me that in the right places, for fair wages and a good boss, there are men, farming men looking for work. Catch a married couple off an emigrant boat and then Mrs Holyman will have some help in the house." He beamed at them, escorting them to the door. "I wish you well."

"New Zealand it is then," said Jeri, and whisked them out of the office and off to find another restaurant where they could dine and make plans.

***

Thank the Lord her men listened and so New Zealand it was. She understood a little more now and today, when her bandages were removed and she would see this room, surely that would help her remember, prompt her mind?

***

"One can only take so much ocean and formal dinners. I don't want to see another ship for months," Melisande said. She had spent a week in bed with what Richard told enquirers was a prolonged attack of travel sickness. It had started like a queasy seasickness but Melisande, thanks to that book, remembered to count days and dates and realised it might be more. That book had taught her much her mother might have told her.

A discussion with Richard and the ship's doctor led to their decision to keep her in bed. Two days later severe cramps and low abdominal pain followed by a heavy menstrual flow ended their speculation and the doctor advised Richard to use preventives for several months.

Jeri barged into their cabin, furious because he'd discovered from the doctor that his sister had been enceinte. How dare Melisande have been with child. He attacked Richard in a round of verbal abuse which exploded into a huge argument they conducted so fiercely, so loudly, that they woke Melisande from her medicated sleep.

"No children until we are settled. I thought we'd decided and you'd organised it."

Richard clenched his jaw, gritted his teeth and swallowed his angry words when Melisande spoke, awake and distressed. "Please don't fall out over something which is not my brother's concern."

Jeri slammed out of the cabin.

"We'll be more careful," Richard said to her, tucking the pillows behind her. Melisande thought perhaps they should. She wasn't ready yet to be a mother, although she wasn't going to tell her bully-boy brother that. And it wasn't fair to yell at Richard when he usually used a preventative. She smiled a sleepy smile as she snuggled into the pillows and down into sleep. They simply forgot sometimes when passion overrode logic. She would enjoy a lazy life on this ship with its steam heating and the electric lighting until they docked in New Zealand. Colonial life on a farm was not going to be as comfortable – she might even make a bet on that with Jeri.

***

A door must be open, she felt a cold breeze. It made her shiver and reach for the shawl Charlotte always arranged behind her.

"The doctor's coming." *Ruth's voice.* "He's attending the men then he'll be coming in here and look at the mess you're in." *Melisande shivered again and a downpour of memories hit her. Arriving in the cold, that was it.*

***

She'd been wrapped up in a great tweed coat, made over from one of her father's, with a woollen Kasmiri pashmina draped over the top and a small lacy woollen shawl tied over her hat and under her chin, yet still she shivered. She stood as close to Richard as she could to steal a little of his warmth and duck the wind. Winter, they would have to arrive in winter. She leaned into Richard's side and he slid an arm around her to snug her pashmina tighter.

"Soon be in port, Lisa." He tugged gently at her head shawl, laughing softly. "It's not really so cold, you'll soon acclimatise, and our journey is nearly over."

She murmured something which might sound like agreement, whilst wondering if it really was the end. India still felt like home and she ached to be there. India offered warmth, beauty and colour, a liveliness and richness of life she hadn't noticed in Sydney and certainly not here. What had this country to equal it?

A long sand spit bordered by a wooden pier flanked the ship's entry into the mouth of the inlet leading to Port Chalmers. The light at the end of the pier, a warning light Melisande thought, winked, rather than blinked at her. It gave off a welcoming feeling, and as the ship slid past it, a breeze from off the shore ahead frisked her hat. She caught the strong scent of dank, heavy soil, a rich scent promising gardens. She liked gardens and growing things, but what plants could she grow here?

***

That was the first good thing she noticed about New Zealand, that green growing scent, and it felt encouraging. She could smell the scent of earth and growing plants here in her bedroom, wherever here actually was.

Footsteps. Charlotte's she believed. "Good morning, I'm Charlotte if you haven't guessed."

Melisande attempted a smile. It hurt far less now to move her facial muscles, but her throat, although less of a collar of solid, bruised and painful stiffness, still did not allow her to speak with ease.

"Let me rearrange your hair, Lisa, here, you wipe your face." She tucked a warm rosewater-scented face flannel into Melisande's hands. "Are you excited? You will be able to see, I'm positive, for your head has healed well."

Melisande wished to say 'Yes.' She managed a croak and Charlotte, between tears and laughter, told her it was good that Richard wasn't here to scold them all for what had happened to his precious Lisa. She remembered the feeling of his hand sneaking into hers in public to tickle her palm or stroke her fingers. Dear Richard, traitor Richard, who'd gone away and left her.

***

Standing where she did on the deck, sheltered between both her men, she slipped her gloved hand into Richard's and he squeezed it gently, turning his head to look down at her.

"A prettier entry than to Sydney," he murmured.

"Oh yes," she agreed, drawn by the squabbling cries into watching a wheeling cloud of gulls.

Jeri grunted. "It looks good land, a touch of England somehow. What do you see, Richard?"

"My wife's future." He tucked her arm under his, wrapped his hand round hers, and they strolled further along the ship's railings. She stroked his palm with her fingers as they continued to watch their new homeland emerge upriver. He pressed hers in return. Perhaps he was correct, perhaps this was where her home, her safe place would be.

The ship took its time slipping along the estuary, and it was the greenness of the riverbanks which struck Melisande. She'd never known there were so many shades of green, and the green made the country look softer, rounder, more … gentle? Something like that.

Port Chalmers surprised. Much smaller than Sydney, the town appeared neat and organised, compact, cupped in a circle of hills. The large spire of a church dominated the town. No obvious naval ships – did New Zealand have a navy? – just two long docking piers, crowded, with a thicket of masts, sailing ships tied up among the steam ships, all loading and unloading in the bustling port. It was difficult to see where they would dock. The port might be small but it was obviously and prosperously active.

Sheltered by a peninsular, the water was calmer than the chop they sailed in on, and despite her qualms their docking was straightforward, even dull. Melisande sighed. If only the next part of their journey could work out as neatly. Jeri had delayed his departure by a fortnight which gave them four weeks to find a suitable estate, or land. He had booked a cabin on a sister passenger ship for England, and their uncle would not be pleased if he delayed any longer. Now they must leave this ship and the holds had to be emptied within two days. Two days! Where would she find a place for all their household possessions? Richard had firmly demanded that Jeri allow them to take the best of the furniture with them from India, and any special thing which his wife needed for her comfort and happy memories. Now she had to take care of it all.

A flock of long-necked black birds swooped in a jagged V across the water. She watched them, distracted. What they needed was a house, somewhere to call home for some months. Persuade Jeri to set her up in house here in this Port Chalmers, as a starting place from which the men could roam freely, finding their paradise, their estate. That seemed a sound plan. How did one find a carrier to remove the crates, and then how to find servants to open them, clean everything and arrange a house? How she wished for Advik and Usha.

Before she could ask her men, Richard and Jeri escorted her back to the cabin, bustling along, talking over her attempts to speak. "We're off to find agents, solicitors, banks and what not," they said, eager to disembark now the passengers' gangway had been extended to the dock side. They collected their documents, placed them in leather wallets, and departed. Melisande followed to watch them bounce down the gangway plank on wobbly legs. The dockside, as crowded with people as a Calcutta street, was a noisy scene, so she merely waved as her men dodged the workers, carts and swaying crates.

She stayed on deck most of the day, watching the unloading, even consulted Customs officers, and other government officials who demanded information about what was in their crates. She wasn't sure who had been more surprised, the officers dealing with the wife and not the husband, or herself having to stand firm and speak out, but she did it.

Officials came and went. She remained, thinking. In order to stay in New Zealand and become members of the community they had to provide evidence of some capital, and a certificate as to health and character. Well, they had all those letters of introduction, bankers' drafts and their marriage certificate.

"Show them to the local Magistrate where you're ready to settle," the government man said, "that will be enough ... Ma'am," he finally added, with reluctance it seemed. Melisande watched him stride away. Was it her youth, or did New Zealand people follow Australians in their independent attitude, their 'I am making my way as I want' air? Jeri would find this difficult. He expected to give an order and have it obeyed immediately, as in India.

Ship's officers, who had been kind to the young family so recently bereaved, paused on their rounds to indicate buildings of interest, the enormous immigration barrack – thank heavens they did not have to go there – and the Presbyterian church, a beacon placed in the centre of the hillside, with its tall spire leading their way to God. They explained about the lovely bluestone which had been used to build the church and many of the government buildings like the Post and Telegraph Departmental office and the railway station, even some of the bigger houses, which they pointed out to her.

Melisande nodded. "As in India. We used stone or brick for the houses."

"Wood's better for houses here, you know, Mrs Holyman. Wood is safer in earthquakes."

The captain, striding past, waved his officers away, but spared a moment to nod politely. A lean, greying redhead, with an absent listening-for-problems air, he'd unbent several times during the voyage to ask if she was comfortable enough on his ship. Here was someone who ought to be safe to ask personal questions. He might have knowledge Melisande could use.

"Are you familiar with Port Chalmers, Captain?"

He paused, "Why yes, Mrs Holyman." He inclined his head again, looked thoughtful, as if arranging the words, then added, "My family come from Port Chalmers." He cocked his head, waiting for her response.

"Can you recommend a reliable agent? We need a house to rent for some months."

The captain's eyebrows rose. "The regional newspaper, the Otago Daily Times, would be your husband's best source of information about agents and houses. Our local newspaper doesn't often carry such information. People know, you see." He fell silent as she nodded and smiled.

"Thank you, Captain. I wonder, as a person with local knowledge, could you advise me about the most pleasant area to select a house?

Agents often don't give one such information, being eager for a sale, and they rarely know about the most reliable shops, carriers and removal men." She gave him a confiding look, but didn't tell him her information about such things came from those useful Australian acquaintances, the Symonds. "I don't think you will be knowledgeable about the best shops though."

The captain actually laughed. "Indeed not, but I know about local property. Would you like a sea aspect?" Melisande nodded. "Let me think. A sea view and a distance from the noise of the railway?" Melisande nodded again. "Bellevue Place or the streets around there. Not too far from the centre of town and the social activities. I doubt you'll be setting up a carriage just yet."

"No, my husband and brother want to begin farming as quickly as they can so we'll only be here until the farm is ready, but thank you, Captain. It helps to have local information."

He gave a half bow then strode off.

Now all she had to do was persuade her men.

**

And that was a thought. Her men. She hadn't been calling for Jeri because ... because ... there was a reason ... she knew there was a reason ... if only her head hadn't fallen apart she'd know. If only she could sort out the 'I must remember' things from the looming fear of some terror.

Doctor Allinson used his cheerful, everything's well voice. "My son, the other Doctor Allinson, is here to see if his handiwork has been effective." He dropped his voice to a pretend whisper. "I taught him, you know," a pretend boastful tone, then back to his usual fatherly reassurance. "I am positive all will be well. Don't expect to see clearly for some time, Mrs Holyman. Now I'm about to remove the bandages. Don't touch the eye pads."

She heard Charlotte and Ruth draw breath, standing near, her dear kind nurses. Her good friends. She needed to remember more. Why were they here with her? Where had she met them? Somewhere in Port Chalmers?

***

The captain had allowed them an extra night on board, providing they accepted that dinner and breakfast were simple, what the crew ate. Melisande, hungry for her dinner, waited for Jeri and Richard in the dining room, a very plain room now, half undressed with linen only on their table and one other. A distracted crew member acted as waiter, hovering with the soup, frequently looking to the door. Late back, her men now kept the waiter and herself waiting again as they cleaned and dressed for dinner. She sighed, heard footsteps striding along the deck, and signalled for the soup.

Jeri burst in, Richard caught the door and closed it carefully, smiling an apology. Jeri slid into his seat with a "What's this?" Richard thanked the waiter.

As the waiter disappeared to bring the next course Melisande examined their faces for any clue, a sign that they'd been successful in establishing money, credentials and a good agent. "Did you have a successful day?"

"Mostly, sister dear." Between mouthfuls Jeri explained about possibilities. "The solicitor is also a land agent …" Richard made a negative murmur. "Well, he knows about the local estates, the large areas of land, because he handles their business."

"We'll have to travel away from Port Chalmers, perhaps be away for a few days, Lisa, my love." Richard took her hand and pulled her to him.

Jeri pulled a face at the endearment and action. "Not in public," he hissed, "show a decent reticence please."

Brothers! He sounded like an embarrassed schoolboy. Jeri ought to make allowances, he wasn't the public. Melisande pulled a disapproving face at him. Jeri pulled one back. Richard laughed and tutted at them both.

The waiter removed the soup bowls and presented them with plates of mutton chops.

"Have you been making plans?" Jeri eyed her sideways, sounding suspicious.

Melisande stared at the mutton chops, a little dubious about this form of meat. "We need to get hold of the local newspaper, the Otago Daily Times. The captain tells me it advertises property. Then I'd like to walk round the town tomorrow and find a house."

Jeri muttered, swallowed his mouthful, and sighed. "I'm not spending money on a house here. We need everything for our estate."

Richard flicked a quick glance at him as he piled roast potatoes and green vegetables onto his wife's plate. "Here try this, Lisa m'dear, fresh Brussels sprouts with sauce and Swiss chard in butter, time to taste new winter vegetables. You'll have to get used to these." He wobbled his eyebrows at her, winked, then he looked towards Jeri, a warning she understood. She pressed her lips together, to let him speak.

"What, Jeri, are our chances of finding our land before you sail? What we want is quite specific. We've been told there might be two properties we could ask about buying within a day's ride of this town. We have yet to check the other agents and the advertisements in the newspaper."

Jeri shrugged.

Melisande looked from one to the other. "Where will you search?"

"We must go inland and beyond Dunedin to see the properties advertised for sale. That's why we will have to leave you."

She opened her mouth to protest. Richard shook his head at her. Jeri butted in.

"The roads are bad, and those back roads and farm tracks are nearly impossible for a pony cart. You have to learn to ride a horse, Lisa – no donkeys here – but that means finding a lady's hack for you. We haven't time."

"Jeri has the right of it, Lisa. You have to stay here until I can help you learn to ride." He leaned over to pat her hand, then turned to Jeri. "But

Lisa's plan is good, Jeri. You want to buy land and build, yet have you thought where we will live whilst all this happens? I still feel strongly that we should spend most of our money and buy an established property which has a good house and farm buildings."

Jeri spluttered. "But the cost."

"An established farm could provide an income for us in our first year; that would balance out our having spent most of our capital. And you know we were told that most of the good land has been sold. We have to wait for another ballot. We've just missed one."

"A ballot?"

"According to Mr Asher, the bank manager, the large estates are being bought by the government and broken up into smaller farms. A lot of the land is already cultivated, and it's a good buy at a reasonable price. Competition is keen, and so people must apply and hope to be the ones whose names are drawn."

Melisande nodded, watching her men as she tasted tiny forkfuls of the strange vegetables. She'd managed to eat her chop, but missed the varieties of fish she'd had at home. Oh dear, she must stop calling India home. One thing in favour of Port Chalmers was the possibility of fresh fish from the fishing boats she'd watched in the harbour. Now how to convince Jeri, who really was being unreasonable.

"Wouldn't staying in a hotel be more expensive than renting a house?" Both men looked at her, Jeri frowning, Richard's mouth quirking the shadow of a smile.

She took a deep breath, tried not to sigh. "Tomorrow we find a house, a carrier and carter. Then you can read the newspapers, make lists of the best properties, hire a horse each and find a map or a guide." She surveyed their expression, let herself scold. "I'll be struggling here, trying to make a home without Usha or Advik, or any servants. I need a person like Advik. Do you think I can hire a cook?"

She noted their shocked expressions and wanted to smile, a rueful smile granted, but she could manage one. Perhaps they might even appreciate the task in front of her and the enormity of what she had to learn.

As the waiter removed their plates and made an effort to clear the table Richard held onto the wine and poured her another glass. "Lisa is quite correct, Jeri. We have to have somewhere for all our household effects, and a home here is only fair for your sister. You know we've been told that buying a property is going to be a task which takes more time than we'd hoped. You might have to leave for England before we complete a sale."

He regarded Melisande with a direct and purposeful expression. "We'll visit the solicitor, Mr Truman, tomorrow together, and I've an idea about servants, something Mr Truman mentioned in passing." He touched his glass to hers. "I promised your father you'd live like a princess." He clinked her glass. "Here's to my promise."

Jeri heaved a sigh, shrugged and gave in.

"Thank you, Richard. Jeri, thank you. I am finding it difficult to know how to do the little I can do. There must be many things I'm forgetting, or just don't know. I'm without any understanding of so many simple things which are needed to make a home. The thought of having a home, a settled place to be for a few months, is a blessing."

Jeri gave her the brotherly smile she'd been missing for months. "I'm truly sympathetic, little sister. Richard and I are also short of knowledge, but at least we know how to find out and Mr Truman says there are men, farm labourers, who need work and can teach us. We'll have to watch and listen. I didn't understand how different this country is, or anticipate the difficulties we might face. I'd hoped for a country more like Britain. Remember those men in India calling New Zealand Little England? But the seasons are back to front. It's confusing, but it's winter here with no need to rush into planting crops or harvesting hay. A house of our own here, a place to stay until we are ready to move is a good idea, little sister, and somewhere to keep safe and lock up our possessions. Give us some time to adapt to this new country."

Richard grinned. "My wife has excellent notions, we should listen more often."

Melisande, lips pressed firmly together, allowed the brotherly slur on her ability to understand to go without remark, too relieved not to have her beloved square piano, Mama's drawings and Papa's books stored in some damp warehouse. She accepted his comments with a thank you.

Houses they discovered in plenty. Melisande, dressed in a sensible walking suit, a severe but Parisian hat, and fine leather shoes, did not take to Mr Truman even though he proved as true as his name, and provided a list of houses his clients would rent 'to suitable people'. He made her feel like a child although he insisted on shaking hands with her and squeezed too hard, expressing sympathy for their recent loss. He then passed them on to his office 'boy' to walk them round. The 'boy', who was not much younger than Melisande, goggled at her, greatly admired her fashionable little hat, and was bold enough to tell her so.

"Paris style, that hat?" he asked, walking them into the main street. "What's it called?"

Jeri and Richard frowned, but Melisande shot them a look, for she realised that this young man might be a useful source of information. He appeared to be nosy and chatty.

"It's a design from Worth," she told him, "He's the most fashionable designer in Paris."

"You're newcomers aren't you? Knew you didn't buy it here. Shame cos I'd like to buy my girl one like that."

Jeri fell in behind her as Melisande walked beside the 'boy', Richard at her other side. He acted like a spotty and gangly youth, which indeed he was, but his sharp glances told Melisande that he had a brain. Her men walked slowly, looking round, but not asking the questions she wanted answers to. She sighed, realising she had to speak if she wanted those answers.

"Tell us about these houses, Mr …?. Are any of them in Bellevue Place, Mr …?

"It's Ron, Missus." He grinned and the pimples round his nostrils glowed pink. "Someone been telling you about the town?"

"Just a little information from the ship. I need to be able to walk to the shops but would like to see the sea."

Ron grinned. "Right Missus. And a view of the sea? How many rooms, sir?"

Richard looked blank. Melisande tried to think.

Ron watched them. "How long will you be staying in town? Mr Truman said he was to organise a year's lease."

Jeri interrupted. "Three months, I'm not paying more."

"We might need a year, Jeri."

Before she could say more, Richard squeezed her arm. "As long as we need," he said.

Ron's eyes swivelled from face to face. He didn't gawp but thoughts flickered in his eyes as he calculated. "Right, lady and gents, you need a gentleman's residence, something with reception rooms, bigger than a cottage."

"Somewhere warm," pleaded Melisande, giving a shiver as a sharp gust blew in from the sea. "We've been living in India, Mr, er, Ron."

Ron stopped again. "India? It's hot there all year ain't it?" He gave a disbelieving laugh. "You'll want fireplaces in every room." He started off briskly. "Let's see this house first."

Halfway up the hill, set back in a large garden, was a square, two-storey stone house. Richard and Jeri nodded to each other. Melisande tried to think as her mother or Advik would. What did one need in a house? Who would cook and clean? Who would garden and grow flowers and vegetables? Gripped by an icy panic which sent frozen shivers down to her fingertips, she shuddered, and squeezed Richard's arm. Richard drew her closer and Mr Truman's 'boy' looked surprised.

"You're right there, Missus. Clever of you to guess. It's a cold house on the shady side and in a bit of a dip. Gets frosts. but it's a real gent's residence with bedrooms up the stairs and a bathroom inside." Ron dug a large key out of his pocket and opened the painted wooden gate for them. He then scampered round them and down the path to insert the key in the lock, open the large front door, and wave them inside.

"It's so dark," Melisande whispered, standing in the long straight hallway. There were brown varnished doors on either side of the hallway and the dim light came through three small glass panels above the front door.

Richard and Jeri stalked along the hall flinging open doors. Ron dithered, decided to talk to Melisande. "Pretty parlour in here, Missus." He gestured to the first room on their right.

She stepped in and found a bare room with a high ceiling, an ornate wooden fire surround and a bay window. Richard and Jeri joined her, their feet clomping on the bare wooden floor. They all looked round and shook their heads.

"We asked for partly furnished houses," Jeri snapped. "We've only brought the basic necessities."

Ron began making excuses but Melisande interrupted.

"Now I see. It's the sun, I'm missing big windows, shutters and the sunlight."

"You don't want sun in the rooms, Missus," Ron's voice reflected horror. "Sun fades the carpets and curtains. Splits wooden furniture. My mam says sun's awful bad."

"Not in India. Houses have shutters to filter the sun into bright light."

The young man stared at her. "Shutters," he muttered.

"Let's see another house," Jeri said. "One with a more sunny aspect."

"Something smaller," Richard suggested. "We haven't a lot of household effects."

"Small enough for me to manage," Melisande whispered, but no one heard. Her stomach clenched. 'How will I manage?' she asked herself, panic howling in her ears, making her shake her head.

Ron rubbed his nose, frowning. "The other two houses Mr Truman suggested are further out, and like this one."

They all looked at each other, not knowing what to do next.

Melisande tucked herself close to Richard and sighed. "Is there nothing with a sea view, more space? I'm not used to living with other houses so close."

Ron coughed and flushed a blotchy crimson, even his earlobes turned red. "If you promise not to tell Mr Truman I told you." Three nods satisfied him. "There's Aurora Terrace. Mr Hammond, the timber merchant, he's a first class builder and carpenter too, he and his men built a house there last December. It was for his mother."

"Oh dear," murmured Melisande. "Did she not live long enough to enjoy it?"

"Nay, Missus. She won't leave her cottage, refused to move. My mam said she were soft in the head not to move. New house has gas lighting, a modern kitchen stove, proper inside bathroom, fires in all the rooms. Nothing were too good for Mr Hammond's mother, and she turned up her nose at it." Ron gave a little laugh.

Richard looked at Jeri. "We could look at it."

Jeri shrugged. "Does this Mr Hammond want to rent it?"

Ron rubbed his nose again. "Well, he'd prefer a sale but it's not an easy sale, only two bedrooms see, no room for live-in servants and it's really only a big cottage, too small for the price he's been asking. But there's not much Mr Hammond won't do. Seems like he's building half the town's houses. This cottage isn't far and it's where you asked for Missus, and overlooks the beach."

Melisande dragged after her men, sighing. Jeri and Richard strode out with Ron and she trailed up the hill after them. It was a pleasant walk, the road tree lined and very countrified, the sea a melodious background murmur. A pleasant place to live if the house proved liveable. She'd think about it. She arrived to find her men staring at a white painted house.

"But it's made of wood," they both cried.

Chapter Nine

Wood, the funny wooden houses, now she remembered. Their little house by the sea. She felt a laugh trying to form and managed a croaking chuckle. She knew where she was.

"Ah, that's an excellent sign," both doctors spoke together. Doctor Allinson junior made encouraging noises as he carefully unwound the bandages from her eyes. "If you would remove the pads, father, please. Now when he removes these pads, Mrs Holyman, try to gently and slowly open your eyes. Slowly and carefully, Mrs Holyman. Before you do, let me wipe them." Using one of her silk cloths, with gentle pressure, he moistened her eyes.

Dim light and blurriness. Blurred shapes but pale ovals and darker outlines, shadows. Oh thank God, she could see. She wept.

Junior Doctor Allinson patted her hand. "Weep away, Mrs Holyman, the tears will help your eyes."

"They look well." Senior Doctor Allinson's comment.

"How is it, Lisa? Can you see something?"

That was Ruth.

She forced the tears to stop, made her mouth shape out words. "Yes, oh yes, thank God. But dimly." She could make out shadowy, blurry forms and profiles. From a throat still stiff and sore, her voice rasped. It sounded old and creaky to her ears, but she had spoken clearly enough for the doctors to understand.

"Do you know where you are?" Charlotte's anxious query. And she didn't, this was not the bedroom she knew from Port Chalmers. It did not smell of the sea.

She tried to shake her head and the jag of pain forced more tears from her eyes. "Port Chalmers?" Her voice betrayed her as she tried not to weep again.

"Keep your head still, Mrs Holyman. That was a severe blow to your skull. Avoid moving your head. You must remain in bed for at least another week, lying on your back or propped up."

"Please don't upset yourself." That was Charlotte.

"If you've reached Port Chalmers, Lisa, you're nearly home. Try to think about your Port Chalmers home." That was Ruth urging her on.

Senior Doctor Allinson clicked his tongue in disapproval. "Now Miss Landry, we will discover the villain who did this to Mrs Holyman, but not if you force her memories." He patted Melisande's hand. "You must not agitate yourself, Mrs Holyman. The memories are not as important as your recovery to full health."

Charlotte agreed. "Don't think of your house, think of your future."

"What future?" she wanted to ask, but the doctors gave her more medicine and commanded her to sleep and dream sweet dreams. Not without Richard, she thought, and knew that he wasn't in this place, wherever this place was. But he had been in Port Chalmers.

***

It was the solicitor's 'boy', Ron who'd found them their home; Ron who led them to Mr Hammond, who was busy farther down the road building another house. That too was wooden. The men worked on the roof structure, putting up timber triangles with much adjusting and calling out. Melisande, bemused, watched the men. It sounded chaotic but they moved as a team. There was a din of sawing and hammering, repeating of instructions and the smell of new timber. Fine sawdust drifted towards Melisande every time the breeze whipped up from the sea.

Ron called up, explaining their visit, and Mr Hammond looked down, eyed them all, touched his cap politely, and shinned down a ladder to greet them. Short, whippy and with an air of 'the boss' he looked them over, bobbed his head in greeting and spoke. "You'll be wanting to see the house then," he said, not questioning them but making a statement.

Jeri introduced himself and "My brother-in-law and sister, Mr and Mrs Holyman," to Mr Hammond, for Ron had forgotten to do so.

Ron flushed up bright red again, ears as well, and rushed into speech. "The gentlemen's looking for land and need a place for the Missus and their stuff while they get sorted."

Mr Hammond sniffed thoughtfully and eyed Ron. "Does Mr Truman know you've come here? I don't have m'house out for renting nor mentioned it to him."

Ron's face darkened to reddish-maroon. He shook his head.

"What's he goin' to say then, when he finds out? Have you shown them the houses he's in charge of?"

Ron ducked his head and mumbled something.

Jeri and Richard looked at each other, but Melisande spoke first. "I think Ron could say quite truthfully that we are not interested in the houses he has shown us because we are from India and want sunlight and warmth." She smiled round at all of them. "Ron then remembered the snug house you built for your mother which faces the sun and has fireplaces in every room." She nodded at Ron. "He hoped to convince you to allow it be rented through Mr Truman's good offices."

"Huh!" Mr Hammond said. "As if I will be doin' that." He laughed and sent Melisande a smile and a nod of approval. "Quick little lady, your wife, sir. I'll take you round my mother's house, but it isn't a gentleman's residence with rooms for servants, just a decent home." He turned to Ron, "You'd better remember what the lady telled you." Turning back to Jeri, Melisande and Richard, he gestured back down the road towards the house. "Come, I'll show you the place."

***

That was when she first panicked, knowing that whilst she'd learned to manage dressing her hair and taught Richard how to fasten and unfasten her undergarments and her bodice she knew nothing of housekeeping. How she should have scolded her men for expecting her to run a house without servants. Coming to New Zealand they regarded as another great adventure. Had they thought no more than that? It seemed not.

***

As they all walked down the road Melisande felt the nervous flutter again within her throat and stomach. She needed servants, help with everything, but how could she explain without making herself look foolish. New Zealand was not India and she'd learned enough to understand that here the colonial custom was to do much for yourself.

"India, eh?" said Mr Hammond, opening the garden gate. "Did you ride around on an elephant then?" He made it sound like travelling to the moon.

Richard explained, with Jeri's additions, about elephants and their uses as Melisande took in a front garden with rose bushes and a lavender hedge. The other plants she did not recognise.

"Good veggie patch behind the house," Ron whispered. "I helped dig it, can come and help you, if you like. You can grow fresh veggies."

The house charmed Melisande. Though small it was light, had high ceilings, and big bay windows in the front rooms with panelled shutters on the inside. Although there were only two good-sized bedrooms, that seemed enough to cope with and the sunny aspect cheered her.

"Mother had old-fashioned ideas," Mr Hammond explained as he demonstrated how the shutters unfolded. "Grew up on the rugged Scottish coast and didn't like fancy curtains which didn't keep out the weather." She wanted shutters like she grew up with."

"I like all the fireplaces," Richard said, "and the bathroom."

"You can collect driftwood to burn," Ron said. "Helps eke out the coal and Mam says wood burns warmer."

"We need an agni," Melisande said with a sigh.

"What's that then?" Mr Hammond sounded puzzled and a little annoyed, as if he thought there was something he'd missed in building the house.

Melisande smiled. "He's the Hindu fire god and what we called our servant who made and attended the fires."

"You had one servant just for fires?" Ron's jaw sagged.

"We had many servants," Jeri sounded terse. "We were expected to."

Richard explained. "In India it's the duty of those with wealth to employ as many people in their community as want to work. Each servant has one small task and must do it well. A sircar, that's a steward, supervises all."

"Oh yes?" Mr Hammond shrugged. "Like the squire and his wife back home in England eh? If you have a good 'un they kept an eye out to see no one went without. If they weren't, you suffered."

"A little like that," Richard agreed.

Mr Hammond looked them over. Three well-dressed youngsters from another country, in deep mourning, and not pioneer immigrants with knowledge and horse sense, Melisande guessed were his thoughts, sure they weren't complimentary.

"Can you light a fire, Mrs Holyman?"

Melisande shook her head, feeling her cheeks warming.

"And what about this?" Mr Hammond led them into the back, where the kitchen ran the width of the house. "This is the latest model kitchen range. A Shacklock. Shacklock's the best. Does your hot water as well as cook."

Melisande stared at the cream and green monster snugged into a tiled recess and shook her head again.

"Eh lass, we'd better find you someone to teach you or your menfolk'll starve."

"We know we need servants …" Jeri began.

"We say housekeeper. You'll not get much help if you keep nattering on about servants. Round here you call a cook a cook, and a general skilled helper a housekeeper." Mr Hammond watched Jeri's face.

Ron interrupted. "I was going to take 'em to the immigrants' barrack. There's quite a few women looking for work."

Mr Hammond shook his head. "Nay, what we need is Miggsy." Understanding dawned on Ron's face. Leaving three puzzled people Mr Hammond walked out of the back door, stepped onto the verandah, and bellowed "Miggsy."

***

Miggsy, of course, dear Miggsy the capable fix-it man. And hadn't she heard his voice here? His mother, the redoubtable Mrs Miggs, who did not approve of Melisande's ignorance, but taught her well, where was she? She'd not be far from her son.

***

Hammering stopped. Back came the yell of 'What?"

"Come here, lad."

Miggsy came quickly, his boots crashing along the road and up the front path. He poked his head round the front door. "What you want, boss?"

"Is your mam busy?"

"Working? Not since the Forresters' last baby."

"Think she'd take an all-day job being housekeeper and teaching this young lady how to run a New Zealand house?"

"Now wait a moment .. " Richard began.

"I need help, Richard, Jeri. If this … Mrs Miggsy?"

Ron and Mr Hammond chuckled. Miggsy coughed his laugh away. "No, it's Miggs, Missus. Me mam's called Mrs Miggs." He hesitated. "You best see her first, Missus. She were burnt bad rescuing horses and ain't pretty. But she can cook and bake, run a house. She's good at that."

"Right, off you go back to that roof, Miggsy boy, and tell your mam at dinner break. Then she can visit Mr and Mrs Holyman at their hotel."

Mr Hammond turned to Jeri and Richard. "Now about the house. What do you think?"

Jeri and Richard swapped looks, uncertainty ploughing furrows in both their brows. Melisande bit her lip, lowered her gaze and prayed hard. She shot an under-the-eyelashes glance at Mr Hammond.

Mr Hammond appeared puzzled, perhaps wondering if a purchase was more to their tastes because he began to speak. "If you really prefer to buy rather than rent …"

"Is it possible to rent for six months but extend the period of time if necessary?" The words popped out of Melisande's mouth. She couldn't argue now with Jeri or demand that Richard see she had a place to live in whilst they went away and roamed the area. It wasn't proper or acceptable in front of other people, but how could they forget what she had explained so carefully?

"I'd buy if I had the money," Ron said. "Now Dunedin is booming people have money to seek holiday homes here. The train makes travel simple and if you don't want to sell you can rent. Nice little money earner renting is, so Mr Truman says."

Richard and Jeri leaned their heads together, muttered, then Jeri spoke. "Buying depends on the price."

Ron's eyes lit up, his pimples pinked up. "Allow me to conduct you back to the office where Mr Hammond and yourself can negotiate with Mr Truman."

Richard offered his arm to Melisande. "We'll look round again if Mr Hammond permits us, and form some plans for our home."

Mr Hammond nodded and departed with Jeri and the chattering Ron.

Richard and Melisande strolled around, deciding which would be their bedroom and wondering if all their things would be enough to make a home. Melisande slid her hand into Richard's gloved hand.

Richard pulled her close. "You're shivering with cold, cuddle closer. I know it's a cottage compared with India, but it is a good place for you to learn how to manage a house, Lisa, my love. We can afford to keep it snug and warm and the gas lights will be time saving compared to lamps and candles."

"It's not the cold, Richard, I'm terrified. I can barely cook, my recipes from our cook are all Indian. I don't know how to buy things here. I don't know where to start, and you are going to leave me. I'll be alone." She swallowed hard, knew her voice had quavered.

"Don't cry, my Nut Brown Maid. You'll find a way to learn, I know you will." He squeezed her hard. "Jeri and I must find our land, but we will have you in this house by tomorrow and you won't be alone. I promise to get you help every day."

She rubbed her cheek against his jacket, fought down the panic. "We'll call it a great adventure, shall we? After all, you are going to learn about farming so we'll both learn together."

"That's my girl. We're off on a grand adventure " He kissed her cheek.

"And the first step is to plan where to meet Mrs Miggs," Melisande replied. "Shall we go and find Miggsy?"

Laughing together, holding each other's arms, they closed the front door and scampered along the road to the building site, dodging the puddles and ducking the gusts of wind.

***

We bought it, that little house. I remember now. Oh, and the wonderful Mrs Miggs. She did learn ... well ... she must have to be here in this house. She wanted a home, that safe haven she dreamed of, but was this place that refuge?

Chapter Ten

Mrs Miggs didn't come to the hotel. She met Melisande at the house the following morning. Miggsy brought the message. "Mam's shy of going out where strange folks'll see her."

"I understand, Mr Miggs," Melisande nodded, remembering the deformed beggars in India.

"Nay," Miggsy laughed, his face crinkled up and his cheeks reddening. "I'm best known as Dan. Me da were always Mister, and I've a ways to go to catch him." He turned to Richard. "An' if you'll let me mam see your missus first, without you, sir, then she can see if she'll be easy working for you. It's hard for her to be gawked at."

"Which means," Melisande said, looking at her husband, "you and Jeri can organise the delivery of all our trunks, boxes and crates from the ship tomorrow." She smiled at Miggsy. "Do you know some reliable men to remove our goods from the ship into this house?"

Miggsy grinned, his freckles stretching across his face. Melisande found him a cheery soul. "Aye, I know several men happy to earn a bit extra and Thomson's Removals is a steady man to cart your traps."

***

Dear Miggsy ... no it was ... she wasn't to call him Miggsy. Now who said that? He'd been such a reliable help. What was it he'd done?

***

Over dinner at the hotel Jeri explained he'd bought Hammond's house. "It's an investment and Richard is correct, you'll need somewhere respectable, suitable to your position here, to live whilst the farm is settled and a house built." He grinned at her. "It's for you, Lisa, to make up for …" he waved his arm around in a sweeping gesture. "all this upheaval. We used your money, therefore it's in your name as well as ours, I insisted you must have it. We've bargained a fair price with an agreement that Hammond may have first offer of its resale." He grinned at Richard. "Money'll be tight for our land until we get our uncle to sign the proper documents."

Richard muttered agreement as he struggled to slice the pork crackling into tidy mouthfuls.

Melisande listened as she tried to eat the mashed potato. How she wished for rice, beautiful light and fluffy Indian rice. And who asked her about using her money? Time to speak to Richard about this, but tonight in their bedroom.

***

Money, that was a problem wasn't it? Something happened and she...she had to have signed documents? But why when her men had arranged everything for her? Thinking made her temples throb. What was it those men of hers had done which caused a money problem? No, it was not them, it had been her Uncle Aubrey. He'd refused to release their funds. If they hadn't bought the Port Chalmers house which they could use as collateral they'd have lost the farm. She remembered struggling with the bank manager who wasn't going to do business with a woman. She'd shown him. She'd cabled her uncle and written a long and detailed letter coaxing and persuading him to release their money. Ruth had been such a help then. Thank heavens for the Port Chalmers house.

***

"We'll move you in tomorrow and be off the following day," Jeri continued. "I've hired those horses, Richard, on the understanding that if they suit we'll buy them." He looked across the table at his sister. "The chap knows we want a lady's horse and promises to put the word out around the farms."

Melisande sighed. "Thank you Jeri, but I don't think I can set up the house in one day, even with Mrs Miggs. Do you think we could eat here tomorrow night and sleep here as well?"

Richard threw her a knowing look full of approval. "That's my practical Nut Brown Maid. It's a sensible suggestion, Jeri. We'll make sure the men unpack and move all the heavy things before we leave and you and Mrs Miggs can spend time arranging the rest."

"Learn how to manage that stove," Jeri said, "and the fires."

Melisande pulled a face at him, gave up on the mashed potato, and tasted the roast pumpkin, which was more flavoursome. How she missed Indian spices. "You find us good land and don't buy without a land agent's advice," she warned him.

Jeri straightened up in his chair, glared, then sniffed with disdain. "You manage the house, my girl, leave us men to manage the business."

Richard raised his eyebrows, winked at her, and smiled.

Melisande smiled back. Silly Jeri, he prickled up like a porcupine.

***

Jeri was so thoughtless. And she did manage the bank and money, despite the problems. Jeri annoyed her with his attitude, as if she had dandelion fluff inside her head instead of a perfectly functioning brain. Richard never did that.

***

The following day meant an early start and Melisande made her way to the house at seven in the chilly dark of a winter morning. She found Mrs Miggs waiting by the front door, escorted by her son. Miggsy touched his cap when Melisande walked up the garden path.

"This is me mam, Mrs Holyman." He touched his mother's arm. "Must get to work, Mam. Excuse me, Mrs Holyman." He clattered off down the path in his large boots.

Mrs Miggs wore a bit of net as a veil and didn't lift it when she spoke. "Morning, Missus. I'm sorry for your loss, 't'always hurts losing parents."

Word certainly flew in Port Chalmers. "Thank you." Melisande saw a solid squarish body of medium height, no real figure, just straight up and down and hidden under a bundle of dull blue and black wrappings and a woollen plaid shawl. She had spent the night worrying about the best approach to this woman. She needed help, Mrs Miggs worked – when she could – as a housekeeper. Mr Truman said she worked hard and her cooking and baking had pleased the people she'd been housekeeper for. How do you not stare and outface a woman so badly scarred? Perhaps honesty was the right approach.

"Good morning," she said. "Shall we go in?" She opened the front door. "Your son tells me you were hurt rescuing horses. That was brave."

Mrs Miggs mumbled something which sounded like, "Had to be done."

Melisande talked over her shoulder as they walked down the hall to the kitchen, Mrs Miggs a pace behind. "I badly need your help. I know nothing about New Zealand houses. I can't cook, I've never bought fuel for fires or the proper stores for a home. I can buy good fish or fruit and vegetables. I used to buy them at the market but only for one meal at a time. Our cook and steward bought most things."

"Are you willing to learn? It'll spoil your pretty soft hands." Mrs Miggs spoke slowly as if forcing her mouth with difficulty.

Melisande pulled off her gloves, waved her hands at her, tried a smile. "I'll learn and they'll learn." She wondered about the voice. Did Mrs Miggs find it difficult to speak? How would she teach if that were so?

Mrs Miggs raised her veil. Melisande's hand flew to her mouth.

"Ain't a pretty sight."

It wasn't. Mrs Miggs didn't have a forehead or left side of her face, she had a mess of red lumpy scars with a slit for her one eye.

Melisande struggled to find words to ease their relationship; pity was not enough. Then she remembered India. "Oh, I am so sorry. It's like being a leper in India, Mrs Miggs. Through no fault of their own they have to face the stares, curses and avoidance. I don't suppose people are kinder here even though they are told it's the scars of bravery."

"Aye." Mrs Miggs shifted her weight to her back foot.

Melisande glanced away. "I'm staring. I'm so sorry and do apologise. But I need to look you in the face when we speak. How can I do that and not upset you?" She glanced back.

Mrs Miggs shrugged, shook her head.

Melisande gave an internal sigh. What could she do or how could she make this woman be comfortable with her? She smiled, looked at her directly again. "The carter will be here some time around noon. What do I do?"

Mrs Miggs broke into the travesty of a smile, her poor wrecked face unable to do more than twitch half her lips upwards, but her good eye sparkled with humour.

"Best get some cleaning done quickly, then."

Cleaning? Melisande looked around at the bare floors and empty cupboards, and she turned a shocked face to Mrs Miggs. "How can we? What do we do?"

"You aim to help?"

"If I can. What's something simple and easy I can do?"

Mrs Miggs laughed, more a coughing gurgle because of her scars. "My boy said he thought tha were a sensible little miss. He's got it right." She looked round the bare room. "You've naught to clean with, Missus, we best go shopping and I'll find some extra help. Will your man pay for extra help?" She actually patted Melisande's shoulder. "Best find you a real worker's apron too. I reckon I can find you a proper black one."

Melisande felt she'd been caught up in a gust of wind and whirled around and about, caught in the vortex of energy. "Er, very well, Mrs Miggs. Can you show me the way?"

Mrs Miggs beamed, well, one half of her face did, and her good eye glinted. "Come along Missus Holyman. We'll get you fitted out, and there's a couple of immigrant women in the barracks in need of work." She pulled the veil down to cover her face and strode down the hallway.

Melisande scurried after the energised woman and followed in her wake as she trod firmly along the path. Mrs Miggs was indeed a formidable force. During their short walk down the hill to the shops she listed what Melisande would need for cleaning and where to buy it all, told her about opening accounts and 'borrowed' the Post and Telegraph Department office errand boy. Willie departed on his safety bicycle to fetch the women from the immigration barracks and found himself commandeered for the rest of the day, carrying messages and orders.

***

Melisande woke herself with a croaking laugh reminiscent of Mrs Miggs' queer rough laugh. How could she have managed without Mrs Miggs and her indomitable determined spirit? How she'd chivvied and driven her co-workers and Melisande. For some minutes as she waited for Ruth to come with a drink and more draughts of that vile medicine her head actually cleared of all aches, noise and zigzags flashes. She began to believe that the doctors were correct and she would get well, and remember everything again.

***

By noon, when the carter appeared with the first load of crates, Melisande had learned the proper way to sweep a wooden floor, how to dust sills, shelves and mantelpieces, and how to lay a fire in a hearth. She'd learned to watch over and instruct the coal merchant's delivery, the firewood man's delivery, and sort out where the grocery deliveries should be stored. Mrs Miggs had been a marvel, a solid support who explained and ordered things as she whirled round the house, obviously enjoying herself.

It was noon. The carter and his men declared a 'smoko', "Time for dinner, and a pipe, Missus." and settled on the crates to eat, smoke and demand hot tea.

Melisande sagged against the door frame of what the women called her parlour and let her knees wobble. She was exhausted. "I agree. It's time for some luncheon," she said, letting a plaintive note creep into her voice.

"She means dinner," someone said.

"Tea, for us and those men," a voice called and she heard water poured, and the kettle clank onto the stove.

"Just finishing this floor, then I'm wanting a cup," said the other voice.

"Where's that boy?" from Mrs Miggs. "Willie? Oh, drat him."

Fortunately for Willie he had been idling away the time between errands by experimenting with the sharp and shiny new chopper, cutting kindling by the firewood stack. He came at the run. "Here, Missus Miggs."

She walked out into the hall, smiled her twisted smile at Melisande and looked sternly at Willie. "You ride down to the bakery, fetch us two of Mr Bream's hot meat and potato pies and two of his apple pies. And bring some more milk." She checked with Melisande. "That'll save us a bit of time, if you approve, Mrs Holyman."

Melisande nodded, managing a smile. Mrs Miggs patted her shoulder. "We've done, we can let the men in when we've eaten." She glared at Willie.

"You get them pies boxed right, Willie. No mashing them up in your bicycle basket or you'll get none."

Willie grinned, dashed out, and sped off on his bicycle.

Melisande wondered what meat pies tasted like, and how could they eat them without a table and chairs? An al fresco lunch in winter like the workmen outside? She went into the kitchen and stood near the hot stove. How she wished for a little Indian warmth. She closed her eyes and rested against the wall beside the stove.

"Ah will you look there, the poor lassie's fagged out."

Melisande blinked her eyes open and saw the three women gazing at her. What pleased her was the fact that all three looked sympathetic, not despising her.

"You'm a quick learner. Missus, you'll do." Praise indeed from Mrs Miggs.

"There's so much I don't know."

Sympathetic ahs and understanding nods soothed her a little.

The stove had heated the room and enough water to use for cleaning and now to wash hands. Melisande copied the women and wiped her hands on her enormous apron.

"I'll make you a couple of aprons your size," Mrs Miggs told her, "and Mrs MacAndrew is happy to come and do your laundry every week."

Mrs MacAndrews beamed.

"Mrs Turvey would do the heavy work for you twice a week," Mrs Miggs finished.

Before Melisande could agree Willie arrived carrying a basket which leaked warm scents of meat and gravy and she felt hungry enough to stand around with them, picnic style, eating, with her fingers, without a plate, a large slice of the meat and potato pie, which was well flavoured with onion and mushrooms.

She looked round at the women, Willie, and the carter holding a battered metal teapot and felt an uncontrolled burst of something like laughter as she noticed her brother and husband standing in the kitchen doorway, mouths a-cock and eyes staring.

"Welcome to the luncheon party," she said with a grand gesture, inviting them in. "Meet our workers. Oh, and would you like a little pie?" She did laugh then.

***

That had been a glorious day. She could smell the pie even now. Jeri had scolded her for 'improper' behaviour. Richard had merely asked her not to repeat that sort of picnic too often. "Needs must when the devil drives," he quoted, "but have a care for your reputation. I understand things have to be different in New Zealand." She'd wondered if her men realised just how different their lives would be socially, and how much physical work they would have to do to prove themselves. In her head she thanked Mesdames Miggs, MacAndrews and Turvey.

***

The ease of the settling in. She had three women who desperately wanted work, a cheeky errand boy, bored and underemployed by his official employer, the Post and Telegraph Department, and a busy carter and helpers who wanted to unload and unpack.

Furniture crates arrived, Jeri and Richard guided the men to the back garden, the crates were opened, and Melisande stood in the doorway instructing them as to which room for each piece of furniture. The smaller crates the men stacked inside the front door, and one man opened them out in the hall, and then the boxes and packages inside she directed into the appropriate places.

"Don't burn 'em, good wood in them crates," the carter said as they departed. "Make a hen house or wood store." He and his helpers put their tools and coats on the cart and strolled off beside the patient horses, who woke up now they were turned homewards.

"It's late," Richard announced when the last empty crate had been stored in the back garden. "Let's finish unpacking tomorrow." He smiled at each of the women. "I hope you can work with my wife tomorrow for we will be away inspecting properties." He handed out shillings, with his thanks, as Jeri tried to bank the stove fire for the night under Willie's instructions and Mrs Miggs's watchful eye.

Mrs Miggs agreed from behind her veil and Mrs MacAndrews and Mrs Turvey beamed. They approved Willie's work and gave Jeri praise for his attempt.

"So much to learn," Melisande complained as Richard helped her into her coat and wraps, before escorting all of them out of the front door.

Jeri locked the door and they parted from the women, heading downhill back to the hotel.

"I think eating in the hotel tonight and sleeping there is an excellent idea, Lisa, my clever one," Richard said, as they hurried. The wind had a nip and the light changed quickly, darkened from dusk into night. They felt cold and grateful for the hotel's bright gas lights and hot crackling fires.

Hearty vegetable soup, roast baron of beef, roast vegetables and thick gravy disappeared quickly. Even Melisande ate her way through a plateful of small servings. A slice of rhubarb pie with custard and cream left her sleepy.

"I'm too tired to think," she said, "but if you men are leaving me tomorrow I will need to know about our money and how to get it from the bank."

Jeri helped himself to a third slice of pie and shook his head. "Lisa, sister dear, you won't need to go to the bank. Ladies don't. I have a fat purse for you. Spend it carefully."

"I will." She thought about the bank and decided she would find out. She was sure women did have banking business. "Mrs Miggs helped me open accounts at the butcher's, grocers and hardware shops. We receive a monthly bill."

Richard sipped his coffee, smiled at Melisande. "You will have to check those bills carefully every month. How's your arithmetic?"

"I think," she replied with a yawn, "I shall not be clever at that, so you will have to help me."

He finished his coffee in one ungraceful swallow and rose. "That's your task as house keeper," he teased, "but I'll help." He smiled and stretched out his hand to her, which made Jeri tut about 'not in public'.again. "Time to retire, Lisa, love of my life. We will leave before daylight and expect to find a welcoming home, a full larder, and you in command when we return."

Melisande muttered complaints, even a small groan, and allowed herself to be escorted to their bedroom.

***

Those first weeks had been hard, even with Mrs Miggs and her cronies. Sometimes she wished her men were less selfish and more thoughtful. Off they went adventuring and Jeri had to sail to England soon. They kept leaving her behind and she needed their support.

Charlotte came to settle her for the night. "Can you see a little more clearly, Lisa, There's so much you need to understand but we are forbidden to worry you with anything until you can see clearly and speak properly again."

"I'm trying" she croaked, wanting to say more to Charlotte about wanting to help.

"We know, my dear friend, we know. We can wait, although it is a great trial and worry. Bless you, my dear and sleep well." She gently kissed the top of Melisande's head and withdrew.

***

A sleepy kiss and Richard had gone, a saddle bag instead of a valise for his few nights away. All Melisande needed to do was eat the large breakfast, then check that Jeri had not forgotten anything, or left anything in his room, and arrange for their luggage to be sent up the hill to their house.

She sat over breakfast making a list, a long list, which grew longer as she kept remembering things Advik always dealt with. She could manage without a lady's maid until it came to socialising at dinner parties and balls, but it took so long to dress herself, ease into that wretched corset by herself, tie the petticoat ribbons, tie on her pocket and fix the dress fastenings, pin plackets and set them straight for access to her pocket. She'd learnt to braid and tuck her hair for daily wear, but for a dinner party or dance she would need help with the more elaborate hairstyles necessary for such occasions. Also getting into her dress without upsetting hair and face was so much easier with a maid. What would happen when it came to the weekly full bath and hair washing which would be so difficult in this colder climate where she couldn't sit in the sun and have

Usha comb her hair cry? Her hair was her only beautiful feature, she knew that. She loved it long, though she did keep it shorter than waist length because it was cooler and easier to manage the weight and thickness of it, but its sheen and thickness were its glory. She couldn't bear to wear little caps to hide it and she surely couldn't manage elaborately dressing it up on her own.

She sipped the last of her tea, too strong and tepid, and wished she could make her men think about the practicalities of daily living. Was she meant to valet their clothes, press their suits and iron shirts? Well she couldn't, didn't know how, and wouldn't. They must think for themselves.

Managing a smile and thank yous to the hotel staff, she grumbled to herself on the short walk up the street, to the left turn. She panicked for a moment, not recognising it immediately, told herself firmly not to be a silly as it was the first turn on the left above the hotel and must be correct, and headed for her new home, continuing, in her head, to list a string of complaints her men should hear. She simply wanted India and home, in the past, as it had been. She found it hard to be brave every day and believe in a better future here, especially now she was alone. She couldn't remember ever being on her own and grief had a way of sneaking back and incapacitating her until she sat and wept for a while. She missed her parents so, and her easy life in India.

Mrs Miggs, Mrs MacAndrews and Mrs Turvey stood on the verandah by the front door with bulging baskets and an eager curiosity to see inside the crates. Miggsy waited with them. Once inside her new home, Miggsy lent his strength with a small crowbar to open every box which needed opening.

"Give us a yell, Missus Holyman, if you need some muscles to move things, me and the boys can lend a hand," he said, before clomping back to the building site.

"Stove's still warm," Mrs Turvey called. Melisande heard the rattle and slur of the kettle going on the hob and then the sound of coal tumbling from the hod onto the fire.

"Let's see," Mrs Miggs said, pushing up her veil over her hair, "we've got your milk coming every day, green groceries, bread and meat in before noon – we'll have to get you learning to make your own bread and scones and cake – but whilst you settle best take advantage of what's on hand and buy."

She looked at Melisande, who pulled a thoughtful face to show that she understood, and then inclined her head with a murmur of agreement.

Mrs Miggs wasn't fooled, nor was Mrs MacAndrews. "Now then, lassie, you'll soon get meals sorted and know what you'll want each day. Best work out a week at a time, saves time."

Melisande sighed.

"That's a grand stove," Mrs Turvey said, coming back into the front room. "All that warmth all day and 'ot water." She turned to Melisande. "A nice stew and a pot of soup'd cook gentle through the day or overnight and you'd bake a bit as well for it keeps heat so steady and constant. We'll learn you how."

"What we'll do," Mrs Miggs said, "is get you, Mrs MacAndrews, to put up a pot of stew, use the bits left to start a stock pot, get the young missus a porridge pot going and set some bread to start. That'll see to meals for a couple of days and let Mrs Holyman arrange the house."

Mrs MacAndrews nodded. "Aye, and I'll get us a bit of shortbread baked for tea and do us a pie for lunch."

Melisande felt her mouth begin to gape. How could anyone do all that before midday? She clenched her teeth together firmly and forced a smile.

Mrs Miggs looked at Mrs Turvey. "There'll be things to wash and clean in them boxes and crates. Can you fix a line outside in't back yard and get that carpet beater we bought, and them scrub brushes, all ready? There's a copper and a pump in the wash house."

Mrs Turvey nodded and stumped off down the hall to the kitchen. "I'll get us a bucket of hot water to start," she called over her shoulder.

"Right then, Mrs Holyman, me and tha'll get your bed made up and t'other bed, with those sheets and blankets we bought yesterday. Then we'll get them curtains beaten and hung. I 'spect most things in them crates'll need a wash and clean up."

All Melisande could do was nod. Suddenly she wanted to sit down and weep, she felt exhausted already, knees ready to sag and give way.

Mrs Miggs eyed her. "You poor lassie. We'll do it all slow and steady. It'll take a week to get all the things unpacked and put up like you want 'em. Don't fret. We'll help."

"It's just …"Melisande shook her head and shrugged helplessly. "It's just that I don't know how to do anything."

"You will. Give us a month and you'll be doing all this cooking and organising yoursen. You'se quick and want to learn. That's what counts. Your menfolk'll be fed and comfortable and that's what counts too." She gave a hearty laugh. "We all had to learn once, and spoiled good food doin' it. I'll show you a quick bread to make for when you've burnt the loaf or forgotten to make one. With a bit of bread and cheese you can feed anyone."

***

She'd been a good teacher, Mrs Miggs, Melisande was sure. She now knew how to make bread, cook a meal, she'd been setting an overnight sponge for the breakfast bread when … when it happened. What it was, her mind refused to even contemplate. but she was getting closer to daring to know. She had to.

***

Melisande managed a shaky laugh and the two of them wrapped themselves in huge aprons and began removing the protective wrappings from the first crate. She scolded herself as she checked the parcels. It wasn't right to feel afraid and she could manage, she could become a capable 'colonial' wife who would have made her parents proud if only they'd been alive to see her.

Most of the bundles of linens, rugs and hangings were fusty, and packages at the bottom of the boxes had been touched by salt water.

Melisande mentally thanked Advik and her Indian servants for their care. Very little had been lost to salt-water damage, the packaging and wrappings had been done well.

Mrs Turvey, eventually joined by Mrs MacAndrews, hustled and bustled in and out, taking things to wash and things to air. They exclaimed over rugs and cushions, and the bolts of cloth Melisande had managed to pack when her brother wasn't looking. How those women could work and still chatter away.

Lunch scented the kitchen with a good comforting smell. They ate standing around a large kitchen table which Melisande did not recognise, nor did she recognise the smaller one near the pantry door.

"Where did they come from?" Melisande asked, wondering what her men had been doing.

The three women exchanged self-conscious glances, not guilty exactly, Melisande noted, but definitely up to something.

"Bit of trading and a promise of payment," Mrs Miggs finally said.

"Ah." Never mind a bit of trading, perhaps this was one of the new chum tricks, she'd have to learn and be firm. She promised herself she'd take a look at the advertisements in the newspapers to find out what was fair and what was exorbitant profiteering. She remembered Advik, drew in a deep breath and stood firm.

"Who made them and what do they ask me to pay?" She shook her head at them. "Please understand. I'd prefer to be asked first. Until our land brings in harvests we have no income and must be careful." She saw the expressions. There, she'd said it, and, by their expressions, not fully believed.

The three women looked at each other. Mrs Miggs explained. "Just thought to help out a bit. Our boys at the timber mill and in the lumber yard, they can get bits of wood and they make simple furniture. You need a kitchen table and a baking board, they need a bit of cash." The women seemed to think that was an explanation.

Mrs Turvey's chins wobbled as she spoke. "One of the lads, he'd knock your crates into summat useful, 'en 'ouse or wood shed." She urged Melisande to agree with nodding smiles and her fat cheerful face belied the fact that she had to live in the barracks until someone employed her or she raised enough money for the authorities to allow her to be a landed emigrant.

It would be remarkable if these women didn't think she was wealthy and able to hand out handfuls of paisa, or annas, even rupees. Oh bother, pounds, shillings and pence, and half pence and farthings and sixpences and whatever she'd forgotten, that was the coinage she had to remember.

Feeling helpless, Melisande looked at the three women. Rupees, money, it wasn't only that. For the first time she began to see how different their lives were from anything she'd known. She tried to reach beyond her own life and think about theirs. "I do appreciate your help and I do need a table but I can only pay what's fair here in New Zealand."

"S'long as it's cash the boys won't fuss," Mrs Miggs promised.

Melisande managed a smile and a nod. "Can they make stout kitchen chairs?"

"Aye," Mrs Miggs said, looking round the bare room. "What'll Mrs Holyman need, ladies, to get this kitchen comfortable?"

"Row of pegs by the door," Mrs MacAndrews said, "and a boot rack underneath. Our George makes tidy small ones." She thought a moment, then added, "If you put one of them cotton rugs of yours there, that'll catch the dirt and wet, save the floors, and I can wash it when needed."

"Yes, saves the mud trampled in, saves me work, and you'll need more shelves," Mrs Turvey said, "an' a slab of cold stone for the little table and in the pantry."

"My boy'll sort all that," Mrs Miggs promised.

Melisande sighed but agreed, and feeling the need to make herself useful and in charge, began unwrapping things from the large box of china. "Who will wash and who will carry?" she asked, smoothing her hands around her Indian pottery bowls, delighted to find them unbroken.

They soon covered the kitchen table with Indian pottery and English bone china.

"I can see why I need more shelves," Melisande said.

Mrs Turvey was much taken with the Indian pottery. She handled it as carefully as she did the bone china. "I'd not care to pay for droppin' it," she remarked. "S'lovely colours, real pretty patterns."

"It's only everyday Indian ware, Mrs Turvey. It's not expensive like the English china, but yes, it's a pleasure to use each day."

***

How she wished her guardian doctor, senior Doctor Allinson, would let her move, and have the window open and the curtains drawn. She'd like to see her pretty Indian pottery again. She'd like to sit in a chair, walk to the bathroom, but all he'd say was, "Don't hasten your healing time, Mrs Holyman. Your health you need for the rest of your life and you've a good reason for being careful."

Yes, she'd lost their child, Richard's and hers, and this time it was a wanted child. Both doctors assured her that the attack and her serious hurts were the reason she had miscarried; given rest, good food and healthy fresh air, she would be able to have more children.

"Oamaru has a salt bathing pool, something for you to try," the doctor said. "Perhaps even a sea voyage to the Pacific Islands. That would be a tonic for you." He checked her pulse once more.

When the doctor left Charlotte brought her luncheon, slops again. She seemed to live on broths and beef tea and soups.

"Might I have a bread roll with this soup do you think?"

"I'll ask the doctor." Charlotte left but Melisande fell asleep before she returned.

***

Someone knocked on the front door. Melisande left the women washing and drying and went to investigate.

The young man – Ron wasn't it? – from Mr Truman's office had a large envelope of papers for her husband and one for her brother. He was in a chatty mood and kept her talking for a good five minutes.

Stopping halfway down the hall to check the contents of a box on her return to the kitchen, Melisande heard her three helpers gossiping away.

"She's a half breed …"

"Nay, too pale …"

"Well, one of her grandparents ain't English, and all this stuff from India she likes … .not proper for a lady," Mrs MacAndrews sounded snappish.

Melisande, indignant, dithered. What should she do? To be Anglo Indian was not socially acceptable in India, obviously unacceptable here in New Zealand too. Should she pretend not to have heard and bring up her antecedents casually in a forced conversation? Or should she march in and announce her pedigree? Either way, her relationship with these women was spoiled. She had wanted to be friendly – as she had been with Usha and Advik – but there was something of a different barrier between herself and these colonial women.

Richard and Jeri weren't here to speak out. She had to set things on the correct pathway now or blight her future in Port Chalmers. She must attack the rumours before they spoiled any social life in the town for her, but she understood that as far as a friendly relationship with these women went she was condemned whatever she did. She'd never find, outside the company of her brother and husband, that comfortable easy feeling of acceptance, that loving feeling of family from her parents and servants that she'd had in India. All lost in this strange new world. Straightening her spine, inhaling deeply and forcing the corners of her lips upwards into a smile, she marched into the kitchen.

***

How scared she had been to face those competent women, women she needed. Gossip she abhorred. She understood the damage gossip caused now she had to face its reality. She smiled to herself. She'd triumphed over the Port Chalmers gossips in the end and caused a shocking scandal.

***

"I don't care for gossip." She straightened her spine and looked each woman firmly in the face. She managed a sweet smile. "My brother and I were born in Somerset, my father was the youngest son of Sir Lionel Allmark. My mother was the only daughter of a gentleman farmer whose family, the De'arths, had owned the land for centuries and were proud to have fought with Oliver Cromwell. And my skin may be olive toned but that is not from Indian grandparents, but living in a hot climate." Still the women would not look at her.

"My husband's family, the Holymans, own an estate in Yorkshire, and they approve and bless our marriage." She inhaled sharply, glared at the three. "Are there any other details you need to gossip about?"

Only Mrs MacAndrews showed embarrassment, although even then it wasn't much of a blush. They shrugged their plaid shawls about them and inspected the floor.

"Well then, I think we'd better finish washing the china." And that ended all chatter for the rest of the afternoon. Melisande noted there were no apologies – that was not the colonial way.

It wasn't the expected differences that caught her, tripped her into fretting and anxiety, it was the unexpected ones. She had always had a friendly relationship with servants, but now she realised that in New Zealand a relationship with servants did not mean the same as it had been with her Indian servants. They had been family in one way, all working for the best outcomes for Papa and Mama, the whole village did, because that meant a good life for everyone. Here in New Zealand that attachment did not exist. These women worked for money and made their own independent lives. They probably knew a good relationship meant a better, happier day's work, but it was not up to them to make this relationship. The task was hers if she wanted to have a smooth-running home and life, and she didn't know how to manage that other than being civil and friendly. She must learn, she would learn, or life in New Zealand would be unbearable.

***

As it was until ... until what? And why did she know that it was unbearable now and that was why she could not, dare not remember? Ruth asked every day how her memory was. There had been men asking once, before ... before what? It wasn't something Richard or Jeri caused. If only the patches of memory cohered in a way that helped her understand.

Chapter Eleven

After a chilly night in a lonely bed, the shadows of grief and fear reaching out to her, Melisande rose early, and found the kitchen stove gave off enough warmth to wake her up and stiffen her spine in preparation for the day's strife. Managing the gaslights and the bedroom fire kept her from worrying about her men and the scrapes Jeri might cause and drag poor Richard into. She hoped they were dry and well fed. There had been talk of camping out, but this was not India with a set pattern to rain. It could rain any time in Port Chalmers as they had discovered, but she had work to do and three helpers to watch and learn from.

Bread baking today, again, and she must learn to like porridge and cook bacon with eggs for breakfast, especially for her men. Fresh bread rolls every morning she thought she could make, that simply meant mixing some flour, yeast and water last thing at night. Setting a sponge, Mrs Miggs called it. Then the rest of the flour and milk and an egg were added in the morning and she had dough ready to knead and bake. Pastry defeated her as yet but savoury pies were something her men had taken to. She must learn. And where were her men? She missed them, and wondered what excuses they would make for delaying and adventuring before arriving home several days over their promised return.

Sleep without Richard never came easy. She'd never been alone in a house before. The creaks and groans in the house at night worried her. The noises were unexpected, some like footsteps, some like a window or door closing, and some as if a person had slapped a hand on the wooden walls outside. The sound of rain on the corrugated iron roof, a musical drumming, she could understand. The wind rattling the windows and setting the shutters to vibrate puzzled her until she sourced the noise, but the house noises unsettled her, made her uneasy.

Miggsy found her walking round the outside of the house in the morning after her second night alone. He called out as he passed on his way to work, "All right, Missus Holyman?"

Melisande, aware of how peculiar she must look, blushed enough to warm her ears. "I wondered if someone had been round the house last night. There was a knocking sound …" Her voice trailed off as Miggsy hopped over the gate and scanned the ground. He tracked around the house, Melisande following.

"No one been here," he paused, looking thoughtful. "D'you hear other sounds?"

She nodded.

"Reckon you don't know about wooden houses, Missus Holyman. They settle at night after warming up in the day." He grinned. "It's like they talk to you. Wood does that as it cools."

"Oh, so it's not . . not people?"

His grin widened. "No one'll bother you, Missus Holyman. Me mam's seen to that. Anyway no peepers in Port Chalmers, our local police sergeant keeps a strict watch. Me mam and her pals gossip away, but they tell what they know straight. People'll watch, they know enough about you now to wait and see you for themselves."

Gossip, Melisande thought, why do people do it? I don't. A wind nipped past, fresh off the sea. She shivered.

"Best go in and have your breakfast, Missus Holyman." Miggsy looked up at the chimneys. "Light a fire too, it's going to blow today. Spring roaring in." He smiled again and strode off to work.

He was quite right about the weather. A cold wind blew in and she lit the fires. More work. Work, work, work. It haunted Melisande that she could not keep up with her helpers and found herself aching and worn out each evening. She hadn't played the piano or sketched or made jewellery since arriving in their cottage home. Mrs Miggs promised that she'd do more cooking and housekeeping once Melisande knew what to do and how to do it, but she insisted that Melisande learn what to do.

"That way you can watch over your cook, Missus Holyman, and make sure all's right and proper."

It was the how which flummoxed Melisande. She'd bought two books about household management and studied them at night. Mrs Beeton and Mrs Acton had much to say about watching servants, and budgeting. Mrs Miggs liked to try the recipes and said Mrs Acton's bread recipes were best but neither authoress knew about setting a sponge properly.

Melisande struggled on, longing for her men. Where were they? Richard promised he'd make certain that Jeri would return within a week. She earnestly wished for his, and Jeri's, return so that they could attend church as a family, but they failed her.

***

Church, that was it. That's where she met Ruth and Charlotte. Now she knew. And hadn't church been peculiar despite the same prayer book?

***

Ron, the solicitor's 'boy', warned her off the Presbyterian church. "Your blacks are too smart," he told her with a cheeky grin, leaning against the door post as he handed her yet another envelope full of documents for her men.

Melisande raised her eyebrows at him, giving him a puzzled look.

"Minister's fierce about proper respect for the dead. Mourning black must be dull, bombazine, no folderols, no frippery, the minister says." Ron grinned. "The old tabbies'll be on the watch and you got shiny silk and pretty beads an' those silver drippy earrings." He grinned some more. "The minister'd have a fit if he saw that fancy black hat of yorn in his church."

He turned to walk down the path, and called over his shoulder, "I wish you dared go. I'd laugh. The minister's such a stern, old killjoy Scot."

He loped away, leaving a bemused Melisande, who'd never been near any religious strife, and only knew her mildly Anglican upbringing from prayer book, confirmation class and Bible lessons with Mama. Downriver to church was not always possible, though her parents had tried to take her once a month. At least bread dough didn't argue or condemn, just this bowlful refused to rise fully to make into a fluffy loaf.

"More kneading," Mrs Miggs explained, "and the dough were too cold overnight."

Sunday morning brought blustery windy weather, and a sea fret of misty moist air which beaded all it touched, covering clothes and hair in a fine veil of silvery droplets. It also brought a strong scent of the ocean, seaweed and a salt taste to the lips. Melisande enjoyed living near the sea; the sound of the water reminded her of living near the Ganges in India. She sighed, forcing her thoughts away from her old home and what had been.

She hoped her men would have returned, but no. Worry nudged her sharply and she wondered what on earth could keep them so long. Mentioning this to Mrs Miggs during the Saturday morning baking lesson brought that cough-rumble which was the Miggs laughter.

"Men that age, like my Miggsy, life's all wanting adventures like they've read in that Boys' Own paper," she said. "Some of 'em niver grow out of it, like this war in Africa them's mad keen to join." She paused, shook her head and sighed.

"Thank the good Lord my boy's got a wise head and a sense of duty to his ma."

Thank the good Lord, Melisande thought, for the African war seemed on everyone's mind in Port Chalmers, that Jeri has Richard to steady him and that they are both going to be setting up the farm. There's scant time for that, never mind time for thinking about running off to Africa. There was talk in the local newspaper of forming a regiment to go out, even the children played soldiers in the streets. Southern Africa was so far away. She'd hate them to go.

Fortunately the wind scoured away the mist, but then it rained heavily. Melisande trudged to church, longing for some Indian sun. The Holy Trinity Anglican church, tucked away up the hill beyond the shops, stood small and solid, made in the blue stone with attractive modern stained-glass windows. It was tiny compared to the Presbyterian church which dominated the centre of the town.

Sheltered under her huge Indian umbrella Melisande joined the queue of people shuffling through the doors. The lack of a porch or covered entrance didn't appear to bother them. Indeed, people smiled at her umbrella. Melisande shivered and stamped her feet to warm them, as the queue of people observed her. The rain had eased, the wind reduced to sneaky gusts which caught one unawares and tugged at hats unexpectedly, and she was glad to enter the church and be greeted by the verger.

"Good morning. Mrs Holyman isn't it? I'm Mr Landry, the vicar's deacon and warden." He squeezed her hand rather harder than comfortable, eyeing her hat and earrings with a sly upwards lift of eyebrows. "Your husband still not returned? I hear Mr Holyman and Mr Allmark are looking at farms near Oamaru."

"Good morning, Mr Landry. Yes, my husband and brother are still away." And I'm not telling you any more, you old gossip seeker. "Will you kindly take care of my umbrella?" She furled it and handed it to him, trying not to pull a face. She most certainly did not appreciate the way the warden judged her. She turned and followed the queue down the aisle, seeking the nearest pew. A swirl of skirts and she was caught up by a gaggle of young women who insisted she sat with them.

She learned, as they all settled and adjusted themselves and their skirts, that they were the vicar's three daughters and the warden's daughter. Around her age, but unmarried, and wearing what they clearly thought to be the most fashionable clothes in town. They shared hymn books and prayer books. Melisande, constrained to explain that her prayer book lay in an unpacked box, felt uncomfortable. She'd never been much in the company of young women of her age and she wasn't quite sure how to respond to them. They fidgeted and whispered behind their hands, eyeing all the young men. Still, they did invite her to Lady's Day at the yacht club, the open day of the art society, a Glee club, and to go walking. She accepted all the invitations, except the Glee club. Remembering Jeri's warnings about socially acceptable behaviour she didn't think that a recently bereaved woman should be singing in a group in public.

***

Ruth and Charlotte and Charlotte's sisters. The beginnings of establishing herself and learning how to make friends with other young women. She hadn't known how solitary her life had been without companions of her own age and sex. And how she valued their friendship now, as they nursed her with such tender care.

***

Hurrying home under a more cheerful sky she found herself overtaken by two horsemen, scruffy, unkempt, unshaven, but her men, riding two well-bred chestnut horses and leading two more, a pretty little bay mare and a comically patched skewbald.

"We have permission to put the horses in the field beside the new houses," Jeri said.

"Do you like the mare?" Richard sounded pleased with himself. "We found her at the Kirkham Stud. I thought she'd be a sweet ride for you." He wheeled his horse round to lead the mare forward and show her off. The mare huffed at Melisande and permitted a gentle stroke.

Melisande smiled up at both her men. "Thank you. She looks an easy ride."

Richard nodded and dismounted to walk beside Melisande. "I have missed you, my love," he whispered in her ear, bending his head to duck round her hat brim.

Melisande slipped her hand into his, for no one could see them here doing this in public, and squeezed. "I am so happy to have you home," she replied. "Have you good news?"

"Oh yes," and Richard, and Jeri grinned.

***

Melisande woke and found she could tell the degree of light coming through the window curtains. Her sight improved, only slowly, but she could see the dawn light. How could she forget her own Ranee, her sweet-tempered mare. She watched the sun rise and remembered learning to ride.

***

Riding lessons commenced in the morning. Mrs Miggs arrived early to take over the housekeeping now the men had arrived, though how she found out so quickly puzzled Melisande. But Melisande proudly presented a breakfast of porridge, bacon and eggs and her own bread rolls and earned high praise from Jeri as well as Richard. Their approval almost made up for all the work and her struggle to learn these basic skills.

They'd talked past midnight about the farms they had found and the two for which they had made formal offers.

***

A little sun sneaked round the edge of the curtains. She could see its warm light. She'd remembered. Her men had been buying a farm It would be logical to assume that this room was in a farmhouse. She eased up against the bank of pillows, cautiously rested her head against them, closed her eyes and tried to find the next cohesive memory.

***

"We've seen two ready-to-work farms. We've offered far less than the asking prices, but we do have the money and so will not involve the sellers in government loans, bank mortgages and large lawyers' fees. It is an inducement to accept the lower price." Jeri couldn't sit still but paced the room, fiddling with ornaments, adjusting lamp wicks, poking the fire. "We checked all the current prices in the government lists and worked out what was correct for the farms we inspected."

Richard laughed "I'm sure we impressed the agent who showed us the first farm. He thought he could convince us the farm was worth double the government land prices. When we told him what the government auction price had been he stuttered and stammered about perhaps making a mistake, and that his first price was in error."

Melisande laughed with them.

"We simply have to wait," Richard said, compelling her to rise and escorting her to their bedroom. "We've some nights to catch up on, my beloved," he whispered in Melisande's ear.

Jeri growled at them and followed behind them to his room.

Chapter Twelve

She loved being loved by Richard. How could she have forgotten their love making? She appreciated his ardour, eager yet gentle and always kind, but she wondered about Jeri. Would he be kind to his wife? And patient? Richard personified patience when he taught her to ride side saddle on dear quiet Ranee.

***

Richard had bought a saddle and a side saddle for the little mare and Jeri, even Jeri, who always insisted on proper behaviour and not upsetting people, said she'd need a split skirt like the one the lady who demonstrated the mare's paces had worn. "Rough riding around the farm would be easier if you're riding astride and a lot of ladies do it, but not in town of course."

Naturally. Jeri tried to instil the importance of being socially correct at every moment. Even Richard insisted that there were set behaviour patterns for a person of their class and status. "It is important or you'll be without social standing and a position," he told her. "You've little understanding of how those old cats who rule the roost in every community can isolate you, ruin your social life, and have a community shun you. In these small colonial communities it's vital that you fit in. Don't you remember society life in India?"

Melisande didn't and thought them overly careful. She had yet to meet the women, meant to be socially her equals, who would try to force her to conform to their rules and judge her by their limiting standards. Some carping she understood was inevitable. Protected by her parents she'd never realised how such social pressure, the spiteful unfavourable comments, could harm a person's position and comfort in their society. She sighed. So much to learn.

The mare stood patiently whilst Jeri and Richard settled the side saddle in place, then serious lessons began. Richard, who had learned to ride with his sisters, had more idea of how a lady rode side saddle, so Jeri led the mare. Her name was Sweet Chestnut for her conker colour and kind nature. Melisande decided to find a simpler name and concentrated on learning how to walk, trot and halt. She'd ridden the donkeys many times as a child but the mare stood much higher off the ground. She was, however, a gentle horse not given to startling or making a fuss. A placid beast suited Melisande.

She stroked the mare's neck. "She's such a sweet animal, a queen of horses. I'll call her Ranee."

Jeri grumbled. "About time you forgot India," he muttered, but Richard said he thought Ranee more suitable than the English word, queen.

"No one can object to the Hindi version, they won't know it means queen," he told Jeri. "Now Lisa, let's see you walk her down the road and back again without Jeri leading her."

Melisande found her centre of balance in the saddle quickly and she discovered that the rhythm of Ranee's long stride was easy to settle into. Even the hammering of the builders did not disturb the mare. She flicked an ear, turned her head to observe, but didn't break her smooth pace.

On their return Melisande trotted ahead of her men and saw, at the far end of the field, on the cliff fence line, a man standing in the field inspecting their other horses. She circled round and back to Jeri and Richard.

"There's a man in the field with your horses."

Jeri sprinted ahead. Richard broke into a jog-trot beside her. Ranee, encouraged with a heel's nudge, trotted too. Richard gave her an approving nod and ran on to join Jeri. They herded the stranger away from the horses.

The three men stood in a triangle, Jeri and Richard shoulder to shoulder, the stranger leaning towards them. Talking at them? Melisande watched with sideways glances as she practised halting, directing her mare left or right and riding in circles. Finally she rode Ranee in a circle near the men.

The newcomer was shaking his head. "You're green, don't know much about horses if you think that. The mare's not fit for country riding. I'll take her off your hands." He glanced up as Melisande halted beside him.

Melisande tried not to stare into those hot brown eyes. He's dark skinned, is he a native, a Maori? she wondered. No, she remembered, Mrs Miggs said the local Maori were busy folk, fishing and farming farther round the bay, and didn't come into town much. Possibly this man had Eastern European antecedents, southern Italian perhaps? She felt his anger which floated like a warm cloud round his head.

Richard stepped sideways to catch Ranee's bridle. "The stud promised to take her back if she's not suitable," he told the man. "How do you find Ranee's paces and behaviour?" he asked Melisande.

"Perfectly mannered and well trained, thank you."

"Then thank you for your concern, we'll stay with our agreement. The stud has a reputation to keep."

The man turned away, walking along the fence line back towards town.

Richard watched him go. "I think we'd better find secure stabling for our nags, Jeri. Best not leave them in this field until we're sure of that man."

"Where's the nearest livery stable?"

Melisande laughed. "Ask Miggsy," she and Richard chorused.

"More expenses," Jeri complained. He groaned and rubbed his head until his hair ruffled up in spikes and crests. "We can't afford it. Our uncle has to release the rest of our funds, and all these women coming every day and …"

Richard caught his elbow, squeezed it. "It's only until we remove and that will be soon." He patted Jeri's back. "Let's find Miggsy first."

***

She must have fallen asleep again for bright sunshine framed the edges of the curtains now, late morning or even noon time? The window had been cracked open and her medicine tray rested on the bedside table. How she wanted to get up and walk about but her uncertain sight, good sense and sore head prevented it, as firmly as the doctor's command. If she remained still and quiet, sleeping most of the day and night, which she couldn't help with that medicine, she would be able to resume a more normal life. She had something to do, papers to sign or persuade someone else to sign them. Which was it?

***

But the acceptance of their offer for one of the farms and the legal papers for it didn't arrive until the day before Jeri's departure. Bustled down to Mr Truman's office to sign the purchase documents, Melisande found herself being instructed in the drawing up of a will. Mr Truman agreed to it, but it was Richard who insisted Jeri and he each make a will making sure Melisande was named as beneficiary and for Melisande to make a will leaving all her property to her husband and any future children. As both Jeri and Melisande were under age – "Only 'til November," Jeri muttered - special clauses had to be drawn up and responsible citizens called to be witnesses. Ron departed to request the attendance of the local police sergeant, the vicar and the minister, whoever was free to arrive within the half hour. Mr Truman ordered tea whilst they waited.

Conversation over tea skirted the farm finances, touched on reliable employment agencies for farm labourers, and expanded over the fund raising efforts for 'the boys off to the African war.'

Melisande pretended to listen as she watched Mr Truman dunk his biscuit in his large moustache cup of tea. She understood his lapse of company manners when she attempted to nibble hers. Consisting largely of coconut and oatmeal it was hard, dry, tasting of coconut dust.

Mr Truman broke off his conversation with her men and twinkled at her, genuine humour in his voice. "My wife always supplies the office with special baking for visitors. If you find eating it impossible, simply discard it in the waste paper basket." He offered her the basket. "Ron removes them for his pig, and my wife never knows how inedible her baking is."

Melisande blushed and dropped her biscuit into the basket. Her men dunked theirs.

"Now gentlemen, I expect to see you ride those fine horses in the parade. We want a grand assembly to impress and persuade the good citizens of Port Chalmers to put their hands in their pockets for more than pennies for our soldier boys off to Africa."

Melisande waited for Jeri to explain that he sailed on the morrow, but he did not. Before she could catch his eye the minister and the vicar arrived and signing the wills prevented her speaking. But she wondered what idea Jeri had roaming in his head now. His trunk she'd packed herself, he had all his letters and documents for travelling. Perhaps he felt obliged to be polite and not refuse? If so he was improving his manners; his arrogance and belief in his social superiority always disturbed her. Papa had maintained that a gentleman had no need of such behaviour, his actions proved his worth.

***

Charlotte brought in her lunch. More slops in the form of a beef and barley soup, but with the beef and barley strained out. However, it was growing thicker, nearer a puree than a soup, and she'd brought a soft bread roll warm from the oven.

Melisande tried a smile, croaked her thanks, began to carefully spoon up the soup. They let her feed herself most of the time now. Charlotte smiled back, sat down in the chair beside the bed and produced knitting from her apron pouch pocket. Baby clothes, a jacket, Melisande thought, and that triggered memories. Charlotte and Ruth taught her to knit, now where did they do that? Not in town. If only she could remember everything in its proper place.

***

"What do you mean, you won't be sailing?" Melisande stared at Jeri and the basket of bread slipped out of her hands, spilling hot rolls all over the table.

"I've cabled our uncle. Three months we need to set up the farm, with a manager and livestock. I've been checking the prices and we can afford good sheep and cattle …"

"But Richard is doing that work whilst you learn the modern methods in England and bring us back seeds and plants and even animals. You said so."

"Yes, well …" Richard began. He rescued rolls from the butter dish and bacon platter, sought the others around the dishes and plates, whilst not looking directly at Melisande. "We have an opportunity to … ah … do a little exploring." He dusted the crumbs from the broken rolls off the linen cloth with the edge of his hand into the palm of his other hand.

"We're panning for gold for a week or two," Jeri said. "Met some fellows when we looked at the farms. Inland from our farm is a bit of a wilderness with a water course where we can pan for gold."

Melisande's legs gave way and she sat her down with a bump. This couldn't be happening. She opened her mouth and tried to speak.

"Now don't flap and fluster, sister mine. You've got this house to make a home and lessons to learn from Mrs Miggs. You've that gaggle of females from church to take afternoon tea with and jaunt about Port Chalmers. You won't miss us and we might find a fortune."

Richard tipped the crumbs into the basket and patted her back with a gentle hand. "I will miss you, my beloved wife, but it is an opportunity to explore and see what lies beyond our farm. After all, someone has to keep an eye on your brother."

Jeri flicked a roll at him. Richard caught it and added it to the basket. "In all seriousness, Lisa, my love, there might be a ballot of the government land beyond ours and we should know if there's saleable timber, or minerals, or possible pasture land to make it worth our buying it.

"Ride out every day, my Nut Brown Maid, practise your cooking and get Miggsy or his workmates to build you a hen coop and poultry yard behind the house. When we come back you and I shall learn how to keep poultry."

Melisande swallowed her scream of frustration. She knew it was useless arguing, and understood that some of their wildness, restlessness, was a way of hiding their grief and controlling it. Moments of quiet and stillness, having nothing to do with head and hands, which meant grief raised its head. She could hide away and weep, but she too had tasks to learn which kept her busy and the grief manageable.

She shook her head at her two silly boys. "Two weeks only for your adventuring. I don't suppose I can explore with you, please Richard? I do so wish to see more of my new homeland."

Jeri spluttered.

Richard shook his head. "You wouldn't like this area. It's full of shrubby stuff, what the locals call bush, tangled up with supplejack and bush-lawyer in hard to penetrate thickets. The supplejack entangles and strangles, the bush-lawyer is covered in large thorns." He reached out and took her hand. "When I know what tracks are safe and know the pathways around our land, we can explore together, Lisa. You'll have to be a good rider too. That's something to work at whilst we're away."

"I imagined you'd refuse me. Please don't leave me alone for longer than fourteen days. Believe me, I shall be counting them."

"We won't." Jeri laughed and grabbed a roll, squeezed it and sniffed it. "Not bad, sister. I begin to think you will manage our homestead."

Melisande eyed him. "Not without a housekeeper and a general helper."

Jeri eyed her back. "Money, my girl."

"My dearest brother, you are the one spending it, not me. What about our uncle? How did you dare to upset his plans once again?"

Richard sighed. "Now then, dear little children. Remember the nursery rhyme: 'Birds in their little nest agree; and 'tis a shameful sight, when children of one family fall out, chide, and fight.' Kindly refrain from bickering in my presence."

Melisande managed a smile. Jeri threw the remains of his roll at him.

"Such behaviour! Jeri, we have to raid the kitchen for stores and provide ourselves with miners' implements and pack a bag. Eat up, my friend."

Melisande accepted a buttered roll from Richard and slid bacon and a broken egg – she must learn to turn them more gently – onto her plate. Then she remembered. "Mrs MacAndrews, who does our laundry, suggested you gentlemen buy work trousers from the local tailor. He has them all sewn, ready made up and will adjust hems."

Jeri gulped the last of his coffee, pulled a face, and sprang up. "We might do that, turn ourselves into local labourers. I'd like to preserve my clothes for England, tailoring here is not what we've had in India. Make haste, Richard. And that coffee tastes more like muddy water, Lisa. Best learn how to make it whilst we're absent finding gold." He shot out of the room before she could reply.

"It wasn't as terrible as that." Richard dropped a kiss on the top of her head, stroked her cheek with a finger, kissed her again in a lingering way, leaving coffee flavour on her lips and her heart aquiver, as he followed Jeri.

Melisande sedately continued her breakfast but thought angry thoughts. She'd explored Port Chalmers gradually, a walk every day to a different place, often with the vicarage girls. She enjoyed a daily beach stroll, finding driftwood, watching the sea birds, smelling the briny air. She'd prepared arguments so that she would ride out to the farm when her men next travelled there and now they'd ventured off to some rugged country place without her. Again. She wanted to see more of this strange country.

"Those men of yourn." Mrs Miggs tapped on the open door and entered the dining room. "No sooner home than roaming off once more, and with half the pantry stores. Life's all marvellous adventures for Mr Allmark. Where's he running to I'd like to know?"

Melisande didn't tell her that the truth was he was running from grief and their future as it might have been. She did understand and wished at times that she could run away too.

"We must send Willie for more groceries, Missus Holyman. Unless you're a goin' on your walk that way?"

"I'll walk to the grocer, Mrs Miggs. Let me make a list." She paused. "I wonder if there might still be a place for me on the boat trip the vicar has organised for his English visitors and some parishioners. Drowned valleys and inlets they talked of, and wondrous waterfalls. We were invited but I hadn't had an opportunity to mention it." She smiled at Mrs Miggs. "Although I wasn't enthused. I've had enough of boats and ships these past months, but this might be a pleasant way to spend fourteen days whilst Mr Richard and Mr Jeri are away adventuring."

Mrs Miggs nodded her head and gave one of her coughing laughs. "That's right good, Mrs Holyman, you show a bit a spirit and go adventuring yournsel. How if I come in on mornings when you're off away, to keep the cottage warm? I could bake a bit, fill them tins with fruit cake and flapjacks, do a stock pot, an' a bit of bread. You'd like a big pot of soup and some stew waiting, wouldn't you?" She tipped her head to one side, considering how to persuade some more. "Your menfolk, happen they come and you're not home, I'll feed 'em too."

Melisande could have hugged the woman. This was her escape. "Thank you, yes, that would be such a help. I hope the livery stable will be as helpful taking care of Ranee. I must call in and see if they will exercise her and keep her safe when I'm away." She reached for the pencil and notepad she kept on the little table. "Now what do we need from the grocer, the butcher and the baker?"

***

And there was that nasty episode with Ranee. "Charlotte," her voice had improved too as the swelling and bruising of the interior of her throat diminished. "Is Ranee safe?"

Charlotte leaned forward to hear. "Oh, you are improving. You're sounding like yourself again. And your memory is returning. We've been so worried for you, and for us, but no more of that. Yes, Ranee is fit and well, Ruth rides her daily. Now finish your soup and then I must give you your medicine. The more you sleep the sooner you'll get better." She brushed Melisande's shoulder with a feather light touch. "We need you to recover."

***

Melisande knew she was right to be worried about their horses. Her men had ridden off on theirs and taken the cob as a pack animal. They kept their horses in the hotel livery stable because it was nearest. Miggsy had recommend another, but Jeri didn't want to walk across town, and it was handy, she admitted, and safe from that man, Donny Boyce. He'd hovered around, and tried twice to buy Ranee. She didn't intend going on this trip and simply leaving Ranee out in the field, and so the livery stable would have to be told to exercise Ranee each day. Melisande did her shopping and then stopped at the livery to ask them to walk Ranee daily. She found the mare gone.

"Where's my mare? What's happened to her?"

The old man who acted as chief groom looked at her. "What d'ye mean? Donnie Boyce came with a paper from your husband and took her away."

Melisande stared. "What do you mean? My husband has sent no such message." She stammered for a moment, the words stuck behind her outrage. "You've let that Boyce man steal my mare."

The old man shuffled closer, too close, leaning over her, sneering into her face. He growled at her. "Well, your husband's away so we'll have to wait 'til he's back. Fortnight was it?" He had a snigger in his voice and defended himself volubly at full volume. "Stop your fussing. The paper was from your husband. I saw it. He's sold her to Boyce."

The bully. She wouldn't be cowed by him. Melisande let anger give her the strength to raise her voice and speak fiercely. "Show me. I don't believe you. My husband is away and couldn't have written a note, nor would he. He doesn't like Boyce and he wouldn't sell my mare." Melisande saw a flicker – guilt was it? – in the groom's expression. Understanding dawned. "He paid you didn't he? This Boyce man paid you to let him steal my horse."

Her raised voice brought the stable boy and a couple of men, gentlemen in suits. Furious and embarrassed she apologised and explained. "I demand to see the manager and I want the police sergeant. This criminal has let a man called Boyce steal my horse."

One of the men stepped forward, and tipped his hat. "My name is Chittock, Mrs Holyman. I am a senior partner in the legal firm of Chittock and Truman. Allow me to assist you." He turned to the boy. "Fetch Mr Swafford. He's the manager," he explained to Melisande. He turned to the old man. "You fool, Barney, let's see you get out of this one."

Mr Swafford scurried in, a note scrumpled in his large hand. He tugged it flat and showed it to Melisande. "I was going to come and visit, to ask you," he said, his voice uncertain. "I know you'd refused to sell the mare." He didn't look directly at her, edged away from her angry expression.

"That is not my husband's writing nor my brother's. And any note from them would be on a decent sheet of paper, not this grubby thing." Melisande's anger cooled and she felt near to tears. "I want the police sergeant here now and my little mare returned."

Mr Chittock turned to Mr Swafford. "This is not the first time a horse has been 'sold' like this from your stables, but this time it's a valuable thoroughbred mare and an owner who is prepared to take legal action. You won't get a thrashing this time, Barney, nor can you buy your way out of it, Swafford. What you will do is fetch that mare and have her back in the stables this afternoon and have Donnie Boyce and Barney in the police station by tonight."

Mr Swafford blustered and sweated. "Impossible," he cried.

"Your hotel liquor licence comes up for renewal shortly. If you don't retrieve the horse I will see you out of business. You've played this trick with Donnie Boyce once too often."

Mr Swafford swallowed, visibly restraining angry words; his face, shiny with guilty perspiration, had darkened to a crimson hue.

"Get that mare back now, Swafford, or I'll have you in gaol too!"

"All right, all right. Wasn't me took the mare but I'll do it."

"Sensible man, and be aware that I'm going to have a chat with the sergeant right now." Mr Chittock turned to Melisande. "Allow me to escort you on your way and please do not be concerned. Your mare will be returned."

Melisande found herself swept out and down into the main street without being able to say more than thank you.

"I've been wanting to catch Swafford in his tricks for some time, therefore I thank you. He's a rogue but we can manage him now." Mr Chittock tipped his hat again and left Melisande by the grocer's.

***

Ruth was sitting in the chair sewing when Melisande next opened her eyes. She beamed at her.

"You do appear to be brighter, exactly as Charlotte said. We've been distracted with worry. She says you're remembering Port Chalmers. Close your eyes again and stitch together more memories whilst I stitch this baby's cap. Do you remember how we taught you to do that?"

Melisande forced her facial muscles into a smile; the bruises were fading, the swellings had decreased and it felt easier now to move her face. "Not yet," she whispered then closed her eyes. The trip to the Sounds, she went on a boat to the Sounds?

***

Having left her orders in the shops and bargained for some fresh-caught flounder from the fishermen, Melisande went to seek out the vicarage girls. She hoped they might be shopping in the main street, that she might see them in the chemist's shop trying new lotions, or strolling to Ritchie's bakery. Miss Fairley's Tearooms was her last resort.

Miss Fairley's Tearooms had become the place for young ladies to assemble after a morning's shopping, or for some afternoon informal club meeting – "without the men" – but Miss Fairley's prices were high and Melisande feared spending too much of her housekeeping allowance if she joined the vicarage girls there every day. Beside which, she was busy with her daily cooking and baking lessons from Mrs Miggs. She was learning and she enjoyed baking. In fact she preferred what they made together to the tearoom's itty bitty petit fours. She smiled to herself. Fruit cakes and those marvellous slabs of cakey-biscuit things like flapjack, that's what her men enjoyed, not bits of sponge cake overly decorated with icing. Also she didn't want to eat the tearoom's fluffy light sponge when, according to Mrs MacAndrews, she couldn't make a decent sponge herself, though Mrs Turvey said her macaroons 'tasted perfect'. Oh bother, the vicarage girls were in the tea rooms.

Settled snugly in the one corner where they had a good view of the street and passers-by were Ruth, the deacon's daughter, and the vicarage girls, Charlotte, Caroline, and Anne, named after queens, their father told her. Ruth, Melisande wasn't sure of, as she seemed a little snappy, but the vicarage girls had been kind – nosy, but kind. They were similar in face and features; looking at them you knew they were sisters, but the oldest sister, Charlotte, was taller, with attractive, wide-set, dark-blue eyes, the youngest, Anne, was plumply pretty, short and very pink and white, while Caroline had the blondest hair, creamy skin and soft blue eyes. She was of mid-height as befitted her middle status.

Ruth's dark brown hair was twisted in curls round her forehead, under her plain bonnet. Most fetching, Melisande thought, and wondered if she should say so. She waved a hand as Ruth noticed her.

The tiny brass doorbell gave a polite tinkle as she entered and before she could speak Charlotte and Caroline called out. She smiled at them all.

"Mrs Holyman, come, come and join us. We're discussing our expedition to the Sounds."

"Have you decided to travel with us?" Anne asked, patting the chair seat beside her. "And will you be bringing that charming brother of yours?"

Charlotte shushed her, but Ruth looked as eagerly at Melisande as Anne did.

"Just tea please, and no, I must apologise for my brother and husband, who have business to attend to for our farm. Might I come, though, because I would very much like to see more of my new country?" Melisande sat on the proffered chair.

"Oh," said Ruth with a pout, "we needed your brother to make up numbers for the dancing."

"And holding our collecting tins, stopping us falling into the streams and being tall enough to reach the best plant specimens for us," Anne added.

Melisande shook her head. "Jeri would be quite hopeless at that. He'd be too busy rushing off to climb the mountains to pay attention to us."

Anne drooped her head, but Melisande saw the expression that whisked across her face, and the confident smile which touched the corners of her mouth. She believed she could attract Jeri, make him come to her.

Let her try, Melisande thought, knowing that Jeri would follow their uncle's advice to make a 'good marriage' and marry whomever Uncle Aubrey approved. The approved one was a wealthy young lady, not a colonial vicar's daughter. She blessed her parents again for their favouring Richard and not pushing her into 'an advantageous match' with one of the 'officers and gentlemen' in the Indian Regiments. She shut away the regret that Jeri held such worldly views and gave grateful thanks for the love which she and Richard shared.

She smiled at Anne, then Ruth. "Perhaps I ought to advise you, young ladies, before you lose your hearts to my handsome brother. He is bound for England and he is promised to a young lady he has known since his school days. Their engagement will be announced officially when he arrives. Our uncle promised it."

"Another good man gone," Anne said, mock solemn, and wiping away an imaginary tear.

Laughter all round before Caroline played hostess. "Do try this cake, there's a delicious lemon filling in it." Caroline offered her a plate with a small yellow cake.

Anne added another petit four. "Try this chocolatey one, it's better."

Melisande gave in and asked when she could visit the vicar to arrange her place on the ship.

***

Yes, that was it. Tearooms and cakes. Melisande stirred, sank back into the drugged sleep, driven by the need to find out what had happened, because it clearly affected her friends. The journey to the Sounds, why was that important?

***

Once assured of Ranee's safe return and having left instructions that Mrs Miggs would be in every day to check on her and young Ron from Mr Truman's office would walk her out, Melisande could attend to the voyage. She feared that the tourist trip to those southern drowned valleys would be difficult. She didn't have Richard and Jeri to protect her from people she only knew politely from church. The vicarage girls would be busy flirting with the young men they hoped to marry. Caroline was newly engaged, her young man had arranged to travel with them, and Anne had the pick of several swain she kept dancing attendance upon her. Four of whom would be taking the trip with them. Ruth would be bound under her father's strict eye, and all other passengers were in their middle years, more her parents' age or older. Who would she dine with? Maybe Dr Gilmour, the senior doctor for Port Chalmers, and his family? She hoped for some intelligent conversation about the fiords, the plants and animals.

She mulled this over as Miggsy carried her bags – Mrs Miggs insisted that her son should play porter – and they walked together to the harbour. She noted that Miggsy had slicked down his hair under a new cap, and wore what were probably his Sunday shoes. No clatter or clomping today.

Their little ship, a coastal steamer named Waikari, had been designed, the vicar said, to take wealthy tourists on journeys of exploration into the fiords of the southern land. As Melisande and Miggsy walked down the hillside road they saw it steam into the port, a tidy and shipshape vessel, all clean white paint and shiny brass work, with gay red and blue trim.

"Looks a better boat than t'usual coastal tramps.' Miggsy remarked as he guided Melisande round the loaded carts, bustling porters and busy dockhands.

She smiled and tried a mild joke. "I hope it smells better, your mother says they usually smell too much of fish."

He grinned. "Aye, happen it will. I'll leave you here, Missus Holyman." He carefully put down her bags, glancing at the vicarage girls, all prettied up and making a fuss. He squared his shoulders and ducked his head at Charlotte, with a smile. She gave him back a quick peek with a fetching smile.

Oh, thought Melisande, as she was swept into the vicarage party, and found her luggage piled onto a cart by one of the eager young men. She just had time to cry "Thank you" to Miggsy before she was escorted up the gangway, leaving him gazing after them. She observed the four launches either side of the boat. They would be going ashore, then, to explore. Excited at the prospect of exploration, she nearly forgot to make a proper greeting to the vicar and his guests.

"Good morning, Mrs Holyman," the vicar replied. "May I introduce my visitors from England, relatives of my late wife?"

She bowed her head in acquiescence.

"Mrs Holyman, Mr and Mrs Quinlan, Mrs Quinlan's brother, Mr Hotchkiss, and Mr and Mrs Sanderson."

A polite murmur of 'How do you dos'.

"Your cabin is next to ours," the vicar said. "Do follow us and we'll see you safely ensconced. I know your husband would wish us to take care of you."

"You're most kind, thank you." Melisande smiled at them and hoped the vicar would allow her the latitude he gave to his daughters for she really intended to read, draw, practise her knitting and crochet and explore. Such activities demanded quiet and peaceful surroundings, not polite chatter about acceptable gossip.

She stepped over the high doorsill into her first class cabin. It was a deck cabin with an excellent view. A brief survey showed a fold-down table, a wide bunk bed neatly made up with navy blankets over a turned-down white sheet, an ingenious little cupboard and a padded chair angled for her to sit and watch the scenery through her porthole window. A simple and comfortable arrangement.

A clatter outside heralded her bags which the youngest Gilmour lad – an awkward sixteen, blessed with handsome looks and a shy smile – carried in for her.

"H … h … here you are, Mrs Holyman," he stuttered, face flushing.

"Thank you. Alexander, isn't it?"

"Yes, Mrs Holyman." He stood, as though waiting.

Oh dear, should she offer him money. Surely not, this was not India or the Australian hotels. Then she noticed his eyes surveying her painting box and sketchpads.

She hesitated, unsure if painting figured in a young man's curriculum in this strange country. "Do you draw?" He nodded. "Are you looking forward to finding new subjects to draw?"

He grinned. "Oh yes. The birds, I like watching birds and trying to paint them."

Melisande was delighted. "Perhaps you can help me learn their names? I know so little of the plants and animals here in New Zealand."

Alexander straightened, lost his awkward edges. "I'd be pleased to help. We have the most remarkable seabirds and our plants are unique. You have yet to hear the morning chorus of our song birds like it is away from the town." He beamed at her and departed with a springing step.

How she wished for Richard to share a gentle laugh at the eager young man.

She unpacked. She'd brought far too much. Not sure about how much dressing for dinner involved she had packed two elaborate gowns, two 'at home' dinner dresses, and forgotten to pack their matching evening slippers. But she had soft shoes for the boat, enough simple skirts and jackets for walking and scrambling up hills and a pair of new, strong walking boots, something she had not worn before in India. Miggsy, bless his kind soul, had told her, when she'd begun her walks along the cliffs and beaches, that a pair of stout boots would be safer to walk in.

"Stop you twisting your foot or turning an ankle … beggin' your pardon for bein' so personal Missus Holyman," he'd said, shifting awkwardly from foot to foot, not looking at her directly, and showing the faintest blush under his tanned skin.

She'd followed his advice, strongly seconded by his mother, using the local cobbler who made Miggsy's boots. Hers, though, were not clomping great worker's boots but fitted carefully to her feet and supported her ankles well. They were a little heavy but Melisande liked the firmness round her ankles when she walked the rough paths. Miggsy had oiled the boots when new and had worked the leather a little with his large hands so blisters had been minimal. He'd oiled, then greased them again for her yesterday.

"Keep the water off better, Missus, with a bit of goose fat, they'll hold up against a slip or two in a stream."

She liked Miggsy, who was always kind, full of common sense like his mother, and – so his mother said – a great-hearted soul like his late father. Remembering his smile she felt uneasy, anxious for his soft heart if he really did hold warm feelings for Charlotte. The vicar would not allow any such connection and would Charlotte truly encourage one? She sighed. Miggsy's skills would make him a perfect colonial famer, unlike her men. He would be able to chop down trees and break in land, build a house, but … always a but … he was not a 'gentleman' with a gentleman's education. The vicar's daughters had been educated to marry 'gentlemen'. There weren't many of them – according to her father's definition – in Port Chalmers.

Papa once told her that education and worldly knowledge made a gentleman, not his birth alone. Melisande wondered about that. Poor Miggsy. If she were Charlotte, what would she do? The social hierarchy seemed more complicated compared to that in India, but it existed. She thought back to her three women helpers and their comments as they tried to fit her into their social system. She sat in the chair, gazing out of the porthole, and missed Richard so much it hurt, a pain under her ribs. She smiled, a real heartache. Jeri would shrug, it didn't affect him, but Richard would stop, think then discuss the problems with her.

Ruth tapped and popped her head round the door. "Excuse me, Mrs Holyman. Coffee, cake and the captain's talk. I'm sent to bring you to the saloon."

"Thank you, Ruth." Melisande gathered herself together, but Ruth stepped in, lingering to look at the evening dress with an envious eye.

"Made for you?" she asked, clasping her hands firmly together.

Ah, she wanted to touch it. "Do you sew, Ruth? Are you one of those clever ladies who can understand how to make a dress just by examining it?" She picked up the dress from where she had laid it ready on her bunk and shook it out so it fell full length and revealed the pieced skirt.

Ruth stretched out a hand to gently touch a sleeve.

"Would you like to examine it?" Melisande offered the dress.

Ruth lifted it into her arms. "Oh, it's so light and soft. Is this Indian silk?"

She twirled around, making the skirt flare out. The delicate pink shade, apple blossom Mama had called it, suited her dark colouring as well as it suited Melisande. The hand-made lace decorating the bodice and as a frill over the top of the sleeve had been dyed a deeper pink shading to white, touches which made it special. Ruth took mental notes of that with little nods as she checked the waist, the sleeve attachment and the skirt hem frill.

"Plain bodice, patterned skirt, a good pattern, one easy to remake as new if you damage the skirt or bodice." She stroked the skirt material, admiring the twining vines and blossoms. "Sensibly economical in pattern and how exotic. But are you allowed to wear it? It's not mourning."

"It is over six months, this is a private party, not a public affair, it is not low cut, and I shall wear a black shawl, cap and gloves with it. It would be proper in India."

"My father will disapprove."

Melisande sighed. "I am sure he would, but my husband approves. And it does seem unfair that my men may simply wear a black armband now and I must continue to wear all black. My walking skirts are black."

Ruth laid the dress upon the bed. "I could make a dress like that, but buying such silk is impossible."

Melisande thought of her trunk full of such beautiful silks, but she had to be careful. Anything that sounded like she was a shopkeeper or trader was not acceptable. "I have some plain pink like the sleeves. I thought to have a dress made from it. Would your father allow a gift?"

Ruth sighed, a vast longing sigh. "My father would not allow me to accept any gift so expensive and certainly not from you." She managed a little giggle. "He does not approve of your husband or your brother." She pulled a naughty face.

Melisande laughed at her expression. "But why does he …?"

Ruth interrupted, inhaled, straightened and produced a deeper voice. "Those Holymans and that Allmark. They come along and flash money around, raising prices." She giggled again, inhaled. "Buying a farm already broken in and producing income. It's not right." Her voice squeaked back to normal as she ran out of breath.

Melisande had never seen Ruth as relaxed, as easy with herself as she now appeared. "Why, Ruth, you're funning with me. Are you anticipating a wonderful trip."

Sullen, quiet Ruth positively beamed. "Papa isn't able to come. Stepmama looks forward to time with the ladies, for my young stepbrothers are with my father and an aunt. The ladies have their knitting and their handiwork, and aim to chat and let their husbands explore whilst they have a leisurely time. The first time since the babies, stepmother says. I am free to be with my friends."

She reached out to catch Melisande's hand. "Come, we are late, and we have a scheme, Charlotte and I. We hope you will oblige us."

***

Dear Ruth and her schemes. She'd had to shape her life, no loving mother to help her. She had taught Melisande much about making decisions for herself. Now, could she remember what their scheme was?

Chapter Thirteen

That first day everyone tried to find their sea legs and a comfortable space on deck. Melisande wrapped herself in her papa's made-over tweed overcoat, still smelling faintly and comfortingly of him, a heavy woollen shawl over her shoulders, and an old fashioned poke bonnet with side wings and broad ribbon ties. She found a place halfway down the top deck. By leaning sideways against the railings she managed to be comfortable and observe the passing coastline.

The *Waikari* sailed near to the shore, close enough to give her a frisson, a whisper along her spine, of fear. She allowed herself a mental shiver and then common sense reared its practical head. This captain had sailed his ship down here many times. She gave herself up to astonishment. The coast, so rugged and wild, rocky and yet green with trees, a real wilderness, astounding in its beauty. It wasn't a savage, terrifying wildness. It was as though the bones of the country, its true nature, were exposed but lightly covered over. Rocks with seaweeds, the trees with lichens and ferns, made a mild, softening effect feathering the wild harshness, which allowed an observer to feel awe yet enjoy the natural world without being overwhelmed.

So this was New Zealand in its pure, untouched state, a kind country in comparison with Australia. She liked it. A brisk wind chopped the waves upon the rocks with a splash of white foam and spumy spray. She might sketch the patterns the spray made through the air; perhaps a design for a brooch could come of it. The wind tugged at her and she retied the ribbons of her old-fashioned bonnet. Charlotte might laugh, but her ears were warm and the bonnet could not be snatched away by a sudden gust as the fashionable little hats or young men's caps or homburgs were.

Aware of someone hovering unobtrusively at her elbow, she turned her head and found Alexander. With a diffident smile he offered a pair of binoculars.

"I brought my father's as well as my own, but my brothers and mother are not interested in using them now. Would you care to use them?"

Melisande gave him her friendliest smile, treating him as if he were a younger brother. "Thank you, Alexander, that was thoughtful of you. Please do point out things of interest to me. I know so little of the flora and fauna of New Zealand."

"Best adjust the binoculars first, then we can try and see the seals on the rocks. We passed some in that other bay. There might be a penguin or two and we should see terns and shags. There are three types of terns we might see."

The enthusiast took off, so. Melisande propped her elbows on the rail, steadied her binoculars and listened to his ready stream of comments. The white-fronted terns skimmed the water, but most of the other birds were on the shore and easier to pinpoint and focus on. It took several attempts before she could find the seals on the rocks. Too rock-like in colour and shape, it wasn't until one raised a flipper that she actually saw it and could tell Alexander. She'd already missed several.

"I think I know how to look for them now," she said, and laughed. "We must sketch them after luncheon."

Alexander blushed, mumbling something about his mother, but the ship's bell, used by the cook to gather passengers for meals, clanged and drowned his words.

Perhaps she needed to speak to Mrs Gilmour, or should it be Dr Gilmour? She really must learn the proper New Zealand way to cope with parents of these adolescents, parents who seemed too strict compared to her own dear mama and papa.

After lunch, a pleasant meal because she had been seated with Ruth and the vicarage girls, most of the party came on deck to watch for the lighthouse on the point. This was where the ship would really begin the journey into the fiords and sounds as it sailed into Preservation Inlet.

Warned by the vicar, the party wore their warmest clothes, gathered in clusters and chattered away. Alexander stayed with his parents, without his binoculars. Did they not approve of his naturalist's bent? Melisande felt obliged to speak to them. She must thank Alexander for his information in such a way that did not embarrass him, and reassure his parents that he had been a welcomed companion. She'd noticed his brothers dismiss him sometimes with a casual contempt she remembered from Jeri at his most lordly. Perhaps here she had the opportunity to improve his worth. Carefully she edged round the English visitors and approached the Gilmours.

"Good afternoon." She knew them as nodding acquaintances from church, but had not held any prolonged conversation with them. Dr Gilmour kept busy with a large number of patients, his wife kept busy with charity work, with those who couldn't afford the doctor, but were, in the vicar's words, 'the deserving poor'.

Melisande had wondered about the deserving poor. Mrs Miggs couldn't pay a doctor's bill. She wasn't regarded as 'the deserving poor'. Her son had a trade and employment, but he'd hesitate to afford a doctor. And what about that handful of dockyard wives everyone pitied, the ones with drinking husbands who beat them and terrorised their children? Were they undeserving poor? She didn't think the doctor's wife would venture into the huddle of houses at the portside where they lived. She'd never understand the distinctions. In the India she knew, everyone helped, and even untouchables were given food and shelter at the temples.

Keeping her puzzles to herself, and wearing what Mama always called 'the social face', which meant a polite little smile raising the eye and mouth corners, and a bland smooth forehead, Melisande extended her hand. "It does not give offence," Mama promised.

The doctor gave her a firm grip and gentle shake. Mrs Gilmour just touched her palm with her own.

"I trust," began the doctor, "my son has not been inconveniencing you with his …"

Melisande saw the blush ascending and rushed in to stop some fatherly comment which would blister Alexander's tender psyche even further. "Why, no indeed, Doctor Gilmour. I wanted to thank him for his information and compliment you on his knowledge of natural history."

For a fleeting moment an expression of surprise whisked across his face, then vanished into his beard. Mrs Gilmour lowered her gaze, but Melisande caught a glimpse of maternal pride lighten her eyes before she turned to Dr Gilmour.

"There, my dear doctor, we needn't worry about Alexander being a nuisance to Mrs Holyman."

"Indeed not, Doctor Gilmour. He has been teaching me about New Zealand birds. I know so little about the native flora and fauna." Melisande smiled at the young man. "I would appreciate his help whenever he has time to spare from his own studies. He will be able to help me make accurate sketches."

Standing at his parents' shoulders, out of their direct sight, allowed Alexander to send her a boyish grin as he murmured some polite acceptance.

"I understand from your brother, Mrs Holyman, that your late father was a considerable naturalist and supplied the Royal Botanic Gardens at Kew and the Natural History Museum in London with specimens of Indian medicinal herbs and plants." The doctor spoke with interest.

Behind his parents Alexander made as if to speak, bit his lip, but looked eagerly at her.

Melisande blinked away the prickle of possible tears and nodded. "Yes, it was his lifetime's work and my mama was his illustrator. They produced several books."

"Indeed. We are the fortunate owners of a beautifully illustrated one of the native flowers of India. My brother is an army doctor with the Indian Regiments and brought it as a gift the last time he was home on leave."

"Exquisite work," Mrs Gilmour patted Melisande's arm. "Have you inherited her skills? I see a drawing pad in your bag."

"I will need many hours of study to attain my mama's skills, but I love to draw and design things." She noticed Alexander making signs behind his parents, tapping his chest and pointing at them. "May I have permission to 'borrow' your son for a short time each day so that he can teach me about the birds and make sure I am sketching the colours correctly?"

Mrs Gilmour allowed herself another moment of maternal pride, but quickly changed her expression back to bland politeness. Dr Gilmour fingered his beard thoughtfully then nodded. "I believe Alexander might spare some time from his studies to assist you. But he must not forget that he has examinations to pass to prepare for university and a medical degree."

"I'm most grateful and promise not to keep him from his studies." Smiles all round before Melisande moved away to join Ruth who was leaning on the railing and gazing at the changed scenery with an expression of amazement.

Their journey through Preservation Inlet gave them a view of distant mountains, dark blue against the late afternoon sky with capes and hats of white snow. Surrounding the ship were little islands, deep dark waters and steep slopes covered with tree ferns and lichens, mosses and bushes. A primordial world.

The *Waikari* snugged itself between a long ribbon of island and the shore. Melisande watched the crew warp the ship neatly between the two and swing the launches down from the ship to the water.

"Landing parties," called the mate.

Melisande saw Charlotte and Ruth waving. She preferred their company even though she was categorised as a married woman. She was younger than Charlotte and Caroline, the same age as Ruth and Anne. They had much in common, being members of the walking parties, tennis club, art society and church choir, but she had caught her man as Ruth naughtily expressed it. They hoped to catch one.

Their launch filled with the English visitors and the vicar. Alexander, whose standing as a young naturalist had become the talk of the party, joined them at the vicar's request. Soon he was answering questions directed at him by the visitors and Charlotte whispered that she'd found a snug, private place on the upper deck, just the place to hide the three of them in full view of any disapproving adult. She and Ruth wanted Melisande's opinion about a private matter when they returned to the Waikari.

The landing parties put in at a small river mouth, more stream than river. Melisande blessed her boots and explored the stony beach, her feet slipping over smaller boulders, scrunching on the pebbly infills. The rest of the party tracked the stream inland and she slowly followed them. The scent of the wet mosses and the ferns, was like nothing she'd known before. Above the splash and spatter of the water round the rocks she heard birds. She found herself marvelling at the wet lush richness.

Alexander came back to find her. "Can you hear the bell birds?" He spoke quietly and raised his arm to show her where to look. She saw nothing, but heard the chiming calls which gave the bird its name.

The shore parties all met for billy tea, boiled up by the cook's assistants.

"Camp style," Ruth said, handing Melisande an enamel mug half full. "Hold it round the top and you won't burn your fingers," she advised as Melisande winced.

The fire, well contained in a circular wall of boulders, burned hot and fast. The stack of cut wood surprised Melisande. Cut into tidy lengths it had obviously been chopped and piled up long before their trip.

The vicar, seeing her examine the wood, explained that the shipping companies kept such piles all along the route for fuel and emergencies. Melisande had a sudden comic picture in her mind of a weary man chopping and stacking whilst ships' crews sneaked in and kept removing the wood.

The crew had provided collecting tins and the English visitors had been filling them with specimens of ferns. They showed their samples to Alexander, who named them as everyone drank their tea.

The ship's bell recalled the parties for dinner and Charlotte and Ruth gathered Melisande between them and sat beside her on the boat.

"We'll show you our hiding hole later," whispered Ruth.

"Not a proper hidey-hole." Charlotte added, also sotto voce, smiling at Ruth. "It's a place not easily overlooked."

"Why not my cabin?" Melisande lowered her voice to match.

Ruth looked at Charlotte and they both gave her a tiny headshake.

"I think," Ruth began, "you don't understand that our families will suspect."

Charlotte gave a soft laugh. "We have a reputation for being mischievous. Our fellow travellers will wonder what we talk about so often hidden away in your cabin."

Ruth grinned. "A hidey-hole's the best. With knitting or handiwork."

"My sketchpad?"

"Oh yes, you could be drawing portraits."

Melisande felt a nervous prickling along her spine. She came on this tour to see the country, learn about the wildlife and rest from all that unfamiliar housekeeping and cooking. Ruth had seemed so quiet, reserved and stiff. Now here she was acting like, well like Anne, who kinder people, like her own father, would call a mischievous sprite. The unkind ones designated her a naughty flirt, a label which also fitted. What plan or scheme were they plotting and why did it involve her?

***

Melisande half woke. Those were good memories, she'd enjoyed that voyage to the Sounds, but there something else. What was Ruth's plan and why did Charlotte need a private conversation?

***

After dinner, Melisande, who had intended to find Ruth and Charlotte's 'safe place on deck, found her cabin filled with all the young ladies. It was an invasion and the cabin door had to be left open so that the crowd could squeeze in. Alice and Martha Ruddkin, the timber mill owner's fifteen- and sixteen-year-old daughters, and Ellen Broughton, eighteen-year-old daughter of the general store owner, joined Anne, Charlotte, Caroline and Ruth, all wanting to see Melisande's Indian silks.

Ruth examining her dress had been accidental and, as a seamstress who obviously sewed at least some of her own clothes, she had been interested from a practical point of view. This crowd of eager viewers were not and she feared their motives. Should she explain that her shawls and dresses were commonplace in India where people of their classes wore silk? Had Ruth told them she had offered some silk as a gift? Oh, where was Richard to talk to? Even Mrs Miggs might help her understand how to tread through this particular maze of social niceties.

Anne led the charge. "Mrs Holyman, my dearest friend, Lisa." She embraced Melisande, "We have a plan, but you must help us. Please show everyone those shawls and dresses." Before Melisande could move she whipped them out of the cupboard, twirled a shawl, flicked out a skirt. "See how beautiful, see the silk ripple and shine?"

Melisande felt herself blush right to her ear tips. "But I only have these things because I've lived in India. Silk is made in India, it isn't made here, you cannot buy such silks can you?"

Anne dimpled up and gave her a wicked glance, turned to her companions and smiled. "But we have designs to improve our local shopping. Miss Broughton planned it. Speak up, Ellen."

"It's wedding dresses, you see, Mrs Holyman. Caroline is not the only young lady looking at a wedding during the next year."

"Coming out ball dresses," breathed the Misses Rudkin, sidling close to touch the dress Anne held.

Charlotte, a becoming pink blush colouring her pale cheeks, touched Melisande's arm. "Mrs Miggs told her son you had a trunk full of silk and could get more sent from India."

"Oh," Melisande understood, and she understood who had told Charlotte, which explained the blush. She nodded. "Miss Broughton hopes to persuade her papa to become an importer?"

Giggles and nudges, faces turned from Melisande to Ellen Broughton, who shook her head.

"No. Pa wouldn't try. We've asked before. He refused to order from Liberty in London and doing that was a simple task we know, for Mrs Gilmour orders and receives Liberty silk and fancy fabrics from London. Papa has forbidden me to order from Liberty, but we thought you might order silk from your supplier in India. I would receive it in the shop which makes it correct for the Customs office."

Melisande blanched. She thought of the silk bazaar, all those little stalls, of the markets where a merchant might come, and she and her mama browsed to find bargains. She'd never bought silk in a shop as these young women seemed to imagine. Then she remembered Advik. He was steward for the new owners of her home. He always knew the best places for bargains.

"It will be difficult. Where I lived one bought silk at the tailor's or in the markets. There are no shops like Liberty."

Disappointed murmurs, downcast faces. Resentment growing as they considered her dresses.

"I could write to Advik, our old steward. It was his task to order anything we needed. He always knew where the best bargains were. He could perhaps post a parcel for each of you, but we must pay him for doing so. Pay for the silk and the postage and his fee for every parcel."

Ruth sighed. "I do not have a generous allowance." She shot a glance at Charlotte who raised her eyebrows. Melisande hoped they would help each other.

Alice and Martha Ruddkin muttered together, then Alice spoke, "We think Mother would be willing to pay."

Ellen Broughton tossed her head, determination clear in her expression. "I have savings and I will have such Indian silk for my next ball dress." She twirled around swishing imaginary skirts, which made everyone smile. "And I will have silks to sell if this … Advik?" Melisande nodded. "If Advik can send enough regularly."

The vicarage girls glowed, Anne and Caroline exchanging mischievous looks, and spoke: "Papa would buy us silks for our wedding dresses."

Heads raised, eyes focused. Melisande thought ears almost pricked up.

"Wedding dresses? More than Caroline's wedding coming soon?" several voices asked.

Anne giggled.

"Anne Polson, have you decided? Are you going to choose from amongst your admirers at last and cease being a flirt?" Ellen Broughton asked. "Some of us have been wanting to flirt a little ourselves."

Laughter grew as Anne refused to say which of her four faithful lovers she'd chosen. "He doesn't know yet," she added.

More laughter and the mood lightened. Melisande knew she'd avoided being regarded as a spoilsport for the rest of the journey. Now, indeed, she was a 'good sort'. "I will try to persuade Advik to do this for you. Why he might even like to set himself up as a trader of silks to New Zealand."

"We'd best tell Mrs Holyman the colour we'd like for our silk and whether plain or patterned," Ruth said. "Did you say two sari lengths made your dress, Mrs Holyman, our so useful friend, Lisa."

Melisande nodded, but no one could decide and they begged for time. Melisande shooed them from her cabin with, "Hurry away and find your favoured ones, your amis. Aren't we supposed to be singing in an informal concert tonight?"

***

That was it. It had been something Indian, about dresses and Indian silks and muslins. She remembered now. The young ladies had wanted silks. She'd written to India and set Advik up as a silk merchant exporting silks and fine muslins to New Zealand. She'd wager her favourite necklace that he'd made a success of it. What a fuss there'd been in her cabin.

The silk and Charlotte. Something happened which would explain why Charlotte was here with her. Silk and wedding dresses and weddings? But whose? And Charlotte. What was it about Charlotte?

Chapter Fourteen

The vicarage girls led the way out and Melisande attempted to close the door behind them, but Charlotte crept back inside and shut the door.

"I wish to ask something," she whispered, leaning against the door. She didn't look at Melisande directly but twisted her fingers in her shawl fringe then took a hesitant step forward, turning her face away, and keeping her voice low. "You know and I don't. My mother's dead, there's no one …" She turned dark red to her ear tips and blurted out, "What's it like … being married? What do they do … the men?"

Melisande plumped down on her bed, opened her mouth, closed it, opened it again, exhaled a gusty amazed breath and finally managed to stutter a few words. "Oh, I can't … oh, why ask me … I shouldn't … it's not right … I mean …" Rational thinking took over from embarrassment; she remembered Miggsy's look and Charlotte's response. "It's Miggsy, isn't it?"

A moan escaped from Charlotte, though she pressed a hand to her lips. "He's Daniel, Dan, not Miggsy." She failed to glare, nodded instead, and Melisande saw tears sliding over her cheeks.

***

How could she have forgotten? And which of them had been pinker with embarrassment? Poor Charlotte was so distressed and Melisande knew she'd dithered and floundered, but perhaps she had been of real help because Charlotte was here, and she wore a wedding ring.

***

"Don't, Charlotte." Melisande rose and tentatively placed her arms round her weeping friend. "Come, sit with me."

Together they sank onto the bed, Charlotte burying her face into her palms, frantically trying to prevent any sound escaping. Melisande reached for one of the small towels folded neatly on the cupboard top. She shook it out and gently pushed it between Charlotte's fingers, then began pat-rubbing between her shoulder blades as Usha used to do to comfort Melisande when she had wept.

Should she encourage Charlotte? Oh dear, what to do, what should she say? She liked Miggsy – no, she must practise saying Dan – she respected Dan. He had all the skills a colonial man needed to make his way in a town, as a carpenter and builder, or in the country, as a farmer creating wealth from the wilderness. Skills she wished her men possessed. But – oh, those inevitable buts – socially he was not a gentleman, not a man Charlotte ought to marry. If they married and lived in Port Chalmers her family might well refuse to mix with them socially, and certainly most of the town's so-called society would cut them off. His mother handicapped them too. Mrs Miggs had been a servant in many of those homes. Still, Charlotte's father was the vicar, perhaps his Christian feelings would help overcome social scruples?

"Does your father forbid an engagement?"

Charlotte, face muffled in the towel as she wiped her eyes and nose, sniffled and managed a few words. "He doesn't know. No one does. I daren't tell. He expects me to keep house for him because no suitable man has asked for me."

"Oh." She didn't know what words to speak to comfort Charlotte.

Charlotte stifled a wail. "I could cope with being the family's disgrace. Dan has plans to move away. We wouldn't live in Port Chalmers. It's not that. I need to know, and who can I ask? Mama is dead. You are younger than me and are married. You know." She buried her face again, shook with sobs. "If I knew, if I dared, I would marry Dan." She raised her head. "He's so good and kind … but I'm afraid. What happens on your wedding night?"

Melisande continued soothing and tried to think. Charlotte quivered beneath her comforting hand and she wanted so much to help her, but help her to the right future.

"Charlotte, what is it you need to know?"

Charlotte, face stifled in the towel, voice muted, spoke. "How it is between a husband and wife. That first night. What happens?"

"Well …"

Charlotte drew herself up, caught Melisande's hand in a frantic clutch, dropped the towel into her lap and the words flowed out.

"Gentlemen are supposed to know, to help their wives on their first night. That's what Papa says. But Dan isn't a gentleman by our standards. I've heard women talking, and workmen's lewd comments." She squeezed Melisande's hand. "When Ruth's stepmother and the doctor's wife talked about making babies they called it 'a woman's lot to be endured', and said that 'women should be thankful for their husbands being gentlemen'. Is it so awful?"

"No, oh no, Charlotte. Please listen …"

"No, you must understand, you are Mrs Holyman, and you are my friend, Lisa. I need your help. Mrs Miggs won't approve, my papa will forbid the marriage, but I am now of age." She gave Melisande a wobbly half smile. "I'm nearly twenty-three and oh, I could love Dan if I allowed myself, if I weren't full of mistrust and misgivings, in dread that he would be bestial, not like a gentleman."

"That doesn't apply to Miggsy – Dan – he's … .could you speak to him?"

Charlotte's pale skin blenched paper white. "Never. What could I say? He's putting his name forward for the next land ballots and has money saved. He hopes to create a farm and has asked me to think about being his wife. I must answer him when I return from this trip. I so want to say yes."

Melisande inhaled, then puffed out her cheeks in a gusty sigh. This was something Charlotte had to decide. "Could you live on a farm?"

Charlotte sniffed, wiped her face again and nodded. "I know how to keep poultry and I'd like to help with the lambs. I like to cook and garden, grow vegetables. I would love to be with Dan on a farm we made together. I keep house for Papa now, I know I could manage."

She swallowed a sob, looked Melisande in the face, her eyes pleading. "My only kind of life in the town is as Papa's helpmate. It is expected that I will not marry, for no gentleman has asked me, and thus my duty is to care for Papa." She shuddered. "I love Papa, but is that all the life I shall have?"

"I understand, Charlotte, indeed I do, but …" But Charlotte, wild in her despair, interrupted again.

"You and Mr Holyman are so happy together. Mrs MacAndrews does our laundry with Mrs Turvey. I heard them gossiping and sniggering that you sleep in the same bed every night and stain the sheets. Is it a trial to suffer?"

Wishing Richard was available to discuss what to say and how to help Charlotte, Melisande paused, then made her own decision. Port Chalmers society would not approve, but knowing that Miggsy – Dan – intended to buy land, a farm which would be away from town, and that he had the skills and determination to succeed and do well, she was certain Charlotte had every chance of a happy life with him, especially as she wanted to do it and seemed to understand the problems ahead.

"Listen Charlotte. My mama and papa died before my marriage. I did not have my mama's wedding night talk. But I did have my ayah – my Indian nurse – and the Indian women servants telling me my wedding night would be a joy."

Charlotte's eyes widened, she stopped kneading the sopping towel.

"Indian women are taught to give and expect pleasure with their husbands." Charlotte's eyes widened, her lips parted with a gasp. "Yes, truly, it can be a pleasure." She knew she blushed right to her hair roots. "What my mama told me, when Papa allowed my engagement, was that she would explain the physical side of marriage on my wedding morning, but that it was something to learn together." Melisande felt the tears gather for she almost heard her mother's voice as she remembered. "She told me that physical loving would sound most peculiar, but was about loving and sharing and caring and that we, Richard and I, would find our way together."

Melisande placed her hands on Charlotte's cheeks and lifted her face to look into her eyes. "We did, by caring for each other, by gentle exploration and loving." She laughed a gentle laugh. "By kissing and touching, slowly learning about each other, and I can't tell you how it will be for you and Dan, but it is a pleasure, truly enjoyable. You must go to him."

"No, no I couldn't ask." Charlotte pulled her face free.

"Listen, oh, please listen. There's something else I've learnt since living in Port Chalmers and having three local women work for me. Gossip. You've lived all your life in the Port, of a certainty you know what gossips will say in spite. They'll say you married your Dan as a last chance, because no gentleman would have you. That he's after your money and trying to make himself a gentleman. Can't you hear them?"

Charlotte nodded.

"Are you sure no one might be saying it now?"

She shook her head.

Melisande thought perhaps some had a suspicion, older women, those nosy gossips, but if she could persuade Charlotte to act quickly then their marriage might have a chance to start well.

"Don't let rumour begin and spoil your marriage with doubts. Find your Dan as soon as we return. He'll be working on those houses near my home. You could come as if to visit me and speak to him then."

Charlotte gave a hiccoughing dry sob, her eyes wet, pink edged, now brightening, filled with hope.

"You must tell him you are afraid. You haven't said 'Yes' because you fear your wedding night, that you love him and want to marry him but you are scared of what happens because you have no mother to tell you." Melisande caught Charlotte's hands. "You know Miggsy, Dan I mean, he's the kindest man I've met, almost as kind as my Richard." She smiled as Charlotte blushed and began to protest her Dan's superiority.

"You tell him before he speaks to your papa, before a whisper catches the wind and blows to him. Make him know you love him, but are afraid, and he'll never heed the gossip as he'll want to care for you because he knows you care for him."

Charlotte drew in a shuddering breath, and another, controlled herself and Melisande watched her find courage. "I will. As soon as we return."

She flung her arms round Melisande and hugged her. Melisande, hugging her back, resolved fiercely that her daughters would not grow up as ignorant as she and Charlotte had been.

She disengaged herself gently. "Shall I find Ruth whilst you use my rose water to cool your face and prepare for this concert? We could sing some nice easy Gilbert and Sullivan, which everyone will know, and encourage them to sing along with us. What do you think?"

Charlotte nodded, dropped a light butterfly kiss on Melisande's cheek and picked up the spray bottle of rose water.

Melisande departed, hoping she'd not blighted Charlotte's life.

The concert had been a scramble of amateur amusements, recitations, skits and singing. Melisande found herself in much demand as a pianist and had to promise to accompany the singers at other concerts. She finally put herself to bed tired enough to sleep and hoping she'd helped, not harmed poor Charlotte's future life. However she slept patchily, troubled that she'd done the correct thing for Charlotte, worrying about Ruth and her mysterious behaviour. She woke the next day, questioning her ability to enjoy the remainder of her supposedly restful holiday and wondering what that day would bring.

Alexander removed her doubts, arriving at her breakfast table with his and his father's binoculars, a sketchpad and an excited babble.

"Dolphins, dolphins in the Long Sound, Mrs Holyman, and they might stay with us when we reach the sea."

That brought everyone onto the deck. A brisk wind in their faces meant most people stayed only five or ten minutes, but the dolphins played around the ship with such charming leaps and graceful arching curves in and out of the water that enough were enchanted and rushed to their cabins for coats and hats.

Melisande and Alexander sketched, peered through binoculars, and corrected each other's work. Charlotte brought Melisande's coat and shawls but refused to bring her 'that terrible old bonnet'. She loaned her a cherry red, woollen tam o'shanter which Melisande pulled down over her ears, never mind how it looked. Alexander's mother brought his overcoat and cap, made him put them on, then watched him fondly as he sketched.

Ruth tugged Charlotte away, sending a wink at Melisande. She supposed they'd gone to the hidey-hole. She spent the next half hour admiring the wild sea, crashing surf and enormous breakers as the Waikari avoided the reef and sailed into the open sea. That day the ship would travel round Long Island, through Anchor Passage, aiming to enter the first of the huge sea valleys. There would be much for Alexander and her to sketch.

She joined Charlotte and Ruth when Alexander's father hauled him off to spend an hour in study with him. She went to the upper deck seeking them. Their hidey-hole was not so much a hidden place as a snug nook on the upper deck which allowed those sitting there to be protected from the wind and to be aware of anyone around them who might be near enough to overhear.

Melisande took her sketchbook. A quick glimpse showed Charlotte had held onto her courage, managing a brave hopeful smile, which she returned. Both young women sat looking industrious and proper, busy with knitting.

"Making baby clothes for the deserving poor," Ruth said as she made room for Melisande to sit between them.

"I haven't fully comprehended who the undeserving poor are," she replied, "in India all are deserving."

Charlotte pondered, but Ruth smiled. "I like that idea," she said. "It has always puzzled me that those wives with drunkard husbands, those families not polite enough to the vicar, or the police, become undeserving." She nudged Charlotte. "Think about poor Mrs Roney who can't feed or clothe herself and her bairns because her husband spends all his money on booze and brothels."

"Ruth! It's not proper to mention such things." But Charlotte spoke with a faint smile and even Melisande only gave Ruth raised eyebrows and a look.

"Pooh hoo, we should. It's not Mrs Roney who is drunk and disreputable, it's her husband. Why do we call her undeserving when she most needs our help?"

Melisande agreed. "Then are you knitting for Mrs Roney, Ruth?"

Ruth gave them both a quick cheeky grin. "Oh no, I must not disobey. The doctor's wife is in charge of who receives the clothes, but as some of the clothes are sorted and parcelled by my stepmother, I can safely slip some to Mrs Roney."

"Ruth!"

"Charlotte!" Ruth mimicked the shocked tone. "I know you've popped baskets of church charity groceries and vegetables from your garden over their gate. Does your father know?"

Charlotte blushed. "Not officially and don't tell, if you do …"

Melisande patted each on the arm. "Peace, my children."

They chuckled, exchanging understanding looks. Melisande began to recognize and appreciate something about young women and friendships.

She smiled on them both. "Mrs Miggs is teaching me to knit and crochet, would you help too?"

Ruth's fingers continued to deftly flick her needles as she spoke. "For payment of … something." She broke off, looked round, seeing no one near, then she spoke again. "You'll be leaving Port Chalmers quite soon."

The tiny hairs in the nape of Melisande's neck prickled a warning.

"Yes, when my men return we will move to the farm."

"They say you've bought a good farm."

"Good land I believe. Half already cultivated."

"With a house, a barn and half-built farm buildings."

"Ruth, I haven't seen it, I'm told so. And I would much prefer to have my parents than this farm their deaths enabled us to own." There, she managed a polite smile and hoped that should prevent any more niggling.

"My father says the Englishman who owned it had grand ideas and the house is a copy of those on English estates. It's a large house." Ruth paused, shrugged. "They say the Englishman ran out of money, returned home to England, married a rich woman, but she refused to sail for New Zealand and so he had to sell."

Melisande's mouth gaped, she snapped it closed and shook her head at Ruth. "They say … who are they? How much of that gossip is true?"

"It is a large house. Timber for some of it was shipped from Port Chalmers." Then abruptly "May I come with you to assist with your settling in?"

Melisande began to understand Ruth. She knew there was an underlying reason for the questions, a means for Ruth to get to what she wanted to say. "Much as I would welcome help I think you have another plan in mind."

Ruth glanced round again, checking where people stood. "Oh, I would help, but when you're organised and things are working then I intend leaving and finding something to do in Dunedin. I want to study, learn, do something other than obey my father and marry the curate."

"Oh, that's why you borrowed our newspaper," Charlotte's voice rose. "You've been reading the notices."

"Hush. I've been seeking a place to stay, some respectable boarding house for young ladies." Melisande strained to hear Ruth's whisper. "Daren't read the newspaper at home as I need permission from my father and he'll watch what I read."

"What about the curate?" Melisande liked Cyril Wadsworth, who would be leaving Port Chalmers for his own parish at the end of the year. He had a rich chocolatey singing voice, an excellent sense of humour, and played the violin as well as the organ. "He certainly like you. Don't you like him?"

"Yes, but I don't want to marry for years. I want more in my life. Look at you," Ruth gave Melisande a poke. "You've lived in England, India, visited Australia and are now in New Zealand, but talk of visiting family in England and India as though it's an ordinary way of life. And you're not much older than me."

Melisande smiled. "By a few months, Ruth, Perhaps you need a husband like mine to do all that."

"Show me another then. No, I have to find a way to work in other places and the money to pay for the travelling."

"Oh, Ruth." Charlotte sighed for her. "What can you do?"

"That's why I need to be in Dunedin. I can learn to type, or tailor clothes, or – well, I don't know what but I can find out. There's art school, even university, but that only leads to teaching, and I don't think I'd care to teach. I don't know what I can do. I must find out."

"Indeed I will help if I can …" Melisande began, but the English visitors drew near to exchange pleasantries and exclaim about the remarkable scenery.

It was. Melisande rose and joined them. The sea valley was hemmed in on each side by massive mountains. The steep slopes were bush covered, but there were slides of differently coloured tumbled rock and slim cascades of white-edged waterfalls. There was much to see and the English visitors proved good conversationalists.

Dusk crept up behind the ship when the dinner bell clattered and clanged. It was fully dark after dinner when Melisande stood on the deck with Charlotte and Ruth. The Waikari had anchored at the end of the inlet. The water lay still, no wind to ruffle the surface, which looked blacker than the night sky. A sheen like glass polished the water to mirror brightness. The stars shone down there at their feet as well as fiercely bright in the sky.

"It is so beautiful," Melisande said. "I feel grateful this is my home."

Charlotte squeezed her arm gently and Ruth murmured agreement. Together they leaned on the railing in friendly silence and Melisande thought the stars might sing.

Chapter Fifteen

Friends, friendship which grew into something special, a bond she treasured. She understood now why Ruth and Charlotte were here nursing her, caring for all her needs without complaint. How could she ever repay them for their constant attendance, sitting in this dim room knitting or sewing or reading to her?

It was Charlotte with her this morning. She had grown able again to feel the passage of a day, knew it was mid-morning. "How can I ..." she coughed, tried again as Charlotte moved to the bed, perched on the edge. "How can I ..." Her voice failed her. It had grown scratchy and hoarse from lack of use.

Charlotte gently squeezed her hand. "Don't fret, you're growing better by the hour. I can see the changes."

"I've remembered the stars."

Charlotte thought, then squeezed her hand again. "The Waikari?"

"Such a debt I owe you, Charlotte."

Charlotte laughed. "You've paid it back, don't you remember what you did for me?"

Melisande leaned back against the bank of pillows and thought. Now what had she done? She could remember Ruth's request. What was Charlotte's?

***

Overnight the feelings of friendship seemed to strengthen. Alexander found himself instructing three young women as the *Waikari* steamed along the coast to Doubtful Sound. The numerous seabirds kept him too busy to be embarrassed in all that female company and he and Charlotte soon started a discussion about which category of albatross it was that had glided over the bow. Melisande admired the little terns skimming the surface like Indian swallows and tried to sketch them.

Ruth thought her own thoughts, elbows on the railings, chin resting in hands. "Most unladylike in polite company," she told Melisande, "and isn't it a relief not to have my father always watching and disapproving?"

The cook's mate rang the bell, announcing coffee and biscuits. In the dining room the captain announced the day's planned trip would be at George Sound, and the launches would take people to a scramble beside a streambed leading to a lake. "Wonderful ferns to collect," he promised, "and splendid views for photographers and artists. Until then, enjoy the passage through Doubtful Sound."

Charlotte managed a few quiet moments with Melisande as they politely allowed their older fellow travellers to exit before them. "Thank you again," she whispered. She smiled, "I've found my courage and won't be defeated by my family or his."

Melisande hoped this remained true. The three sisters always seemed affectionate, but would that bond remain when their father refused her engagement, Charlotte disobeyed, and so their fiancés, Caroline's lawyer, just beginning his career, and Anne's newly chosen, a doctor in his final year of training, along with their families, made her a social outcast? Melisande wondered how strong their love and loyalty would be.

"Charlotte, if things prove to be impossible, if your family are distressing you, please accompany Ruth, come with her when we remove to the farm."

Charlotte tucked her arm through Melisande's and gave it a gentle squeeze. "I'll think on that idea and discuss it with Daniel."

Alexander popped his head round the doorway. "Come and see this waterfall, Mrs Holyman, Miss Polson, and there are tui singing. I've brought the binoculars."

"I do hope you've completed all today's study tasks," Melisande said, attempting a severe tone, as they followed him onto the deck. "Your father will be most displeased with me if you've failed to complete everything." She flashed the boy a quick grin.

He grinned back. "There's a dance this evening and I am to study then. I don't like dancing."

Charlotte laughed. "I do. I'll leave you to your sketching and go to our hidey-hole to find Ruth. We'll enjoy the scenery from there."

She left them and Melisande sketched her fill of the cliff sides, the trees and shrubs, the waterfalls, and even attempted a tui under Alexander's critical tuition. The views she called splendid but the end of the Sound, called Hall's Arm, left her breathless. Snow-covered mountain peaks, wispy layers of cloud, the rainforest in many shades of green, and the still-dark water. Finally the dolphins again, performing a ballet against that backdrop. She struggled to fill her sketchpad with the magnificence and wished her mother could see the scene.

She slipped away from dinner early, not wanting to sit out during the dances and make polite conversation when she had so much beauty inside her head which needed some form of expression. She expected a quiet night, but Ruth came knocking.

"I knew you'd be doing something artistic," she said, partially opening the door and slipping round it into the cabin. She closed the door and leaned against it. "May I stay for a short time?"

"No partners you like?" Melisande teased.

"Your brother isn't here." Ruth tried to sound light hearted.

"Oh Ruth." How could she explain? "Men like my brother are not free to marry as you are. He's the spare." Ruth quirked a questioning eyebrow. "Heir and a spare? Our uncle only has one surviving son. If cousin George dies my brother is the heir, heir to a title, wealth and a large estate. My brother must marry, and his wife must be someone like himself, who knows that social group, who can entertain and behave in the presence of dukes, even royalty." She shook her head sadly. How could she kindly point out what society insisted on and how Ruth didn't fit there? "It's the lot of younger sons who are not direct heirs but might be. They must consider the family heritage, and so my brother will marry someone my uncle chooses or approves of. That way he gathers prestige for the family and perhaps political influence. My brother is keen to try for Parliament when he's older, but needs the right wife and my uncle's support."

"I wish him well then, for that wouldn't be a person like me." Ruth sounded resigned, not bitter. "Where's the place of love? What happens if your brother does not like the chosen one?"

"My uncle would never force a marriage and my brother has been fortunate in that he spent his school years in England, living with my uncle when not at school. He socialised with a number of suitable families, has a fondness for one young lady." Melisande sneaked a quick look at her sketches.

Ruth's shoulders twitched in a tiny shrug. "I suppose that's it, then," she said. "Is it the same for younger sons of all English gentlemen's families?"

"Some are lucky and inherit money from relatives, a godparent, perhaps their mother. Then they don't have to be so careful about marriage. Most must marry someone with money, influence, and from the same social circle or a higher one in order to achieve that."

"Why can't they work, like real people? What is wrong with farming or accounting or being a doctor? That explains those so-called gentlemen who come out here from Britain and work up on the high country farms, but it's only for experience, for growing up to be responsible or whatever they make of it. Not for life."

Melisande stopped wanting to get on with her drawing and listened to the tone of Ruth's voice. "It's not easy, younger sons usually have the army, navy, church and perhaps law or medicine, although that is more unusual." She saw Ruth's face, mouth working as though swallowing an uprush of emotion, like a lump in her throat, noted that her eyes glossed over with … with tears? Ruth, crying?

"Do you wish to talk of it, to tell me about it?"

"He was one of the shepherds on the farm where my uncle is head shepherd for an English family." She turned away, shrugged, straightened. "I was sent to help my aunt with her new baby. He was some relative of the owners, a son of a second son he told me."

"Did he have a name?"

"Not saying. I can't."

"Oh, Ruth, don't cry." Melisande went to her, tentatively put an arm round her, but Ruth turned and bawled into her shoulder, a wrenching combination of groans and sobs.

Melisande patted and rubbed as her ayah used to do until Ruth could stand on her own and speak again.

"He promised to write, when he returned to England. He never did."

"Oh, Ruth."

"Four months we had, and he was kind, talked of balloting for land and making a farm for us. His last night we went to the local dance and danced all night. He said he loved me, and he'd write. Oh, Lisa, I loved him."

Melisande could only hold Ruth close and murmur her regrets. "Perhaps he meant to write but found himself trapped by family expectations."

Ruth sniffed and wiped her face and nose on the hand towel Melisande had provided. "I can understand that, but why didn't he write and explain?"

Melisande shook her head. "Cowardice? A hope you'd soon forget? Someone preventing his letters being sent? Do you have an address?"

"No. I tried to find out, but my uncle said he didn't know, and the estate manager refused to tell me."

"Perhaps he's going to return. Does he know where to find you?"

Ruth laughed, a wobbly one, but she did laugh. "Mrs Holyman, Lisa! Fairy tales! Reality doesn't touch you does it? Such a romantic you are, locked in adoration of your beloved husband. Hoping for a like miracle for others."

"Ruth, that's … that's, well, why shouldn't I wish that others have a marriage like mine?"

"It's all very well for you with your money and family. You can afford help, servants and pretty things. Marriage is good to you. What about women like Mrs Roney and her marriage? What about my aunt stuck out there in the high country, miles from neighbours with no help and too many babies? If that is what marriage is to be for me then no, I don't want it."

"The curate will be able to pay for servants, he will have position and place, he's going to his own parish and will soon become a vicar. That wouldn't be a bad marriage. He's a good man."

"I don't love him. I can't forget Hugo and it hurts." Ruth dropped onto the bed and buried her face in her hands, weeping again.

Melisande hovered, then sat beside her. "I am so sorry, Ruth. Will going to Dunedin help you?"

Ruth sniffled. "At least I will find something to do, some work where I can earn money and keep myself. What would you do if you lost your husband, lost your farm, had years of failed harvests or something? How could you keep yourself?"

"I don't know."

"Well, best you find out in case an accident happens."

"What a horrible thought. Stop it, Ruth we'll both be weeping soon." She tapped Ruth's shoulder. "Come let's take a turn on the deck, smell the night air, admire the stars, or are you going back to the dance?"

Ruth shook her head. "A walk, I can't go back to the dance with my face all pink and puffed up, my eyes swollen. Beside which I haven't had a partner, because I've been avoiding the curate, and don't wish to be the wallflower again."

Melisande wrapped her coat around Ruth, wrapped herself into a thick woollen shawl and tucked her arm through Ruth's. "Come and let the beauty of this place soothe your hurts." She opened the door for them, wondering why some people had such difficult lives and thanking God for her easy one. How could she complain about the death of her parents and leaving India, when to others she had Richard, comfortable wealth and social standing, a good life? What did Ruth have?

***

"Ruth, I've remembered I promised to help Ruth. That's why you're here. Is here our farm? Why can't I remember it?"

Charlotte laughed. "You see, you are getting better. Now take your medicine and have another long sleep and see what else you can bring to mind. It is so important that you can tell us what happened." Her voice changed, her hand clutched Melisande's. "Our lives depend upon it."

Melisande blinked and tried to shake her head, a foolish move for it made her ears clang and bars of light danced behind her eyes. Tears of frustration stung her cheeks. "I don't understand."

"No, but you will. There is so much we cannot, dare not tell you. It's why only Ruth and I are here with you and why Doctor Allinson senior lives here with us to watch you. When you remember you will understand. Here, drink your medicine and sleep your way to wellness. Think about the Waikari."

***

Doubtful Sound. She'd never forget that part of the trip. Over breakfast, another outsized feast of lamb chops, thick slices of ham, eggs, sausages, potato cakes and fresh bread rolls, the captain explained that the ship would return from Hall's Arm at the end of Doubtful Sound, double back and turn into Thompson's Sound, and then sail out to sea again. They would pass by three lesser Sounds, Nancy, Charles and Caswell, which were, according to the captain, 'Pleasant, but on the small side and nothing like as spectacular as George Sound,' which was to be their next place to visit.

Melisande, growing accustomed to New Zealand breakfasts, had eaten rather more than she normally did.

"I feel sleepy," she whispered to her companions. "I don't usually eat such a large breakfast."

She linked arms with Ruth and Charlotte. "Come along, let's be 'three little maids from school' once more."

They giggled.

"Shall we promenade on the deck?" They went up in high spirits and walked round and round the deck, planning Melisande's removal to her farm and their proposed visits.

Also promenading up on the deck were the sweethearts, for the vicar allowed Caroline to spend her free time with her fiancé, Mr Victor Searle, and Anne allowed her newly chosen one, the doctor's son, Mr Douglas Beattie, to escort her, although the engagement was not formally announced. They made a charming set of couples in love which lent a gentler atmosphere to a day of buffeting wind, crashing waves and spume floating past.

The couples delighted the vicar and his companions, all of whom became nostalgic, full of tales about first loves and reminisces about where they had met their spouses. Melisande and Charlotte thought the atmosphere rather sweet, Ruth did not.

After coffee and biscuits Alexander came to educate Melisande further on New Zealand birds, particularly how to check the eye and upper part of the bill to decide which kind of albatross or seagull it was. He had discreet drawing lessons which Melisande was careful to disguise as comments about plumage and colouring, for his father did not approve.

Melisande could honestly see no harm in helping a talented youth, although she would talk to Richard later to assuage any feelings of guilt. Beside which, she thought, his mother approves and so would my mama.

Ruth and Charlotte disappeared, plotting something for Ruth, but the English visitors wanted Alexander's expertise and joined the two of them at the stern railing. Mr and Mrs Sanderson had a keen interest in birds and a good eye for drawing, making helpful comments. When the ship's bell announced luncheon Melisande had several sketches which pleased her, and a feeling of satisfaction.

"A good morning's work," she told Alexander's mother who came to escort her son to the dining table.

When luncheon finished, shortly after the Waikari had sailed into George Sound, the ship nosed into a sheltered cove and anchored close to the shore. Launches delivered everyone to a streambed, mainly tumbled rocks and pebbles with a trickle of water.

"Pretty little lake up top," the mate told them. "Follow t'streambed and ye can't go wrong."

Charlotte walked ahead with her sisters and father. 'I shall make the most of being together with my family for I may not have them much longer,' she'd whispered to Melisande. Melisande thought her courageous and told her so. Ruth hung back, waiting, hoping to avoid the curate, for Cyril Wadsworth had been in their launch.

Thanking Miggsy – no, Dan – for the strong boots which supported her, Melisande clambered and scrambled over the rocks behind Ruth, relishing the amazing ferns and the unique scent from the wet soil, the ferns and tree ferns. Heavily damp, mossy and earthy, the scent of the News Zealand bush filled her nostrils The rata showed vivid scarlet blossoms, the flowers were amazing fluffy spikes like so many large stamen. She plucked a few to help her drawing and thought how her mama would have loved painting them. The scrubby manuka had smaller apple blossom like white flowers with a faint sweet scent. So much for her to sketch and take in and remember.

"New Zealand bush is amazing," she told Ruth, stopping yet again to draw a large daisy flower.

"I suppose it is." Ruth was urging her along.

"I'm so pleased I came on this journey. It has made me value and enjoy a place I was afraid to make my home. Look at this clearing. Mossed rocks, trickling streams of clear water, sculptured stones, and manuka blossoms. And that scent of old forest and earth. It is …"

Ruth nipped her arm, gave a little squeak, and fled on up the streambed as Cyril Wadsworth strode into the clearing.

"Miss Landry," he called, but Ruth carried on sliding between, and slipping over, the boulders beside the streambed as though she had not heard.

Melisande closed her mouth and wished she knew a stronger expression than 'oh dear'. Perhaps one of the Indian ones would do, she thought. 'Phut' had a solid explosive sound to it. Now here she was, having to make excuses or pretend she hadn't seen Ruth run off. "Oh, phut," she muttered to herself, expecting indignant outraged male feelings to radiate from the curate, although he was a gentleman and wouldn't express them aloud.

She looked at Cyril Wadsworth as he came towards her, gave a little shrug and essayed a smile, which he returned. He was such a good man, in his early thirties Ruth said, which perhaps made him more tolerant and patient. At the moment his eyes held a hurt expression, but his mouth continued to smile.

"Miss Landry is avoiding me. Have I hurt her feelings, do you know, Mrs Holyman?" He looked after Ruth, who was now a distant figure, and suddenly laughed. "She manages the terrain like a mountain goat, I admire her ability … oh no, she's slipped. Excuse me, she's fallen."

He whipped round and hurried off, Melisande following after, anxious about Ruth.

"Are you badly hurt, Miss Landry?"

Ruth was leaning against a large boulder, her right foot raised as she struggled with boot laces. "I've twisted my ankle, I think."

Melisande, relieved, sighed – at least that was a minor injury. "Ruth, here let me help with your boot. We have icy cold water in this pool, and you can sit on this flat-topped rock, bathe your foot, and then I can bandage it for you."

"Excuse me, Miss Landry," and the curate put his hands round her waist and lifted her up onto the rock. He laughed at her outraged expression. "Mrs Holyman is here to see to propriety, and I want to talk to you, Ruth."

Melisande, not sure how to answer, bent to unfasten the boot, but Ruth was tick-ticking her other boot heel against the rock. Melisande looked up and took note of Ruth's stubborn, even defiant, expression. She was about to say something disastrous, and Cyril Wadsworth didn't deserve to be the recipient of more hurt.

"Mr Wadsworth, please. Ruth is …" she hesitated, desperately searching for the right words, "upset." And phut, that wasn't correct, but nothing she could say would sound anything except feeble.

The curate hesitated, settled himself against another boulder. "Miss Landry, your father gave me permission to speak to you, and I would like …"

Ruth, indignation turning her cheeks and forehead pink, interrupted. "No one asked me if I wanted you to speak to me."

"Hush a moment, Ruth, just listen," Melisande patted her knee, "and let me bathe your foot."

Ruth ducked her head, angry and embarrassed. A smothered sob caught Melisande's ear.

The curate thought, a puzzled look on his face. "I believed," he mused aloud, "that all young ladies want to be married. We have been friends, Miss Landry, Ruth. I hoped to find a moonlight nook on deck and ask you to consider my proposal." He sighed.

Melisande, greatly impressed, admired his patience and restraint. "I think perhaps Ruth seeks more than friendship in her marriage," she offered tentatively.

"I understood, from your father's comments, and your behaviour, that you, Ruth, were more pragmatic than romantic. The clergy, you know, must be careful in their choice of wives, and you are most suitable."

Ruth spluttered, caught her breath and glared. "I suppose you mean that I am suitable, because I am not pretty like my friends, nor do I flirt or behave in any manner which might cause comment. My behaviour is controlled by my father. Did you expect to control me?" Her voice rose.

"Hush now, Ruth, and do keep still." Melisande poured cold water onto the bruised flesh from her cupped hands. "How do your foot and ankle feel now?"

"Borrow my handkerchief, to bind the ankle," the curate said, offering his large white linen one. "And no, Miss Landry, I expect you to control yourself, knowing what is fitting behaviour for your situation."

Ruth muttered something which Melisande was pleased the curate did not hear, then spoke aloud. "Not all ladies wish for marriage, but most who do expect love."

"But affection can grow into love," the curate replied. "After all, none of us marry our first heady frantic loves."

Melisande was having none of that. "I did and I'm sure many others do."

The curate shook his head. "Very few of us are fortunate enough to fall in love with someone we can marry. Indeed, often those we first fall romantically in love with are not suitable."

"Mr Wadsworth, I think you mistake schoolboy crushes for real love. My husband was my first and only love. I know it was the same for him."

"Truly?" The curate turned thoughtful. "But then you are younger than he is. I wonder though, would he have loved you if you hadn't adored him and shown him you did?"

Melisande froze, her hands stilled. Yes, indeed she had always adored Richard because he had understood the power of names. At fifteen it had been puppy love from her, growing into the powerful emotion she now held for him. But Richard had always … or had he? He'd spent his free hours with the family, almost a second son to her parents. There'd never been the hint of another love in his life. Now she would never be sure until she asked him. Would he have loved her if she hadn't always been there, always loving him, from puppy love to true devotion? The curate had spoiled her day, sown a seed of doubt where she'd had none.

Ruth touched her hands. She unfroze and blinked fiercely, tried to assume a controlled, calm voice.

"That was not kind of you, Mr Wadsworth." She rose, took on an air of hurt dignity. "To suggest that …"

He slid with a clatter into the streambed, full of apologies. "Indeed you are correct. I was thoughtlessly musing out loud and to have entertained such an unkind thought, never mind uttered it, is not a good or godly thing to have done. I apologise and wish I could unsay those words."

Ruth levered herself to her feet. "Well, it's too late now, and how you could say such a thing, Mr Wadsworth, when we have all witnessed Mr Holyman's behaviour to his wife? He is devoted. I would wish for such devotion."

"Say no more." He pulled a rueful face and held out his arm. "Let me lend you my arm and we can hobble back to the launch. I believe the men are making tea for us."

Ruth inclined her head in a stiff little bow. "You may return, Mr Wadsworth. Mrs Holyman and I are determined to see the little lake." She sniffed in disdain. "Come Lisa, we can hobble together." She grasped Melisande's arm, leaving her with no choice but to support Ruth, and they progressed slowly up the stream, Ruth wincing and muttering, Melisande hesitating between scolding and laughing.

***

Oh, dear prickly Ruth. How she made Melisande laugh and yet garner an understanding of what friendship needed to become, the valuable treasure she now knew it to be.

And here was Ruth this night, sitting with her, the oil lamp close to her lap to light her sewing.

"Hello Ruth. Is it late?"

"Good, you're awake. Come, let me settle you for the night. I have rose-scented soap and the kettle is warming by the fire to give you hot water. Then shall I read to you? It's Sunday, would you like today's psalm and Bible readings?"

"I'd like that." The fire, a low glow of warm red, was burning coal. She could smell the sharp mustiness of it. She preferred the dance and crackle of wood flames but coal lasted better overnight. If burning coal made life less difficult for her friends then she wouldn't object.

Chapter Sixteen

How the curate's comments had stung, jabbed their way into Melisande's thoughts, little barbs catching her mind with their points when they popped into her memory. Had Richard only noticed her because she had clearly adored him? The curate now stood in her disfavour as strongly as he did in Ruth's.

George Sound was wonderful but marred by a prick or two of anxious thought. Even the totally breathtaking Milford Sound, the last Sound they were to visit, had her watching Caroline and her fiancé up on the deck and wondering about their relationship.

Ruth, hobbling with a slight limp, was cross and bothered by what the curate would say to her father, who obviously expected her to return home with a fiancé.

"Now I know why he let me come without him. I wonder if my stepmother knows and has been watching?" she hissed at breakfast. "I must have an escape planned so that I will be able to appear calm and repentant when I am berated and punished. You have to help me."

"I give you my word I'll try, and I'll think of a way to aid Charlotte too. It must be painful to see both her sisters now engaged."

Ruth managed a smile. "Poor Charlotte, she's been allotted the spinster sister's lot and it isn't fair." She frowned, pondering Charlotte's state. "She is as pretty as her sisters, but more serious, not a charming flirt. They captured husbands, and she hasn't. If she'd been without sisters she'd be married by now. Vicar's daughters are sought after." She grinned her cheeky grin. "Not so a warden's daughters. Now I'll help you by speaking to all those who want silk, I'll write down their colour preferences and yardage." She squeezed Melisande's hand and scampered off.

***

Melisande opened her eyes. Her sight had improved. A warm glow of relief cheered her. Dawn light sneaked between the curtains and window frame. She clearly saw the fireplace across the room, the fire a dim red glow. Ruth had taken care of it before she'd gone to bed. How they watched over her and cosseted her. No birds called, no poultry woke and squawked, no one clattered outside. The silence reminded her of the peaceful tranquillity of the Sounds. She had to persuade Richard to escort her back there. She closed her eyes and thought about what more she'd done for Charlotte and Ruth because of their growing friendship. She had a hazy idea that it been fun.

***

Milford Sound was extraordinary. Melisande found her coat and the unfashionable bonnet and took herself to the quiet of the deck to gaze at the scenery. Magnificent mountains, with a topping of snow, which streamed down the sides in a manner reminiscent of runnels of icing on queen cake buns, rose straight up from the sea. To Melisande they looked delicious, almost edible. Mitre Peak topped them all and held the eye. The water was dark black and still, the mountains made twins of themselves as reflections. Streams poured down sheer cliff faces as waterfalls, tumbling from a great height as thin wavering ribbons or solid white furies. The recent rains had increased the water flow, so the mate told her. In contrast to the cover of trees in varieties of green were stark rock faces where vegetation had slipped away. Wonderful lichens dripped and dangled from branches and mosses covered any available surface.

At the head of the Sound the Lady Bowen Falls thundered down in a torrent of spray and avalanches of water, an awe inspiring sight, but

Melisande preferred Sterling Falls. Nearly as tall as the Lady Bowen Falls, these were tucked in a nook, which refined the spray, allowing it to make rainbows. She sketched, astounded by the beauty surrounding her, and knew she had to persuade Richard to accompany her one day and see for himself.

On their return to the sea, halfway down the sound, the Waikari sailed into Harrison Cove and anchored there so that the launches could bring people to the shore for a walk around a glacier melting into the water. The rain, which had been only a light spasmodic spotting, turned into a downpour which cut short the walk and prevented billy tea being made.

Back on the ship Ruth caught Charlotte and insisted that Melisande come to the hidey-hole to formalise a plan.

"Not in the rain," Charlotte protested.

"It will have to be in my cabin, this one time," Melisande said. She wanted to draw. The mountains and waterfalls of Doubtful Sound were nothing to Milford Sound's grandeur. She'd seen so much she wanted to commit to her sketchpad, and finalise those sketches in preparation for paintings.

"Mrs Holyman, Lisa, pay attention. I beg you. I need to be so important to you that you must have me as a helper when you remove to the farm." Ruth grasped Melisande's sleeve, tugging in short jerks so Melisande couldn't draw.

"I will send a formal invitation, but I wonder if your father will listen to me. Perhaps I can persuade Richard to deliver the invitation or at least make it seem important."

"Babies," Charlotte said. "Ruth, you could hint that Lisa needs help for that reason."

Melisande's eyebrows rose, as did her voice. "I'm not prepared to lie. Richard would never forgive me."

"No, no, not you, Lisa, Ruth and I can hint." She smiled at Ruth. "I am determined to help you to a chance to make another life." She turned to Melisande. "You don't have to say anything. It would be a natural, much desired event, and, of course, you wouldn't want to be talking about it until you began to show."

Ruth gave a squeak, blew a kiss at Charlotte and rushed away to find dry clothes. "I'll be back and I'll bring my knitting. Remember now, I'm in your cabin, out of the rain, teaching you to knit." She fled.

Charlotte hurried to speak. "We will arrive in Port Chalmers in two days' time, at midday, the captain tells me. I'm hoping to walk with you, I must see Daniel. I am afraid, but I know you're quite correct and I must speak, explain to him." Her eyes shone with hope and joy. "I do love him, you know. My family will never understand, but he is such a good, kind man. I know him well. His father was the carpenter who came to our home and made clever alterations to the doors and stairs for my mother to help her during her illness. Daniel helped him. He used to listen whilst I read to my mother and he would recite poetry with me which Mama loved."

"Your perfect gentle knight. I agree, he is. I've just realised, Mrs Miggs knows when I am to return. She might send him to carry my bags. In which case you could walk with us and I'll give you privacy." She lowered her voice in case Ruth should dash in. "I have been thinking about your future. Tell him that you have an invitation to come with Ruth to help me with our removal. I hope my brother might hire him to help. I believe there is building work to do on a barn and sheds. If you find yourself forbidden to marry him …" Ruth flung open the door. "Later," she finished and smiled at Ruth.

"Did you see Alexander, Ruth? He wanted help with his waterfall sketches."

"In the saloon. He's alone if you want to give him a lesson. Oh, and there's to be entertainment tonight and a dance for our last night. We've been requested for our version of 'Three Little Maids' and more Gilbert and Sullivan songs." She pulled a rueful face.

Melisande laughed. "We are popular. Very well I will play, but you must sing,"

"Only if Charlotte and I can borrow your Indian shawls."

"Only if you will go away and let me draw in peace."

They did.

***

Both the Doctors Allinson were pleased with her progress. "Your sight is much improved," Young Doctor Allison told her. "And your head wounds are clean and knitting together well."

"I wish I could remember more, I cannot even hold onto which day it is or even the date." Melisande complained, sounding so sad that both doctors hastened into reassuring speech.

"If you continue to be calm and quiet and rest you will remember," they said.

Melisande sighed. More rest.

***

The return to Port Chalmers was strictly a sea sailing, no lovely slow trips into the drowned valleys they'd missed out before. Ruth kept Charlotte and Melisande busy knitting and crocheting. Melisande learned to make crochet squares and had nearly finished a simple baby's hat. Charlotte's attention drifted. Ruth helped her unpick the missed pattern stitches in good humour.

"I don't care what my father will say. I have hope for a different future. I'll hold my tongue and be still. Only, Lisa, dear Lisa, how soon are you removing to the farm? If I know it's soon I can bear anything."

Melisande had to laugh. "For you, Ruth, I promise it will be as fast as we can arrange the men and the transport. Yes, it will be soon." and 'soon' became their watchword.

On the last two evenings there was a general relaxing of formalities. Melisande played the saloon piano and sang with her friends. Their fellow travellers sang with them. It made a memorable time for everyone. How long the comfortable feeling would last Melisande couldn't be sure, but she hoped that it had eased her position in Port Chalmers. Now she had a good idea of how to become part of a social group she thought she could do it again after they'd moved to the farm.

As Ruth still avoided the curate, dodging off in the opposite direction as soon as she saw him, he gave up trying for a conversation but came to stand at the deck railing beside Melisande after breakfast on their last morning. "Would you be so kind as to tell Miss Landry that I will try to soften her father's attitude? I know he will be angry but I'll tell him that I believe there is hope for an engagement in the future." He smiled at her in a way that made her feel like a silly young miss and not a responsible married lady. "I hope there might be. I'm fond of Ruth and I know her position at home is not a happy one."

He leaned against the railing and watched the waves for a moment. "I believe that you and Miss Landry are planning your removal into the country, to your farm." He gave a soft chuckle. "I am certain Ruth has other plans too. Please chaperone her and keep her safe." He turned to go and Melisande bit her lip to stop her mouth sagging open. He really did care for Ruth. "Tell her typing and bookkeeping would be useful for an independent future life." he said. "Oh, and helpful in a curate's wife if she changes her mind," he added softly as he departed. Melisande clutched the railings and wondered how he knew what Ruth aimed to do. She debated whether to tell her what Mr Wadsworth had said, then determined against it. Ruth in a good temper was easier to be with.

She only had a few moments admiring the sun's sparkle on the wave crests before Alexander peeked round the corner, saw she was on her own, and came to lean on the railing beside her.

"Thank you, Mrs Holyman. I'll practise what you have taught me. I want to be as good as your mother at painting plants and birds, so I'll take your advice and not upset my parents, especially father. I can study art when I'm at university. There's an art school in Dunedin and I can attend lessons as well as take my degree. When I'm of age I can paint."

"I hope so, Alexander, and I should be thanking you. Thanks to you I have learnt a great deal about New Zealand flora and fauna, and I have some reasonably accurate sketches of the birds and flowers. I'll seek that copy of Buller's Book of New Zealand Birds you recommended too." She smiled at him. "It's been a wonderful trip for painting hasn't it? I hope to persuade my husband to accompany me on another trip and we can enjoy seeing those beautiful sights together."

The bell clanged as Charlotte arrived, calling, "Morning coffee, Mrs Holyman." She smiled at the young man. "Oh, Alexander, your mother is looking for you. Something about packing and tidying your cabin."

Alexander blushed, muttered and fled.

"Nearly home, Lisa." She gripped the railing, her knuckles white mountains, her lips pressed into a thin line. "I so hope Dan is waiting for us. I've told my sisters I am going to walk home, stopping at your place first to pick up some samples of silk for them to choose from. They will manage Papa and I have time to … oh, if only Dan has come to carry our bags. I can talk to him. Oh, Lisa!" She grasped Melisande's arm in a pinching anxious clutch.

Melisande patted her hand gently. "Well, I can turn that into a truth as I have silk pieces we could use as samples. And I hope Miggsy – Dan – is waiting too." She sighed. "Letters. I'll have to write a long letter to Advik about silk and money transfers and postal addresses, and I ought to write again to my uncle and to Richard's family. We sent proper bereavement notices and a wedding announcement, and our travel plans by telegraph cable, but I've only sent two letters since than. Jeri has written, but I really must too."

"There's the bell again. Come for coffee, Lisa, and look, there's the Port Chalmers bar, the sand spit." Charlotte actually trembled. "I am fearful, afraid I won't say the right words."

"You will, Charlotte. Think of what your life will be if you don't speak to Dan. Let's drink strong coffee and laugh. You're with your friends."

It took an eternity to arrive in the harbour. Melisande fidgeted in her cabin, hoping to hurry on the arrival by pretending to be busy. It didn't work.

Ruth swept her out to join the crowd on deck, then vanished herself.

"I'm hiding in the saloon until most passengers have departed. I'll exit last if I can. Avoid my father if I may."

Charlotte decided that might work for her, too, and disappeared. Melisande waited by the deck railings eager to see if her men had arrived. Surely Richard would come to welcome her home if he was back from his and Jeri's latest adventure?

The Waikari had a snug berth in a privileged position along the jetty nearest the shore and not down at the busy wharf end with the cargo ships. The captain tucked his ship neatly into dock and Melisande eagerly scanned the crowd. Yes, Richard stood on the dockside looking up for her. She raised her arm in a polite wave. He saw her and responded with a cheerful two-armed wave and a grin. A quick look round, good, no one would see her for they gazed shorewards, so Melisande quickly blew him a kiss and laughed. And behind Richard stood Miggsy – phut – how useful that expression was, it made a lovely fierce sound – she must call him Daniel.

***

She'd never asked for Richard. Her beloved man. Her traitorous man. Now why would she know that? How was it she could remember Richard and where he was. Jeri had to go to England, she knew that. She still hadn't stitched together her memories properly. Charlotte and Ruth, with Doctor Allinson watching, refused to tell her anything and did no more than nod at her remembrances or add pieces of their own with the doctor's permission. She must, must, must remember for herself. There were other people in the house, she heard them moving around but she wasn't permitted to see anyone except the doctor, Charlotte and Ruth. And surely Charlotte had accepted Daniel. What had happened?

***

Melisande looked round. Where was Charlotte? There, by the rails, looking in the wrong place and enclosed by her family. Ruth stood next to them, beside her stepmother. All this bothersome secrecy. If only the vicar would behave as a true Christian ought to behave, grant Charlotte his blessing and welcome Miggsy – oops, Daniel – as a promising son-in-law. 'If wishes were horses then beggars might ride,' as Mama used to say. Melisande moved to join their group and waved to Richard again, making sure to include Daniel in her smile of greeting. Ruth, thank heavens, noticed Daniel.

"Miggsy came with your husband, Mrs Holyman. Mr Holyman must expect you to arrive with a cartload of trunks and tins of specimens and has enlisted extra aid." She gave a cheeky grin, quickly suppressed when her stepmother glanced her way.

Charlotte's head snapped right as she tried to see. She finally caught sight of Daniel, flushed, then paled as she sent a pleading glance towards Melisande.

Once the gangway settled firmly on the dockside, Anne and Caroline fenced their father between them and escorted him off the ship. "Charlotte has a little task to organise with Mrs Holyman, Papa," they told him as they swept down the gangway. "Choose well, bring us as many silk samples as you can carry," hissed Anne as she leaned in to give a sisterly peck on the cheek to Charlotte.

Charlotte nodded; Melisande smiled.

Ruth departed with her stepmother. Her father stood waiting on the dockside to escort them home. She pulled a face as she passed them, and slipped a note into Melisande's hand.

"Instructions," she whispered.

Melisande and Charlotte bade her farewell, and waited as though politely allowing the vicar, the English visitors, and the doctor's family to precede them. Charlotte, wanting to be the last to leave, prevented Melisande from following with a firm grasp on her jacket sleeve.

"Wait, please wait."

"Courage," Melisande whispered. Charlotte's hands trembled; she locked her fingers together. Melisande tucked a comforting hand under her elbow and led her forward.

By the time they reached the dockside Richard and Daniel had arranged a cart for their trunks and found their bags.

Richard tipped his hat in greeting, Daniel raised his cap.

"We'll carry these for you ladies," Richard announced with a grin and a flourishing bow, as one conferring a great favour. Melisande laughed, even Charlotte smiled. Daniel reached over the cart and picked up Charlotte's carpet bag.

"Did I find the correct trunks and is this all, my dear?" Richard asked.

Melisande nodded and stood as close to him as she dared in public, to touch his hand. "I've missed you." She spoke softly.

"And I you." Richard raised her gloved hand to his lips. "Pardon me, Miss Charlotte," he added, giving Melisande's hand a gentle squeeze as he released it, placing it under his elbow. "Would you allow me to escort you too?" He offered her his other arm. "Miggsy kindly promised to play at porter as he had to be on the dockside with an errand about a missing shipment of building supplies."

Oh, phut, Melisande nearly said aloud. She exchanged a stricken glance with Charlotte.

Richard, usually so quick to observe and understand any undercurrents, failed to do so. He tucked Charlotte by his left side and with Melisande on his right, led them along the dock and onto the pavement.

"We can enjoy a gentle stroll home and you ladies can tell me of the wonders you have seen on this fabled trip. I'm most envious."

They proceeded up the hill with Daniel a step behind them, following with all the bags.

Melisande sought some way to partner Charlotte with Daniel. "Richard?"

"Yes, my dear?"

"Ought Daniel be carrying my bags when you are here. Is it fair? Oughtn't you be helping as he has Miss Polson's bags as well?"

Richard opened his mouth, felt a quick squeeze, noted the meaningful look and realised something was occurring, some happening of concern to his Lisa, about which he knew nothing. He stopped, released both of his ladies, and turned to Daniel.

"Miggsy," a sharp dig made him remember. "No, I'm to be more civil and remember that your name is Mr Daniel Miggs. I apologise." He was grinning, Daniel appeared bemused. "Mr Miggs, Daniel, Daniel if I may. If you would be kind enough to carry Miss Charlotte's bags, I really should carry my wife's."

"Nay," Daniel began, but Charlotte turned her head towards him. Melisande thought she whispered to him. He stared at her, and must have noticed something in her face for he nodded, passing over Melisande's bag.

Melisande caught her husband's arm as he released Charlotte to grasp the bag. She propelled him forward so that they walked a few paces ahead.

"What …?" began Richard.

"Oh, do hush, please do. And listen please. No, don't look back. Let them walk together behind us a little." She gave him a pleading look. "Do you really think that you and Jeri can farm this property you've bought? Can you fix fences and build barns, plough and …?"

"Lisa, what are you talking about? Why on this good earth are you asking about my ability to farm? What notion is in your head, my dear that …?"

"We need a Miggsy, a Daniel, to help us with that farm. I am sure you mean to learn some skills, my love, but you need help."

"Well naturally, Lisa, Jeri and I plan to hire a manager, but I don't understand why. …"

Melisande nudged him around with her elbow so that he could take a quick glance at Daniel and Charlotte.

"I don't see … oh." For Charlotte moved so close to Daniel that she appeared to be leaning on his chest. She raised her head, spoke, then blushed rose red. Her head drooped so she didn't see Daniel's face lighten, colour with a triumphant flush, as his arms encircled her waist.

"Good Lord," muttered Richard, "the vicar's daughter. Is Miggsy mad?"

Oh Charlotte! Halfway up the hill where everyone could see. Melisande shook her head but felt pleased. Charlotte had grasped her courage and spoken, and it appeared all was well between them. And, oh, the look on Daniel's face, so … so tender as he dropped a kiss on the top of Charlotte's head, which buried more firmly against his chest. Melisande clutched Richard's hand, rubbing her cheek against his shoulder.

"Oh, I see," Richard commented. "Have you been playing cupid my romantic, soft-hearted love?" But as he modified his words with a public embrace and kiss, Melisande knew he was more amused than annoyed.

"Don't you see, we need help, they will need help. Of a certainty we can help each other."

Richard tutted. "Have you no common sense my love? This is a social disaster for them. Now I understand your comments." He turned and strode back to the couple. "Not in public, you lovebirds. You'd better come to our house and I'll talk some sense into your heads." But he spoke with a smile.

Charlotte blushed again, and broke away from Daniel's embrace, startled and embarrassed. She trembled, but Daniel caught her hand with a look so full of loving and caring that she visibly strengthened, her face glowing, and they began to walk up the hill again, lagging behind to exchange more words.

"If her father and his mother are difficult, we could take them to the farm couldn't we, Richard?" Melisande whispered.

He opened their garden gate, escorting her through with a thoughtful nod.

"Talk to Daniel. We need help, you need help. He has ideas and plans which could work with ours."

Daniel ushered Charlotte through the gate, grasped Richard's hand and shook it firmly. "I'm grateful to you. I know what you must think, but it will work out. I've planned. Now I'm off into your kitchen to tell my mam. Best you wait in your parlour, Mr Richard, with the ladies, for Mam will not be happy and she'll be mighty noisy."

Richard nodded, shepherding the ladies to the front door.

"If you'd allow my Charlotte to wait in your parlour, I'll come for her to take her to her father and ask his permission once I've made Mam understand I will be marrying Charlotte Polson, vicar's daughter or no."

***

There had been a wedding. She was sure of it. Melisande thought until her headache tightened to a heated throbbing band round her skull. Oh and the appalling fuss, she remembered that. Mrs Miggs had been furious. She should talk this over with Charlotte, check to see that what she thought happened had happened. She needed the comforting reassurance that her memories were correct, because she was beginning to allow that dreadful lurking 'thing' to take shape and it scared her badly because of who it must involve. Charlotte would help her remember.

Chapter Seventeen

Daniel was right. His mother's first shriek hit around high e flat and rivalled the Dunedin train's whistle. Melisande grimaced, her musical sensitivities offended. Charlotte started, clapped her hands to her ears, and Richard closed the door, leaning against it as though to add extra solidity and prevent the yelling becoming clear words and not mere noise.

"Phew!" he exhaled noisily. "Mrs Miggs certainly has powerful lungs. I think we should sit and be comfortable, ladies."

Melisande smiled at Charlotte. "Take that chair, Charlotte. Be thankful Mrs Miggs won't be allowed to speak to you, so this is all you'll hear."

"It's enough."

"Don't worry. She's a fond mother and adores Daniel, is rightly proud of him. She won't be able to disassociate herself from her only child forever, and she'll want to know her grandchildren."

Richard, still leaning against the door, agreed. "Miss Charlotte, the worst she can say is that your marriage is not socially suitable. She can have no complaints against you, the vicar's daughter, and I think it might be wise to pretend you haven't heard this argument."

Charlotte blinked, pressed her lips together and then managed a smile. "Yes, I believe that. You're correct. Daniel and I must be the forgiving ones."

Mrs Miggs stormed down the hall, still yelling, her feet stomping, the floorboards bouncing. She slammed open the front door so it crashed into the wall. Voice raised again in a bellow, she screamed, "She's only marrying you because no one else has asked her." She then stomped down the path and clattered out through the gate, banging it behind her.

Charlotte looked as if she'd been knocked breathless. Melisande rose and whisked across the room to comfort her, but Daniel opened the door and came in.

"Oh, Daniel, my Daniel, that isn't true, I …"

He knelt in front of Charlotte, took hold of her hands. "Nay lass, she'd never make me believe such a thing of you." He pressed her hands between his, turned his head to look at Melisande. "It's you I thank, Mrs Holyman, for knowing that. For what you said to my lady. I bless the day you came from India with your different foreign ways, both you and your husband."

Melisande felt the blush ascend from her toes in a rush, and seethe into her cheeks. Whatever Charlotte had said, she thanked goodness they had been words that Daniel believed.

He smiled at them, then looked back at Charlotte, who smiled and glowed under his gaze. "We'll go speak to your father, Charlotte. At least he won't deafen us."

She breathed in, straightened her spine, even gave a little gurgle of laughter. "No, he'll pray over us and send me to my room, and then he'll refuse you and banish you."

"Aye, likely that's what he'll do."

Richard interrupted them. "What will you do if he confines Charlotte to her home and forbids you to speak to her? He'll be thinking of Anne and Caroline and their engagements. Have you some plan to avoid this?"

Daniel stood up and assisted Charlotte to her feet. "I told you I'd been planning, Mr Richard." He put his arm round Charlotte's waist and eased her to him. She leaned against him, head on his chest. "I have your word you'll not spoil it, Mr Richard, Mrs Holyman?"

"Of course," Melisande said; Richard concurred.

"I'm thinking to pretend to be angry and heartsore and leave town. I've a building job near Oamaru will take a good four or more weeks. It's a cash job with living in supplied. You best be a good daughter and comply, my love, but be ready after four weeks. There's a good bit of work up that way and I reckon I can find us a house to rent. You look round after morning service at church on the sixth Sunday and I'll be there waiting outside in a pony cart to fetch you off to Dunedin and a wedding that same day." He cuddled Charlotte to him, smiling fondly. "It'll be our first steps to our farm and that fancy home I'll build for you."

"If you need to send messages to each other we'll do that for you," Melisande smiled on them both. "And Richard, what about our plans?"

Richard nodded. "Yes, now's the moment indeed. Daniel, do you know the property we've bought?"

"Aye, I know of it, not seen it though."

"Take a look when you're in Oamaru. Go out one Sunday and see if you would care to finish those farm buildings for us. That's a well-paid building job for you. Could you manage a farm? We need a manager and there's a good house goes with that job."

Charlotte's eyes shone. "To have a friend nearby, oh, Daniel. Surely you could manage a farm?"

"Aye, well I'd need to think about it. I'd manage cows and sheep and hay making, but corn crops, harvesting and sowing I don't really know. Never done it."

Richard frowned. "That's a blow." He turned to Melisande, raising an eyebrow.

"Wouldn't we need another farmhand anyway, Richard? We could hire an older experienced farmhand couldn't we? Find an older farming couple who'd welcome Daniel's physical aid? A housekeeping wife for me and an experienced farmhand for Daniel? I know we can hire in people like a ploughman for I've seen plenty of advertisements in the newspaper and on noticeboards from farm workers. And at harvest time we'd hire a harvest gang. That's what farmers do, don't they Daniel? You could manage that, do you think?"

Daniel, under a battery of hopeful eyes, flushed and nodded.

Richard shook his hand. "We all need to think about it, Daniel, but the building work is there for you whatever you decide. Please consider the manager's position."

"I will, Mr Richard, and thank you. I'll come to your farm after this Oamaru job. I'll surely think of being manager if it gives my Charlotte a nice house and a friend nearby. I'm balloting for land up that way, so maybe we can settle near enough that I can work for you if I can't manage for you."

He offered Charlotte his arm. "Come, my lady, I've to ask your father for this hand of yours." He tucked the offered hand under his arm and escorted her out.

Melisande turned to Richard and gently encircled his neck so that she could stand on tiptoe and kiss him. "I think they'll make a good and happy marriage," she whispered, kissing him again, "like ours."

Richard grasped her round the waist, whirling her out of the parlour, down the hallway into their bedroom. "Let me show you how I've missed you," he said and began nibbling her neck as he unbuttoned her shirtwaist.

Melisande giggled and started to work on his tie.

***

Ruth brought the dinner, the doctor followed her in. More medicines, more slops but no more bandaged head. Melisande smiled, the muscles in her face working even more easily.

Her eyes could follow the doctor's moving finger and she could see and describe the items he had Ruth place on the mantelpiece.

"Yes," the doctor nodded, "I do believe we can allow you to have more light. Just morning and evening light, two hours of each and no bright sunshine," he warned Ruth.

He walked to the window and moved aside one curtain a little. "Excellent, you'll have a pleasant view of paddocks and the manager's house. Nothing too exciting or disturbing."

"Now is there anything you desire which I might give permission for, Mrs Holyman?"

"My husband," and Melisande found herself crying, tears washing away the soreness in her eyes, flooding her cheeks to drip on her gown. She turned her head away, embarrassed and cross with herself for being a watering pot.

Ruth mopped her face with a towel and the doctor tisked and shushed in his fatherly way. "I think you know I can't do that, Mrs Holyman, but you're very near to remembering everything. Be brave, Mrs Holyman. We cannot, must not, tell you. You must remember and you will."

She had to swallow another draught of medicine to soothe her nerves, keep her tranquil and resting, and to be reassured again by the doctor that all would be well.

Ruth tidied her up again. "You will remember," Ruth said. "Do you remember why I'm here?"

She didn't quite. Something to do with Charlotte and Mrs Miggs again?

***

Mrs Miggs failed to appear in the morning although her cronies did; it was scrub-the-floors and washing day. Mrs MacAndrews and Mrs Turvey liked to work together, for laundry work required plenty of hot water and the heavy work on floors and in the kitchen needed hot water too. Melisande found her mother's advice, that servants work best when their tasks make sense, was true for Mrs MacAndrews and Mrs Turvey, who worked away, their energy fuelled by their chatting. She greeted them cheerfully and received a flat response.

"Mrs Miggs ain't well today," Mrs MacAndrews said, and disappeared to the washhouse.

Mrs Turvey had a knowing look on her face but said nothing about Daniel, only that it was a good blowy day for drying, and she'd better get on, as she followed Mrs MacAndrews. Melisande bit back further remarks, pressed her lips firmly together to prevent a smile and concentrated on preparing breakfast.

Jeri was last to breakfast, having had a long meeting with Mr Truman the previous evening, and thus been late to bed. He devoured porridge and a ham omelette, several rolls and marmalade.

"Well done, Lisa, your breakfasts are good and those rolls are improved. Muffins and crumpets next. Get Mrs M to teach you."

Melisande bobbed a mock curtsey This was the time, since Jeri was in a good mood, to broach the subject of Daniel and Charlotte, and Ruth, and visits to the farm. Ruth's note instructed Melisande to persuade Richard to speak to her father, asking if he would permit a friendly visit from Ruth to assist his wife. She knew Richard would agree, persuading Jeri was the problem.

"We need to talk about the farm, Jeri."

Jeri's head jerked up, and he set down his cup of coffee. "Have you told her?" he demanded of Richard.

Melisande paused, gave Richard a reproachful look. "What is this?"

Richard shook his head.

"Letters," Jeri said. He drank the remains of his coffee, searched his inside jacket pocket, and produced a bundle of papers, rather creased and folded.

"Our uncle is not pleased. He has forbidden us to buy land here, forbidden your marriage and demands that we 'come home' at once."

Melisande gawped, gathered herself, clapped her hands to her mouth and cried, "Oh phut."

Her men boggled at her, stared at each other, then Jeri waved his hand at Richard. "Did you teach …? Good God! You deal with her," he said.

"Lisa, where did you learn that word?"

"What? You mean 'phut'?"

Jeri looked shocked. "Lisa!"

"What's the matter? It's Hindi, means useless. You must have heard Advik use it, Jeri."

Richard raised his eyes to heaven, shook his head at her, but she saw the smile wrinkle the edges of his mouth. "Lisa, my love, don't speak that word here or anywhere except India."

"But why?"

"It sounds like a most offensive English word which no lady would ever know or have heard. It's crude, rude and appalling."

"Oh, my goodness." She began to laugh. "I didn't want to swear, you see, so I found a useful word in Hindi, to say when I was cross, or so I thought." She sat and laughed until her eyes watered.

Richard shook her gently by the shoulder, laughing and chiding her. "Please don't say it again. Try 'drat', that's a politer word to use. Oh, and you'll be pleased to know that my parents have approved of my actions if not our hasty marriage. My mama wanted a glorious English wedding."

"So did I." Melisande didn't mean to say that but the words sneaked out.

"I know, I will make it up to you," he dropped a kiss on the tip of her nose, "and I'll tell her so, when I write tonight. What we must sort out is this threat from your uncle. It's serious, Lisa, because your uncle controls your funds."

Jeri frowned. "I've spent a fortune on cablegrams, and now I've got to get a letter written today. You must write too, Lisa, explain about our parents' blessing on your engagement, because if our uncle cables India, and the bank here, it could halt everything. I had to give him our banking details for him to give permission to release the English money. Once the cash is spent we'll be without support unless we persuade him to change his mind."

"Oh, Jeri. And you, Richard, why didn't you tell me?"

"Jeri's been holding the information," Richard's voice told Melisande he was still annoyed. "I wasn't informed until we failed to find more than a speck of gold."

"Jeri, how could you? I might have helped, sent a cable, reassured our uncle, written to …"

"Lisa, it's nothing for you to concern yourself with. Richard manages your finances and I manage our family funds."

"But I can help with our uncle."

"Yes, by writing and persuading him. Coax him into a good humour." Jeri slammed out, leaving a bewildered Melisande who turned to Richard.

"Jeri deliberately didn't inform your uncle until it was too late for him to stop us leaving India for the colonies. That's what has enraged your uncle."

"Oh, no."

"Oh, yes."

They looked at each other and Melisande wished she'd cabled her uncle and then perhaps they could have stayed in India. She bit her lip on the words threatening to spill out in anger.

Jeri barged in, frowning. "I need writing paper." He slumped into a chair.

"Are you telling me, brother mine, that with our uncle's help we could have stayed in India?"

Jeri scowled. "No, no, no. Don't drag out old history, little sister. Our uncle would have ordered us home. He believes he should control our money and our lives."

Melisande pulled a face at him, swallowed back hard words. "Papa always said his brother had an overly strong sense of being head of the family, always issuing commands for the good of the family name."

He rubbed his hands over his face and through his hair. "I do miss them, you know, Lisa, Papa's advice and Mama's wisdom."

Melisande patted his shoulder. He always could disarm and charm her into forgiving him. "Don't say that, I'll start weeping."

He stood up and hugged her. "Don't or I might too. I'll write that letter now, you and Richard plan our move out to the farm."

"Wait a moment, Jeri. We need to talk about the farm."

"Oh, Melisande. Now? There's so much to do and I must write this letter."

"Yes, now. If we are to make this farm our lives and livelihood it must pay …"

"I know that …"

"But do you know how to make our farm earn an income?"

"Really, Lisa, I do have some understanding …"

"But do you? Please sit and listen, Jeri. Richard, please persuade him and help convince him." Richard nodded. "And you need to listen too."

She stood in front of them and laced her fingers together, seeking the words. "I've heard you both complaining about the attitude you meet, you grumble most after church. Patronising you call it, Jeri. Do you know why those men speak like that?"

"What do …?" Richard placed a restraining hand on Jeri's arm.

"Wait, Jeri, let Lisa speak. I know, from what she's been telling me, that she has been thinking about our future here. She has sensible ideas and we should listen. I've already acted on one. I expect she's going to tell you."

"Thank you, Richard." She blew him a kiss which made Jeri frown again. "Most people here think we're like the man we bought the farm from. Spending too much money and then failing because we don't know what we're doing and are too gentlemanly to work hard ourselves. We are not, you are not, colonial pioneers, men like Daniel Miggs, who can turn their hands to anything. You've not been seen taking off your jackets and working with your hands. They think you're playing and will tire and move away. It annoys them because the farm is a good one with plenty of land for growing corn. Wheat and barley fetch good prices, even our poorest soil will provide a crop of oats. And our pasture is good, should fatten beasts and provide winter food for them."

Jeri stared. "What do you know …?"

Richard interrupted. "No, Jeri, let Lisa explain how she knows all this and why it's important. You've felt insulted once or twice when someone's said to us 'you gentlemen'. So have I. Let's listen to the explanation."

Melisande paused, collecting her thoughts. She must explain well so that Ruth and Charlotte would be welcomed and she could form an alliance of mutual assistance with them, bringing Daniel Miggs in as well. She wanted that team.

"I learned so much on my trip on the Waikari. The vicar's English visitors were curious, asked questions. It meant many explanations to them about life in New Zealand. I heard comments which have made me aware of how many people regard us. Even Ruth – Miss Landry – and Charlotte – Miss Polson – they know more than we do about farming life." She saw the look of disdain on Jeri's face.

"Yes, they do, Jeri. A vicar's daughter helps those in need. Mr Landry has a small acreage where he grows barley. This isn't our estate in India, where we had workers for everything. We had experienced people who planted and harvested the jute. We need a team. We haven't family to rally round and work together. We must find people who will work with us for mutual aid and success.

"On the ship the general consensus was that those who have done well in New Zealand, if they didn't have a fortune to spend, were those who worked as part of a family group or who had a mutual support group to do the big tasks together."

She drew in a deep breath. "I want to help my friends and they want to help me. Ruth is in disgrace because she's refused to marry the curate. Charlotte is in disgrace because she intends to marry Daniel Miggs …"

Jeri started. "Good lord. It's true then?"

"How did you …?"

"Apologies, Lisa. I didn't mean to interrupt again. Last night I stayed on for a drink with Mr Truman, and Doctor Gilmour and his junior partner Doctor Beattie were there. Seems there was a rumour that the vicar turned Miggsy off his doorstep quite smartly and told him not to come back or try to see Charlotte again. Everyone was speculating as to why."

"Then you can see how we can help them and they can help us."

"Oh no, Lisa. The social consequences are such that we don't want to be involved."

"But we won't be in Port Chalmers will we? And if Daniel – do stop calling him Miggsy, he's a grown man – comes and finishes that barn and outbuildings, that's helpful to us. He's valuable to us, Jeri, because he's a good worker and he knows which men to employ who'll work well too. We help him by paying him well and if he accepts the post of manager then he'll have a house and Charlotte and I will have each other's assistance and company. You haven't thought how lonely it will be out on that farm with no one but ourselves. Ruth, Miss Landry, needs a place to escape for some weeks. She would be a welcome helper as well, as I set up the house and learn some new routines."

"My sensible Nut Brown Maid is correct, Jeri. I've offered Daniel the building work and the manager's position. We need a man of his talents."

"More than one, Richard. I've looked at the newspapers and talked to people. If we offer a little more than the usual wage and show our willingness to learn and work we might find helpful people. You'll have to take off your jacket, Jeri, and put your back into shepherding or cattle watching or firewood chopping and stop junketing about on boys' adventures."

"Just one more adventure, little sister, then I'll be a good farmer for us after my uncle has taught me management."

Richard and Melisande exchanged looks and sighs of exasperation.

"Oh, Jeri. If Mama was here she'd tell you to stop such childish behaviour."

"Heed your clever sister, Jeri. You know I have plans to breed work horses. I know something about that, but how do we grow the food they need?"

Jeri pulled a wry face, opened his mouth, but Melisande spoke over his first words.

"Yes, we have to grow corn. At the very least oats and barley, and make hay, Jeri, and finally we need to hire a married couple, an experienced farming people. There are advertisements in the newspapers of couples looking for work. Or we could use an employment agency. This way, Jeri, I have help with running the house and if the wife is an experienced farm worker she'll teach me how to care for poultry and young animals. Her husband can be a source of knowledge for Daniel and you two. We hire in an extra ploughman and a harvesting team when needed. There! Oh, and I mustn't forget to tell you why Ruth needs to escape her father but I'll explain all that later."

Jeri looked at his sister and then at Richard. "You agree with all this, do you?"

"Yes, I do. And I am ashamed that we've not thought well enough or seriously enough about what we need to do to make this new life a success. I bless my clever, practical wife." Richard drew Melisande close and kissed her forehead. "Would you like me to speak to Mr Landry, ask if he would permit Miss Landry to help you settle into your new home? Shall I try the vicar for Charlotte – Miss Polson, that is? Say that we'd heard of a problem and being fond of Miss Charlotte thought it might take her away from any scandal and set her mind on other things?"

Melisande chuckled. "You might tell him you've heard that Daniel has gone to work in the south, Invercargill possibly." She warmed her cheeks with a blush. "Perhaps hint that in your wife's condition you are anxious to have friends and help for her?"

Jeri looked shocked. "You aren't …?" Richard and Melisande shook their heads. "Good lord. Then are you two actually encouraging the match?"

Richard laughed. "My romantic wife believes they will be the perfect colonial couple. We've got Daniel as an example to live up to, Jeri."

"Hah! Give me some paper please, and I'll write that letter to Uncle Aubrey now. Lisa had better take command in the kitchen then write her letters and you, Richard, can go and charm the locals."

***

Melisande sighed. "One tiny hint, perhaps, dear Charlotte."

Charlotte frowned. "Well, perhaps, as you are so near to the memories we need from you." She pressed her lips together, ummed and gave her a name. "Mrs Miggs."

"Oh, now what did I do for Mrs Miggs after she was so angry with me?"

Charlotte refused to say more and performed her nursing duties, singing softly and teasing Melisande about what she'd done to upset Port Chalmers. As she left, with Melisande tucked in for the night, she turned in the doorway and whispered. "We are forbidden to tell you more and dare not for fear of the consequences to those we love."

Ruth had been hinting for some time that Melisande's memory had great importance for them all. Melisande closed her eyes, willing herself to sink into those patches of memories and stitch them together without giving herself a headache. She was beginning to understand that she must be careful, not from fear, but for her friends.

Chapter Eighteen

Richard succeeded in charming Mr Landry. He failed with the vicar. "I'm sure he believes that Miss Charlotte will run away," he reported at lunch. "I gather she's kept in her room."

"Oh, poor Charlotte. I wonder if Ruth has spoken to her."

Ruth had. She arrived, escorted by her father, who deposited her at the front door and intended to collect her later as well. She rushed in full of the news. She found Melisande in the kitchen struggling with a leg of lamb.

"Here, let me." Ruth nudged Melisande to one side and, after checking to see whether Mrs MacAndrews and Mrs Turvey were working within earshot, began to tell her tale in a whisper. "Charlotte wants to marry good old Miggsy! Did she tell you on the ship? Ah, I can see she did. You might have let me know. She's in such disgrace."

"I know. Poor Charlotte. But what about you? Did the curate explain to your father as he promised to do?"

"He must have because my father thinks we are going to be formally engaged next year." Ruth frowned. "I am determined to be far away by then, thanks to you. And your husband asked for my help in exactly the proper way and I am allowed to accompany you as you are in a delicate condition." She grinned.

"Oh, Ruth. Cyril Wadsworth is a good kind man to prevaricate like that and fool your father, and he in holy orders too. He is fond of you, you know."

"Yes, well I'm not getting married for years if ever. He can find someone else to feel sorry for."

"Dear Ruth," Melisande shook her head. "What fibsters we are becoming. Goodness me, and did my Richard actually suggest I was in an interesting condition?"

"Oh no, he hinted most elegantly, and my stepmother nudged my father, understanding dawned, and he gave permission for me to help here and accompany you to the farm." Her face had a rosy glow of excitement, her eyes bright with anticipation. "I won't return. I'm going to learn to type and keep accounts. You'll have to help me in return for my assistance."

"Well, I'm not sure …" Melisande began, and laughed at Ruth's expression.

Ruth smiled back. Oh you, Mrs Lisa Holyman, you! Then she frowned. "But what about poor Charlotte? You can't approve surely. It'll mean social disgrace here in Port Chalmers."

"Daniel Miggs is a good, kind man, capable of making a good livelihood and running a productive farm. He has all the skills. He would be a wonderful husband …"

"But not for the vicar's daughter. She's a lady. Daniel Miggs is a carpenter, a builder, a workman; his mother cleans houses. That makes him a worker not a gentleman."

"And Daniel Miggs is a gentle man who adores Charlotte. She could be truly happy."

Ruth pulled a face and concentrated on basting the lamb. "Can't see why she wants to be married anyway. Stuck out with Miggsy alone on a farm somewhere." She sighed.

Melisande squeezed the obvious retort between her teeth, and sprinkled rosemary on the potatoes.

With the lamb roasting in the oven, and the rice for the pudding soaking in its Indian style spices, Melisande led Ruth to the parlour to make lists. Ruth's organising skills were outstanding. She knew Port

Chalmers and its people in a way that Melisande never could. She knew who were the best carriers and carters. She knew who would pack furniture properly. "You need Thomson's Removals."

"I agree, Thomson's Removals again."

Letters were written and dates set. Richard and Jeri argued and then agreed over each suggestion, but it was definite. They would be removing in four weeks. The afternoon sun had long disappeared round the other side of the house when Ruth rose to depart.

"I'll catch my father walking up the hill. I am not being collected like a parcel."

"Don't forget to set your bread," she reminded Melisande, "and Mrs Miggs will be back tomorrow, she's ordered Daniel off to Invercargill where she's heard there's work for him."

"I don't know how you learn all these things so quickly. Poor Daniel and poor Charlotte, I wonder if the vicar will let me visit Charlotte? Will you try asking again, Ruth?"

Ruth pulled a cheeky face. "I learned from Daniel, who was walking to the sawmill, and I promised to see Charlotte today. And I'll return each day to help you pack personal items." She departed, escorted by both Richard and Jeri, to give a good impression. They had Melisande's letters to post as well as theirs, and they intended to bribe Willie, the post office boy, and Olly Ogden, the grocer's boy, to run errands for them during the next few days.

Peace, time for a quick walk along the beach, time to think and cease worrying and ban anxiety. Melisande skewered her hat firmly with the longest hat pins, found warm gloves and slipped into her warmest jacket. She left by the back door and her boots rang out on the path, reminding her of Dan's big boots. She looked at the houses he'd helped to build. One was finished and for sale, one half built and a third was in its foundations. And there was Daniel himself with his, what was that expression, his mates – that was such a New Zealand expression – and Mr Hammond too. She waved and turned towards the beach path.

She had barely taken five steps when "Mrs Holyman!" echoed behind her. She stopped. Now who was that? It was Mr Hammond, striding down to meet her with Daniel and his mates at his heels.

"I hear you've hired Miggsy boy, and he's hired the rest of my gang, You and Daniel stealing my work force away." He shook his head and pulled a fierce face at the young men, then smiled at Melisande. "Make 'em work hard. My building work's slowed until I sell another house so I'm not holding them to my contract."

The young men looked bashful but muttered a chorus of "What contract?" Mr Hammond elbowed the nearest and wagged a finger at them all.

"Nay lads, you settle your hours now with the lady, and I'll take this darn fool," here he scowled at Daniel, "and pay him what I owe him and try to knock some sense into his wooden block of a head."

Daniel shrugged. "I'm off south 'til the fuss dies down."

"You find yourself a nice lass down there and bring her back to please your ma. Get rid of these daft notions." Mr Hammond stomped off.

Daniel raised his eyebrows, shrugged, winked at his mates and followed.

The young man calling himself Tommy introduced the others as Paddy, Vic and Doug. "We're a team with Daniel," he explained.

They promised to arrive the following morning to see what needed crating up in the household, and Tommy and Paddy promised to travel with the crates going by train whilst Vic and Doug would help Thomson's men with the carting of the goods out to the farm.

Vic and Doug touched caps and strode off. Tommy and Paddy hesitated, watched their workmates out of earshot, then begged pardon for interrupting her walk.

"Dan's told us you're helpin' 'im?"

Melisande nodded.

"He said to talk to you or your man. That right?"

She nodded again. "Both my husband and I know his plans and offered Daniel work."

"Then 'tis right if we to pack some of Miss Charlotte's things and a bit of furniture o' Dan's with your stuff? Seems you've got a place for him to live?"

"Yes, if he's accepted the position of manager then there is a house. But how are you to take Miss Polson's things without her family knowing?"

Tommy and Paddy grinned, touched caps and walked off. "Best you don't know, Missus," they called over their shoulders.

Melisande puzzled over the comment, decided she truly would prefer not to know, and continued on her delayed beach walk. She simply must speak to Charlotte.

When she returned Richard and Jeri were arguing over what to do with the Port Chalmers house when they moved out to the farm.

"I knew we shouldn't have bought the place." Jeri's voice neared a shout. "Now we're going to lose money if we sell back to Hammond."

"It's Lisa's home and we should rent it out. There are plenty of people needing a house. Mr Truman can manage it for us. The rent will be useful cash for Lisa if we ..." Richard broke off when he saw Melisande in the doorway.

"Lisa, my love, do I smell roast lamb? Shall I carve for you and Jeri can arrange the table for us?"

Melisande gave them a Look. "'If we ...?' Do you have something to tell me?"

They both shook their heads.

"Later," Richard promised as he followed her into the kitchen, Jeri close on his heels.

She found the oven cloths, removed the joint and set it on the table to rest, then pulled the dish of Indian rice pudding off the hot plate, whisked the dish of bread rolls out of the warming oven and pushed the rhubarb pie into it.

"Good lord, I am honestly impressed, little sister. Not one servant in sight and you've managed all this? Not bad, Lisa, still short of a soup course and a fish course but we're nearer to getting a proper meal."

Melisande, dishing up the potatoes and fishing out the rest of roast vegetables, looked up with an oven-heated face. "If you want a full dinner then you can help me. It isn't easy and I'm still learning." She sounded as cross as she felt.

"Don't be upset, Lisa love," said Richard, picking up the carving knife. "You are a marvel and you will have help always, I give you my word. We've Mrs Miggs until we leave, then Miss Charlotte and Miss Ruth can help until we find someone from Oamaru."

Jeri grinned. "Oh, I think we'll always need a trained cook. But dear Lisa, sweet little sister, now you can bake a cake or two, don't you want to keep sweetening us up?" He'd found a large square fruit cake sitting in its baking tin on the rack above the hot plate.

"Jeri, don't you pick the nuts off that cake. Just bring the warm plates please."

Richard began carving thin slices of lamb. "My oldest sister is married to a real countryman, a squire farmer." He arranged each slice carefully beside the joint. "When they were very busy, with harvesting or wool clipping or on a Sunday when all the servants had a day off, they'd eat in their great kitchen all snug and informal. Not if they had company of course but I was never company and it saved my sister and her family a lot of work. What do you think, Lisa?"

She smiled. She and Mrs Miggs had often eaten luncheon in the kitchen on busy days, but she'd never confessed this. "I am tired," she said, "and it's warm here and everything we need is within a step or two or arm's reach. Yes, please."

Jeri swished the Indian cotton cloth off the small side table, threw it on the large table, and began setting plates and cutlery as Richard continued to carve and Melisande placed the dishes of rice and vegetables in the centre.

They sat down and sang the family grace before Richard served the meat.

"If Lisa will play tonight," he said, "we can sing for our supper and think about what to do with this house when we are living on the farm."

***

Oh, now she remembered. In fact she felt proud of herself for doing a good deed and making her own decisions. Perhaps this was the moment she grew into a self-sufficient colonial woman, or was that later when Richard ... no, she'd not dwell on what Richard had done. She knew, almost from the beginning, what he had done, but she'd preferred not to remember.

***

What to do with Lisa's 'little house' settled itself in the morning. Mrs Miggs bustled in the back door and began clattering in the kitchen as Mr Landry escorted his daughter to the front. Ruth promised to return in time to help her stepmother with her half-brothers at five o'clock and rushed Melisande into her parlour, closing the door firmly behind them.

"I've seen Charlotte again. She's still confined to her room. She's politely asking why it's impossible for her to marry Daniel Miggs." She looked amazed. "I always thought of Charlotte as timid, a sweet little mouse of a character."

"Oh poor Charlotte, but I wish she'd been timid. This is no time to be brave. She should be compliant and apologise. How is she?" Melisande stopped. Ruth was not party to their plans.

Ruth tilted her head, gazing at Melisande with her bright brown eyes. A knowing look of surprised comprehension lit up her face and she grinned.

"You're helping her ... does she mean to elope?" Ruth's voice lowered in a shocked hush.

Melisande said nothing, forced herself to think of icy cold snowy mountains to prevent a blush rising. A trick her mama had taught her and it usually worked.

Ruth covered her mouth with both hands to stifle a peal of laughter. "Mrs Holyman, you are going to be in such trouble with our society families." Laughter stifled, she looked at the silk shawl Melisande wore. "Poor silly Charlotte, stuck out in the lonely wilds with no one but Daniel Miggs. What a life. Shall we … would you gift Charlotte that length of silk you told me about and I'll make her a wedding dress? I could make her a very simple, well cut, elegant dress – I have some lace to make a detachable front which she could add for special occasions, something really …" her voice faded away.

"Why Ruth," Melisande embraced her, "such a kind person you are under all those grumps and prickles. I'd be delighted to give Charlotte some silk for you to tailor a dress, and I have a box of trimmings and lots of silver buttons. And yes, we are helping Charlotte and Daniel, but I may not tell you more without their permission. But I may tell you that as we are moving we've offered to carry some of their goods with ours to the railway. If you as much as give away a hint of this to your family or the vicar or anyone you will not come with us."

Ruth chuckled. "Oh my friend Lisa, you will be rightly accused of interfering where our respectable senior ladies dare not. It's good that you are leaving town. The senior society ladies hate people who upset their plans. They call them meddlers and busybodies. And no, if Charlotte wishes to escape her boring future, who am I to hinder her."

They were still laughing when Mrs Miggs knocked on the door and walked in without waiting for an answer. "I'll need a bit of time for m'self. Need afternoons this week, Mrs Holyman." She didn't acknowledge Ruth, just spoke abruptly and turned to go.

Melisande assumed she was concerned for her son. "Daniel wouldn't want you to worry. I'm sure he will write soon."

Mrs Miggs gave her cough of a laugh. "Nay it's me needing to worry. They've turned me out of me cottage. I've got 'til end of t'week to pack up and go."

"Why?" Shocked, Melisande caught her arm to prevent her leaving.

"Do you owe rent?" Ruth asked. Mrs Miggs shook her head.

The front door opened and Richard and Jeri walked in, only to stop by the parlour door as they saw the trio.

"Hello? Is something happening?"

"Richard, Jeri, Mrs Miggs is being forced out of her home." Melisande couldn't believe it, patted Mrs Migg on the arm.

"It's because of Daniel isn't it?" Ruth looked at Mrs Miggs. "Did they tell you?"

"Nay, they sent Ron with a letter and a message to say it – as if I couldna read it m'self."

Jeri's mouth gaped. Richard looked amazed, then spoke. "Who owns the cottage? Is it Mr Truman?"

"He's in charge. It's a group of them, those solicitors own some and the doctors own others and Mr Truman manages the rents and contracts."

"I find it hard to believe Mr Truman would do this without a real cause," Jeri said. "What did the young clerk, Rob, isn't it? What did he say, Mrs Miggs? The owners must have a cause to use to eject you, surely that's the law?"

"Maybe, Mr Allmark, but I'm paid up and the house is kept goodly well. I suppose it's the vicar and them thinkin' if I'm gone then Daniel won't be back."

Melisande and Ruth made sympathetic murmurs, looking to the men.

"I think, Jeri, you and I shall have a word with Mr Truman. If it is about Daniel, then Mrs Miggs won't find another place to rent."

Richard regarded Mrs Miggs thoughtfully. "Do you have friends who'll take you in? Have you family in Dunedin or elsewhere?"

She shook her head.

Melisande had a niggle of an idea, and smiled up at Richard. "We might help about that, if we think hard. Shall we go now and speak to Mr Truman? Jeri, would you come too?" She released Mrs Miggs with another pat on her arm. "Please, Mrs Miggs, could you prepare the meals and the bread, and leave me a list of tasks and we'll do our best to keep you in your home. We'll be back for luncheon."

Mrs Miggs nodded, thanked them gruffly, and trod off to the kitchen.

Melisande checked her men: hats, gloves, good boots, yes they'd outface Mr Truman. "I'll fetch my coat. Ruth, come with me please and let me find you that silk. You could begin work on it." Ruth seemed about to argue but then agreed and followed her.

"You're correct. I'd best keep away, Lisa, my father would follow the majority and want Daniel Miggs forced away. I must not be seen to be part of any protest."

Melisande understood: she smiled and found the silk. She left Ruth spreading it on her bed and hurried her men to town.

Ron ushered them straight into Mr Truman's office, invited them to be seated and spent five minutes discussing Ranee and the mare's wellbeing before departing at the sound of footsteps advancing down the corridor towards them. Mr Truman appeared, fluffing his moustache, and dusting crumbs from his cheerfully bright checked waistcoat.

Melisande smiled to herself. No wonder he was chubby if he took a little something this early in the morning. He obviously enjoyed his food.

"Late breakfast, bit of a rush job overnight," Mr Truman explained. "Welcome the Holymans and Mr Allmark. What problem may I help you with?"

"The rush job wouldn't have been an eviction notice would it?" Richard asked.

"Ah, now why would that be of concern?"

Melisande forgot her promise to be discreet and quiet. "How can you throw Mrs Miggs out of her home? Her rent is paid; she's a good tenant. What reason do you have?"

"There you have it, I'm afraid. Now don't be upset, Mrs Holyman. I'm sure your menfolk understand these social matters, but …" he waved his hands in the air, wafting away the idea of female understanding.

Richard murmured a warning to Melisande.

"Is her eviction because of her son?" Jeri demanded. "Have you ensured that she won't find another place to rent? It's despicable and will prove a most unpopular move. Daniel Miggs, Miggsy, is well thought of and popular in the whole community."

"Nicely put in a nutshell, Mr Allmark. But not so popular in certain circles. Between ourselves I don't like doing it. Daniel Miggs is a popular young man, as was his father. His mother suffered that nasty injury helping others, then the untimely loss of a good husband, and now her son has upset her. I did advise the owners that forcing her from her home will cause a great deal of ill feeling against them and their families."

"Then why do it? Why hurt an innocent woman by turning her out of the house she's lived in for years?" Melisande and Jeri spoke together. "She doesn't want Daniel to marry Miss Polson."

Richard looked at the solicitor. "Removing her won't solve the problem."

Mr Truman sat down in his office chair and swivelled it from side to side. He sighed. "I am sorry but Messrs Broughton, Ruddkin, Searle and Beattie were driven by a power greater than theirs in this type of matter. As was I."

Melisande stared, her men looked at each other.

"What father wants to see his daughter marry beneath herself? He might be persuaded through affection for his child, if the man is a good man, but no fond mother is willing to see her social status and her daughter's damaged by an unsuitable attachment." Mr Truman shook his head. "In these small communities it means the whole family being social outcasts, never invited to the best social events, ostracised." He looked at Melisande. "That kind of treatment is much harder on the ladies."

Melisande chose her words carefully. She might harm Charlotte's prospects if she spoke the wrong words. "Miss Polson told us that if she married Daniel Miggs they would live far from Port Chalmers."

"Makes no difference, Mrs Holyman. She sets a bad example to other girls of her social standing."

Jeri snorted. "They're hardly aristocrats."

"No, the vicar might claim distant relationship to a more aristocratic lineage, but the others are upper-middle class and precious about their hard-won status." Mr Truman spoke sharply.

He was one of them, Melisande realised. "Messrs Broughton, Ruddkin, Searle and Beattie, the likes of the Gillespies and Gilmours, they've earned their status and their wives are proud of it. Miss Charlotte Polson is letting the side down and must not be allowed to do so."

"And so Mrs Miggs must suffer too?" Richard stood up. "I see. We can't save her home and Miss Charlotte cannot marry." He faced his wife, offered her a hand to raise her and pulled a warning face at her as she opened her mouth.

Mr Truman shook Jeri's hand, made a sort of bob-bow to Richard and Melisande. "My wife thinks Miss Charlotte only thought of the Miggs boy because no other man has offered for her. She says she'll recover and do her duty to her father." He offered the words as a reassurance, it sounded to Melisande, as much for himself as to them.

"Very likely," Richard replied as he escorted a furious wife out of the solicitor's office. "Not a word," he hissed.

Jeri closed the door behind them and bustled them outside. "Phew," he said. "Even I can see that poor Miss Charlotte would have a better life on our farm with Mig … Daniel."

Melisande beamed at him. "Then would you escort Richard and myself to the vicarage? I want to suggest to the vicar that Ruth and I making a new dress for Charlotte for her sister's wedding would distract Charlotte, and I think you two might try suggesting again that as we are soon moving to our farm beyond Oamaru, might it not be a good idea to remove Charlotte with us and take her away from the gossip and unhappy situation?"

She dimpled a sisterly smile at Jeri. "If you could be aristocratic?" she suggested. "Give off an air of importance that might brush off on Charlotte?"

Richard choked, but Jeri grinned. "You mean the Indian Maharajah air? Delighted to oblige. Hints of trips and occasions for Miss Charlotte in improving upper-crust society perhaps?"

Melisande chuckled, Richard shook his head. "You're quite mad," he said, but he tucked Melisande's hand under his elbow and grasped Jeri's arm. "Let's have luncheon and then we'll go to make a polite morning call on the vicar."

***

But the vicar had not been 'At Home' to visitors, especially the Holymans and Mr Allmark. Charlotte was 'Not Available' either. Oh yes, she remembered it now. How they'd been made to feel insignificant, like some annoying pest and it was hinted that it might be to the good of Port Chalmers if they were to leave soon.

Chapter Nineteen

At last, she was allowed to get up and walk, well supported, around her bedroom. Melisande gave the doctor a smile which no longer caused the skin over her skull to twinge, nor did her face feel stiff. He also allowed her to see herself in the dressing-table looking glass.

She gave a muffled squeak when she saw how much of her lovely hair had been cut away. While her front hair seemed untouched, the hair round the back of her head had obviously been shaved away, and she now had a soft fuzz of regrowth which looked a more reddish brown than her usual hazelnut brown.

Charlotte and Ruth quickly consoled her. "It's regrowing well," said Charlotte.

"I'd cut it all short and keep it tidy under a cap until it's long enough to wear normally," Ruth said.

Melisande sighed.

The doctor scolded her. "Mrs Holyman, at least your hair will grow back and cover the scar. Often the hair round a scar does not regrow." But he did smile and compliment her on her returning health.

"When will Mrs Holyman be ready to ..."

"Miss Landry," the doctor snapped. "We need to see Mrs Holyman recovered enough to walk round her house and spend her afternoons in the fresh air sitting out on the verandah."

Melisande puzzled over the anxiety in Ruth's voice and on Charlotte's face. "What is it that troubles everyone so? Why may I not leave my room, or see visitors, and isn't there a housekeeper?"

"I will decide when you're ready, Mrs Holyman, and that is not until you have remembered what happened. Then you will be ready to answer some very important questions." He guided her back to her bed. "That's a sufficiency for now. Rest and remember. Other people need you to remember."

She did her best.

***

Melisande hadn't mentioned her idea about Mrs Miggs with Ruth present. It was a family matter to discuss first with her men, but she did mention to Mrs Miggs that they hadn't given up, and would continue making attempts to keep her in her home. "But if that fails we have another idea which might help. And I am certain that you know how angry your friends will be." She smiled at the disappointed woman. "I think that the Truman, Broughton, Ruddkin, Searle, Beattie, Gillespie and Gilmour families will find it difficult when they need help from, say, a carpenter, or builder, a cook or laundry maid."

"Nay, people need money," Mrs Miggs shook her head then cough-laughed. "But people might be a bit slow or lacking at their tasks."

Melisande was still laughing when she arrived at the dining table with the hot bread rolls. She shared the joke.

Ruth sighed. "Now I know why my father has problems with people working for him. I am grateful to you, Mr Holyman and Mr Allmark, for allowing me to escape to your farm. Otherwise my stepmother would have an excessive amount of household tasks for me."

That created more laughter and Melisande found herself smiling at Jeri. This was the first time since their parents had died that she and Jeri had laughed like this, family together.

She looked at Richard. He understood and smiled back. Perhaps New Zealand would become the place where she could make the home her whole being reached out for.

After Ruth had departed, reluctantly, for home Melisande gathered her men to walk to the kitchen to speak to Mrs Miggs.

"Don't let her think it's charity," she hissed in Jeri's ear. "And we only ask the same rent as she's been paying."

Jeri choked, stopped abruptly. "We need money, you'll need money …"

She pinched his arm. "We help each other. We need Daniel and Charlotte. Mrs Miggs might well move to live with them, another pair of hands to help. Port Chalmers is growing, so Ron says. We might sell the house for a better price in another year."

Jeri muttered but moved on.

"Explain that it's helping us because we don't trust Mr Truman to oversee renting the property out," she suggested to Richard as they entered the kitchen.

"Mrs Miggs," Jeri began, "I think we can help each other."

"Oh yes, Mr Allmark?"

"Do you want to remain in Port Chalmers even though you've been wrongly thrown out of your home? I expect you've been threatened too."

"Aye, I'm told there'll be no work for me."

"Do you think that's true?" Richard asked. "Will you really be banned by everyone."

"My friends won't heed. Them as fancies themselves will."

"You mean there'll be less work?" Melisande asked. "Will there be enough for you?"

"There's always housekeeping wanted." Mrs Miggs nodded her head, sure of it.

Jeri looked at Richard, who spoke for them. "We wondered if you would care to rent this house, for no more rent than you've been paying of course, because you'd be caring for the property for us."

"It would comfort me to know that you're looking after my little house," Melisande said. "And if your son settles out of town and you wish to live with him, well, we know you will have kept this house in excellent condition, ready for sale."

Mrs Miggs stared, wobbled, sat down in a rush. She eyed the Shacklock stove. "I could do a bit of baking on that stove. Sell a few pies and cakes. The same rent?"

"Richard nodded. "We'll put it in writing for you."

"I do thank you kindly," she managed to say, then pulled herself up, straightened her spine. "We'd best arrange moving in as you move out. Use the same people."

And so the great move began.

It was a good thing, Melisande thought, that they hadn't converted the crates and packing cases into a hen house or firewood. The trunks, stored in the wash house, had to be cleaned, the crates and cases brushed out, and everything wind dried and scoured before the packing could start.

Richard and Jeri rolled up their sleeves and were dreadfully underfoot. Fortunately, before Ruth vented her feelings in a way which would have horrified them, Mrs Miggs swept them out with her broom and a message enquiring about moving the horses. Ridden? On the train?

Dan's mates, Tommy, Paddy, Vic and Doug, worked hard moving and crating. Tommy and Paddy began to sneak Daniel and Charlotte's bits of furniture into the house and pack it for them. Jeri and Richard finally found work they could usefully do and began moving packed goods to the station and onto the hired removal carts.

Melisande worried about Charlotte, who hadn't been seen even in church. At the end of the week, when Ruth arrived, showing her the nearly finished dress, and asking for lace and buttons, Melisande enquired after Charlotte.

"Did you tell her to be compliant and obedient?"

Ruth laughed. "She's told her father she's of legal age, over twenty-one, able to decide for herself and he has no right to lock her in her room."

Melisande gaped, she knew she did. "Charlotte said that? Truly love is a powerful motivator. Was her father shocked?"

Ruth shrugged. "She also whispered a message for you. She wants to know what day you are leaving Port Chalmers. She wants you to know she is not going to be allowed to go to church."

"Oh," Melisande paused, thinking. "Ruth, is Charlotte's bedroom upstairs?"

"Yes." Ruth chuckled, went to the door to check where Mrs Miggs was, and returned to whisper. "This is all like some tuppenny romance isn't it? You expect Daniel to climb up and elope with her? Or hope Charlotte can climb down? There's no handy tree, alas!"

Melisande found herself chuckling too. "No, and I'll say no more. Only I'll ask if you think the vicar might be persuaded to change his mind and let me visit her?"

"No. You are a persona non grata. There's a suspicion that you might encourage Charlotte and, of course, about your foreign ways." She tutted and wagged a finger in Melisande's face.

"That is troubling. I wonder what we can do. You can't be caught with a note or message. You must be seen as one who thinks Charlotte is a fool."

Ruth pulled a face. "You know I do."

Melisande hesitated, not wanting to scold. Then she gave a quick laugh. "I have it," she declared, opening the cupboard to find her rolls of lace and button box. "You could be part of it, Ruth. Only if you take part you will be in such disgrace with your father. Would he forgive you after a time?" She offered Ruth a handful of delicate, twisted silver wire lover's-knot buttons she'd made. "There, these will look well with this lace, Ruth. Ruth?"

Ruth started. "Do you know, Lisa, I've never really been a happy part of my father's family. There was always an aunt or cousin for me when I was a child, but when father remarried, and my half-brothers were born, it was as if they were father's family and I merely a pair of hands to work and save them money."

"Oh, Ruth."

"I think, Lisa, that if whatever you are planning will stop my father running after me then I might take part."

"It will and it will cause quite a scandal. But it's the only thing to do and it might be fun." She began to explain and Ruth's face turned a dull red as she tried to swallow her shouts of laughter. She took herself and the dress off to Charlotte and promised not to tell her anything until Saturday.

"Yes, warn Charlotte that she mustn't look hopeful or seem cheerful, Ruth."

Melisande spent the time waiting for her men to come home consulting her lists, ticking off things done and circling things to do the following day. She hummed as she worked: 'O young Lochinvar is come out of the west … So faithful in love, and so dauntless in war, There never was knight like the young Lochinvar.' Ruth couldn't ride, but Daniel had promised a horse and trap so that was Ruth's transport settled. She had her sweet-natured Ranee to ride, and her men had their horses. An elopement it would be.

After dinner, in the kitchen again, for the dining furniture had been packed and sent on, she spoke to her men. "We must send a message to Daniel. Charlotte isn't going to be allowed to come to church as we'd thought."

Jeri looked blank. Richard remembered Daniel's plan. "Difficult," he said.

Melisande shook her head. "I'm thinking of 'Saint Agnes Eve' or perhaps 'So faithful in love … There never was knight like the young Lochinvar.' What do you think?"

It was Jeri who roared and laughed; Richard who uttered a shocked 'Oh no!"

"Oh yes, next Sunday morning, when the community is in church or chapel, we can swoop down on our horses, with Daniel and his horse and trap, invade the vicarage, and carry off Charlotte."

"Good Lord, Lisa …"

"We intended to leave on the Monday, let's go on Sunday. We can ride as far as Dunedin, stay for the wedding and then take the train on to Oamaru. That will save three or four days' riding to Oamaru and horses can rest, travelling on the cattle train with our household effects which arrives only an hour behind us."

Melisande gave her brother a mischievous glance. "It will be fun," she said, "and it's time we looked on this colonial life as seriously hard work, but we can make it a pleasure. If we can do that we might succeed."

Richard sighed. Jeri grinned. "I'm all for it," he said. "One in the eye for a stuffy, snobbish group of provincials."

"We won't be forgiven." Richard ruffled his hair and frowned. "What happens if Lisa … we … need to live here again? I thought Mr Truman laid out the problem well, all those strong feelings Charlotte's marriage will give rise to amongst people who would be our social circle."

Jeri scoffed. "Once I'm returned from England and our farm is running well, we'll have money, and money always attracts society."

Melisande walked to Richard, leaned against him. "Don't forget that we are gaining by helping Charlotte and Dan. We need them."

Richard dropped a kiss on the top of her head. "I give in, my sensible Nut Brown Maid, I'll book the horses on the train from Dunedin to Oamaru."

"Don't reserve seats for us here in Port Chalmers," Melisande patted his cheek, "We can book seats in Dunedin, that way we keep people wondering."

"How do we let Dan know, sister mine? He's without an address."

"I know how to get a message through to him. Tommy and Paddy are moving the last of his and our things tomorrow. They're taking Daniel's on the train through to Oamaru where he will be picking them up. I'll tape a letter onto a box for him and give them a message as well."

Richard looked around. "Bare rooms, boxes and crates. I'll be pleased to leave."

"It's a mess." Jeri kicked at a crate.

"And we'll be living in a mess for some time, brother dear. You're going to be moving a lot of furniture."

He groaned. "Let's hope we have as much hot water in the new place. I'll stoke the stove for baths, you two plan this Lochinvar escape for Miss Polson."

***

She had planned the elopement hadn't she? And caused a scandal in Port Chalmers. But Charlotte's happiness had been more important and bonded them all together against disapproving society. She had followed Advik's advice and surrounded herself by people who had skills she needed to make a success of this new life on their farm. And she believed her plan wasn't as selfish as her conscience sometimes scolded her about, for all of them gained from her plans. She must make sure her plan succeeded.

Chapter Twenty

Sunday came too quickly. Melisande had thought Tuesday to Sunday would give her enough time to get organised, until she realised that it was Saturday afternoon and she hadn't even arranged with Mrs Miggs about keys. She'd just have to leave the back door unlocked, so that when Mrs Miggs turned up on Monday to move in, she would find the keys on the hook in the kitchen where they always hung. Perhaps it was just as well she didn't speak to her, since Daniel's Lockinvar act would leave her furious. As for their part in it, well, she gave thanks that they would be miles away from her tongue and temper.

Ruth had been organised: she intended to slip out of church and cross the road to the vicarage when they arrived to swoop in and rescue Charlotte.

"It's madness, Lochinvar indeed," she kept telling Melisande, but she borrowed the book of Walter Scott's poems and read all about young Lochinvar.

"Yes, but it will work," Melisande kept reassuring herself on Sunday morning as she chivvied her co-conspirators. She knew Daniel had been warned, and he'd responded by organising a horse and trap, which Paddy would bring. They would all meet at the vicarage at fifteen minutes past ten, after the morning services had begun. Almost the entire Port Chalmers population would be in church or chapel, including the vicarage household. No one should be around to see. Charlotte, who was expected by her father to be reading her prayer book at home, following the service in that way, had been warned by Ruth on Saturday evening and threatened with disaster if she even looked cheerful or gave other optimistic signals to her family.

Melisande stood on the doorstep and dithered – had she considered all aspects of this escape? – whilst Jeri and Richard stood by the gate.

"You can't do any more, either the plan will succeed or it will fail," Richard said.

"Stop blethering," Jeri said, "and hurry along."

She heaved a great sigh, shrugged, and left all her problems on the doorstep. She slid an arm through each of her men's and marched off in step with them.

At the stables Paddy had all their horses saddled, a neat carriage mare and a good sized trap ready, and himself and Tommy, Sunday tidy, offering to help.

"Miss Polson's got a few bits to carry to the trap," Tommy explained as he pulled himself up to sit beside Paddy. Paddy clicked his tongue, the mare flicked an ear and walked on.

Melisande envisaged a quiet approach, a discreet entrance to the vicarage and a quick, quiet getaway. As they left, crossing the road and going downhill towards the church, Daniel appeared from the side street. He ran up the hill to meet them and leapt onto the driver's bench, taking the reins from Paddy. He wore a neat suit and a trilby, not his usual cap, a gentleman's appearance, and smart shoes – no boots today. His grin, like a fat slice of a new moon, split his face open from ear to ear.

"Let's rescue my bride," he said and set the mare into a trot.

Melisande could see him breaking into whoops and yells. She cast an anxious glance at Richard and Jeri, and found them grinning. No help there. She pressed her horse close to the trap. "Quietly, Dan, we must be discreet until Charlotte is secure."

"Aye, I know that, Mrs Holyman, but I've got the papers all signed and correct and a special service booked. There'll be a wedding in Dunedin and then she's mine. Worth a bit of a smile that, Mrs Holyman."

Tommy and Paddy had moon-slice grins to echo Dan's.

"We'll get you in, mate," Paddy said. "We'll be fetchin' a bit of a chest for the vicar, so I'll be charmin' the maid in the kitchen, and Tommy'll nick the bedroom key."

Dan eased the mare up the slope as Tommy winked at Melisande. "'S'a good thing we aren't in the vicar's flock," he added.

"Or the minister's," Paddy said, another grin splitting his face. "We're wicked 'Oirish paddies', them evil Romans d'ye see."

They both roared and slapped hands.

It was no use, the affair promised to be a ludicrous riot. Melisande allowed Ranee to trot and took comfort from Richard riding beside her.

The group clopped down the hill, an assemblage of determined people sure in their task. Melisande stopped worrying about luggage at the station, or catching the train. She decided that if she had to leave Port Chalmers this way, it meant a memorable leaving. She chuckled to herself.

Once they reached the flat stretch of road a couple of horse lengths from the vicarage Tommy and Paddy leapt down and strode briskly along the road and up to the gate. They propped it wide open and stepped up to the door. Paddy knocked and they were inside by the time Daniel had halted the mare beside the gate.

Melisande checked Ranee and looked across the road and up the side road towards the church. Where was Ruth? It would be dreadful if she'd been delayed by her father, or had to stay at home with tasks for her stepmother.

Before Melisande could imagine more disasters Ruth appeared, slipping out of the church and speeding down the side road. She crossed into their road and ran to join them.

"My bag's with Charlotte," she said, huffing between each word. "Quick, Daniel, let's fetch her. My father's suspicious."

They both went inside, dodging Paddy and Tommy, who carried out a padded lady's chair and a chest.

A muffled shrieking and thumping broke out.

Paddy grinned. "Oops-a-daisy, that's the maid discovered I locked 'er in."

"Lend us a hand, Mr Allmark, there's a little desk and two cases yet," Tommy called.

Jeri thrust his reins into Richard's hand and ran inside. Richard gave Melisande a look. "We'll wait."

Ruth dashed out with her case and bag, loaded them into the trap, and climbed aboard. "They're coming."

Paddy and Tommy arrived with the last bits and pieces, loaded the trap and scrambled into the back. Jeri dumped a bag into the cart and mounted his horse.

"My father," Ruth moaned, looking over to the church. Melisande and Richard glanced that way. "He's gone back inside. He's seen us, he'll be getting the vicar."

Daniel appeared, crossing the threshold the wrong way according to tradition, with Charlotte cradled in his arms, her face so bright with joy she was a little sun of lovelight. Melisande, content, her misgivings settled, beamed at Richard.

"Soft-hearted romantic," he whispered, then, "Shall we go?" as Daniel carefully settled Charlotte on the trap seat and took up the reins.

"We'd better," Ruth said, her voice rising in a panic. "They're coming."

"Giddy up," yelled Tommy, and Paddy whooped. The mare launched into a startled trot, all the other horses, upset, took off too and a triumphant cavalcade sped away.

Melisande had a snatched view of a group of people gawping, standing outside the church in an agitated cluster, watching them as they fled. She didn't know if she should laugh or feel remorse, but looking at Daniel, with his arm around Charlotte, and their faces radiant, happiness flowing between them, she thought perhaps gladness was in order. This journey to Dunedin she would never forget.

***

Ah, now she understood Charlotte's remarks. They'd set off with such hopes. She'd been full of hope because Jeri had listened, when Richard had made him, and agreed to Ruth coming to help her, to have Daniel and Charlotte in the manager's house, and to look for an experienced farming couple to help them all. She'd feared to be on her own with Jeri and Richard having no farming skills, the three of them creating a financial disaster which would see them retreating to their uncle in England without their capital. Jeri had splashed her money around, she was sure. Without knowing the particulars she knew her brother.

***

Dunedin and a wedding. Nothing like an Indian wedding of course, but Melisande determined to make it a joyous occasion unlike her own rushed service had been.

First there was a fuss at the railway station, getting the horses settled. Paddy and Tommy had intended to drive the mare and trap back to Port Chalmers that day, but decided to stay for the wedding, which meant another fuss as they tried to find a place to leave the mare. In the end the livestock manager at the station agreed to keep the mare and trap for them after they bribed him with the promise of a crate of beer.

Then they all walked into town. Ruth wanted to impress Melisande with the magnificence of Dunedin. "Look at the buildings, such grand stone work, clean wide streets, all done in just fifty years."

She certainly was impressed and her head swivelled from side to side like a clock pendulum, trying to see all that Ruth pointed out, but then Ruth had never seen Calcutta or New Delhi.

Melisande kicked Jeri on the ankle as she squeezed Richard's arm, preventing them from uttering disparaging or belittling remarks. After Calcutta Dunedin was a tiny place, but Ruth said the gold rush had brought Dunedin wealth and prosperity and one could see that in the city buildings and its generous layout. A university, a boys' college and a girls' school, a museum, art gallery and some beautiful churches, so many elegant stone buildings.

"It's a city to be proud of," she told Ruth, as they walked to the hotel. She meant it too.

Daniel had booked a room in the Grand Hotel. "A place for my Charlotte and you ladies to pretty yourselves for the wedding," he explained. "And we'll be staying for a couple of days to enjoy the city. I've reserved us a table for a wedding breakfast as well." He patted Charlotte's hand. "No one's going to say you didn't have a proper wedding, no rushed up affairs for you, my lady, a real celebration we'll have with witnesses." He grinned at Melisande, Richard and Jeri. "And my mates can tell it all around Port Chalmers when they get back."

Paddy and Tommy roared and would have thumped him on the back but for Charlotte's nearness. Melisande swallowed down the words she might have said about planning weddings to Richard and Jeri, because she saw regret in Richard's eyes. Jeri even gave a shrug and a rueful glance at her.

The Grand Hotel lived up to its name. It was held to be the most expensive and most luxurious hotel in the southern hemisphere, so Ruth whispered to Melisande, and she wondered where Daniel had earned enough money to pay for it all.

An extravagant stone building, with three floors above the ground floor and designed, so the receptionist informed them, by a famous Italian architect, it was indeed very grand. The building towered over the street with arched windows and a magnificent entrance into a huge reception area with gilt and plush and columns; it even had a lift. Tommy and Paddy goggled at the lift but pointed out the bar. Jeri approved of the luxurious atmosphere and wanted to book rooms for them too, but Melisande reminded him that they had the horses to settle and a train to catch. She privately thought that Charlotte would not want witnesses in the morning and that the newly-weds needed a little time to themselves.

Truth to tell she envied Charlotte, her Daniel really was an exceptionally thoughtful man, perhaps an inherited trait, for his father had that reputation too. That thought pricked a memory about what the curate had said about first love, and his wondering whether Richard would have loved her if she hadn't adored him and shown him she did.

As they waited in the reception area whilst Daniel signed and registered himself and Charlotte she turned to her husband, speaking softly. "Richard, was I your first and only love? Would you have loved me if I hadn't shown that I adore you?"

Richard looked puzzled, then smiled his special smile which always made her heart jump. "Well now, I think Ellen was my first love, she used to let me sneak sultanas and made me tiny loaves of malt bread and saved me supper if I was in disgrace. Then there was my sisters' governess, an adorable French mademoiselle …"

Melisande pinched his arm and he laughed. "Be serious," she commanded.

"I watched you grow from fifteen to eighteen and saw the self-conscious girl become a self-aware woman, someone I cared for. I admired your artistic talents, saw you magic jewellery out of silver wire, and manage your parent's daily affairs for them. Yet if you hadn't shown me how special you thought I was I might not have been as quick to love you, because you were Jeri's sister and I worried that loving you might affect my deep friendship with him."

Melisande frowned.

Richard grinned. "But I couldn't help falling in love, my love, and although it's pleasant to have good friends, I can manage without friends, but I can't manage without you. I acknowledge that you are my first, one and only love." He sneaked his arm round her waist and snuggled her close. "In fact, I adore you," he whispered in her ear.

"Will you two behave in public, please," Jeri hissed at them.

Ruth stared, flushed. "We'll go and help Charlotte, shall we?" she asked, turning towards the stairway.

Melisande squeezed Richard's hand, then hurried after her and they both caught Charlotte and swept her off up the stairs behind the young porter carrying her case. The men took Daniel into the bar.

The first-floor bedroom made Ruth gasp. "It's got its own bathroom," she cried, dashing in to examine the porcelain fitments and try a tap.

Melisande liked the occasional table and chairs set in the bay window. Charlotte sat on the edge of the bed and gazed round at the pictures, mirrors and tasteful floral wallpaper, and gave a contented delighted sigh. Ruth emerged from the bathroom and peered at herself in the looking glass.

Charlotte stood up. "I am so proud of my Daniel, he's arranged everything perfectly." She opened her case and took out a beautifully embroidered blouse with pin tucks and a frilled collar and sea-green tailored skirt and jacket. "There, my wedding outfit, with extravagant hat. And I've brought the dress you made me, Ruth, the shawl you gave me, Lisa, I'll be elegant enough for the Grand Hotel at dinner tonight."

"Charming," Melisande said, struggling out of her riding habit and into a tailored near-black purple skirt with its matching jacket and frivolous hat. "You'll be a beautiful bride."

"Thank you," said Charlotte, looking at Melisande, "for not wearing full mourning at my wedding." She turned round so that Melisande could button her blouse.

Ruth was struggling into a white blouse with lace inserts. She'd added a half veil and a cockade of feathers to her ordinary hat. "One day," she said, shaking out the jacket and skirt she'd worn on the journey, "I'll have money enough for a whole wardrobe of clothes. Meanwhile, help me dust down my skirt, Lisa please, and tug my jacket straight."

They aided each other, pinched cheeks and rubbed lips, dusted noses, and decided they were fit for a wedding.

Charlotte hugged Melisande. "It's all thanks to you," and she kissed her on the cheek. "I'm so happy. I pray my father will forgive me and my sisters will visit, but I have you two dear friends and a good house and dearest Daniel. We will prosper." She smiled at them both, drew herself up, lifted her head. "I feel like a queen. Let's go to my wedding."

They tripped downstairs and found Paddy handing out buttonholes to the gentlemen. Daniel offered a posy and a tender smile to Charlotte. Other guests in the hotel lobby looked, began to guess, and smiled.

"Do you think," Richard whispered as he took Melisande's arm, "they've realised we're a wedding party?"

Jeri offered Ruth his arm. "It's an obvious conclusion to draw. We are somewhat conspicuous. Come, the carriages await." He whisked them out of the entrance, sweeping Daniel and Charlotte with them. Paddy and Tommy, grinning, brought up the rear.

Two hansom carriages took them to the Court House, another large edifice designed to impress. Blocks of cream stone set around doors and windows and in bands across the building brightened the grey-brown masonry. More cream stone in the turrets and finials, and gothic-style carvings made Melisande think the building had a fairy tale castle appearance. It was impressive in its own New Zealand way.

Once inside their party was escorted to a side room where a portly full-bearded gentleman waited for them. Daniel led Charlotte forward and the simple service began with their names and finished with a cordial wish for a happy future. Daniel had wedding rings for them both, made from gold he'd prospected. He slipped Charlotte's ring onto her trembling hand, then she nervously slid his larger one onto his finger with both hands.

Perhaps awed by the rather intimidating interior, Paddy and Tommy waited to cheer until they stood on the pavement outside. Daniel refused to allow them to kiss the bride.

"That's my privilege, find your own lasses." However, he didn't embrace Charlotte in the street, but patted her hand and tucked it under his arm. "My lady expects a little decorum, having been taught how not to behave in public places," he said. The look he gave Charlotte must have made her heart rejoice; the look she gave him in return must surely have made him the happiest man in Dunedin.

Melisande believed it did, sighed, and glanced at Richard. "Do you remember our wedding night," she whispered, and saw him grin.

Jeri had escorted Ruth into the carriage, Melisande and Richard stepped up and made Paddy and Tommy crowd in with them. "Give the bride and groom a few private moments," Melisande said.

The wedding breakfast was a generous spread of good food and Jeri and Richard bought two bottles of champagne for the toasts. Tommy and Paddy called it fizzy pop, not a real drink. Ruth pulled a face, Jeri declared it not a bad vintage, but Daniel and Charlotte sipped and swallowed without noticing.

Richard stood. "I ask the company to raise their glasses and wish long life, health and happiness to Charlotte and Daniel."

"To Charlotte and Daniel," returned a chorus, and the maître d' trotted over to wish them well and offer an elaborate dessert of meringue, fruit and cream as a gift from the management.

They finished the champagne in a series of toasts to the success of the farming venture, their new lives, their new manager and their future together.

Ruth and Melisande slipped away to change and collect their bags. They returned to find Daniel promising to be at the farm in three days.

"Tommy, Paddy, Vic and Doug will come to help with the building when that last house is done. Mr Hammond's not got ought else to build 'til he sells them houses and it's getting near to summer and hay time," he said. "We'll need barns for storage."

"And we'll be needin' a bit o' work," Tommy added.

Melisande and Ruth embraced Charlotte and farewelled the men. Richard and Jeri shook hands all round and they left the Grand Hotel with Jeri muttering regrets for not staying there.

"To the station and do stop grumbling, Jeri dear." Melisande tucked her hand through Ruth's arm and let her men follow behind them.

***

Melisande watched the daylight fade, allowed Ruth to prepare her for the night and thought. Now why had the farm become the nightmare which had ended with her attack? She shied away from unpicking these last memories because she must take care. Her friends had warned her as much as they dared with the doctors Allinson honour bound to hear and report to the police.

She knew that everything she hoped for, all her plotting to achieve a comfortable home like they had had in India, was at risk. Her cherished plan, to form a circle of mutual support, of helpers helping each other, would collapse if she blurted out any of her memories without context. She must remember in silence and stitch them together in the best way for them all. Here, she knew, was a case where the best for one was indeed the best for all. Charlotte and Daniel had a good start to their married life, a home, work, friendship and the chance to achieve Daniel's ambition. Ruth had her friends, freedom and a possible future when she finished her studies. She'd riffle through those memories which were tied up with Richard's traitorous action, Jeri's totally selfishness and … and … someone else.

She needed to regain her strength and walk through this house unaided, look in every room, see everything, so that she could find her memories, control that fear, and save them all, and one in particular. There were people here she should know, people not allowed to come near her. Why? She must make connections, important connections which affected everyone, she mustn't guess, she mustn't speak until she knew what she had to say, even if it meant stitching the pieces together in a new pattern.

So what did she remember about the farm? She walked round her bedroom. Would the doctor allow her to walk round other rooms under his guidance? She wasn't certain she could walk that far yet. Perhaps a room at a time? She would ask when he woke her to give her the last of her medicine.

She woke before the good doctor. Dr Allinson senior reclined comfortably in a large armchair she did not recognise. Seated close to the fire the elderly man had dozed in its warmth. The poor man had been talking with her until well after midnight. He'd thought her fit now to have memory prompts and had given her a list of things she might remember because they were events important to most people: Christmas, birthdays, Easter in the church, any parties or picnics, singing in the choir? What had her experience of a sunny December been like? That one had made her laugh because her part of India had sunny Decembers, but he was from Scotland where December was a cold winter month. Perhaps a cough would wake him? She needed to tell him she had holes, memories which just would not clarify in her head until she'd walked through the rooms in this house. She'd had such a shock when she'd learned the date. She knew that she and her men had sailed into Port Chalmers in September 1898, but she couldn't remember their first Christmas. It must have been in their own cottage but she didn't remember it although Charlotte had mentioned a dance and a party.

She struggled to remember Richard's birthday, with the certainty that they would have had a splendid dinner. How did they celebrate Jeri's coming of age? The official party was to be in England, their uncle had arranged it, but what did they do for him that first November in Port Chalmers? It pained her that she couldn't remember. And she reckoned the days incorrectly between Richard and Jeri coming home full of the farm, their offer, it being accepted, and the legal details settled before the move out to the farm. She remembered a swift event, but the dates didn't match. It had been a much slower affair. Did it matter, these holes? Did it mean she'd never retrieve all her memories, and what if she'd lost some really important memory? She did so want to talk to the doctor about walking round the house, but he looked comfortable and rested; she'd feel badly if she woke him now. He'd been a solace and companion during her nightmares, more a father figure than the watcher and guard she knew him to be.

Chapter Twenty-One

The doctor had agreed. Melisande woke early and greeted Ruth with a safe memory, eager for her walk.

"I know what my men did." This morning felt good, one where Melisande woke without a dull ache between her eyebrows, and only the prickly feeling of hair regrowing at the back of her skull. Ruth, carrying a can of hot water, with towels over her arm and a pot of soothing cream balancing on top, plopped everything on the floor, helped her sit up and took her hand.

"That's good ... er ... and what was it?"

Melisande squeezed Ruth's fingers. It still felt a feeble effort but better than before. "You were furious." She managed a gentle laugh.

Ruth squeezed back. "I still am. Charlotte will be in later to take you out for a gentle stroll. The doctor allows it and will accompany you."

Melisande smiled and vowed to herself to keep her lips sealed on any memories the walk provoked until she knew she had them all set in a way which would harm no one she cared about.

***

The Oamaru railway station impressed not. A new station was under construction elsewhere – 'Be finished in the New Year,' the stationmaster told them as he tried to move them along the platform. This gave the station at the end of Wansbeck Street an air of not being all there. Richard and Jeri looked for a porter and a trolley, and information about the arrival and care of their horses.

Melisande, tired and dusty, brushed down her skirt and looked at Ruth. "Are you familiar with Oamaru? A cup of tea would be …"

"Life saving nectar," Ruth responded as they stepped aside and watched their bags, cases and boxes piling up.

"Shall we organise transport for ourselves, Ruth, whilst the men sort out everything else?" Melisande hunted in her sensible leather satchel for the notebook in which she had addresses and necessary information.

Richard and Jeri left the guard's wagon. "Another hour to organise," Richard called as they joined Melisande and Ruth. "We'll stroll along to the hotel with you and leave you ladies enjoying refreshments whilst we poor thirsty men must return and send our goods on their way."

"Knowing you, I'm sure there'll be a beer along the way. How many public houses did you tell me Oamaru has?" Melisande pretended to scold as she took Richard's arm. Jeri escorted Ruth with a flourish and made a rapid turn to spin them all round to face away from the station.

"I want to see your expressions when we turn round the corner into town," Jeri chuckled. "They use a special local material for the major buildings."

"Oh," Ruth smiled. "I know what you mean. Whitestone," she explained to Melisande. "They're very particular about it."

Before Melisande could ask what whitestone actually was, Jeri and Richard marched them smartly left from Wansbeck Street into Thames Street.

"Wait 'til you see what they've done with it," Jeri said, as they turned the corner. Melisande halted and stood stock-still in amazement.

Thames Street's road was not yet sealed and tarmacadammed, so it was rutted and pitted and dusty, but it was broad, spacious and lined with impressive stone buildings, the stone a bright white. No, not merely impressive or grandiose, such as would be seen in a capital city like New Dehli or London. On the right of the street were – "Good gracious, are we in Greece?" she asked, staring at the enormous columns and pedestals, the huge entrance doors and all the intricate details she associated with the classical ancient Greek buildings.

Richard grinned at her. "That's only a bank. We'll walk you down the street, then you can see all the buildings. They've used the stone everywhere."

"Civic pride," muttered Ruth as they walked, "trying to put Dunedin to shame."

Jeri laughed at her. "Vainglorious you mean? Well why not show some pride in your achievements. It's only some fifty years isn't it since this town was planned and built? I say good for them in making such a strong emphasis on how civilised they are." He pointed across the broad roadway. "See there's an Athenaeum, these people have time to spend on literary and scientific studies. And it's the Mechanics' Institute as well, even the Courthouse is designed on an Athenean scale." He grinned at her.

Ruth gave in with a reluctant, "I suppose so, but I'll always be a Dunedin girl deep inside."

"To the hotel, ladies, we'll explore the town tomorrow and the next day for we must see to those matters of business, in particular banking and … and other things," Jeri finished with a quirked eyebrow in Richard's direction.

Melisande gave him a Look, at which he laughed and Richard bustled her along the pavement so that she couldn't argue in public, and whisked her into the Criterion Hotel on the corner of the next crossroads.

"Trust Jeri to choose the most expensive hotel," she whispered, for indeed the large whitestone building made a four-square declaration of solidity and status.

Richard patted her arm. "It's the last time he'll be able to for a while so let him enjoy being the expansive gentleman. He'll soon learn that the farm will have to eat money before we can spend money."

After a stodgy luncheon in the hotel restaurant, a digestive-easing stroll became necessary. Thames Street had been quiet before lunch, just a couple of carts, a pony trap and a few busy people. Now there was an almost military air. Part of a military band, just a drummer, a bugle boy and two pipers, wandered down the middle of the road. Two officers trotted by, followed by a trooper leading a string of three horses.

A group of small boys tagged after them cheering and calling, and Melisande saw Jeri's face light up with eager excitement as he turned to look after the officers.

Richard had seen his expression too, shook his head at Melisande, and turned Jeri back to face them.

"We have a farm to organise," he warned Jeri. "Set up our future before you even think of playing soldiers. Let's find the Oamaru Borough Council Chambers and sort out rates and taxes." He handed Melisande a pamphlet. "Would you and Miss Landry care to stroll the street following this guide? The hotel manager handed me it 'especially for your edification.'"

Ruth pulled a face. Melisande sighed. "Very well," she said, tucking her hand under Ruth's elbow and beginning to read aloud from the pamphlet.

"'Thames Street is a notable thoroughfare, flanked on the east side by banks and retail business places and shops. On the western side are the Corporation offices, the post office, the Athenæum, gaol, police station, courthouse, offices of the Waitaki County Council, and business premises and residences.' Shall we explore, my dear friend?"

They linked arms and strolled off laughing at the fulsome language the writer of the guide used to compose his masterpiece.

***

And so they did explore and found the shops satisfactory. It was a pleasant little town, Oamaru, with a comfortable air of prosperity. Melisande thought she could grow to like it and wished she was well enough to ride Ranee and go shopping.

She sighed and let Ruth help her stand. She could almost wash by herself now, and then she had her walking exercise to do. The doctor granted her permission to walk from her room to nearby rooms. Today she was to walk to the drawing room. If the late summer weather had settled into a calm warm day she could even go onto the verandah and sit in the rocking chair. Summer nearly over already, she'd missed most of winter and all of spring this year, thanks to that blow to her head.

Charlotte hovered, Ruth helped and Melisande made a shuffling progress along the hallway to the drawing room. The scents enveloped her in a familiar fuggy embrace, roses and honeysuckle, warm grass and soil, and Indian cedar wood. Arranged round the fireplace were her two comfortable chairs, an Indian rug covered the floor, her chest and piano lined the far wall. Pictures from home — India she meant, she chided herself for she really must start calling New Zealand home — hung on the opposite wall and her favourite heavy silk curtains framed the French windows.

"Oh," she cried, for standing in the open French windows were two women. She blinked and memory came in a rush. "Mrs Lightfoot!" Mrs Lightfoot, along with her husband and sons, was part of the farm, but Mrs Miggs? "When did you arrive, Mrs Miggs? Please say you've forgiven Daniel and Charlotte."

Both Doctors Allinson stood watching her. Young Doctor Allinson glared at the women and held up a warning hand. "You may not speak." Both women gave her looks which could only be described as entreating as they gazed at her hopefully.

Did that mean herself or the women? "Who? Why?"

"Good, no more." said Doctor Allinson senior, and dismissed the women before catching Melisande's arm and guiding her to a chair. "There are people waiting to speak to you but only when you can tell us what happened that night."

But Melisande shuddered. She couldn't think about that night yet, not until all the memories of what led up to the attack were filed neatly in a safe order, but she would remember the farm.

***

The farm, oh, the farm. They made a cavalcade entrance trotting down the drive, the hired drivers with their big hairy Clydesdale workhorses pulling the loaded wagons in the rear, Ruth, driving the new pony trap in front of them, and Jeri leading the way on his bright chestnut gelding. Melisande craned her neck to see the house and let Ranee trot to catch up with Richard, who rode on ahead to keep Jeri company. The long driveway had been flattened, smoothed and gravelled; it was in a better condition than the road from Oamaru but who would fill in the ruts and dips when weather scoured it? So much work ahead and her men oblivious.

Down the gentle slope, round a corner and there – a tidy wooden villa with a small lawn and flower beds in front, a vegetable garden tucked away on the right-hand side. The paintwork looked fresh, the verandah rails shining white. It might be as pleasant a home as her Port Chalmers cottage had been. Melisande smiled.

"Richard, Jeri, I thought you told me our house was a large one?"

"That," said Jeri, "is the manager's place."

Ruth, guiding the pony and trap to the right of Melisande, exhaled an envious sigh. "Lucky Charlotte, to have this as her first home. No wonder Daniel agreed to be manager. There's even a planted veggie garden."

"Wait 'til you see our place." Jeri grinned as they rounded the sharp bend. There, standing in a wide circle of gravel, with hedged lawns to each side, a rose garden with a fountain apiece, was a long rectangular building, wood on top of the bright Oamaru whitestone base. One third of the house was made of the local limestone, a brilliant white, then the walls up to the roof were wooden, interlocking tongue and groove planking painted a sandy brown, a pleasing contrast to the white stone. An ornate verandah ran the full length of the building, rising to a peak over the front doorway to make an elaborate portico. The columns supporting the verandah were as decorative as the iron filigree trimming the roof. Either side of the massive wooden front doors were four pairs of French windows, evenly spaced, blank of glass as the blinds were drawn. The pitch of the corrugated iron roof, lower than on a town villa, plus the blind windows, gave the house a solemn appearance. Chocolate-brown, bright-red and a soft dark-green paint had been used to highlight all the window frames, sills and corbels beneath. It did look impressive, but a stately dowager of a house rather than a friendly home. Melisande foresaw much work to make it the home she so wanted.

"This is only the front," Jeri explained. "There are two wings. The building is like a capital E without the middle stroke. What do you think?"

Melisande stared, then stared some more and gave him a Look. Fortunately, Richard laughed, and then Jeri saw the funny side too.

"How are we going to live here?" Melisande shook her fist at her men. "Not enough furniture, no curtains or carpet. How am I to keep this great place clean without an army of servants. How do we stay warm? What about water?"

"I'll send you good furniture and stuff from England," Jeri promised.

Melisande made an exasperated noise.

Richard leaned over, caught her hand. "We can live in one wing and open the rooms when we have the furniture and fittings." He smiled, coaxing her to smile back. "There are three enormous water tanks catching rain water plus a well. We have three bathrooms and look at all the chimneys, Cape Cod-style, in the centre of the house. We'll be warm, and I knew you'd like the place because there are interior shutters on most of the windows too."

Ruth, who had driven the trap round to the back of the house in search of stables, came scampering back, laughing. "Come and see, Lisa, and then I promise to help you murder these men of yours."

***

It was panic and chaos for three weeks, Melisande smiled to herself. She felt justified in her insistence that helping Ruth, Charlotte and Daniel would help Richard and Jeri, and herself, of course. So it did, but it wasn't until the

Lightfoots became part of her equation for colonial survival that their lives as farmers truly began. She remembered that quite clearly.

Oh, and wasn't Josephine Lightfoot peeved when first they met. Such a pet she was in, when she tromped onto the verandah and banged on the front doors.

Melisande rested against the chair cushions and remembered. How Mrs Lightfoot had come huffing, puffing like a steam engine boiler about to explode, and all ruffled up about hay. And then she'd seen the look on Jeri's face, mirrored on Richard's as they finally understood exactly what they'd done. She smiled to herself, as she'd been so self-restrained, noble even, and hadn't pointed out that she had warned them. Wasn't there an old saying about ignorance being blissful, until one discovered the necessity of knowledge? My goodness they'd been ignorant, but she mustn't be smug or complacent, for she'd been cocooned in ignorance too. Thank the Lord for Mrs Miggs for her education, and the Lightfoots for theirs.

***

"Hay, Mrs Lightfoot?"

"Aye, what do you reckon on it? All that stuff stored in your barns."

Melisande and Ruth had just finished helping in Charlotte's kitchen and were about to begin on Melisande's. They'd worked out a daily plan to see that both houses had a stock pot on the go, some slow-cooking meat on the back of the stove, and some bread always set, some rising and some cooking so that they could get on with unpacking, feeding all the men, and trying to place Melisande's vegetable garden in the most productive site. She couldn't have managed without her friends.

"What's happening?" Melisande dusted off her hands on her apron and hurried to see what the fuss was about. Ruth and Charlotte followed.

A red-faced, dumpy woman had backed Richard and Jeri against the front door frame. "What about that hay in yon barn? My man made it an' stored it. Did you think the wee folk magicked it for ye?"

She leaned towards Richard, chin raised, the angry red patches flaring brighter on her cheeks, then turned to Jeri and glared. "Well?"

Melisande's hand flew to her mouth. She glanced sideways at Ruth and Charlotte. Their expressions nearly undid her. Ruth, choking back laughter, caught Charlotte's shocked face and smothered her laughter into a sort of cough. Melisande tried to still her own mirth but the look on Jeri's face. Oh dear, what should she do?

Charlotte knew what to do. She smiled at the woman, bravely ignored Richard and Jeri, and stretched out her hand.

"That's her upbringing," Ruth hissed into Melisande's ear. "Her upbringing as a vicar's daughter."

The woman's head darted round, and she glared at the three of them. "Don't you reckon on what's been happening either? House pretty clean was it? Where's my pay then, and what about our hay?"

Charlotte reached out tentatively and took the woman's arm. "Please come in and explain to us over a cup of tea, Mrs …? We don't know anything about money or the hay." She looked at Richard and Jeri.

Melisande, much impressed, nodded at her husband, grasped his elbow, tugged him towards her and flashed a warning at Jeri. "Oh, please do come in and explain," she said. "We really don't know why you're upset."

Ruth spun round and hurried off to see to the kettle. Jeri gestured the women to go inside. Richard escorted Melisande, murmuring "What in God's good earth?" in her ear.

The angry woman stamped inside, darting glances about at them all and the interior. They escorted her through the entrance hall, down the hallway past the enormous dining room, still empty, and into the other large room next door. There were only four enormous rooms along the front of the house and the other two were bedrooms with dressing rooms and baths. This room Melisande had turned into their main living room because she hoped it would be warm enough with a fireplace at either end.

Jeri became the genial host. "Do please sit down Mrs …? And excuse our unprepared state for we are still settling in."

"Lightfoot, I'm Mrs Lightfoot, as if you didn't know."

Melisande hastened out to help Ruth and met her carrying a laden tray. "You take that," Ruth said, thrusting it into her arms. "I'll get the scones. It's a good thing we've been baking for the men's smcko."

Melisande set out the tea things and Charlotte took over arranging the cups and saucers as their angry visitor berated Richard, who was struggling to keep Jeri silent with a firm grip on his arm.

"Please do sit down, Mrs Lightfoot, and would you like tea? We've hot buttered scones if one would please you." Melisande took a seat in the chair opposite the woman. "Can you explain about the hay?"

Mrs Lightfoot broke out in a series of hisses and splutterings. "Who d'ye think's been managing this place until it sold to you? Who's been farming here for you?"

Melisande looked at her men, as did Ruth and Charlotte. Jeri and Richard exchanged glances, eyebrows raised. Richard nodded at Jeri who spoke first.

"The land agent told us the owner had a local man in charge when he departed for England. We understood that this local man had been paid by the former owner to continue taking care of the farm." Jeri at his lordly best, avoiding any trace of blame coming his way.

Melisande sighed. 'Trust Jeri,' she thought and flicked a glance at her husband, who quirked an eyebrow and smoothly took over speaking to Mrs Lightfoot. Melisande poured cups of tea, Ruth handed round milk and sugar, Charlotte offered a plate, napkin and hot buttered scone to each person. Mrs Lightfoot almost refused.

"Are you telling us that this local man hired your husband to make our hay and has not paid you?" Richard asked politely, and in a gentler tone than Jeri's.

"We paid an agreed fee," Jeri said, anxious to avoid more problems, "to cover any extra expenses. The agent should have dealt with all this."

"Oh, you did, did ye, and who took yer money? Because it were meant for my man."

"Then why," exploded Jeri, "isn't your man here to say so? We've done everything correctly, the agent has your money. Why haven't you spoken to him?"

Mrs Lightfoot's chin rose, her considerable bosom lifted and she all but levitated off the chair. "My man is there right now, but we know Mister Sutton's nasty little tricks. You'll have to fix 'im."

Richard murmured to Jeri, then spoke. "Is it that you want Mr Allmark and me to speak to this Sutton character for you?"

Mrs Lightfoot flashed a shifty sideways glance at them so swiftly that Melisande only saw it because she was facing the woman. She doubted her men had caught it. "Yes," a flat answer, with another sideways glance.

Richard smiled at Jeri, who nodded his head. "We have everything in writing. Mrs Lightfoot. It's all set down, what to pay a man to care for the farm, what to pay a hay making team, we took advice on fair payments."

"That Sutton man just took your money and let the farm go. He paid one of his pals to keep the house paddocks tidy but the rest of the farm were left until my man ran stock on it."

"New chums," sighed Melisande, "and new chum tricks."

Mrs Lightfoot cocked her head. "Aye, well, you come out, well-heeled youngsters, in mourning, bound to be wi'out much nouse." She suddenly grinned, like a boy. "You've truly had it all writ and signed for?" Jeri nodded. "That'll learn that cheat Sutton, and his pal who's claimed our hay money."

Charlotte cleared her throat. "If I may Mr Holyman, Mr Allmark?" Jeri nodded, Richard waved his hand. "I think Mrs Lightfoot's husband might have spoken to mine. He's actually been farming this land without official permission because …"

"Aye, well, maybe he shouldna …" Mrs Lightfoot interrupted, pinking up with cross embarrassment this time, and a touch of guilt. "He's a good man, a good farmer and he dinna want to see this farm go to the bad." She drank her tea in one go. "He were manager here for t'old gaffer, him that stayed in England." She grinned again. "Right soft he were on his lady, made everything of the best an' as she'd a liked it, then she refused to come so he went to persuade her and niver came here again."

Charlotte smiled at Melisande and Ruth. "Mr Miggs, Daniel," she said with a smile and touch of a blush, "he thought, seeing that Mr Lightfoot knew the farm, that perhaps Mr Allmark and Mr Holyman would care to offer him employment to assist Daniel managing."

Mrs Lightfoot positively shone with eager delight. "And you young ladies will be needing a hand now, won't you? My oldest son'll work with his da but my young one, fine boy, can dig out a patch of soil and put in your veggies. There's a right good place behind the house near the kitchens and the poultry yards. I can help set that up. Have you got your chooks sorted and bought sheep 'n' cattle beasts yet?"

Richard and Jeri frowned at each other. "I think,' Jeri began, "we'd better organise a meeting between Mr Lightfoot, Mr Miggs – Daniel - and ourselves. We need a plan, but tomorrow as we are riding to town we'll see our agent and this Sutton fellow. Then in the evening, if Mr Lightfoot would care to walk us round the farm and buildings we can see how to arrange everything with him."

Mrs Lightfoot finished her scone in two bites and jumped up. "Let's see how you're managing the kitchen," she said to Melisande, "and I'll show you the best place for growing them veggies and we can look out about your poultry yards." She seized the tray and trotted out of the room. Ruth, laughing, followed her.

Charlotte paused at the door, "I'll take the men's scones and tea, and I'll speak to Daniel about Mr Lightfoot." She went without waiting for a reply.

Melisande eyed her men. "What a woman, I can see it'll be impossible to keep her out of the kitchen." She arranged her features into a scowl. "And would going into town have anything to do with a muster and parade?"

Jeri didn't even blush. "They need officers with good horses and some experience. We've lived in India and travelled. We're valuable."

"You are to go to England, our uncle commands it. Richard is needed here. This African war is not a game, an adventure. It's war. Oh, please think of us all Jeri, please think not just of adventures for yourself, but of this farm and all it needs."

Jeri shrugged. "Our uncle would want me to fight for Queen and country. He doesn't mind, rather me than his heir, I suppose." He grinned. "You can't stop me, little sister." He turned on his heel and departed.

Melisande caught her husband's arm as he turned to follow.

"Richard, please, you can't go to South Arica, you can't leave now. We've so much to do, setting up this farm, you establishing your horses and learning what you need to be able to farm and succeed. I've played my part, learned to be a colonial housewife who can cook and clean and keep house. You must stay." She lifted his hand to her cheek, then kissed it. "And I don't want you to go, to be fighting and killing people."

"Oh Lisa, my love, I know. I'd rather stay but someone has to look after Jeri." Richard caught hold of her hands, pulling her to him. "Lisa, my own dear one, I truly would prefer to stay with you, but without me there to restrain his impulses and watch out for him you know your brother will do something rash." He slid an arm round her waist, brushed his head gently against the top of hers. "He is my brother – by law and by friendship - I promise to keep him safe and to return him here as soon as we've shown these Afrikaners who is boss." He kissed her. "Now go and subdue that terrible woman and make her know you are the mistress here."

***

And so they did. She remembered that now. Oh, and how cross she was. "And you laughed at me, Ruth, and scolded me for not wanting my men to be prepared to fight for Queen and country."

Ruth squeezed her hand. "I changed my mind, didn't I?"

Melisande nodded and kept her words unspoken, safe in her head. But most young men thought it a glorious thing to do, a great adventure to be a soldier for the Queen and show those Boers who was boss.

She was ready to face the last memories. She'd wait until Doctor Allinson senior took his rest – he still sat with her most nights, allowing Charlotte to be home with Daniel for an evening meal, and letting Ruth retire around ten each night. Then she'd speak to him, tell him she knew what happened, but first she'd speak to her friends.

"I think I'm as well as I'll ever be as an invalid. If I am to recover fully I need to try to be mistress of my home again. Can you arrange a meeting with both doctors Allinson and that noisy policeman, Sergeant Webster, who kept yelling at me and tried to shake me until you and Daniel prevented him, Charlotte. He will want to know who did what that dreadful night."

Charlotte paled and nodded.

"I think I have most of it now. There are patches and gaps in time, I'm so frustrated as I can't get days and weeks in their proper order. So much still seems unreal and doesn't match what you say." She paused, thinking of the times during the past week when Doctor Allinson allowed her to play 'Do you remember?' with Ruth and Charlotte, only to discover that she had different memories. Sometimes they'd corrected her remembrance of times or months. She massaged her temples, sighed and prayed for the strength to say the right words and ease the tension she felt building around her. "I think a walk outside and through the kitchen is just what I need at the moment. We can steal Mrs Miggs's shortbread and see what's cooking."

Melisande looked at her friends, and they looked at her. She dared not warn them that she knew to guard every word she spoke to the doctors and the police. Even if her memories were faulty there was one extra death to account for and she had a feeling, because her friends were afraid, that she must remember slowly who was where and doing what that dreadful night.

"I'd like the meeting in two days' time in the afternoon." She noted Ruth's clenched fingers and Charlotte's trembling hands, which she quickly hid behind her back.

"Charlotte, you mustn't worry any more, it's not good for you to do so in your state." She smiled as she glanced at Charlotte's gently swelling belly. "Is that why Mrs Miggs forgave you both?"

Ruth managed a chuckle. "Oh, she came in a rush, ostensibly to help you, Lisa. Daniel set her up in the end of the east wing. She has a tiny apartment of three servants' rooms and keeps house for you. Mrs Lightfoot does the same for Charlotte and both of them have driven me mad with their pickling, preserving and baking in your kitchens every afternoon and evening."

Charlotte's lips wavered into a slight smile as she absently stroked her stomach. "My mother-in-law is not allowed to stay with us until Daniel is satisfied she will be kind to me. She and Mrs Lightfoot have been in competition to see who could cook and manage a house the best. The men have been wonderfully fed."

Ruth gave a little shudder. "But we have been treading on eggshells to avoid praising one above or in front of the other."

"Are Tommy, Paddy, Vic and Doug and his young brother, Vince, wasn't it? Are they here now?"

Ruth shook her head. "They come and go as work suits them, though Vince is often wanted at home. They all helped with the harvest, but as they were not here when you were attacked the Sergeant did not require them. He's already taken statements from them." She clutched Melisande's hand. "Oh do tell all and clear up the mess your attack has left us all floundering in."

"Hush, Ruth, no matter what we've had to bear, our worries and suspicions and mistrust about who …" Charlotte's voice tailed away. "At least we have not been ill nor suffered the pain and permanent damage Lisa has. She has her life but her vision and hearing will never be as they were." She stroked her stomach again. "I still have my child. She lost hers."

Always loss, Melisande gritted her teeth, bit back words. She'd understood from early on in her recovery that her injuries meant the loss of the child which she'd only just become aware she carried. Doctor Allinson reassured her that she would be able to have more children, but in her heart she felt its death to be murder. It was hard to forgive her attacker.

"Enough, Charlotte. Let's have this meeting, and with all involved, with the Lightfoots, and Daniel, present.

"Sergeant Webster will insist on it." Ruth reached out and gently eased Melisande to her feet. "Let's take that walk."

Melisande, walking carefully with a watchful friend at either hand, began to understand what she must do to protect all she had achieved in her home. She must be sure to keep everyone safe.

Chapter Twenty-Two

They held the meeting in the drawing room at noon. Melisande resolved to be mistress of her home and the lady of the house. She intended to command the meeting, as if she were an actress giving a heroine's performance. She borrowed some of her brother's assumption of superiority, tempered with some of her husband's reasonableness. She dressed for the part, insisted on having her hair carefully arranged and the back of her head hidden under a pretty cap. Doctor Allinson left the bedroom so that Melisande could dress, and Ruth helped her into one of her formal day dresses, one from India she'd thought too English Grand Society to wear before, but it was perfect for the part she must play. She warned Charlotte and Ruth to guard their expressions and not correct anything she said. She knew, keenly understood, that they all had to live together after this meeting without any doubts about what had happened and who had hurt her. No more mistrust or suspicions, everyone must be freed of every scrap. She felt sure she could manage the meeting if her friends held their tongues and the men did as requested and acted as stolid witnesses.

She made her way to the drawing room, leaning on Doctor Allinson senior's arm and attended by Ruth and Charlotte. They had arranged a comfortable chair for her by the fireplace.

"Make it like a throne," she had whispered to Ruth, "and see Charlotte settled nearby." They had organised the room perfectly. She sank gracefully onto her chair and tried for a regal posture. She'd show that rude sergeant how wrong he'd been to so malign her friends.

Young Doctor Allinson escorted Sergeant Webster into the drawing room.

"Please fetch Mrs Miggs and all the Lightfoots," Melisande said to Doctor Allinson junior. "Everyone needs to hear what happened."

She waited whilst people settled, women on the few chairs, men leaning against the wall behind their women. Mrs Lightfoot twisted her hands in her apron skirt. Mrs Miggs darted glances at Charlotte and her son. Daniel rested a gentle hand on Charlotte's shoulder and she folded her hands neatly one over the other in her lap. Samuel Lightfoot had his hands behind his back. In the space beside him where his older son Thomas should stand was their younger son, James, but generally called Laddy.

Sergeant Webster marched across the room to face her chair, tugging a notebook from his tunic breast pocket into the palm of his hand, and producing a stubby pencil from inside the notebook. He gripped it tightly between his fingers.

"This is all I know – all I remember, Sergeant Webster. You tell me my friends, Daniel Miggs and his family, and the Lightfoot family, all these people are under suspicion of murder."

"Indeed, Mrs Holyman, there's three men shot dead and must be accounted for."

Melisande shifted in her chair and Ruth brought another cushion to support her back. "There were more than three men." She held up her hand to stop the Sergeant speaking. "I understand what you say and hope to prove to you that your suspicions are unfounded. This is truly what I remember and know to be fact, and my people here are not responsible."

Sergeant Webster turned to the doctors. "Has Mrs Holyman been isolated? You're sure none of the men spoke to her? Have Mrs Miggs and Mrs Lightfoot been near? Are ye sure that she hasn't misremembered or made up something?"

Melisande felt her friends take offence, and she gave the sergeant one of her Looks.

Young Doctor Allinson glanced at his father, received an encouraging nod, then spoke. "Mrs Holyman has been guarded by myself and my father. Miss Laundry and Mrs Daniel Miggs, who you yourself proclaimed to be free of suspicion, have only been near her when one of us has been present. She's made as complete a recovery as she ever will. She has followed our instructions carefully, no one has prompted her or supplied any information."

Sergeant Webster humphed, looking disgruntled and grumpy as he opened his notebook to a clean page, licked his pencil lead and waited.

Well, he would have to wait, if he expected her to denounce a murderer. Melisande ordered the last memories, as she now knew them.

"I can't denounce someone, sergeant, without you understanding what led up to the attack."

***

It took several weeks before Melisande grew used to the size of the house, the empty rooms, the bare floors and blank windows. Her bedroom she shared with Richard as she had at the Port Chalmers cottage. That room she made sure looked and felt comfortable with Indian rugs and hangings, her Indian paintings and one of Mama's. The large dining room remained empty except for an enormous mahogany dining table which Daniel had found for them in Oamaru at a house sale, but the other larger front room with two fireplaces became their drawing room, a place to entertain visitors and display Mama's wonderful flower drawings, Papa's books, the Indian works of art and the rich silk fabrics. She tucked her piano in the alcove made by the two bookcases, and placed chairs around to make a snug place for them to entertain themselves. She thought to have more large sofas but couldn't find any suitable in Oamaru.

"Wait for a house sale," both Ruth and Charlotte advised. "Those old fashioned large sofas you want often turn up at farm sales," they said, and

Daniel promised to look out for sale notices whenever he went into Oamaru for building supplies.

Jeri had insisted she arrange his bedroom in a sternly masculine fashion. The east wing they left empty, all but one pleasant sunny room with a good fireplace for Ruth, though Melisande began to plan which rooms would be for guests and which for a nursery and their children. The west wing had her morning room, a small study for her men, and a huge kitchen, divided into work areas, two sculleries and pantries. Even Jeri allowed that the main part of the kitchen made a convenient but temporary area for eating and organising.

***

She sighed. Life flowed in her memories, she knew that real time escaped her. The things she remembered melded into a flow of episodes. She thought of the time spent writing all those letters, making Jeri and Richard sign legal and banking documents so that the Oamaru Bank would allow her access. All those letters coaxing and soft soaping her uncle so that he would forward the remainder of their funds. Friendly letters to Richard's parents, whom she'd never met, inviting them to come and stay on their colonial estate. Didn't it sound grand? And it would only exist if she convinced the sergeant that her 'family', for that was what they now were, had nothing to do with the death and disaster. Her people — and hers they were and must be if this house and farm were to become a safe haven like her home in India had been — her people were owed an apology for the suspicion he had laid upon them. And she'd have it.

Everything depended on her leaving no finger of suspicion touching the shoulder of any of her people. They must all be free of it and feel free of it or her community, her family would be destroyed.

"It was after we farewelled my brother, Mr Allmark, my husband, Mr Holyman and, to our surprise and his mother's distress, Mr Thomas Lightfoot, Sergeant, that the trouble began."

She paused to let the sergeant write a few notes. Oh didn't trouble begin, creeping upon us, sneaking around us, and you did nothing Mr Policeman, she longed to tell him.

"First, Ruth heard someone outside her window, it must have been after midnight, wasn't it Ruth?" As she agreed Melisande carefully rearranged those newfound memories flickering through her mind like pictures in a magic lantern display. First Jeri and Richard departing.

***

Everyone went to cheer the troops. Melisande and her people, her family, trotted back from the railway station where the troops had left for Port Chalmers and the ships to sail them to South Africa. It had been a great celebration and display, a waving of flags and rousing cheers, Richard and Jeri made a brave show on their horses with the other officers. Thomas had, perhaps wisely, knowing his mother, said nothing until he jumped down from their cart and ran to join the troops, shedding his coat and revealing his uniform. His father sighed, but Josephine, too shocked to speak, clutched her heart and nearly slid off the cart seat. Young Laddy, only fourteen but a big lad looking all of sixteen or seventeen, swore, caught his mother, and begged his father to let him go too.

"Under age, Laddy," came his father's terse reply and his mother grasped him in a great embrace, clutching him like the tortured soul she was, her grip stronger than iron bars. "You shallna go, we need ye. Eh, son, don't be breaking my heart." And she sobbed into her apron all the way home.

After that display Melisande dared not become emotional too, although she longed to weep and rage at her selfish men.

Daniel put it into proper perspective. "Aye, well, it's a war our country fights on behalf of our Queen and we owe our duty to her." He took Charlotte's arm and led her back to the pony trap. "Some of us have to stay and bring in the harvest and pay the taxes for the war."

They didn't stay in town among the jubilant and excited crowd, not for a meal or even a cup of tea to make time to rest the horses. Slowly they returned to their homes for a quiet evening; even the horses caught the mood and plodded along solemnly.

As they turned into the farm's long driveway, the first part of which the Lightfoots now used as access to their little farm, Laddy glanced to the right. "He's back, Da, look," he actually snarled in anger, his voice a growl. He would have leapt out of the cart, only his father barred his way, thrusting out a rail of an arm to block him.

"Nay, Laddy. It's to provoke us, leave it be. If there's been any mischief you 'n' me'll settle them, but quiet like. He's got friends and influence in Oamaru."

All Melisande could see from her vantage point on horseback, across two large fields, were two dark silhouettes on the Lightfoot's farm boundary. One thin and nobbled like a stick, the other with a weird shape where his head should be. Was it something over his head? "What's wrong with that one's head?"

Josephine Lightfoot coughed a laugh of sorts, Sam Lightfoot guffawed as Laddy snorted. "They're both wrong in't head," Laddy said. "Nay, Mrs Holyman, that's the beeman, him'll have been at his bees. That's his bee hat he's wearing."

A stick man and a bee man, Melisande said to herself. Why did she think they spelled trouble?

"Doubt they'll trouble us," Sam said. "Not while we've got them Irish boys, Dan's builder mates, around." He looked across to Melisande. "There's bin loose tongues, on a Saturday night, beer talking, Mrs Holyman."

Josephine pulled a face, shook her head and became strongly Yorkshire in her speech. "You watch out sharpish round your place, Mr Miggs, leave nought out, tie all down, shut up them fowls and owt valuable. There's jealous folks about."

She turned to look at Ruth and Melisande. "And watch yoursen lasses. Beeman's a daftie, follows t'other's lead. Bit of a fool but t'other he's a right bad lot, fancies himself a man for the ladies, thinks he's a right gay dog." She smiled with bared teeth. "He's a dog all right, a dirty dog, that's why we call him Rex."

"An' talking of dogs, Ma …"

"Nay then, Laddy …"

But Laddy ignored her. "You need some watch dogs, Mrs Holyman …"

"Laddy," his mother warned, then turning to Melisande she explained. "The boy's right soft on animals, he's a one to save owt sick and dying. He's taken in a hunting dog and her three pups and I've told him to get rid of 'em."

"I can't shoot 'em Ma, and the pups are half grown an' too old to drown."

Melisande and Ruth exchanged glances, Charlotte looked at Daniel then glanced back at her friends. Daniel sighed.

"One each as guard dogs?" Melisande suggested.

Daniel tried to dissuade them with comments about 'soft hearted women' and the fact that this was a working farm, but he said no more when Charlotte caught and held his hand, giving him a loving smile.

"We could use a dog to protect the fowls," she said.-

"That's right kind," Josephine said.

"Nay, now then, no more chatter." Sam Lightfoot nodded at Melisande. "Me and Mr Miggs and his mates'll see all's trig and trim, make sure Rex and his pals are seen off." He flapped the reins and clicked his tongue at the stolid carthorse and they moved off, the black horse almost trotting now, eager to be home.

Daniel made the cob walk on, and Charlotte and Ruth both turned on the trap seat so that they could stare at the figures. Melisande urged Ranee into a trot to keep up.

***

"That night, Sergeant, Miss Landry heard someone tapping at her window."

***

Melisande had taken the opportunity of an early night to rage and weep into her pillows, and consequently fell into a deep sleep. She woke with a start to find Ruth tugging frantically at her shoulder

"Lisa, Lisa, there's someone at my window, shaking it and trying to open it."

Melisande jolted awake. "Light the lamp," she said, struggling from under the bed covers. The match flame quivered so badly in Ruth's hand as she lit the lamp that it took her two attempts. Melisande threw her a shawl and draped the bed coverlet around her own shoulders.

"Let us be sensible. There is no wind, no storm and no reason for the window to move." Melisande linked her arm through Ruth's. "Therefore let us shed a little light on the matter and confront this trespasser." She picked up the lamp.

Ruth shivered. "I don't believe in ghosts," she declared, her voice wobbling.

"Then let us, dear friend, concentrate on that," said Melisande as she wheeled them both round and out through the door. She marched them down the hallway. "Take heart, Ruth. We're going to grasp a curtain apiece and fling it back crying firmly, 'How dare you. Go away.' And we won't scream even if we see a round fat face or a pale ghostly shape."

Ruth managed a giggle. "I might."

They paused in Ruth's doorway. "No, you won't because you are prepared to see a person standing there." Melisande nipped her arm. "Ready?"

"Yes,"

"Let's run."

Together they ran to the window, each caught hold of a curtain and flung it back crying out "How dare you!" But only blank glass filled their gaze.

"Ah," Melisande said.

Ruth dropped the curtain, reached out a trembling hand. "I didn't dream it, Lisa, there was someone there." She touched her arm. "Please believe me."

Melisande put down the lamp. "We can prove it for you, Ruth. Either the night witch stalked your dreams or someone was there. Come, help me raise the window."

It was huge, a sash window with counterweights hidden in the frame. It had two large catches which took both Ruth and Melisande a two-handed effort to undo.

"Ready Ruth? One and a two, and a heave."

The sash cords were in good repair for the window lifted smoothly upwards. Ruth picked up the lamp and dangled it out of the window so they could spy the flowerbed below.

"There," she cried. "You can see where you and Charlotte planted the bulbs. The soil's tramped down and those boot prints are bigger than Laddy's, and he's the only one who's been digging around there."

Melisande gave a shiver, then shook herself. "It's a well-made window, the catches are strong and can't be shaken loose. " She glanced at Ruth, held her gaze. "My window has shutters. Daniel has Tommy, Paddy, Vic and Doug working with him to finish the stabling for Richard, and whilst they're still here, he's planning to get them to make hen houses, store sheds and everything Sam Lightfoot thinks we could use. Doug's best at fine carpentry after Daniel isn't he? He could make some shutters for your room and eventually for all the rooms without them."

Ruth, still looking as pale as her white nightgown, darted quick glances into the shadowy corners of her bedroom.

"Meanwhile, Ruth, my dear, let's go back to my room." Melisande pulled the coverlet tightly round herself. "It's a little eery standing in the dark in this empty wing of this wretched barn of a house." She seized Ruth's hand and they fled down the hall, back to the warmth of her room. With her William Morris chest slid to rest firmly in front of the door, the shutters, and thank God they were inner shutters, closed tightly with the bar in place across them, she managed a smile for Ruth before they hastily settled under the covers.

"All secure, let's try to sleep," she said and, surprisingly enough, they did.

***

"And so it began, Sergeant. The Stickman and the Beeman filled with rage because we had made them pay back the hay money, and stopped them using our land. They believed that without Mr Holyman and Mr Allmark in the house they could bully and intimidate us women. And indeed they tried."

Sergeant Webster made some under-breath comment.

"Yes, Sergeant?" Melisande adopted the tone she'd heard her mother use with Advik when — rarely — he overstepped the line, taking some decision upon himself without consulting Mama first.

Sergeant Webster frowned. He obviously disliked being chided by a young female, clearly would have preferred to deal with Mr Holyman not Mrs Holyman.

"Let me continue, Sergeant. I could list the damaged fences, broken water troughs, trespass and theft. And you didn't help us when they walked our two house cows off the property, even though young Mr Lightfoot — Laddy here — saw it happen."

"The lad stood too far away to be sure."

Laddy stirred, opening his mouth, but his father dropped a heavy hand on his shoulder.

"You left us to find our cows," Melisande, tone reproving, told the sergeant, but she wasn't going to tell him how they organised a schedule to protect themselves. He must learn nothing which would make him suspect there was a regular nightly inspection and walk around the property. He must believe the shotgun wasn't in the house, that it was she who'd alerted them all to the intruders. After all, that was nearly all the truth.

***

In the morning the joshing and joking quickly stopped when the men saw the imprints in the flowerbed.

"Two men," they all agreed, "and leaving clear footprints."

After that everyone crowded into the kitchen whilst Josephine Lightfoot growled about dirty boots and treading dirt all over her nice clean floor, but flung enough chops, eggs, and left-over boiled potatoes into skillets to feed them all whilst Ruth and Charlotte handed round tea or coffee and Laddy sliced, toasted and buttered a couple of loaves.

Melisande planned, using a notebook, to sketch the farm, manager's house and the Lightfoot's farmhouse, their boundaries and where the boundary coincided with the ghastly Rex's. She asked Sam Lightfoot and Daniel to find the places where the dogs needed to be kennelled at night to protect everyone. She waited until Tommy, Paddy, Vic and Doug were on their second mugs of tea before broaching the subject of their staying on a few weeks longer.

"Would Mr Hammond need you for building work?" she asked.

Tommy and Paddy shrugged, looked at Vic and Doug, shrugged again. "Inside work I'm thinkin'," said Paddy "He's plenty of carpentry for us to do over winter. He'd be wanting us then."

Melisande knew that Vic and Doug supported their mothers and Paddy and Tommy stayed in a strict Catholic boarding house. "No one to miss you?" she asked. "No sweethearts? And what about your parents?" she asked Vic and Doug.

They shook their heads. "Glad to see us wi' our boots under others' tables," Doug said.

"More room for me brothers," Vic explained. "Me mam's always wishing me a lass of me own and a place to be which ain't hers."

Daniel smacked Paddy on the back and elbowed Doug. "Landed on your feet, haven't you? They wouldn't want to be leaving such an easy workplace if there's work going, Mrs Holyman, now would you lads? All that good food, and they're set in the new shearer's quarters we've built you, a neat little cottage it is with bunks, a stove, and even a bathhouse, a bit o' the best, eh lads? It's a good lay for a working man." He winked at the four of them. "And I've kept the bulk of their money in the account so they'll be off home with enough to bank for their own bit of land and a house, if they've owt in their noddles."

"Give over Dan," Vic said. "We don't all fancy being big farmers. I'll be banking mine now you've showed us how, for I'm after a carpenter's shop with Doug here."

"To be sure," said Paddy, Tommy nodding in agreement. "We're all lookin' to be as well set up as Dan here now we've got this banking with interest worked out."

Melisande looked at her workers and thought fond thoughts of her parents and Advik, who had taught her that if servants and those who came to do work were spoken to in a civil voice, treated fairly and well, then they would work well. She smiled at them with a genuine affection, remembering how Richard and Jeri had started to explain banking to Daniel, who'd laughed and said he'd been banking away his earnings – at good interest – for years and could manage banking for the farm.

"Mr Hammond's a good boss as well as a strict Methodist. He tries to get all his lads to bank their earnings, better than drinking them he'd say. He's right an' all."

"If you can stay then there's plenty of work which Mr Miggs and Mr Lightfoot can arrange with you," Melisande promised them, "and would you be willing to keep a watch patrol for us?"

A general nodding of heads, and muttered 'ayes' and 'to be sures'.

Daniel and Sam worked out which hour each of them would cease work and walk around the yards, garden and the big house, and set a night watch of four hours a person, using the biggest hay barn as a base.

***

"I think you will remember, Sergeant," Melisande elongated her spine, lifted her chin, at her regal best, "the drunken rowdies who threatened us."

***

It was a memory they preferred to forget. The stickman, 'Rex the dog', and his pals, with enough beer in them to forget sense and wag their tongues to foolish talking, came in the afternoon. Led by the stickman, four of his rowdy mates rushed up the driveway with the beeman at the rear. The stickman, who spent too much time standing on their boundary fence line watching, must have been spying that afternoon for the rowdies lurched up the driveway when Sam Lightfoot, who was to be the guard after the noon meal, had hurried off with Tommy to show him which part of the farthest boundary fence needed strengthening. Daniel was away helping Paddy, Vic and Doug to build a sheep walk and pens in the back sheep paddock down the dip beside the valley.

Unaware of the problem staggering towards them Ruth and Charlotte sat hemming curtains in Melisande's snug morning room whilst Melisande wished aloud for one of those sewing machines she'd seen in India as she sewed bobble braid along the length of a blind.

"I would like that Nifty Knitter," Charlotte said, "think of all those stockings a family needs and the time it takes to knit good ones."

They had all laughed as they remembered the eager woman who'd demonstrated the knitting machine in the public room of the Oamaru Athenaeum and her pleasure when she'd sold one to a bachelor who wanted one as a bribe to turn his lady friend into his wife. Then Laddy's three half-grown pups, together during the day and kennelled comfortably in a sprawl near the hen run, gave voice and then yelped, a series of pained cries. Ruth jumped up, ran to the side window and called out.

"There's that Rex man and others reeling up the drive, and one's shying stones at the pups."

"Doors," Melisande said, darting out to close and lock the outside kitchen door. The others followed her into the kitchen.

"I closed the front doors when I came in, but what do we do?" Charlotte asked.

"Make a noise?" suggested Ruth.

"Yes, bang some pots and pans out of the window and hope Daniel can hear."

Charlotte handed round the enamel pans and the lightest of the saucepans and Melisande opened the side window.

"This is ridiculous," she said, "but all together please, one, two and a three." She bashed two pans together.

The three of them made a fine noise, but it was the weather which saved them. It'd been a grey, dull day with a rain-heavy sky which spat frequent weighty downpours of rain, one of which had started some moments ago. The rain bounced fiercely on the iron roof and chuckled down the drain pipes, soaking everything in seconds. Out in the paddock Daniel, reckoning that he and Paddy could finish the pens, sent the best carpenters, Vic and Doug, up to the house, into the dry, to the big barn, to make Ruth's shutters. They came pelting up, saw the rowdies yelling, and collided into them in a muddle of flailing arms and staggering bodies before the verandah steps. Above the clatter of the pots and pans there was a babble of voices calling out.

"Ye canna keep the pussy all to y'sen." The rowdies shoved and thrashed at Doug and Vic. "Let us at 'em."

"Rex had 'em. We want 'em. Don't you keep 'em for yoursen." This now with fists punching at Doug and Vic who dodged out of their way.

"Open up, darlins and spread your legs for us." The leader tried to mount the steps. "We want pussy, nice pussy."

The rowdies began a chorus of what Melisande first heard as "Phut, phut, phut. We wanna phut Give us a phut."

Melisande remembered Jeri's shock and Richard's shocked but gentle chiding when she'd used that word. "What is that word they're ...?" she began, turning to her friends. Charlotte and Ruth looked aghast, hands clasped over their mouths, their horrified faces telling her more than any words they could utter.

"This is terrible," they both said, dropping their pots on the window sill.

"Rape," whispered Ruth between her fingers, "fuck means rape, Lisa."

Melisande reached out and they all grasped hands, clutching tightly, as they watched Vic challenge the leader as Doug ducked round the other side of him.

In a well-practised move Doug and Vic each grabbed an arm and stuck out a foot, tripping the rowdy forward as they thrust him backwards to ram the others. As the group collapsed, Laddy hared up the drive while Sam, Dan, Paddy and Tommy came hurtling across the paddocks.

Melisande stopped trembling and cheered as the rowdies, including the stickman, were soundly grasped and shaken into quietness.

"How dare they!" She looked at her friends, "Are you coming?" She swept out of the kitchens, marched down the hall to the front door, and flung it open. Ruth and Charlotte tagged on behind her to peer over her shoulders.

Laddy leapt up the steps to stand in front of Melisande, his hands bunched into fists. "I won't let 'em near you, Mrs H," he promised.

She patted his shoulder gratefully as the rowdies, the beeman and the stickman, subdued and yanked into submission, knelt, bent over, or grovelled face down in the driveway.

"How dare you!" She stood at the top of the steps, Laddy beside her, anxiously guarding her. "You drunken scum." She raised her voice and poured out the words with disgust and scorn. "My husband and brother are absent, fulfilling their duty for Queen and country, or you would never dare show your faces here. Now you know my estate manager and farm manager have your measure and they and my workers can trounce you soundly. Don't dare show yourselves here again. And you can be sure the police will hear about your trespass and threats to us women."

"As for you – Rex Weston," she addressed the sickman. "We know you to be a dirty lying dog. Don't you try this sort of trick again, for if you set foot on my property again I'll let the dogs and men teach you a lesson you'll never forget."

Melisande glared at him then turned to smile at her rescuers. "Thank you, Paddy, Tommy, Vic and Doug. If you, Mr Miggs, and you, Mr Lightfoot, would escort these …" she curled her lip at the rowdies, "these filthy animals off our land and make sure you have names for the police, I would be most grateful."

"Our pleasure," Daniel said, as he and Samuel, with eager support from the others, yanked the rowdies to their feet and hauled them off down the driveway, dragging the protesting men so roughly they scraped tracks in the gravel as they went.

Laddy stayed by the front door. "I'll let you borrow Hector," he said.

"That was beyond nightmares," Charlotte said, shuddering. Ruth patted her arm and shook her head.

"It was alarming." She turned to Laddy. "Thanks to your puppies we had a warning. I'd welcome your great big hound, Hector, even in the house. What do you say, Lisa?"

Melisande had been watching the departure. She nodded. "I think we all need an extra smoko, don't you Laddy? And yes, we'd love to have your Hector, mud, dirt, hairs and all in the house. He's a great big hound and you've trained him well. He'd send them off."

Laddy grinned. "You saved the pups, Mrs H and persuaded me mam to keep their ma. She'll be our watch dog and do fine an' Hector'll eat anyone you stick 'im onto."

"Mrs H?" Charlotte chided gently.

Laddy didn't even blush, he just grinned, and it was Melisande who admitted, "As Holyman is such a long name to say, Charlotte, I did allow Laddy to use it."

"S'alright, Mrs Miggs, it's to use just for family like, ain't it, Mrs H?"

Melisande reached up as if to clip his ear. "But with respect," she warned him, hand hovering.

They all managed a laugh and Melisande felt a warm, happy sort of glow. She'd done it. Got these people united as a supporting group working and thinking like a family. Nearly like India, for if Laddy could see the value of being family, then his parents probably did too. Success!

Chapter Twenty-Three

Sergeant Webster, pencil still poised, coughed. "What are ye trying to say, Mrs Holyman?"

Melisande touched her head, as if it was hurting, then rested her forehead against her hand. The doctors stirred, she heard their feet scrape on the wooden floorboards as they made to rise.

She raised her head. "My memories are painful, not my head," she told them and looked at the Sergeant. "We'd been enjoying a farewell celebration ..."

***

It had been a good day for finishing things. Josephine Lightfoot had been preserving and pickling with Charlotte, clearing the Miggs' vegetable garden ready for early potatoes and winter vegetables. Ruth had finished the first set of her business studies classes that afternoon. Laddy and his father had finished selling off some of their fat lambs and fetched the house cows back from the bull and Paddy, Tommy, Vic and Doug had finally finished Richard's stables, tack room, feed shed and exercise barn. To celebrate, Daniel had driven to town to do the farm banking and bring home everyone's wages and Melisande promised a sing-along tea instead of a celebration supper because the lads wanted to catch the early carrier's cart into Oamaru and then home to Port Chalmers on the first evening train. They'd be missed but all of them promised to be willing workers when Daniel needed them.

Everyone came to a kitchen tea in the big house, even the Lightfoots. There was good fruit cake baked the previous day. Mrs Miggs would be proud of her, Melisande thought as she cut it and prepared meat pies, Ruth made sandwiches and Charlotte and Josephine brought pickles and spreads. Daniel brought beer and Sam and Laddy brought themselves. It was a feast enjoyed by all in an informal picnic fashion, sprawling on the verandah and round the big kitchen table with much joking and teasing. Everyone waved Paddy, Tommy, Vic and Doug off from the back verandah. The young men raced round the house and down the drive in high spirits, shouting and shoving and promising to return. It had been a good meal and they had their well-filled bank books in their pockets.

"I'm sorry to lose them," Daniel said, "but it'll be a bit of a rest not having to keep them up to their tasks." He turned to his wife. "A quiet evening in for us'll be a restful change."

Charlotte smiled up into his face and Ruth and Melisande watched Daniel escort her to their home, slipping his arm through hers and guiding her carefully round the rougher patches of gravel.

"You know," said Ruth, "he always treats Charlotte like that." She sounded wistful.

"You mean with tender concern, courtesy and respect?"

"Yes, and you were quite correct, Lisa, Daniel's more of a gentleman than some so-called gentlemen I've known. Charlotte did right. She's made a good marriage hasn't she?"

"She has, like mine, and they'll prosper, leave us one day to work a good farm of their own, and he'll build her a gentleman's home, not to show her family and Port Chalmers' society how wrong they were, but because he wants to give her a home worthy of the lady he knows she is." And, she thought, half ashamed of herself, he won't leave the comforts Charlotte has here until his farm can provide her with the same comforts. And that's good for us and our farm. She shook those selfish thoughts away. "He understands what she's lost marrying him, her family have cut her off, her father won't baptise her children, she has no family now except us."

Ruth sighed, gave herself a little shake. "Charlotte's shown such courage, I didn't know how brave she could be. I don't mind being distant with my family because they've never really treated me as a part of them, but Charlotte loves her father and sisters. It must hurt that they spurn her." She smiled. "You and I will be sisters and family for her, and now I'm going to run down to help Josephine Lightfoot; I won't be more than an hour, I'll be back before dark. She's wanting to lay out a new dress and cut down some of Sam's old shirts for Laddy. That boy's grown again."

They both laughed and Melisande waved her away. "Off you go. I must write to Richard and Jeri, there's a special post going out to the soldiers at the end of the week." She twisted her fingers together, trying not to frown. "I wish we'd heard from them, the newspapers have so little information."

"No news is the best news," Ruth said, and skipped down the steps.

Melisande didn't mind the empty house, well, not during the day. She called Hector away from the front door where he'd been guarding them and took him through the kitchen to the outer door.

"Away you go," she told him, opening the door for him. "You trot off and inspect the fowl runs and veg garden for intruders." The dog nudged her hand and pattered outside. "I think you understand every word I say," she said, laughing at herself and such a whimsical idea.

She settled in her morning room at the desk which had been her Mama's and added the final piece to her letters. She wrote daily, adding a few lines to her letters to Richard and Jeri, until they were finished. She enjoyed telling of the every-day incidents, wishing to keep them abreast of any changes and hoping they would be impressed with her management. As she finished relating details of the farewell party for Paddy, Tommy, Vic and Doug she remembered that they'd used most of the bread in the party sandwiches. "Drat," she said. There was probably enough for breakfast but bread they must have. She'd set the yeast, liquid and a little flour to form a sponge overnight, then she'd only have to add the remaining flour in the morning and the the bread would be ready to bake after breakfast.

Dusk touched the edge of the sky as Melisande bustled into the kitchen. She lit the table lamp and threw a little wood on the kitchen range. She'd warm some milk for Ruth, who liked her cocoa made with all milk, whereas she preferred half water and … where was Hector? The hound usually leaned on the door when he heard her come into the kitchen, and huffed noisy puffing sighs until she let him in. Then he'd ask for a pat before collapsing by the range with a contented sigh.

"Hector," she called, and pattered across the kitchen to open the back door. She almost tripped over him. The hound lay across the doorway, a solid lump blocking the way, but his head looked … it was wrong shaped and his coat had splotches of stuff … funny-coloured patches. "Hector?" She bent forward to see better. Something gripped her tight around her neck, throttling her. She was wrenched up to her feet, swung about, and slammed face first into the door frame. She smelled sweat, stale beer, some kind of fetid tobacco, felt a solid mass push against her as a hand moved up from the back of her neck to the back of her head and shoved. Her forehead crashed into the door frame again. Her vision exploded into spears of light as she cried out. She heard a grunt and a hand slapped across her mouth, crushing her lips against her teeth. It hurt.

Boots clumped up the steps. "Don't bash her senseless, she's gotta tell us."

"She'll tell, I'll see to that."

Out in the house kennel her puppy barked once then yelped.

"Told you to deal with all of them bloody dogs." A different voice.

Three men? Who? And what did they want?

"Rex is."

Four men. What could she do against four men? Reeling, her head beating a sickening tattoo, Melisande found herself shoved back into the kitchen and thrust into a chair. She couldn't think easily through the stabbing pains in her head. She bent over her lap, clutching her head, trembling, making it seem as though she might faint. She needed time, she needed an idea, she needed some way to reach help.

Oh, oh, Ruth ... Ruth hadn't arrived yet. She'd come in the front door, that being the nearest way in. She must find a way to make a noise and warn her. Ruth would fetch Daniel and the Lightfoots.

The men pushed and shoved round her, a solid wall of angry muscle ringing her in, forcing her to breathe air full of ripe beer, stale tobacco smoke and unwashed clothes. She choked. Someone poked her back, a vicious jab.

"Where's the money?" A low, fierce voice, eager and greedy.

"Tell us." They pressed closer, one man pinched her arm, the one behind her breathed heavily, spraying moisture on the back of her neck. She couldn't prevent herself trembling.

"What money?" Her voice came out as a thready squeak and she lifted her head slowly to try and make out who they were. Surely two of them were those rowdies who'd bothered them previously? Swaying, she squinted blearily as though she couldn't see properly, was liable to faint.

"Quick, make her say."

"The money, Sutton saw yon manager man get a load of cash at the bank. We wants it."

Ah, now she could stall them. Melisande knew exactly what to say, and how to say it.

"But the money's gone, not here. Truly." She let her voice quiver, added a touch of panic so her voice pitched higher and would travel farther.

Sounds of disbelief grew. A hand twined in her hair at the nape of her neck and yanked. Another swore.

"Truly, I give you my word, on my honour," she cried out, the grip on her hair making her eyes water. "The men were paid today. Their work is finished, didn't you see the new building, the stables and sheds? They left on the carrier's cart. They've returned to Port Chalmers on the early train.

The money was for them and they have it. We don't." She sounded scared. It wasn't difficult.

The grip on her hair tightened as the men cursed and muttered to each other.

"Lying slut." A rough hand slapped her face.

"Get Rex in here. He's the one said there were hundreds to take."

Now, how to convince them? Melisande whimpered, flinched. The fewer men inside the better her chances. "Please, don't hurt me," she squealed, hoping Ruth would hear the noises when she returned. "Let me show you. We keep any money locked in my desk in the room next door." Her voice quivered.

One man remained behind her, but the other two moved off to the side so that she could stand. She had no chance to rise on her own as the bully behind yanked her up by her shoulders.

She staggered, straining to hear any sound indicating Ruth's return, and deliberately wobbled, placing her feet as though she mistrusted their reliability. To no avail.

"Can't walk, eh?" Two of the men, and she was sure they were those rowdies, dragged her across the kitchen, the other walked beside her. "Now where's this room, and don't be foolin' us or you'll get it worse." They hesitated at the doorway.

"No, no, it's here. Don't hurt me." She made her voice squeal again. "This door on the right," she said, her voice raised even higher in panic for she thought she heard the front door open.

They pushed her against the wall. "Stop, please stop." She cried out loudly. "Please, you're hurting me."

"Lisa? Lisa what ..." It was Ruth calling out.

"Run, Ruth, run for Daniel. Help! Help!" Melisande screamed.

The men holding her swore, slammed her down on the floor, and charged down the kitchen wing's hallway. Melisande was sure they'd not reach Ruth, she was by the front door, the main hall's length away. Melisande sagged down the wall as though collapsed, unable to move.

The third man glanced at her then took a step away down the hall. She slumped over, he took another couple of steps.

Now, now she could go. She pushed herself up and off the wall and fled through the kitchen yelling for help. She shot out of the back door, nearly tripping over Hector's body, lurched upright and bolted down the steps screaming until her ears rang. She hurtled down the path beside the house in the fading light aiming for the front and the path towards Charlotte's house. She kept sobbing and screaming. Noise, she had to make as much noise as she could draw breath to make. Hope blossomed, for lights shone outside. She heard Charlotte's voice calling her and Daniel yelling.

Ruth shouted, saying she'd fetch the Lightfoots, and Daniel ran towards the house, roaring in a fury. "Stay in the house, Charlotte. Lock yourself in," he bellowed as he set their dog free. It came running with him, barking fiercely.

Melisande staggered towards Daniel as he charged up wielding what looked like a large chunk of firewood he'd picked up from their verandah woodstore. "What's happening?" he asked, looking all round.

"Four men, three in the house." Melisande gasped for breath. "In the hall going to the front door ... that Rex man's somewhere about too."

Hollers and yells came from the paddock.

"There's the Lightfoots, go join Charlotte, Mrs Holyman. I'll clear the house." Daniel then yelled in response and charged down the path towards the kitchen She heard his boots slam on the wooden verandah floor and the back door crash against the wall..

Melisande, shivering, slowly, cautiously stepped down the path towards Charlotte's home. She hadn't taken more than three steps when a large shape loomed into her sight and grabbed her. The fourth man, holding her with a pinching grip round her arms, and reeking of hair oil. That dirty dog Rex.

"Quiet," his hand flailed across her face, trying to cover her mouth.

She found herself being dragged towards the back of the house again, when Daniel's dog rushed upon them, barking excitedly. Her captor swung her round so that the leaping dog knocked into her.

She deliberately overbalanced, pushing her weight on top of the man so that he fell down underneath her. She wrenched herself free, clambered up, kicking him as hard as she could, then turned to run back down the path towards Charlotte's house. She heard him staggering up to his feet, tried to dodge away, but tripped and fell.

"Stay down!" Who was that? Surely not Josephine Lightfoot.

A shotgun boomed and Rex collapsed face down with a grunt behind her. Melisande squealed, she couldn't help it. Her ears rang and her head felt as if it would explode. Who was shooting? In the darkness all she could see of the Rex man was a bulky bundle of clothes. This was terrible and terrifying and her head was going to split apart. Ought she try to help him? She brushed his shoulder but it was a pulped mess. She recoiled and pushed herself off the ground to a wobbly stand. A touch on her arm startled a stifled squeak out of her, but it was Laddy who appeared beside her.

"Ma's coming, leave 'im Mrs H. Let's get you inside. Da's up front helping Daniel." He put an awkward hand under her elbow to escort her. They'd barely walked three paces when they heard a scrum of men crashing out of the front door and onto the verandah.

"Da and Mr M'll drive 'em off, Mrs H. I'll go check the kitchen. You stop here, Mrs H. You're all right, Ma's at hand." Laddy patted her elbow and ran up the path and onto the back verandah.

"Hector!" the cry came, wrenched out of him as he discovered the dog's body. Melisande staggered round the corner of the house to find him on his knees keening.

"Killed his dog, have they?" Mrs Lightfoot appeared out of the dark, and what a blessing, she carried an outdoor lantern. She also had a shotgun tucked under one arm. "Vermin! You take my arm, Mrs

Holyman, and we'll get you inside." She made a strong support of her free arm round Melisande's ribs and they moved slowly towards the house.

"Laddy, go help your da," she commanded in that mothers-must-be-obeyed voice. "Howling won't help but you can get in a few licks and feel better for it."

"I'll kill them," he snarled and raced into the kitchen, his feet thudding as he belted through and down the hallway towards the front door where the fight was still full on, a noisy crashing mess of grunts and thuds.

With Josephine's aid Melisande hobbled to the verandah steps, tottered up them and inside. She shook and trembled as she leaned on Josephine, hoping to catch her breath as she collapsed into her chair by the range.

"That's a nasty shock you've had, Mrs Holyman You sit there in the warm and I'll make sure them rogues are rounded up." She hurried out of the back door, loading both barrels of the shotgun as she went.

Melisande touched her throbbing forehead and tried to think, but boots crashed down the hallway and a raging devil, stinking of sweat and fear, incoherent with rage, raced into the kitchen from the hallway. Melisande swung herself behind the chair, groping for the lamp on the table. She grabbed the handle, swung the lamp at the brute, the big bully man who liked to hurt.

He roared as the hot lamp hit him. Snarling, wild, and desperate to escape, he crashed into her, propelling them both forward, ramming her into the back door post, deliberately smacking her head against the hard wood. As she collapsed Laddy charged back into the kitchen, chasing the bullyman. He clutched the shotgun. Melisande slid down the door frame and hit the floor as the man and Laddy tumbled off the verandah in a wild struggle for the gun. She heard Josephine scream at her son, the shotgun boomed once, twice, and then silence, all sound and sight vanished in an enveloping darkness.

Chapter Twenty-Four

"Mrs Holyman, Mrs Holyman. What happened? Who shot those men?" The sergeant, tetchy now, grumped at her.

Melisande paused. No lies, if she could avoid it, but if she had to tell half truths or avoid mentioning a fact to keep her family, her home and her farm safe, she'd find a way.

"I am so very sorry, Sergeant but I can't say who fired the shotgun which killed the men." That was true she couldn't – and wouldn't say.

She hoped the faint sigh escaping behind her didn't reach the sergeant's ears. She'd warned Ruth and Charlotte not to appear anxious or look at the men. Now she had to hope Josephine Lightfoot understood and kept that unresponsive expression on her face. She couldn't risk everything they had achieved so far to make her safe, comfortable, stable home by guessing. After all she did not truly know, she could guess but that was not certain knowledge.

The sergeant looked grim, pinched his mouth in a line, and tried to compose himself enough to speak.

Melisande waited until he opened his mouth. "I can tell you that Mrs Lightfoot and her son were attending to me in the kitchen when that big bull of a man came roaring in from the hallway. He grabbed the shotgun which Josephine held, tussled it out of her arms, bashed her with it, knocking her flying as he fled out of the kitchen door. Laddy bravely tackled him and they wrestled out on the verandah, but the man escaped. He had the shotgun."

She allowed the sergeant to collect his thoughts before speaking again. "As I collapsed Mr Miggs and Mr Lightfoot ran into the kitchen from the hallway." She inclined her head graciously at the frustrated sergeant. "The Lightfoot family and Mr Miggs were in the kitchen when the shotgun boomed twice outside. Mrs Charlotte Miggs and Miss Landry were locked inside Mrs Miggs's home."

The sergeant examined the faces of her friends and helpers. No one appeared guilty, all were nodding or murmuring agreement.

"So you're all agreed then. You were all in the kitchen when the shotgun was fired outside?"

Ruth and Charlotte shook their heads. The Lightfoots looked at each other. Laddy gazed across the room at his mother before nodding.

"That's right," Josephine said stoutly, glaring at the sergeant.

"Everyone was too concerned about my injuries to have chased outside and grabbed the shotgun. But have you thought, Sergeant, that those men were furious with Mr Weston? He'd told them that Daniel, Mr Miggs, had withdrawn a large sum of money from the bank in Oamaru. They came to steal it, but it wasn't here. Doesn't it make sense that the four men, desperate to escape and angry with Weston, had a violent argument and one of them used the shotgun?"

The sergeant gave up, folded his notebook into his breast pocket, and puffed his chest out in a huff of breath, exhaling noisily through his nose.

"You owe everyone here a public apology," Melisande said. "In the form of a statement in the newspaper perhaps, but something where everyone can see that you have, thanks to my recovered health, solved the problem of the deaths. It's quite plain to me that the men, disappointed and angry, beaten off by Mr Miggs and Mr Lightfoot, argued, fell out, fought over the shotgun and only one escaped."

She hesitated. Dare she push a little more? "Are you certain now, Sergeant, of the events from the attempt to rob me in my own home to the rescue by my friends?"

"Indeed, Mrs Holyman, you've been clear." He coughed. "Very clear."

"Then why, Sergeant, have you made all this fuss and persecuted and threatened us? We have complained several times about Weston and his friends. You have done nothing – no, don't make excuses – you did not help us."

"It were you, Mrs Holyman," the sergeant pointed an accusing finger. "You were moaning about Laddy and guns. You pointed the finger at him and your men, so to speak."

Both doctors interrupted. "How many times have we told you that the mutterings of an unconscious person, particularly a delicate female with serious head injuries, mean nothing."

Dr Allinson senior actually tutted and waved an admonitory finger at the sergeant. "From what Mrs Holyman has told us she remembers, it could so easily have been her anxiety for the boy not to be hurt as he tried to stop that brute which made her call out his name."

Dr Allinson junior nodded. "Of a certainty, what the lady spoke in that unconscious state would be not factual but emotional, of no importance to you, Sergeant."

"Satisfied, Sergeant?"

"I'll have to be."

"Then good day to you, we are going to hold a celebration party. Daniel, if you would be so good as to escort the sergeant out." Melisande turned towards the doctors. "Gentlemen, if you wish to join us in celebrating my recovery, and the removal of any stain of suspicion from us all, please do. You'd be welcome." She gave them her warmest smile and hoped that Ruth and Charlotte had been confident enough to do as she'd asked and spent a little of her emergency savings on some extravagant foodstuffs.

The doctors laughed and Dr Allinson junior said he'd stay for a celebratory toast but then really had to get back to Oamaru and their practice.

Dr Allinson senior lent Melisande his arm and they made their way slowly to the dining room. "I'm grateful to Mrs Miggs for readying my belongings for a departure today and will leave with my son, but not until we've toasted your recovery." He patted her arm. "Now you are to be sure to be careful and avoid any strenuous work or exercise until the end of the year."

"I'm thinking of your advice about the salt water baths in Oamaru, Dr Allinson. And perhaps a sea voyage to visit family in England."

The doctor gave her a little bow as he released her into an armchair. "An excellent idea, a sea voyage could be most restorative," and he went to fetch her a drink from the small kitchen table carefully disguised under one of her prettiest Indian cloths. The main table shone with a glassy sheen and more of her Indian mats and cloths protected its gloss from the assortment of plates and bowls. Under the variety of good food smells she thought she detected beeswax polish and smiled. Bless Ruth and Charlotte, Mrs Miggs and Mrs Lightfoot. They'd made a brave show for her. She accepted her drink and allowed the doctors and her friends to toast her health, the end of suspicion, and a better prosperous future.

She waited, content to let the talk flow around her. She knew what she'd said had been the right, the only thing to do. She felt the lifting of anxiety in the atmosphere within the dining room as her people let the weight of suspicion drift from them. The police sergeant had finally accepted that they were not guilty of murder. She thanked the doctors again and they bid the company a courteous goodbye. Charlotte and Daniel escorted them, with the Lightfoots entrained behind, to send them off with more thanks.

Ruth remained to stand beside her and they waited in an easy silence for the others to return. When plates were filled again, Josephine Lightfoot caught Melisande's eye and tipped her head in a silent thanks. Mrs Miggs tentatively offered tea to Charlotte with her lopsided grimace of a smile and sat beside her. Daniel gave them both a nod of approval.

Melisande stood up and made a little speech. "There aren't words enough to thank you all for the care you have shown to me. To Daniel, for organising the managing of the farm, to Mr Lightfoot for his farming skills, to Ruth for her help with the accounts and bookkeeping, to Mrs Miggs and Mrs Lightfoot for helping

Charlotte and Ruth manage the housekeeping and Laddy for managing the gardens. I know how difficult it must have been, waiting for me to remember, with the sergeant insisting on knowing what happened and you only having parts of the truth." She smiled round at them and blinked away the possible tears.

"I need to ask for your help a little longer. I wish to follow the doctors' advice and sail to England, but not for my health only. Ruth and I are going to bring our men home. You valiantly kept the news of the war from me and of the epidemic and them being shipped to England until I was fully recovered, but I shall return with my Richard and your Tom, Josephine, and with Ruth's help all four of us will benefit from the sea air and come home ready to work."

She raised her wine glass. "Here's to our future plans, to the Miggs family farm, to the Lightfoot's future farming successes, Ruth's exciting travels and my safe return with our men."

"The future," everyone cried.

That's it, Melisande thought. I've done it, made myself a colonial home and life which has a fortunate future. She smiled again and sat down.

"I'm going to England," Ruth said, amazed.

"Both of us," Melisande reminded her.

Charlotte, enclosed within Daniel's arm, laughed. "We've set loose," she said to him, "a pair of wild colonial girls. Will England be safe?"

The laughter dissolved all tension. Everyone knew what had actually happened and they were all relieved they no longer had anything to conceal.

Daniel raised his glass again. "To our wild colonial girl, our friend Lisa, who has put things aright."

Melisande, heart full, could only bow her head as they cheered and toasted her. Home at last.

RESOURCES USED

I used a huge number of books, DVDs and online collections from the museums. These are a few favourites.

'Pay Dirt' The Westland Goldfields from the diary of William Smart'

'Plain Tales From The Raj' BBC Publications

'The Raj: the making and unmaking of British India' by Lawrence James

'Begums, Thugs and White Mughals' by Fanny Parkes and William Dalrymple

'Hobson-Jobson: being a glossary of A Glossary Of Anglo-Indian Colloquial Words And Phases, And Of Kindred Terms'

Run, Estate and Farm by W H Scotter

Captain's Log: New Zealand's Maritime History by Gavin McLean

National library of New Zealand photographic collection

Waitaki Museum and Archive -Te Whare Taoka o Waitaki, photographs collection

Hocken Collection New Zealand

'Constance Astley's Trip to New Zealand 1897-1898' edited by Jill de Fresnes VUP

'Port Chalmers and its People' by Ian Church Otago Heritage Books.

P and O Shipping History of the cruise ships.

'The History of Otago' by A H McLintock

'Letter to Emma -Early Oamaru through the eyes of the Sumpter family.' edited by Fiona McPherson.

FREE PRIZE WINNING SHORT HISTORICAL STORY FOR YOU

https://storyoriginapp.com/giveaways/2431a908-6f6a-11eb-9d8a-0f5ef124708f

ABOUT THE AUTHOR

p.d.r. lindsay is a member of the Writer's Choice writers' cooperative and a keen supporter of New Zealand writers. *'Wild Colonial Girl'* is her fourth published novel. Born in Ireland, educated in England, Canada and New Zealand and having lived and worked in many different countries she calls herself a citizen of the world, writes about the many cultures she has observed and which stimulate her preference for writing serious historical fiction.

Writer's Choice a writers' publishing collective

We publish quality fiction for readers' enjoyment

Thank you for taking the time to read *'Wild Colonial Girl'*. If you enjoyed the novel, please do tell your friends and/or post a short review online, just a few words = just a few words – 'I enjoyed this book' – are all that's needed. Word of mouth is the author's best friend and reviews tell others you enjoyed the book and that they might too.
Thank you again. p.d.r. lindsay.

90% of our readers go on the enjoy another Writer's Choice novel. Order them online, through Kobo, Amazon or Smashwords or the local bookshop. Check them out at the website: www.writerschoice.org

p.d.r. lindsay www.pdrlindsay.co.nz.
Novels:
    'Jacob's Justice' – short listed in the UK unpublished novel competition
    'Tizzie' –short listed in the MM Hubbards Historical Fiction Award, Editor's choice in the Historical novel Society Review and short listed in the HNS novel competition.
    'Bittersweet' - long listed Wishing Shelf Awards

Short Story Anthologies:
    'Women Waking Up' prize winning short stories
    'Blokes muddling Through' prize winning short stories
    'Tales From Old Japan' new collection of recently published stories

    'Benjamin's Adventure' a children's bed time story
    12+ Short Stories to choose from in the Writer's Choice Shorts collection.

Sharon Robards - www.writerschoice.org or at www.goodreads.com
    'A Woman Transported

'Unforgivable'
'Playing With Fire'
'Burnt By The Flame'

G.J. Berger - www.writerschoice.org or at www.goodreads.com
'South of Burnt Rocks, West of the Moon' winner of the San Diego Historical Fiction Award
'Four Nails' winner of the San Diego Historical Fiction Award

 www.ingramcontent.com/pod-product-compliance
Ingram Content Group UK Ltd.
Pitfield, Milton Keynes, MK11 3LW, UK
UKHW021328180426
11947UKWH00017B/1500